D1522050

The Apprenticeship of
Big Toe P

The Apprenticeship
of
Big Toe P

A Novel by
Rieko Matsuura

Translated by
Michael Emmerich

KODANSHA INTERNATIONAL
Tokyo • New York • London

Note: Japanese names in this book appear in the Japanese order, surname followed by given name (except on the jacket, title page, and copyright page).

This book has been selected by the Japanese Literature Publishing Project (JLPP), an initiative of the Agency for Cultural Affairs of Japan.

Originally published in Japanese in 1993 by Kawade Shobo Shinsha, Tokyo, under the title *Oyayubi P no shugyo jidai.* Copyright © 1993 by Rieko Matsuura.

Distributed in the United States by Kodansha America, LLC, and in the United Kingdom and continental Europe by Kodansha Europe Ltd.

Published by Kodansha International Ltd., 17-14 Otowa 1-chome, Bunkyo-ku, Tokyo 112-8652.

Library of Congress Cataloging-in-Publication Data

Matsuura, Rieko, 1958–
[Oyayubi P no shugyo jidai. English]
The apprenticeship of Big Toe P / Rieko Matsuura ; translated by Michael Emmerich.—1st ed.
    p. cm.
"Originally published in Japanese in 1993 by Kawade Shobo Shinsha, Tokyo."
ISBN 978-4-7700-3116-7
I. Emmerich, Michael. II. Title.
PL856.A81980O9313 2009
895.6'5—dc22

2009005459

The Apprenticeship of Big Toe P

Prologue

I had met Mano Kazumi just a few times. She was a good friend of an acquaintance of mine, and that was how we were introduced. It had been two years since I'd last seen her.

About a month ago Kazumi rang to pass on the sad news that our mutual friend, Ayasawa Yoko, had died. Then recently, early one morning, she called again, saying she wanted to discuss something with me, and would I mind if she dropped by in an hour. Groggily I tried to call up an image of her, but none came, and I drifted off back to sleep unable to put a face to her name.

I was roused by a barrage of knocks on the door, and suddenly remembering Kazumi was coming over, I made a mad dash to the door. When I opened it and saw her standing there timidly, the memory of her came rushing back and superimposed itself neatly over the person before me.

"It's been a while," Kazumi said, bowing slightly, smiling shyly.

Yes, the slight plumpness of her cheeks, the droop of her lower eyelashes, and the lovely arc of her lips, the fullness of which comes as a surprise because her mouth is so small . . . yes, yes, this is the Mano Kazumi I knew—the woman who did her best not to attract attention as she sat beside Yoko. At first glance Kazumi has the sort of face people describe as cute, but upon closer examination the observer notes that her eyes and nose are somewhat precariously balanced, giving her the expression of a child on the verge of tears—a look that was half funny, half sad. I had secretly thought of her as "the Young Woman with the Funny Face."

I hastily folded my futon and stuffed it into the closet, and invited Kazumi into my room. This was the first time she had ever set foot in my apartment. She settled down at the *kotatsu* and eyed the cramped six-mat room as though it were something rare.

"No computer or anything. Doesn't look like the home of a novelist," she said.

"I'd be happier if you said it doesn't look like the home of an average Japanese. I don't have a VCR or a CD player either."

"Are you poor? You know, Yoko was always puzzled by you. She used to wonder why you didn't get a job."

I changed the subject. "Have the rites taken place yet?—for the forty-ninth day after her death?"

"Yes, three days ago," Kazumi said, somewhat sadly. "I have to say, you never want to be the person who discovers a body. I had nightmares about it every night until the rites. I didn't tell you how she died, did I? She had on a prim white dress—the sort of thing a well-bred young lady would wear, nothing like her usual loud clothes. But then she had this heavy rope around her neck—didn't go with the dress at all. It was so creepy— when I found her, I couldn't tear my eyes away."

Yoko had hanged herself in her apartment, tying the rope to the bathroom doorknob and throwing it over the door. She was twenty-two. She had carefully done up her hair and made up her face before doing the deed.

"She called me the night before. She had left her car with one of our customers, and she wanted a ride to the office the next morning. So I went over to pick her up, and . . . there she was. I mean, why would she ask me to come get her if she planned to die?"

"Because she wanted you to find her."

"You think so?"

I couldn't tell whether Kazumi was being naïve or obtuse. It reminded me of an occasion when the three of us had gotten together, back when Yoko was starting her company and was planning to hire Kazumi as her right-hand woman. When Yoko stepped away briefly, Kazumi confided in me, "You know, M., I don't understand why Yoko asked me to join her company. It's not like I'll be able to do the bookkeeping or anything." "She asked you because she trusts you, of course," I said. And Kazumi replied,

"Do you think so?" She had the same incredulous ring in her voice now that she'd had then.

Yoko was just the opposite of Kazumi—she always saw more to things than met the eye, and her sense of what more there was tended to be quite jaded. Her cynicism, in fact, was the basis for her new business, as she explained—rather enthusiastically for her—when she returned to the table. "It's like the sex trade—only what we sell isn't sex, it's love."

"I didn't know you could sell love."

"You can, actually. Of course, some love can't be bought. But young women these days are no less infatuated with rich men than the professionals are."

"At least that's what people say."

"Do you realize what that means? Women aren't necessarily calculating, choosing their partners on the basis of the math."

"Oh? What are they doing then?"

"A surprising number of these women seriously believe in the purity of the love they feel for a rich man—that it's got nothing to do with the fact that they're getting expensive gifts and meals at good restaurants. In their mind, they're not calculating anything. They really believe they love the guy. And yet, while they may *believe* it, it isn't entirely true. Because even though they keep telling themselves, *He's so kind, and I really love him,* the moment their honey drops out of his Elite Street life or comes down with a terminal disease, the moment his loaded parents go bankrupt, they start singing a different tune. All at once, without any qualms whatsoever, they say, *I thought I loved him, but I was wrong,* and then, with hardly a moment's hesitation, they throw him over. There are plenty of women like that. And when they meet the next wealthy guy, they say, *This time my love is real.*"

"You hear that kind of story a lot, it's true."

"After observing these young women at close range, I realized that it wasn't in me to criticize them; on the contrary, I couldn't help but marvel at their ability to rouse passion within their breasts that really felt like love, even if they were deceiving themselves, and to do it for a profit. That's when it struck me—that *I* could profit from this ability of theirs."

"People are quick to fall into pseudolove even when there's no profit involved. There are plenty of romantics just dying to fall in love."

"Exactly. So I started thinking: If there're women who have the ability to hypnotize themselves into feeling love, or something closely resembling love, then it ought to be possible to cultivate that ability, to perform the hypnosis expressly, so that women could coax themselves into falling in love with one particular man. Of course, people have preferences, there are limits to what they can accept, and on rare occasions a man might simply be beyond their capacity to love; but for the most part they should be able to fall in love with almost anyone, regardless of appearance or personality. That was my idea."

"By making women *believe* they're in love."

"Yes. A woman who can consciously make herself believe that the love she feels for someone is pure even when her real motive is profit—in a woman like that, it ought to be possible to hone that ability even more, so that even if she does something less than pure, she can still tell herself she's dating the guy because she loves him. It has nothing to do with the contract they signed or the money she's getting from him. For these women, that sort of thing shouldn't pose a problem."

"In theory."

"My company recruits these women and trains them in autosuggestion. We teach them to look actively for things in men that they can feel good about, even when the men are short and bald and fat and hairy, and never say anything unless it's to brag or tell a dirty story. We teach the women to pick up on little things—the attractiveness of a man's fingernails, say, or a charming vulnerability in his bad posture—and then take that faint gleam of warmth and amplify it, so that they start feeling something akin to love. The important thing isn't to give a convincing performance, making them *seem* to love the man; our women have to be skilled at putting themselves in a state of virtual love. This is what distinguishes us from the usual sort of escort agencies."

"In other words, you're selling love that's almost like the real thing."

"But we're not pimping. All we do is introduce women with love to offer to men who come looking for it. Our sole aim is to provide a helping hand, to do what we can to foster a lovelike alliance between a woman and a customer. Needless to say, it doesn't concern us in the slightest whether the couples have sexual intercourse, or whether the pseudolove blossoms into actual love and ultimately leads to marriage. You've heard of these clubs that introduce potential marriage partners? Our system lies somewhere between them and escort agencies. Except that we're not about either marriage or sex—we're about love."

I had been nodding as Yoko earnestly described her plan, but now the time had come to express my doubts. "I kind of wonder, do you really think men will be interested enough in love that they'll go to all the trouble of seeking you out? And even if some are, will they be content with pseudolove?"

"M.," Yoko said, her voice oozing with confidence, "do you know what men and women want in this world? They want love that isn't a hassle and doesn't hurt, love that's carefree and fun, love that doesn't become a burden. No one's looking for the real thing, actual love that can be painful and get in the way of other things—not at all. They just want the tasty bits. I've created an enterprise that meets those needs."

"So will you take customers yourself?"

"No. I'll just manage things."

"Why not?"

"Because . . ." For the first time, Yoko hesitated. "I don't want to."

"But why?"

"Because I'm not good at lovelike things."

"Then what motivated you to start a business like this?"

"I didn't have a motive. I just had an idea. And I didn't have anything else I wanted to do."

I'll never forget the somber smile that crossed Yoko's face as she said that. She was a haughty young woman, but there was also something touchingly pathetic about her.

Sitting next to her, Kazumi did not contribute to the conversation except to smile from time to time at a phrase her friend used. As far as I could tell, the two of them were good friends but not a pair, if being a pair meant thinking and feeling the same way about things. No, their friendship was cemented by the combination of Kazumi's innocence and susceptibility and Yoko's affection for Kazumi. It made sense that Yoko would feel at ease around Kazumi, but since Kazumi couldn't quite comprehend Yoko's sensibility, Yoko must have been wounded often in the course of their long acquaintance.

Kazumi sipped her tea, sighing, then said, "If I had a friend I wanted more than anyone else to discover my body, I would never consider suicide."

"Were there any signs?"

"No, I don't think so. Yoko was cheerful as ever, right to the end. She might have grown a little quieter, but we saw each other six days a week, you know, and didn't have that much to talk about . . . I'm so slow on the uptake, it's possible I just didn't notice. She used to tell me all the time, 'You're so dense, Kazumi, you don't get it.'"

Before I could stop myself, I blurted out, "No surprise there."

"What do mean . . . ?" Kazumi said, her eyes wide. "You think I'm dense, too?"

"You see . . . ," I began, "you're really nice, very easy and obliging, but you're not what I'd call sensitive . . . or perceptive."

LOVESHIP, the love-distributorship that Yoko founded, was a success. The company was given such extensive coverage by the mass media that before long everyone knew about the peculiar business scheme this twenty-year-old woman had launched. Naturally, people were interested, not only in the operations of the business, but also in the woman behind the company. The weekly magazines were flooded with interviews and articles with predictable headlines like "Meet the Mastermind behind the New Trade in Love: Brilliant, Beautiful, and Only 20 Years Old." The young woman in the pictures that ran with these articles didn't look at all like Yoko, however, and her name was reported as Uzuki Misa. Yoko had been savvy enough to prepare a dummy in advance.

LOVESHIP grew steadily. The office moved from an ordinary middle-class apartment to more spacious quarters in Nogizaka. Some of the women who had registered with LOVESHIP joyfully tied the knot with their customers, and scenes from their wedding ceremonies were broadcast on daytime television. Another woman went on to become a TV personality and released a collection of nude photos. A number of rival companies sprang up. There was no shortage of fodder for the media.

Yoko herself didn't get caught up in the excitement. Six months ago, when I'd talked with her on the phone, her tone was anything but. "I'm about to open a cultural center on the side," she said flatly. "To teach cooking and stuff."

"You'll have the women on your list attend?"

"Yes. But we'll also bring in young women from outside. That will help us scout new members."

"You're really working hard."

"Yeah, but I hardly care anymore. It's no fun."

"Why not?"

"Watching all the people flock to the company, watching the media, it's made me hate people. I guess it's true . . . I don't appreciate the pathos and humor of life. The women disgust me the most. No ambition at all, no will to go out and clear their own path . . ."

"Why don't you just give it up then?"

"Yeah, I know."

I was suggesting she give up the company, but she gave up living instead.

I decided not to tell Kazumi about the darkness I'd heard in Yoko's voice.

"So what's going to happen to LOVESHIP?" I asked Kazumi.

"Another company bought it. I don't mind. I'm drained," she said. Then after a brief silence, she added, "I feel like Yoko put a curse on me."

"Why would she do that?"

"Because I didn't give her any attention. I didn't try hard enough to understand her."

"Whether or not you understood her, you know she was very fond of you."

"Then why did she make me discover her body?"

There was unexpected vehemence in Kazumi's reply, and I flinched. "You think she wanted to hurt you?"

"I'd rather not believe it."

"This is just speculation," I said, choosing my words carefully, "but I wonder if, by forcing you to discover her body, she was trying to create a bond between the two of you."

"There's been a bond between us for ages."

"A stronger bond. Almost like physically leaving a mark on you."

From the expression on Kazumi's face, it was clear she didn't get what I was saying. I let it go at that. "So what did you want to talk about?"

"Right, I almost forgot." Kazumi sat up straighter. "I had a dream the night before last."

"About Yoko?"

"No, Yoko wasn't in it." Then, after pausing to exhale, she enunciated each word: "THE BIG TOE ON MY RIGHT FOOT HAD TURNED INTO A PENIS."

"What?" I stared at Kazumi. "What turned into a penis?"

"The big toe on my right foot."

First it's a clearinghouse for love, then it's a toe that becomes a penis. What was it with these two women? The thought of it was so crazy that I burst out laughing. Which made Kazumi grin a little, too. And then she told me about her dream:

"It was a pretty short dream, not so dramatic or anything. I just realized, all of a sudden, that the big toe on my right foot was a penis. I didn't feel surprised because that's how things are in dreams, and it never occurred to me to wonder if something so absurd could actually happen. I simply accepted it; to tell the truth, I felt kind of knocked out, like, Wow, I've got a penis! A penis isn't such a big deal if it's on someone else, some guy, but it feels wild and fresh when it's your own and you're a woman. I had this surge of emotion; I was thinking, Yes! This is amazing! Because now I could experience that eternally mysterious pleasure—a feeling women can never know: orgasm from sensations that male genitals feel. This was all happening in a dream, so the thought of what a pain it would be if such a thing actually happened never crossed my mind. I just thought, Yes! This is amazing! And then, without losing a second, I started to fondle it."

I burst out laughing, slapping the table.

Kazumi continued, "And you know, you can actually feel things in dreams. Just putting my hand around my toe-penis was enough to . . . I don't know how to explain it . . . it felt so *good*. This sweet wave rolled over me—it felt kind of ticklish, like it was quivering or something. And then when I started massaging it, my toe got bigger, and the pleasure got bigger, and I could feel the climax coming, and my chest was pounding, and then—" Kazumi lowered her voice, "the climax came sooner than I thought it would. And it didn't feel as good as I thought it would, and the pleasure had hardly begun to spread through my body when my toe-penis started to shrivel up. I couldn't believe it. It was such a letdown, and I was muttering to myself, What the hell? Is that all there is? That's all the pleasure men feel? And then I woke up."

Somewhere along the way, I found myself listening very intently to her story. "Just putting my hand around my toe-penis was enough to . . . I don't know how to explain it . . . it just felt so *good*." There was no doubt—judging from the expression on Kazumi's face and the intonation of her words—this was a person remembering, tenderly, the thrill of sex. Her story was so vivid, so powerful, that I thought *I'd* grown a penis on my big toe. I knew I didn't have one, but still I tried to make my toe get stiff. So before I could laugh off Kazumi's dream as incredible, and delightful, I had actually tried to experience it.

As I sat wriggling my foot, Kazumi turned a suspicious gaze on me. "Is something wrong?"

I was about to answer when she cried out gleefully, "Don't tell me you actually have a toe-penis!"

"Please," I laughed. "But after having a dream like that, don't you feel a little anxious? Don't you ever think, What if I really do grow a penis on my toe?"

"Absolutely! It's been worrying me constantly!" Kazumi reached down and wrapped her hand around the tip of her foot. "I keep thinking, What if that dream comes true? Because in real life, it would be a real hassle to have a penis like that. Since that dream, I've had the urge to take off my sock and check several times a day. It was the first thing I did this morning, too—as soon as I woke up, I looked at my foot." Kazumi moved her hand back to her heel. "Right now, the urge to take off my sock is so strong that I can hardly stand it." Her fingers found their way back to the top of her sock. "I wonder, M.—do you think you could do me a favor and take a look?"

Kazumi kicked away the *kotatsu* quilt with her black-socked foot and thrust her leg out in front of me. I need hardly mention that removing other people's socks is not my thing.

"Are you serious?"

"Just take a look, please. Hurry."

Unable to resist her urgency, I grudgingly inserted my two index fingers into the top of her sock and pulled.

I stared, entranced.

THE BIG TOE OF HER RIGHT FOOT WAS A PENIS.

Chapter 1

True, M.'s eyelids did flutter when her eyes landed on the penis on my big toe, but she didn't gasp or cry out. She simply sat there, my sock dangling from her hand, gazing down at the thing.

There it was . . . my big toe. From the first joint downward, considerably more fleshy than it had ever been—and now shaped rather like a mushroom. I hadn't gotten used to the transformation of this toe of mine. Every time I took my sock off, I couldn't stop staring at it: the reddish tones, strikingly different from my other toes, and the smooth skin, missing the whorls at the tip of the toe. But the most extreme change was in the shape of the toenail. It now bulged out like a hemisphere, about a half inch across, and gleamed like a pearl up near the head. From where M. sat, on the other side of the table, she could see its underside, which was shaped like a heart, the kind on playing cards, but upside down.

M. put my sock down and folded her arms. "It's true . . . You've got a . . . *thing*." She spoke softly, but unable to conceal her excitement at seeing something so phenomenal, so inexplicable, there was fire in her voice.

I smiled wryly. When I decided to let someone else see my toe, I thought of M. first, and the reason was she could be trusted not to react in a tiresomely extravagant way. She wouldn't be uncool and make a fuss; she wouldn't blush and look away; she wouldn't get speechless or serious or clutch her head in her hands. I was right.

"Upon closer inspection," M. said, examining my foot from various angles, "it's not exactly the same as a man's. There's no foreskin, and there's no hole. And you can see where the toenail was. But, I have to say, it's pretty close to a real P."

"A real P?"

"A P-nis. A penis, I mean. I feel more comfortable abbreviating it, don't you?"

I wasn't sure how to respond. M. looked totally serious.

"Can I ask you a few questions?" she said.

"Sure."

"This *thing* of yours doesn't change into a rose or something when you sneeze, does it?"

"Nope."

"It doesn't assume this form only when there's a full moon? Nothing like that?"

"No, it doesn't seem related to the moon."

"And it wasn't done by a plastic surgeon?"

"Please. I sincerely doubt that anyone, even the most discriminating pervert, would go to all the trouble of having something like this attached to this spot."

"Yes, I suppose you're right." M. chewed her lip as she turned things over in her mind. "I don't know, though. No matter how closely it resembles a P, there's no way a real P could just materialize on a big toe like this. So what do you think it could be?" M. said, reaching out and brushing her fingertips along the length of my toe-penis, stroking it from base to head.

I don't want to think she was teasing me, or that she was being vulgar. I mean, she had to have been perplexed, and she acted without thinking what she was doing. But her stroking was too soft, too delicate. A sweet shock jolted my toe-penis, and blood began rushing into it, in time with the beating of my heart. I jerked my foot back and covered my toes with my hands.

"What's wrong?" M. stared at me, surprised.

Now was not the time for such a question. My penis was pressing against the palm of my hand.

"Hold on. Does your *thing* get an erection?"

"I told you that, didn't I?"

"So it's just like that dream you told me about. You weren't born with it, it just appeared one day, all of a sudden. And it has the same physiological response as a real P. Is that it?"

I was too caught up in the task of controlling my erection to reply. The toe had grown to more than twice its usual length, and was flopping about on its own. I pinched it to make it shrivel, but this only egged it on into even greater flights of dynamism; it got warmer, it pleaded for more stimulation. Unfortunately, whatever my toe-penis wanted, I also wanted. I would have loved to satisfy its urges right then. Of course, I couldn't do that in front of another person. I was annoyed with M. for having thoughtlessly got it going.

M. grabbed my wrists and pulled them away from my feet, exposing my toe, whose transformation was now large and complete. I was humiliated and turned my face away.

"It's your fault," I sobbed.

"My fault!" cried M. "I just touched it a little, that's all!"

"So you've taken a liking to this *thing* of mine?"

"Maybe it's not used to being touched. It's very excitable," M. said, unfazed by my sarcasm. Like a compassionate physician, she peered at my toe-penis. "What do you usually do when this happens? Dump cold water on it?"

"Very funny," I said, my shoulders sagging. "You think since it's not your problem, you can just treat it like a joke." I sounded almost tearful. A few moments ago M. had told me I wasn't sensitive, but she was no diplomat herself.

"I'm not treating it like a joke at all," said M., who got to her feet and went into the kitchen, returning with a cold wet towel. I took it and wrapped it around my toe. It was March and the water in the tap had been so cold that the towel wrapping my toe sent a shiver down my spine. I felt the blood vessels in my toe contract.

"Sorry about that." M. aligned her knees properly and bowed her head in apology. Removing the wet towel, I saw that my toe-penis was gradually regaining its composure. I breathed a sigh of relief.

"So when did this happen?" M. asked, picking up where she'd left off.

"The day before yesterday."

The dream I'd told M. about happened two days ago, late in the afternoon. The day before had been the forty-ninth day since Yoko's death, an event marked by certain rites of passage. So the instant I lay down in bed that night, there was Yoko again, deep in my thoughts. I was exhausted, emotionally drained, but was afraid to go to sleep. A little after noon the next day, I was overcome by sleepiness.

I don't think my nap lasted more than three hours. When I awoke, I felt queasy. My body felt unusually warm, my limbs charged with energy. I got the feeling that the fatigue I'd been feeling ever since Yoko's death had dissipated a little, so I made to jump out of bed and cook dinner for the first time in a long time. But my body wouldn't move so quickly; I was still basking in the aftereffects of my dream, and the big toe on my right foot was still tingling.

What a dream it had been . . . absolutely ridiculous, and fun. Who could've come up with something like that? My big toe turning into a penis! I mean, it's not like I never wondered how it would feel to have a penis, but I never seriously wanted one and I never seriously wanted to know what it felt like to be a man. Why would I have a dream like that?

More than these musings, though, it was the pleasure still coursing through my big toe that kept me thinking about my dream: The thrill of discovering a penis sticking out the end of my foot. The fantastic sensation that came over me when, without any hesitation, I reached down and wrapped my fingers around it. How the excitement intensified when I moved my fist up and down it. Just a dream, but I was tantalized, experiencing pleasure like that. The orgasm was a bit of a disappointment, but that could have been me—my own inability to imagine how a penis feels at the big moment. I could do much better when I was awake, but that was only because I con sciously superimposed onto the proceedings the sort of orgasm I was used to. The unusual location of a penis on my foot must have made it hard for me to do that in my dream. What a waste! If I could have the same dream again, I'd have everything down pat, including the orgasm.

When you dream something like this, you've got to tell someone about it. Someone who won't wrinkle her brows, someone who will listen with interest and talk about it and laugh. The person who came to mind was Yoko. And all at once my fluttering heart sank. Yoko was dead. I no longer had a friend who would listen to me without qualification, someone

I could talk to without embarrassment; Yoko had known me better than anyone else in the world. I might live for decades more, but I would never find another person who would be as good to me.

Yoko was by no means the sort of person one might describe as kind. She had a tendency to either like or dislike people intensely, and if it was the latter, she showed it in no uncertain terms. It was not her best trait, but I never said anything to her about it. As I far as I was concerned, though, she was a wonderfully engaging, truly precious friend.

Once, when a bunch of women friends got together, someone tossed out the question, "What would you do if you could be a man for a day?" Without missing a beat, Yoko shouted, "Castrate myself!" When someone in the group responded with, "That's the absolute height of narcissism!" Yoko shot back, "I'd prefer to be told it's the height of romanticism." How would Yoko have interpreted a dream in which my toe had turned into a penis? Actually, it's just the sort of dream Yoko might have had herself.

It occurred to me, as I lay in bed, that Yoko hadn't been in my dream . . . This brought on an overwhelming sense of foreboding that prompted me to throw off the covers. And that's when I discovered the real, undreamed transformation that had taken place in the big toe of my right foot.

Needless to say, I was surprised. I couldn't believe my eyes. Nor could I distill the emotions gyrating in my chest. This transformation was peculiar, to put it mildly, and I didn't know what to feel. I switched on the lamp by my bed, and there it was. I wasn't so sure I wanted to touch it. Not because it was too bizarre to be believed, but because the moment my fingers came in contact with that toe-penis, arousing the sensations that slumbered within it, I knew there would be no turning back. I would no longer have the option of simply relishing the pleasure, treating it in the breezy, lighthearted manner of my dream. I would find myself having started down a draining, arduous path.

Of course, I gave in to the temptation of my new toe-penis—gave in to the lure of its physical form, which is only inadequately described as freakishly beautiful. I held my breath and slowly, ever so slowly, stretched out a hand to my foot.

But just before I made contact with the toe-penis, my hand froze, hanging in midair. The telephone had rung. I turned over, actually glad for the interruption, and plucked the receiver off its base, which was on the floor.

"Hey, it's me. So you are at home!" The familiar sound of Masao's voice was comforting, but it wasn't enough to calm the extreme agitation that had taken hold of me. "Mind if I come over?" he asked.

Of all the times to choose! Ordinarily Masao preferred for me to go to his apartment, rather than coming to mine. Rarely did he want to come to my place. "Why, what's going on?"

"Oh, nothing, really. I just don't want to be here if that bastard Haruhiko shows up, that's all. He called and said he wanted to see me. I lied and told him it wasn't a good time because you were over, but he said that was fine, he didn't care. What a jerk. So I yelled at him and said, Look, I said no, and I mean it! and I hung up. But you know how Haruhiko is— nothing stops him. You can bet he'll barge right in."

Haruhiko was one of Masao's friends from school. They had been close ever since their freshman year—they got part-time jobs at the same store and went on trips together and all that—but about three months ago Haruhiko stole the girlfriend of a friend of theirs, so now no one wanted to have anything to do with him, even with graduation around the corner. Haruhiko was definitely a strange guy. I met him once when I was with Masao, and the moment Masao left the room he leaned over and said, "Stealing other guys' girlfriends is kind of a hobby of mine." "What got you interested in such a hobby?" "I don't know, no logical explanation, just the way I am, I guess." "Maybe you should get your hormones checked."

"So," Masao continued, "I don't want to be here if I can avoid it. Besides, I haven't seen you for a while. Hey . . . what's wrong with your voice?"

"Is there something wrong?" He was right, I sounded shrill. "I had a weird dream."

"You sound different. Is someone with you?"

"No, I'm alone."

"Are you sure?" Masao fell silent, apparently trying to detect some sort of sign; then, his tone solemn and deliberate, he said, "I want to hear you say you love me."

I burst out laughing. Masao was a worrywart. We hadn't seen much of each other since I started working at LOVESHIP, and he was afraid I was seeing someone else. As a matter of fact, a year and a half ago, he worried that that someone was Haruhiko. "He said he made a pass at you." Nothing ever happened, but I had a pretty hard time convincing Masao of this.

"Look, don't just try to laugh me off!" Masao was growing agitated. "Your laugh doesn't sound natural!"

In the extraordinary state I was in, I found it impossible to stop laughing. That was all it was, but of course Masao didn't know this, and he started getting more suspicious.

"Hold on . . . Haruhiko's not with you, is he?"

"You think there's something going on?" I asked.

"No, I guess I don't," Masao said, his tone softening. "But you swear no one's there with you?"

"I've never even looked at another man!"

"You're right, you haven't," he said, then added. "Matter of fact, I'm not so crazy about other men either."

That made me laugh.

"So can I come over?" he asked again.

"No, no! Not today, okay?" I could hear my voice grow shrill again. "I don't feel well."

Gracefully, he gave up, "How about tomorrow or the day after?"

"I'll come see you the day after tomorrow." And that was the end of the conversation.

I had been lying on my stomach while we talked; now I sat up. What would Masao think when he found out I had a penis? I was still a woman, so maybe it wouldn't bother him, but he wasn't going to be very happy about having to look at it. If I could keep him from seeing it . . . but of course that was impossible. In the spring I would be returning to college—I had taken a year off to work at LOVESHIP—and we were going to get married when I graduated in two years. It wasn't the sort of thing you could keep hidden for the rest of your life, and even if you did manage to, think of the stress. When I saw him the day after tomorrow, I was going to have to come clean.

On the other hand, what if my big toe returned to normal by tomorrow?

What if it was just an illusion that my next deep sleep would dispel? If that happened, it would be a terrible waste not to have spent tonight carefully examining my toe-penis while I still had it.

Coming to this conclusion, I eagerly stretched out my hand and took hold of my toe.

"So your toe didn't return to normal that night?" M. asked.

I shook my head.

"Did you go the hospital?"

"For what? Do you think they could do anything?"

"No, I suppose not. If I were you, I probably wouldn't go either."

"The best that could happen is that I'd end up some doctor's guinea pig."

"So what did you do yesterday?"

"I spent the day at home." Before these words were even out of my mouth, I'd broken into a grin. M. smiled back; she knew.

"Well, how is it?"

"Perfect. I mean—" I paused. "Of course, I have no way of confirming whether the pleasure I felt is really like it is for a man."

"It's not able to make babies, is it?"

"No, there's no ejaculation."

"So it's an organ devoted purely to pleasure."

M.'s bluntness made my cheeks grow warm.

"You're right," I said, quelling my embarrassment. "This is one tool that won't make work fun and easy, and won't make the world a better place."

"Oh? I think it could make things more fun, don't you? After all, it seems quite capable of maintaining an erection."

"What are you saying? What's so much fun about this *thing* of mine?"

M. peered at me quizzically, totally not understanding me. A few seconds passed, and her lips eased into a smile. "I'm saying that you can use your penis, not just to amuse yourself, but to give pleasure to others."

"Hold on, hold on. Just what sort of person would actually want to get pleasure from a *thing* like *this*?"

M. seemed at a loss for words, and a bit sorry for me. "There are all kinds of people in this world, you know, and they're into all sorts of things."

"Are you talking about weirdos? Well, it just so happens that I'm not that weird, and neither is Masao, so this *thing* of mine isn't going anywhere."

M. heaved a sigh, seeming exasperated. "Do you have any idea why something like this happened to a person like you?"

"I wish I did!" I said. Then I started to ask M. about what was really on my mind: "You know how I said that I felt maybe Yoko had put a curse on me?"

M. was about to take a sip of barley tea, but now turned to look at me.

"This happened," I said, "the day after the forty-ninth day rites."

M. put her cup down. "Is there a reason why you think she might have put a curse on you?"

"No. But who knows. Yoko could have harbored a grudge against me, right? Without my knowing? Everyone says that I'm dense."

"I don't know much about these occult things," M. said, turning away. "Assuming for the time being Yoko had something to do with this thing that happened, what makes you so certain it's a curse? Maybe it's a gift. A curse would be a lot more devastating."

"That's precisely the point. I have this feeling that Yoko has sent me a riddle, a riddle that isn't devastating, that doesn't mean much at all, simply to confuse me, and right now she's heaping curses upon me in the next world for being such an idiot, such a dunce."

I had spent the whole day before thinking: Yoko had been very good to me, it was true, but had I ever been good to her? The fact of the matter was, I hadn't been able to do anything for Yoko, not a thing. Or maybe it was more accurate to say that she never gave me an opportunity to do anything for her. She never discussed her problems with me, never shared her thoughts. She would tell me bits and pieces about her life if I asked, but at a certain point she would just put an end to the conversation. And to tell the truth, I have hardly any idea how she spent her time or what she thought about. She knew Masao was my boyfriend, but she had never mentioned whether she was seeing anyone herself.

It hurts to think this, but maybe I wasn't a very good friend to Yoko. She thought I was the kind of person who could get along with anyone. In fact, there were plenty of people I didn't like, but I think what Yoko meant was that even where our friendship was concerned, I was only close to her because events had brought us together. In other words, I hadn't *chosen* to be friends with Yoko. That was true, and not only in her case: I had never once actually chosen a friend. I couldn't imagine what standards one might use for doing that.

Presumably my understanding of things is much shallower than I realize. That's what it means to be dense. That's why I wanted M.'s insight; she wasn't so dense. Did Yoko hate me?

For a long time, M. said nothing. I suspected her view of things was pretty clear; she was simply trying to decide how to put it. I could understand that much.

Finally, M. offered a reluctant reply. "I really can't see why Yoko would put a curse on you. I mean, it's not as if she ever hesitated to say what an idiot you were when she was alive, right?"

"That's true."

"This *thing* on your toe might be some sort of message from Yoko, I agree—but even if that's the case, maybe you don't need to figure out what it means right away. It's only been two days; you can't know if it's good or bad yet . . . For the time being, why don't you just enjoy it?"

I nodded, but there was something M. wasn't saying. At the moment, though, I felt too vulnerable to keep trying to get her to say it.

My sock had been lying on the floor the whole time we'd been talking. I scooped it up and slipped my foot back into it.

"I want to ask you one more question," M. said.

"What is it?"

She hesitated again, then fired away. She was tossing all discretion to the wind.

"What would you do if Yoko were still alive, and she asked you to put your toe-penis in her?"

♥ ♥ ♥

Masao was waiting for me at the wicket at the train station. I wouldn't go so far as to say that all my worries faded when I saw him standing there, but I did feel a kind of peace—the relief that signifies a person's arrival back at a place where she was meant to be. I take more pleasure spending time with people I know well than I do getting to know new people. So I always try to keep up my relationships for as long as possible. At this point, I had been going out with Komiya Masao for three and a half years.

Masao was dressed casually, a beige jacket over a blue sweatshirt. He was carrying a bag with leeks poking out the top. When I got through the wicket, he wrapped his arm around me.

"I had nothing else to do, so I thought I'd come meet you."

"It'd be nice if you had nothing else to do more often."

As we walked down the stairs that led out of the station, the shopping arcade across the way came into view—it was another familiar sight. I had been coming to Masao's apartment here for three and a half years, but I wouldn't be coming anymore after this month, because in April Masao was moving into a company dormitory for single employees. A few more visits and I would be saying goodbye to this part of town.

"So did Iwai barge in on you the day before yesterday?" I asked.

"Haruhiko, you mean? I'm happy to say he did not." Masao said, looking annoyed. "Yamagishi said he called him, too. That guy sure has some nerve."

Masao may not have been aware that he still called Haruhiko Haruhiko, and not by his family name. He always called the other guys in his group by their family names—Yamagishi, Hatakeda, and so on. Calling him Haruhiko was a lingering trace of the close friendship they had once had. Masao used to tell me, "Haruhiko's kind of strange, but he isn't a bad guy." Haruhiko, for his part, once told me, "Masao doesn't look like a slob, so, you know, I can introduce him to my other friends."

"You can't forgive him?"

"How the hell could I? Imagine how Hatakeda must feel!"

Hatakeda was the guy whose girlfriend Haruhiko had stolen. The girlfriend was also Hatakeda's first, so he was in pain. For whatever reason, Hatakeda was unlucky in love. Maybe it was his awkwardness. He was a pleasant guy, he wasn't bad-looking, and he also happened to be enrolled at one of the better-known universities, which helps; but he just couldn't find a girlfriend. His buddies coached him on how to go about doing it, and it worked! He met this girl, whereupon Haruhiko—who had been one of his buddies coaching him—came along and wooed her away. Hatakeda was so miserable that no one could bear to look at him.

Among the group of friends, Masao was the angriest at this turn of events. He was also the most disappointed, because Haruhiko had been his closest friend.

"I mean, of all the girls out there, he has to go and steal Hatakeda's! It's inhuman, if you ask me."

"Aren't you being even more cruel to Hatakeda, talking like that?" He and his friends used to mock Hatakeda behind his back because he was such a loser with girls—until this business happened with Haruhiko.

Masao snorted, then mumbled without looking at me, "I wouldn't talk. That company you were working for was pretty inhuman, too."

I let that go. This wasn't the first time he said something nasty about LOVESHIP, and I knew that if I said anything in defense of Yoko's enterprise, it would put him in a foul mood. Masao had been unhappy I was working at LOVESHIP, and had absolutely hated the fact that I was so close to Yoko. He had disliked Yoko, and she returned the favor. So much that she would sometimes ask me, sadly, "Do you *seriously* like that guy?"

What would you do if Yoko were still alive, and she asked you to put your toe-penis in her?

M.'s shot zinged back to me. It had come so completely out of the blue when she said it, I was left stammering.

"What . . . what are you talking about?"

M. wagged a hand in the air, annoyed. "There's no point getting all shocked. Just think about it."

"You're telling me you think Yoko was a pervert?"

"Different people have different ideas of what's kinky and what's not. Before you try to make up your mind about that, can you just give me an answer?"

"But I can't even entertain the idea!"

"No, I suppose not," M. muttered. "That's the way you are, isn't it?"

She could say whatever she wanted; it was impossible for me to imagine putting my toe-penis into anyone. Even if I screwed up my courage and tried it, the mere thought of someone's warm, moist vagina or anus—enveloping my toe-penis—was gross! That wouldn't change no matter whose orifice it was.

The notion that Yoko might desire my toe-penis also struck me as laughable. Supposing she was sexually frustrated, she wasn't so lacking in dignity that she would go ahead and satisfy herself with whatever happened to be available. M. had a reputation as a dreamer; I wasn't sure I could dream anything as wild as this!

As we neared his apartment, Masao dug his key out of his jacket pocket, and I started feeling nervous about my big-toe P, which was, at the moment, sitting quietly in the tip of my plain-toed shoe. I would have no choice but to tell Masao this evening about this bizarre development of my body. I had coolly taken stock of my situation the day before, concluding that it wasn't so earth-shattering as to cause Masao to lose his head. I had prepared what I would say:

All that's happened, really, is that one of my toes has changed shape— I'm no different as a person from who I was before. Basically, the only problems we'll have to deal with are that I'll no longer be able to wear shoes with pointed toes, and I won't be able to walk around barefoot in the presence of other people, so we won't be able to go to the pool anymore . . .

Cardboard boxes were stacked in a corner of the apartment in anticipation of Masao's move; his apartment wasn't spacious to begin with, and this made it feel cramped. Masao opened the window, but the impression of confinement didn't go away—not with the wide expanse of concrete wall the window opened to.

"This apartment was pretty livable until last year, when they built that place next door."

It was some sort of house, as far as we could tell, that had suddenly sprung up on the neighbor's land, taking over part of the back garden and depriving Masao's apartment of sunlight and breezes. To make matters worse, the person who moved in was in a band: when the windows were open, it was like the guy's piano and synthesizers were right in the room with us. Masao moaned about how his quality of life had declined, but the rent was cheap for an apartment with a bath, and when air-conditioning season arrived and the neighbor shut his windows, the sounds were muffled, so Masao had decided to stay in the apartment for another year, until he graduated.

There wasn't any noise today.

"Funny, it's been noisy again these past few days." Masao stood on tiptoes and peered out. "The windows seem to be open."

I hung up my jacket as Masao tried to clamber up onto the windowsill.

"I want to get a look at the bastard's face while I still have the chance."

All we knew about the pianist next door was that he was a young guy. He was a pretty amazing player, able to dash off boogie-woogie arrangements of Mozart and stuff like that. Masao grumbled about what a pain the guy was, scrunching his lips into a frown, but much of his annoyance might have stemmed from envy, since he couldn't play a note himself.

"What good will that do?"

"You're not interested?"

"Not in the least."

Masao slid down off the windowsill and stood beside me at the sink where I was washing vegetables. "You have way too little curiosity," he sighed, reaching up to bring a ceramic pot down from its shelf. "You know, I've seen his woman."

"Whose woman?"

"That guy, the pianist, his woman. Talk about heavy makeup."

I glanced at Masao. His expression was irritatingly jolly.

"Haruhiko would like her, I bet," he continued.

"And you? Do you like her?"

"She's not bad—to fool around with."

My hands fell still. My gaze wandered to the big toe of my right foot. Masao patted me on the shoulder, sensing something amiss.

"Hey, don't take it the wrong way. All guys talk like that."

I barely noticed this gratuitous remark. I was focusing instead on the fact that I had just been made acutely conscious of something I had never given a moment's thought to before, something now specifically relevant to my own life.

"Has it ever felt gross to you?" I asked, looking up. "I mean . . . when you're doing it with a woman?"

For a moment Masao seemed at a loss, maybe because the question seemed totally out of context, but his answer was perfectly clear:

"Never. It feels good."

"But isn't it all gooey inside? Doesn't it make you want to pull out?"

"I thought that in junior high," Masao chuckled. "But once I actually experienced it, it felt good—nice and warm. I suppose there were girls who made me feel gross . . . or maybe not, I don't know. Why are you asking? You just got curious all of a sudden?"

I had been planning to break the big news to Masao as nonchalantly as I could, impressing upon him that it really wasn't a big deal, but now that he was standing in front of me I had to catch my breath. His mouth was hanging open; he had no idea what was going on. I decided to give myself a few seconds' grace by placing the vegetables into the colander. Then, just as I was licking my lips, preparing to launch into my tale, the phone rang, and Masao trotted off to answer it.

I had no choice but to return to my cooking. I put water in the ceramic pot and set it on the stove. I retrieved the chicken from the bag at my feet. All along, I kept hearing this: *Once I actually experienced it, it felt good— nice and warm.* Would that be true for me? Did female genitals make male genitals feel good, period? Was that the way things were? Without realizing it, little by little, I began to picture myself enjoying the tactile sensations of being inside a vagina. Then I came to my senses. What was I doing?!

Behind me, Masao banged down the receiver. Then he stomped over to me with a scowl on his face.

"That was Haruhiko," he said, practically spitting out his name. "Sniveling asshole asked why I won't listen to his side of the story."

"Shouldn't you just do him the favor of saying your friendship is over? That's how you feel, right?" Then, in part because Masao had no reply to this, I pushed some more: "Seriously, you two are acting just like schoolgirls."

"Yeah, thanks. Sorry to bother you with my petty concerns," he said, then walked away.

"Are you mad?"

"Oh no, not at all," he said. He sat down at the table heavily.

If you're mad, why don't you just say so? Getting sulky and denying it—you can't get more schoolgirlish than that. Of course, the whole way Masao and his buddies interacted was always like that: not only were they glued to each other at school, they also worked and traveled together every holiday. They were so intensely intimate that even schoolgirls would be embarrassed to act that way in this day and age. And now they were ganging up on one of their number, making up their mind to ostracize him . . . My use of the word "schoolgirl" was not inappropriate.

Nevertheless, I had something important to say this evening. With Masao in a foul mood, there was a danger the discussion would lead to our breaking up. I hadn't said anything awful enough to merit an apology, but maybe I should say I'm sorry anyway. As I skimmed the scum from the broth, I tried to think of a way to make Masao feel better. And then all of a sudden it occurred to me: *Would it really be so terrible if I broke up with him?*

The thought came as a surprise. Until then I had never seriously considered that option. It was true that on three occasions during the three and a half years since we met at a Shinjuku pub and started dating, we had talked about breaking up. The first time was when I started working at LOVESHIP, which led to a change in the rhythm of our day-to-day lives. The second was when Haruhiko lied to Masao about hitting on me. And the third time was just recently, when Masao suggested that we move in together once he started his job and I refused. We actually separated for about three months the first time, and I didn't see him until he called to say he realized he didn't like being apart. All that time, deep in my heart, I had been hoping our relationship wouldn't really have to end.

I've never wanted to break up or stop being friends with anyone. Once I connect with someone and we become friends, I stay friends with that person for the rest of my life; if I develop feelings for a guy and we start going out, it seems perfectly natural that we should get married and stay together until we die. Yoko said thinking like this was way too naïve, but in my view everyone around me was caught up in a game; they were making something simple much too complicated, going through the same motions time after time, getting together and splitting up, getting together and splitting up.

Could it be that Yoko's death, by forcing us to part, had changed me? I had the feeling that, even if I did break up with Masao, I would be okay. Just look how well I was doing since I had to say goodbye to Yoko. Hold on . . . what am I trying to say? That I liked Yoko more than Masao? No, that's confusing two different things. It's a mistake to compare friends and lovers as though they were on the same plane.

A puff of steam billowed up. The pot was boiling over.

"What the hell are you doing?" Masao came over and adjusted the flame on the stove. He peered into my eyes. "Are you pouting?"

I shook my head. For whatever reason, Masao's mood had improved; he nudged my back, saying, "Time to switch places. Take a break." He started to grate daikon, muttering to himself that he hadn't really been angry anyway. I decided to take him up on his offer and relax.

In the wake of Masao's lightening up and a mellow dinner, I found myself feeling quite different from before: no trace remained of my earlier willingness to split up. Masao was a nice young man who was easy to talk to and who didn't make people feel uptight. It's a wonderful thing, the existence of two different sexes. No matter how attractive one may find other people of the same sex, there's no possibility of ever becoming more than friends; with members of the opposite sex, however, one can be friends and lovers and even spouses, all at the same time. How happy I felt as I sat there drinking my coffee. Masao seemed to be feeling pretty easy, too.

"What was that about earlier? Asking if I find sex gross?"

"It just occurred to me that I'm glad I'm a woman." I felt so giddy I might as well have been drunk.

"Yeah, I'm glad you're a woman, too."

"Oh?" I said, grinning. "How would you feel, like, if I had a penis?"

"A woman with a penis? Isn't that a problem?" Masao had been infected by my silliness. "Or are you talking about a hermaphrodite? I'd be okay with it if you were like that. I don't think I'd like to be penetrated, though."

"What! I wouldn't do that!" I laughed so hard I fell over.

"Besides, I know perfectly well that you don't have a penis."

"I didn't," I cried out merrily, "but I got one a couple days ago!"

Masao feigned surprise, his expression fantastically exaggerated. "Wow, how did you manage that? Did you take a dip in the Fountain of Salmacis or something? Were you brought down by the curse of Simone de Beauvoir? What about your female parts? Still healthy?"

"As fit as ever. The penis isn't there—it's on the big toe of my right foot."

Masao's expression turned solemn. His manner remained exaggerated.

"Hmm. Sounds like everything's fine then. No problem if it's just the big toe of your right foot. You're still a woman! Have you jerked off? If you don't know how, I can show you a few tricks, my charming underclassman."

It dawned upon me that my confession had been a bit too blithe. Masao jumped on top of me.

"Maybe we should have a contest—see who's got the bigger penis. Come to think of it, you kind of look like a boy, you know? Let's pretend we're gay!"

Masao wrapped his arms around me. Immediately my breasts began to tingle, and all the strength drained from my body. I was having all sorts of first-time experiences today, and my powerful reaction to this simple hug was yet another. The fact was, the words Masao had just whispered had put me in a trance. *Boy. Gay.*

"I think you're really cute. You know, actually, I've liked you for a long time." Masao was throwing himself into this little drama in earnest. "I can see you're surprised. But the truth is, love doesn't distinguish between the sexes."

That last line was hilarious, but I didn't laugh. I had been swept up in the sweet waves of sensuality rolling through my chest. When Masao put his lips on mine, I simply let him do as he pleased. I was helpless even to kiss back.

"You're as convincing as I am," Masao said, lifting his lips from mine for a moment. Then he kissed me once again, very gently. The scene he was acting out was of two young men kissing for the first time, so the movement of his tongue in my mouth was light and tender, more so than I had known in a long while. It sort of felt like when we were going out in the beginning. Except that I couldn't recall ever being as excited as I was now. I had *become* the character I was playing, the boy whose love for an older boy was being fulfilled—and this had me extremely excited.

And what about Masao? Had he ever touched me the way he was now? In the early days of our relationship he was rather clumsy. It was like he was doing what he'd read he was supposed to do, without really understanding what was going on; it wasn't like he was doing something he wanted to be doing. The same was true of me, to a certain extent, but it had to have been even more so for Masao. Because it was like he was caught in a fierce struggle with the blind desire he felt. If he stopped trying to keep his desire in check and allowed it to run rampant, it would be frightening; and when, after we had already been together a few times, he let that desire run free, I got so unnerved I thought I was going to throw up. But now, each move Masao made was brimming with love, and it all came naturally to him. He was sensitive to how I was feeling, but he was overflowing with confidence and showed no hesitation. His caresses were relaxed and in control. I'd never experienced anything like this, even after we had grown accustomed to each other. The only thing that had changed once he got used to me was that he had started cutting corners.

Was it because he was pretending I was male that he was able to touch me like this, or had the shift in perspective in our sex play elicited a style of lovemaking he had never tried before? Masao was always saying that he had no sexual interest in men, had no homosexual tendencies, so perhaps it was the latter. All the same, I couldn't dismiss the former so easily. It made sense that these caresses—which I was responding to because they were less calculated, more spontaneous and genuine—had been enabled by the fact that, in Masao's mind, he was making out with someone of the same sex. For a moment, I found myself thinking: *Homosexual love isn't so bad—gay love . . . between two men . . . Maybe I wouldn't have minded being born a man, after all . . .*

Masao's fingers started undoing the buttons of my blouse. He whispered, his tone sweet, "It's okay. This isn't a bad thing we're doing—it really isn't." I had never known Masao was so into acting. "People write literature about being gay, you know."

"The truth is, we'd be better off if women just vanished off the face of the earth—who needs such stupid, dirty animals anyway?" I said, marveling at my own ability to improvise. "And if they're not going to go away, at the very least they ought to keep their mouths shut and stay out of the way like the objects they're meant to be. That's what they are—tools to satisfy the desires of straight men, those fools."

"Ah, you're so clever."

"It's only natural that I know about these things! I'm a transsexual," I said as Masao uncovered my breasts. "I had the operation done in Singapore."

Masao guffawed as he pulled down the zipper of my skirt. By then it had entirely slipped my mind that I had a penis.

"Chopped it off, huh?"

"I felt so much better afterward," I said.

Masao eased my underpants down, planting kisses on my thighs along the way. Deep in my being, something tightened. I was feeling a more heightened sexuality than I ever had. The pleasures I was anticipating as he undressed me, however, were those of a woman. Allowing my eyes to shut, I waited.

A yelp from Masao, and my eyes popped open.

"What the hell is this?!" he yelled.

He was clutching my sock in his hand, a look of utter disbelief on his face. I leapt up, flustered, suddenly having to confront the reality of what was happening. On the big toe of my right foot there was a penis. And though it was only mildly excited, it was definitely getting erect.

"What happened to you?" Masao's voice was trembling.

"I had them move my thing when they chopped it off," I said, in the hope that a joke might break the tension. "Seemed like such a waste, you know."

Masao looked mortified.

I took a deep breath. "I told you, I've been like this since a couple days ago."

"Don't joke with me, please."

"It's the solemn truth."

"How come you're so calm, then?"

"It's already been three days."

Masao pressed the hand holding my sock to his forehead. "Oh my god. This is just too wild."

"Calm down. It's really not that wild. Are you listening to me? That's the only part of me that's changed."

Masao opened his eyes a crack and cast a sidelong glance at my toe-penis. He shook his head.

"Sure is weird, huh?"

I felt a bit hurt by this. But for now, calming Masao was my first priority. "It's better than having one sprout on my forehead, isn't it?"

The fact that I blurted this out probably indicates that I wasn't exactly in a normal state of mind either. Masao didn't say anything. He just kept crouching there, silently. Noticing that I was naked, I scooped up my underwear. Masao didn't look up, even when I started putting my clothes back on. When I zipped up my skirt, I plucked the sock from Masao's hand. Then, finally, he looked up. There was a nasty gleam in his eyes.

"So you wanted to be a man. Is that it?"

"Hardly! And I haven't become a man."

"No, but you wanted to be one. Deep in your heart you yearned for a penis."

"Don't tell me what I wanted or didn't want."

"I've read Beauvoir."

"Well, I haven't!"

"Whether or not you've read her isn't the point."

"Exactly—the point is whether or not you're willing to acknowledge that I'm still a woman."

"Don't try to make it my problem."

We weren't communicating at all. I was close to tears. What the hell was Masao so angry about, anyway? It wasn't as if I had grown a hideous wart or something. I had simply acquired a new organ that looked just like one he had himself.

Suddenly there was a pounding on the front door. Masao spun around. For a moment he seemed unsure how to respond; then he got to his feet.

No sooner did I hear the click of the bolt turning in the door than someone exploded into the room. The thought that it might be a burglar flashed through my mind and I started to stand up, but the person who came barging into the apartment, his face so dazzlingly red that it was clear he was drunk, was none other than Iwai Haruhiko.

"What the hell are you doing here!" Masao shouted.

Haruhiko paid no attention to Masao or me and plopped down in a chair. Masao sat next to me, furious.

"So sorry," Haruhiko said brazenly. "Hope I'm not interrupting."

"I asked you what you're doing here," Masao replied.

The tension between these two men was so thick that, rather than being angry at Haruhiko for butting in at just this moment, I got swept up in their agitation.

Haruhiko opened his bloodshot eyes so wide they bulged. "Like you don't know! Sneaky bastards."

"If we're sneaky, you're too open."

"Open about what?"

"About the fact that you're a scumbag, for instance. You've got 'pig' written all over you."

"What, you're talking about Hatakeda's woman?" Haruhiko said, suddenly seeming reasonable. "I feel awful about that. I didn't mean to hurt Hatakeda. I realized what I did was wrong, so I dumped her."

"What good does that do? It's too late! She won't go back to Hatakeda."

"He's better off without her. A flake like that . . . acts so prim all the time, but the second some guy makes eyes at her, *bam*, just like that, she flits off with him. She wasn't right for Hatakeda anyway."

"Don't be a son of a bitch. You seduced her."

"You know how I am! I make eyes at women as a way of being polite, that's all! I didn't really mean to make a pass at her!"

I was staring at Haruhiko. I couldn't figure out how this guy could be such a lady-killer. He wasn't handsome, he didn't dress well, he wasn't refined. He wasn't a smooth talker, and he didn't seem either considerate or sincere. In fact he was precisely the opposite: he ogled women's bodies so shamelessly it was rude. Masao was right—he had "playboy" written all over him. How was it possible that so many women fell for him?

Come to think of it, Yoko had had no problem with Haruhiko. She liked his head-on approach to life. The time when Masao and I went out for drinks with them, they seemed to get along fine. And Haruhiko seemed to like Yoko, too, even if he said later, "I like strong women, but I wouldn't want to try anything with her."

"The thing is," Masao went on with his inquisition, "you treat women like objects."

"I don't mean to! It's just that sooner or later after I've been going out with a girl, I get tired of her."

"Then why do you go on chasing them?"

"As if it's possible to stop! I *need* women, man."

"Then go to the baths or something."

The way these two men were going on, it was like I didn't exist.

"You're totally misunderstanding me. Whenever I start going out with a girl, I'm always praying that this time it's going to work and I'll be able to go on loving her."

"Sounds good, except it's bullshit."

This was getting uncomfortable. Was there any point in my staying? On the other hand, if only Haruhiko would leave, then Masao and I could continue our discussion. I wanted to prove to him, in the most practical of ways, that I was as much a woman as I had ever been. I decided to wait it out.

"C'mon, have I done anything bad to you?" Haruhiko pleaded, his voice rising.

Masao didn't answer.

"You and I were such pals. And now you're going to end it because, just once, I did something to some other guy?"

"Pretty sickening choice of words, don't you think?"

I agreed with Masao there. Haruhiko sounded like a husband who'd had a fling and was begging his wife for forgiveness.

"What's the big deal, anyway?" Haruhiko answered, trying a different tack. "You were always making fun of Hatakeda yourself. As I recall, you said he was a total loser who couldn't get laid if his life depended on it."

"That's completely different."

"Who cares about Hatakeda? What does he matter to us?"

At this, Masao looked Haruhiko right in the eyes. "It's true. He doesn't matter," he said quietly. "Not to me, anyway."

Haruhiko's expression softened. "Yeah, well, the same with me."

"No, it's not. You've got something against him."

"What are you talking about?"

"You stole his girlfriend because you've got something against him."

"I don't have any grudges against that clown."

"Then maybe you have some sort of complex about him?"

"A complex about him? What?" Haruhiko was on the verge of breaking into laughter when suddenly his expression froze. After a few seconds, his face relaxed, and he smiled. "Maybe *you're* jealous of Hatakeda?"

"Huh? Why would I be?"

"Because I stole his girlfriend instead of yours." Haruhiko said, his tone triumphant.

Now it was Masao's turn to freeze. I had no idea what was going on.

Haruhiko gestured in my direction with his chin. "I told you I hit on her, right? That was ages before I made a pass at Hatakeda's stupid girlfriend."

Masao swiveled his head listlessly in my direction.

"He's lying," I said.

"You just didn't notice," Haruhiko responded immediately. "Because you're so naïve. You're way too good for Masao, you know? I bet you've never been with anyone but him, right?"

"Haruhiko . . . ," Masao intoned.

Ignoring him, Haruhiko leaned toward me. "Let me tell you something, my innocent thing. Once Masao and a woman I picked up and I—we had a threesome."

At that, Masao lunged at Haruhiko, kicking the table away and toppling the boxes piled in the corner.

I don't know what happened after that, because I grabbed my backpack and jacket and ran out of Masao's apartment. I kept running until I was exhausted.

Chapter 2

I was in a daze for three days. So much had happened in so short a time that while I wanted to make sense of my new situation, to figure out what was happening to me, I couldn't concentrate. I muddled through the days mechanically.

The two things that I couldn't get out of mind were the vague anger, mixed with shock, on Masao's face when he discovered my toe-penis, and the bond between Haruhiko and Masao, so intimate as to exclude everyone else. Haruhiko's claim that he and Masao had been involved in a threesome with some woman certainly hadn't pleased me, but it was less that than the bizarre, twisted feelings the two men had for each other—the sense that they were more than just "friends"—that I found unbearable.

For some time I had suspected that Masao was seeing another woman on the side. He himself had intimated, though half in jest, that he was sleeping with someone else. This didn't bother me. It would have been entirely different if this other woman had hurt our relationship, but since this wasn't the case, I saw no need to pressure him to be faithful. Needless to say, the thought of going out and having a fling of my own never occurred to me. My women friends couldn't believe it. "And you say you really like him?" they would ask.

This business about the threesome came as a shock, however. Sex—kinky sex in particular—was a frequent topic of conversation among my friends, so I had acquired a rich store of knowledge on the subject. But I never thought I'd know anyone who was actually involved in threesomes or spouse swapping or things like that, even if I fully expected to encounter individuals with more common predilections, like homosexuality or

S&M. And here was my own lover taking part in a threesome! Somehow I found myself laughing, even though it wasn't funny. Laughing made me feel a little better.

A drive might have taken my mind off things, but the car I had been using wasn't mine; it had belonged to LOVESHIP. I didn't feel like doing anything else. My toe-penis was no longer tempting. The phone didn't ring but once, stopping before I could pick up.

On the fourth day, Masao called. "I'm nearby," he said, sounding anxious. "I'm sure you have your own ideas about what's going on, but I don't want our relationship to end this way."

"Are you and Iwai gay? Is that it?"

"No, absolutely not. But at least let me explain."

When he arrived, Masao was pale, and he kept rubbing his eyes.

"Haruhiko has a peculiar way of relating to people. When I say people, I guess I really mean guys. I don't think he's gay or anything. It's just that . . . he cements his friendships with guys by having their private parts touch. Of course, I'm talking metaphorically. He exposes his emotional weaknesses, the aspects of himself he's ashamed of—exactly the kinds of things people don't ordinarily share with others—as a way of getting close to a person. It works because he doesn't try to get the other guy to reveal his own private parts. If the guy Haruhiko has exposed himself to happens to have a similar shameful secret of his own, it's a done deal. Because the other guy can't help sympathizing very deeply. He sees Haruhiko as a true, rare friend. He's able to cover his private parts, keep them out of sight and out of mind, and concern himself instead with Haruhiko's. And yet the fact that he feels such sympathy for Haruhiko reveals that he, too, has precisely the same shameful private parts."

I didn't know what Masao was talking about at all, but I nodded.

"Once the two guys become partners, connected by their private parts like this, they're enveloped in a sense of well-being that is, in a way, sensual. Even though they're the same sex. As a matter of fact, it may be better than a partnership between a man and a woman. Men and women come together by fitting their sexual organs together—their literal 'private parts,' in the usual meaning of the word. But you know, lately I've been thinking that maybe it's not right to refer to the genitals as 'private parts,' as if they were something that had to be hidden, something to be ashamed of. After all, we all have them—they're perfectly ordinary. Sure, it can feel great to connect with someone via genitals, but when you allow your *emotional* private parts to touch—the parts of yourself you're most ashamed of—this relief washes over you, and you experience this amazing sense of trust in another person. You want to lean on him for support, and you put yourself entirely in his hands. I got caught in this web of Haruhiko's, and for a while I was totally into him."

Masao sighed deeply. It was hard for him to talk about when it was something he didn't even want to think about.

"I really hope it won't make you angry when I say this, but the truth is, there was a time when I depended on Haruhiko even more than I depended on you. I used to hang out with him, go drinking with him, telling myself that I didn't need women. That was when you started working at LOVESHIP, the three months when we didn't see each other. That's when Haruhiko invited me to go with him to this woman's place, and I went."

My whole body tensed. Masao was staring intently at me, trying to read my expression. I couldn't bring myself to say a word.

"I spent these last three days mulling things over. Trying to make up my mind if I was just going to say that Haruhiko was lying. But I didn't want to lie to you. Because you've never lied to me. I could bear you looking down on me for doing something dumb, but I couldn't bear being rude or disrespectful or lying to you. It would be like piling on the infidelities."

"Why did Iwai ask you to go with him to that woman's place?"

"He probably wanted to cheer me up, since I was such a mess."

"And he thought sex would cheer you up?"

"Maybe he figured woman troubles could be cured by a woman."

"And were you cured?"

Masao met my gaze silently. For some reason my heart was beating wildly. Then Masao lowered his eyes.

"There was something wrong with me then," he said.

"Was that why you wanted to break up?"

"Yes. I didn't really *want* to break up, not deep down. So when you told me you didn't want to break up, I was overjoyed. I was just being stubborn, that's all."

"Why? What was the—"

"I thought that maybe you didn't really like me that much."

I hadn't the foggiest that Masao felt that way, and a stab of pain went deep inside me. "But I told you so many times that I loved you," I said.

"I wanted you to love me more," he replied hoarsely.

I buried my face in my knees, which I had drawn up against my breasts. My heart ached so badly it felt like someone was drilling a hole in it. I couldn't raise my head.

"You always act so indifferent," Masao went on, his words drumming pitilessly into my ears. "I always thought that when a girl is really into a guy, she wants to be with him all the time, like they're a pair, and she always wants to do stuff with him. You're not like that, you're cool, and so I thought that something was missing, until it dawned on me that that's just the way you are. And that was when I realized what an immature boy I was."

It's painful to find out that, without knowing it, you've been making someone suffer. You feel helpless because there's no guarantee you're going to act differently, and then you're just going to keep on making the person suffer. Was I born with this coldness, this inability to communicate warmth, which made people I truly cared for want more and more? Had Yoko wanted more from me, too?

I had never craved affection so much that it caused me pain. The signs of affection I got, freely and spontaneously, were always enough. Why weren't people more like me in this way?

Masao was saying that when two people let their emotional private parts touch, they experienced great relief and trust in each other. But this made no sense to me. I mean, I could understand it in general terms, but I couldn't understand going to such extravagant lengths to get there. Couldn't people learn to feel trust in everyday interactions? Why were they so full of doubt and suspicion? What a way to live. "Emotional private parts"? Now physical private parts I could relate to, especially lately . . .

"You follow me?" Masao asked. "I felt unsatisfied for a while, but then I

44

settled down. I've been really happy with our relationship, and I've come to realize, I really have, that I like you exactly the way you are. I don't care if your big toe has turned into a penis—I don't want to lose you."

I looked up very slowly. Masao's cheeks were flushed.

"If you're not sick of me, I want to stay together."

My eyes clouded over, and I nodded without hesitation.

That was three days ago, and here I was, back in Masao's apartment, in bed, where we'd been spending most of our time. Making out after making up is great, because it feels fresh and new. Some couples are always fighting, even though they love each other, and I'm sure part of the reason is that heightened intimacy that comes during sex right after the disagreement ends.

But Masao and I weren't just making love in bed the last three days. We spent a good deal of time studying my toe-penis.

For starters, Masao wanted to see what it could do. When I told him I didn't want to, not with him looking, he called me a hypocrite, since I'd once asked him to masturbate while I watched. So I had no choice. But as I expected, under his gaze my toe-penis wilted and refused to comply.

"Aha! Impotent!" Masao chuckled. "You see how sensitive guys are? It's not as easy as you might think!"

As far as I knew, Masao had never experienced any impotence himself; he was only saying that because he liked being the one with more experience.

I had no more success when Masao turned his back; it was only when I made him leave the room that my penis revealed itself in its most splendid form. "Wow!" he cried, when I called him back. "*Very* impressive."

I was impressed myself. Ordinarily my penis just crouched there quietly at the end of my foot, the size of a slightly swollen big toe, but when I fondled it, it grew to a startling length, reaching almost seven inches. Good thing it didn't seem to react to visual stimuli, because I would be in trouble if I started getting an erection walking down the street.

Masao wanted to see my penis have an orgasm, but I couldn't get there, no matter how much I stroked it. When I touched it in front of Masao, I felt no pleasure.

"You're a shy little guy, aren't you?" Masao said, talking directly to my penis. The conversation, to tell the truth, sure wasn't like a man and a woman talking.

"What do you think about when you're playing with your toe-penis?"

"Nothing."

"Nothing? You just jerk off, that's all? You don't imagine anything, or look at anything, or read anything?"

"No, nothing."

"Hmm. Maybe you're not mature enough yet."

"That's what happens when you mature? You start imagining things?"

"Yeah. Try it next time. It'll feel even better."

"I don't know. If I imagine too much, I could turn into a pervert."

"Not if you don't think about weird stuff."

"What should I think about, then?"

"Think about me."

And we both laughed.

"It feels like I've just acquired a younger brother," Masao murmured. "I never really wanted a brother, but I don't know, maybe it would have been nice."

This, surprisingly, didn't bother me at all, since the intimacy between us now was unlike anything we had felt in the past, when we were only lovers. We were closer than ever, on friendlier terms. We were intimate the way we were the moment just before Masao first set eyes on my toe-penis, when we were acting out our little gay drama.

The brotherly feeling vanished, though, each time we made love. I remained a woman through and through. I had this toe-penis, it was true, but it didn't lead us to try anything new. When we made love, Masao ignored my penis completely. In fact, he never touched my penis, even when we weren't having sex.

"I only touch my own thing; I'm not interested in touching anybody else's. Once, at high school camp, I took part in a circle jerk. You were supposed to jerk off the guy next to you. I didn't want to do it, but you can't refuse when it's just guys, you know? I really hated it. I mean, I didn't mind somebody doing me, but it was hard to do it to the next guy. You know what I mean?"

"No, I don't."

Until Masao started talking, his penis had been in my mouth.

"A woman wouldn't understand. I remember when I was in junior high how I thought my penis grew uglier every day."

I wasn't sure how common Masao's feelings about his penis were. His penis didn't strike me as ugly at all, and neither did my own. If I *had* found it ugly or gross or anything like that, I wouldn't have been able to have sex with him. The first time I saw a penis I was shocked, but I got accustomed to the sight. The first time Masao pushed my face against his crotch I was disgusted, but I got used to that, too.

"So," I said, "you don't mind having other people do you—you just mind doing other people."

"What do you mean?"

"Well, you love it when I use my mouth on you."

"On my penis, you mean?" Masao laughed. "But you're a woman, right? You mean you don't like it?"

"I don't dislike it." Even as I said this, I wasn't sure I liked where this conversation was going. I didn't particularly want Masao to put my penis in his mouth or anything.

Masao, who had been lying on his back, rolled over and looked at me.

"I like it when you suck me. Because I feel that you love me. A girl wouldn't put a penis in her mouth unless she really likes the guy, right?"

Dense as I am, this was one time when I had an immediate response: "Sounds like you think your penis is dirty. You feel loved because I'm willing to suck your penis even though it's dirty."

"Yeah, like that." Masao nodded.

"You won't feel loved unless I'm willing to go that far?"

"No, I'm not saying that. But of course I want to feel that I'm loved deeply."

Now I was confused. *I wanted you to love me more*, he had said, and now he was saying, *I want to feel that I'm loved deeply*. He was so consistent in his needs. A few days ago, I was worried he was so starved for love, his life was plagued with doubt, but now he was starting to look like a demanding, spoiled kid.

At the same time, I realized that, in Masao's eyes, an act I had engaged in as a simple expression of love had a weightier meaning—for him it was a sign of "deep love." I felt a surge of emotion. It seemed that my performing fellatio was important, and he took more pleasure in it than he otherwise would have precisely because he thought his penis was dirty. Even a warped sensibility had its advantages.

On the other hand, he showed no hesitation to shove a part of his body he considered dirty into the mouth of someone he loved. *You're a woman, right?* Masao was assuming that a woman feels less revulsion for a penis than a man does. But at the same time, he had agreed that he felt loved *because I'm willing to suck your penis even though it's dirty*, and he himself had said *a girl wouldn't put a penis in her mouth unless she really likes the guy.* So he could only experience deep love if the woman thought his penis was dirty? Was the pleasure he got from fellatio based on a kind of cruelty?

This was all *very* confusing, and a welter of emotions churned in my breast. I tried to see things in a more positive light: Masao's characterization of his penis as something dirty was really just a conceptual game, and in his heart of hearts he didn't actually believe this. That's why he was able to put it in my mouth. He didn't hate his penis. But if so, why did he refuse to touch *mine*? Why did he pull back whenever his leg brushed against it?

I was thinking all this, gazing up at the ceiling, when Masao leaned over and peered into my eyes.

"Do you want to feel deep love?" he asked. And he began to perform an act that he viewed as an expression of *deep love* for a woman. I liked this act, but I didn't *need* it. If he didn't do it, I was fine. I had never thought of the act as a measure of his love for me. Though now that he had told me this was *deep love*, I did feel sort of grateful.

Masao changed positions. Now it was my turn. Guided by Masao's hands, I moved my face closer to his partially erect penis.

I caught my breath. All of a sudden, Masao's penis looked dirty.

♥ ♥ ♥

The spring sunlight streaming through the window warmed me. I could hear the bell at the elementary school ringing. It was early afternoon, and

I was alone. I stripped the sock off my right foot, doubled over, then gently slipped my big toe in my mouth. At first it had a faintly dusty taste, but that quickly faded; then the toe had no taste or smell at all. The half sphere of the nail was hard against my tongue, but its surface was as smooth as if it had been polished, and it didn't feel unpleasant at all. The toe itself soon grew accustomed to the warmth and softness of my mouth. It felt as comfortable in there as a person feels in bed.

With my tongue I tickled my penis. I ran my teeth against it lightly. I squeezed my lips around it. I coated it in saliva. It began to grow. I sucked on it, tightening my cheek muscles. Pleasure ran through the length of my toe-penis, and it became fully erect. In this doubled-over position, my back started to hurt, so I took the toe from my mouth and carefully, lovingly, began to lick it, the way a mother cat licks a kitten. Though it was part of my own body, it almost seemed like a pet. It was such a cute little thing. I had never felt this way toward my vagina. I suddenly now understood why men take their genitals so seriously, whether they hate or love them.

When my leg and neck muscles began to ache, I lowered my foot to the floor and wrapped my hand around my toe-penis. I stroked it up and down, which was very easy to do with all the saliva on it, and the sensation was sweet. In the future I would know what to do when I played with it.

I imagined myself doing this with Masao. He kisses me; he removes my clothes. Before I know what's happening, he's naked, too. Just as I begin to feel cold, he lays his warm body down on top of mine. This is always a wonderful moment. Masao's tongue moves from my lips to my ears, from my ears to my shoulders. The hair hanging over his forehead tickles my chin. I love the prickly feel of his hair at the back of his head. The little pit at the base of his neck makes him look strong. I take Masao's face between my hands, bring it up to my lips, and kiss him. As I draw my lips away, he smiles. Then he lowers his face to my breasts.

I stopped stroking. Masao had said I would like doing this more if I used my imagination, but it was more distracting than exciting. And even a little depressing. I lost any interest in this pursuit of pleasure.

As soon as Masao's penis started to look dirty to me, intercourse left me high and dry. Putting his thing in my mouth became an ordeal that I got through only by not thinking about it. When that part of sex was over, the disgust I was left with prevented me from feeling any excitement or pleasure. I just lay there gasping, like a fish out of water. The rocking of my body as Masao thrust in me might as well have been happening to someone else.

I'm not saying his touch was repugnant to me. I just didn't feel anything. His heavy breathing might have been steam rising from a pot on the stove; his sweat and saliva were like condensation dripping from the ceiling over a bathtub; his caresses felt like a massage with a dry towel. It was the same the next time we had sex, too. And the next. I had never felt *nothing* before, not even the first time we made love, as frightening and embarrassing and painful as the experience was.

A young woman at LOVESHIP told me that after she had an abortion, she couldn't enjoy sex for several months. That changed, but if while lovemaking she ever found herself in the same position she had been in on the operating table, she couldn't go on. My situation wasn't quite the same, but I worried about being permanently scarred. Will I ever recover? Will everything ever be as it was before?

I wasn't certain whether Masao noticed the change that had taken place in me. I tried to keep him from noticing, putting his penis in my mouth as before, fighting the nausea. I'm sure I could have refused, but I had been performing that act for three years and I wasn't sure how to say no now.

I had no problem putting my own penis in my mouth, because the thought that it was something dirty never once crossed my mind. I began to wonder how it would be to suck the penis of someone other than Masao. Would I be able to do it? This made me feel I was being unfaithful to Masao, but surely there was no harm in thinking . . . I tried to imagine the scene, except that I couldn't picture it with any specific guy. And supposing I could, shouldn't he have some say in the matter?

The next time we had sex, I asked Masao to lie on his back. With my lips and fingers, I moved across his body, touching his Adam's apple and his chest, his seedlike nipples and his firm upper arms. I thought this change of position might change my mood. But as I made my way from one part of his body to the next, my mind went blank, and I went on automatic pilot.

Masao lay there luxuriating, arms and legs spread. "I feel like a woman," he said.

"A woman? Why a woman?"

"Because I'm lying here passively while you do what you want."

This grated on my nerves. "You really think that makes you like a woman?"

"I mean, I bet what I'm feeling right now is how girls feel in bed."

For some reason, his saying this wounded my pride. So I went on the attack. "All right, you want my penis? You want me to do you?"

"Don't be an idiot," Masao said, pulling away. "Keep your thing away from me. You'll make me into a faggot."

I placed my hands on Masao's chest and, trying to keep calm, I said, "I'm not a man, Masao."

Masao laughed and pulled me down on him. "I know that. So we're like lesbians now?"

I didn't like that either. I squirmed and tried to get away from him. "No we're not!" I shouted. "You're a man. I'm a woman!"

"You got into it when we were pretending we were gay."

This was true, I was shocked to realize. What was going on here—I was fine with male-male sex but not with female-female sex?

"If I come back as a woman in my next life, I'm going to be a lesbian. I can't imagine sleeping with a guy," Masao suddenly volunteered.

"Do you really want to be reborn as a woman?"

"I wouldn't say I *want* to. I just wouldn't mind if I was. But I'd want to be really pretty."

"If you had the choice to be reborn as a man or a woman, which would you be?"

"Ideally," Masao answered seriously, "I'd like to be born as the only man in the world. Everyone else would be a woman."

This made me burst out laughing, and I suddenly felt more comfortable lying on Masao's chest.

"All right, say you had to be reborn as either a woman or a gay man?"

"That's a tough one. If I'm gay, then I'm supposed to like men, right? So maybe I'd choose to be gay."

This came as a surprise. "Why?"

"I don't know. Maybe because, emotionally, I feel closer to men than women. And because I'd still have a penis."

I found myself lifting my head and extracting my body from Masao's embrace. I felt a knot in my belly, I didn't know why, and wrapped my arms around my waist. I could feel some strong emotion inside me. Evidently I was very, very angry. "In that case," I said, my voice involuntarily rising, "why wait? Why don't you just *be* gay!"

Masao put his arms behind his head. "What the hell are you talking about? A person can't just *become* gay."

"So you wish you had been born gay?"

"Are you kidding! A faggot doesn't have it easy. I mean, I wouldn't want to spend my whole life in the closet."

Come to think of it, was the fact that Masao had sex with women proof that he *wasn't* a faggot? He thought penises were dirty and he didn't like the idea of sex with men, but he felt no qualms about sticking his dirty penis into my mouth *at the same time* that he emotionally felt closer to men than women. He was so confused, his emotional life so riddled with contradictions, he couldn't possibly be normal! . . . But then who was I to talk? I had a penis.

"You know, *I* wouldn't mind being reborn as a man and having a woman I could do whatever I wanted with," I blurted out. But I was as shocked as Masao to hear what I had just said. I had never even thought such a thing before, and yet the words came out as if I'd written them in my diary. What was going on?

The taste in my mouth was suddenly bitter. I hated what I had just said. I didn't *really* think that. Nor did it turn me on. I meant it as an ironic jab at Masao—maybe not at him *per se* but at this whole dumb business. But my attempt at irony had flown right back in my face, and what I was left with was this bizarre picture that was sort of half *sado*, half *maso*: It was me reborn as a man, with the penis between my legs stuffed into a woman's mouth. And the woman with the penis in her mouth was me.

I wiped the vision from my mind. What was going on? I was a healthy, normal woman; I had a terrific guy I was going to marry; I wasn't dissatisfied with life. Everything was fine, but suddenly this grotesque change had forced itself into my life.

"Unrealistic. No woman is just going to let a man do whatever he wants with her," said Masao. "Just think about yourself."

Did I detect some anger in what he was saying?

Alone in my room now, after the last three days with Masao, I leaned back against the wall, clutching my toe-penis. I had the feeling that my relationship with Masao was turning sour. A lot of this was due to changes in my own thinking, which, no doubt, the appearance of my penis had sparked. No . . . that was claiming too much. My penis was just an innocent bystander that gave me pleasure when I was alone.

I began massaging my innocent bystander, which caused a wave of pleasure to undulate up my right leg, making me think it was about to dissolve. A certain amount of feeling seemed to be communicating itself to my female parts. But only my toe-penis had a climax.

I was lucky, I guess, that there seemed to be no intimate connection between my penis and my vagina. Masao, who professed dislike for penises, would have been horrified to see my toe-penis getting hard during foreplay. Once, after sex, he glanced down at my foot and said, "Good boy, you keep quiet down there," and "You can ask her to come out and play later on." He seemed pleased, as I was, to view my toe-penis as an independent organ.

But Masao had to remember how, that time when we were pretending we were gay, my toe-penis had gotten a slight erection without being touched. Why *had* it gotten hard then?

It was true I'd never been so aroused before. On the average I had an orgasm once out of every three or four times we had sex. But I was pretty sure I would have climaxed big time then if our sex hadn't been interrupted midway. Not that I had to have an orgasm; I enjoyed kissing and stroking most. They were the whole reason I shared my bed with Masao.

My body had lost feeling, but pleasure could still be coaxed out of my toe-penis. The one time M. had barely touched it, I'd gotten erect. Masao wasn't going to be of much help in that department, though; it was like he was scared of it. A couple evenings ago, he'd said, "Try using your left hand sometime. It's like someone else is doing you."

"Someone else?"

"Well, doing yourself is always best because you know exactly what you want. You get a different kind of pleasure when someone else does you."

"So why don't you just have someone do you?"

"That's ideal, of course, if you have that option."

"All right, then—will you do me?"

"Nope."

I was pretty sure he would refuse, but not with outright prejudice like that. "Maybe I should try and find someone who will."

"Sure, go for it. Just keep it limited to your penis."

I didn't like Masao treating a part of me like an alien. He was obviously conflicted about it; it was always on his mind. "Could you put your penis inside you?" he asked.

"If my bones were like elastic," I said, laughing.

Masao tried to twist his own leg into his crotch, as if he himself had a toe-penis, to no avail. "You're right," he said. "Sure is a waste, though, considering the size of what you've got. It might be better for you than I am."

I couldn't believe it: Masao was comparing the sizes of our penises!

I'd stopped enjoying sex, and now this. What next? I still liked him, he seemed to like me. But that could change.

The night before, we had gone on a cruise around Tokyo Bay. The wind on deck was cold, and at some point, before we knew it, we were snuggling. There were two other young couples on the deck leaning against the railing, snuggling just as we were. Gazing at the lights on shore as they grew smaller in the distance, I began to feel as if Masao and I were still the way we had been before: a couple made up of an ordinary woman, with no toe-penis, and an ordinary man, with a penis. As long as we forgot about sex, we were still lovers, still on good terms.

As we stepped into the warm cabin, we found ourselves in front of the glass doors of the boat's restaurant. People were eating away; unfortunately, we had neglected to make a reservation. As we walked away, a crew member in a white shirt and black bow tie called out to us from the counter.

"There's a nice place over there," he said, pointing.

We thanked him and walked toward the open door of a café. It was a small room with windows on two sides, allowing you to look out at the nightscape without being exposed to the wind. We were the only ones there.

"This is great!" Masao said.

In the dim light of the room, his complexion looked beautiful. We ordered wine. The waitress left once she had brought it, leaving us alone.

Masao leaned back, looking out the window. Quietly, he sighed, "I wish I could be a child again, before I knew anything."

"You'd think you're an old man, the way you talk." Had the sight of airplanes taking off from Haneda made him sentimental?

"I'm only twenty-two, but I'm feeling old," Masao said wistfully. "I have no dreams left. Starting next month, I'll be a work slave."

"You can't expect to stay a student forever."

"Enough platitudes, thanks."

"You'll be able to do all sorts of things that you couldn't do before."

"For instance?"

For instance . . . get married. I could've said that, but I didn't. Because all of a sudden I wasn't sure whether or not our engagement was still on. Masao must have been thinking the same thing. After a pause, during which fireworks exploded into the dark night sky, he asked:

"What would we do if we had a kid with a penis for a big toe?"

"We won't. My penis is acquired, not hereditary."

"How do you know? Maybe it's in your DNA."

"No one else in my family has a toe-penis."

"Maybe you'll be the one to hand it down to future generations."

"I wouldn't mind even if we did have a baby like that."

"I would."

Masao's tone was clear, decisive. I didn't know how to reply.

"She'd have a terrible time of it—a girl with a penis on her toe. She'd be bullied in school, and of course no boy would want to have anything to do with her."

I knew Masao didn't mean this as an attack on me; he was worrying about the daughter he could very well have with me, sometime in the future. Still, his words stung me.

"And think how awful it'd be for a boy to have a penis on his toe. It's not like that would make him twice as masculine."

Was Masao saying he didn't want to marry me because our kids could be born with toe-penises? Was that what he was getting at? I didn't want to ask; maybe I was too scared to. He was silent now, and so was I, just staring at the rocking surface of my wine.

This moment was interrupted suddenly by a family of six strolling into the café. A man, who looked to be in his fifties, threw himself down onto a chair and bellowed, "What a view!" A waiter brought slices of melon for the group, then departed, leaving us alone with them in the room now alive with conversation and the clinking of silverware on plates.

Masao glanced in the direction of the group, apparently regretting their presence, then returned his gaze to me. "We'll have to think carefully about having children," he said slowly.

That was what Masao had said last night. He was assuming we'd get married but at the same time worrying about the kids we'd have. I was worrying that we might not actually make it that far. We'd been planning on marriage two years down the road, but how safe was the road—assuming that my toe didn't return to its former state . . . or that Masao didn't learn to love it as it was?

Would all men hate my toe-penis as much as he did? Did all men think their penises were dirty and consider fellatio confirmation of a woman's love? I suddenly wanted to find out. One thought led to another: If I made love to another man . . . someone I liked, would I enjoy it? I felt on shaky ground. I'd never thought these things before.

The next evening, still feeling uncertain, I set out for a small eating establishment in Shibuya where I was supposed to meet Masao. It wasn't a trendy place; it was old, on a dingy street, and it hadn't changed in the years we'd been going there. It was dimly lit, and had chairs with awful checkered upholstery and plants covered with dust, and it was perfect for the glum way I was feeling.

Somewhere along the way there, I got turned around and had to retrace my steps through the obnoxious Saturday crowds. The kids hanging out and the grubby middle-aged men looking like wannabe yakuza—they all got on my nerves. When I finally found the place, Masao wasn't there.

I sat down, ordered a cup of coffee, thinking how much I liked this place. When we first started coming here, we were as innocent as could be, happy just sitting across from one another, gazing into each other's eyes. The night before each date, I would stay up late deciding what to wear. No matter that the train was packed, no matter that I stumbled on the sidewalk, I was full of excitement, coming here to meet Masao. But now I found myself getting irritated over the most trivial things.

Masao showed up after ten minutes.

"Sorry," he said, out of breath, "hope you weren't waiting too long." Alongside his coffee, the waitress brought him a warm towel, which he wiped his face with as he glanced around.

When he put the towel down, I noticed a red stain. I looked at his face; blood was oozing from a spot on his lip.

"What happened?"

"A little altercation."

"What? Who with?"

"I don't know. Bastard rammed into me with his shoulder. Pissed me off." He pressed the towel to his lip.

It was clear that our relationship might already have passed through some major change.

♥ ♥ ♥

It was warm the day before Masao's move into the company dorm, and we were in T-shirts, packing his various odds and ends into cardboard boxes. Masao accumulated things—he owned, for instance, not just one iron but three: a dry iron, a steam iron, and a "fashion steamer" that let you steam clothes without taking them off the hanger. He had a lint-remover, something even a woman like me had never owned. With all this stuff to deal with, the packing took longer than expected.

I was poking around his closet when I came across a box of sanitary napkins that I had bought ages ago, opened, and then forgotten. I tossed the box into a bag that already held underwear I had brought to the apartment at some point and also forgotten.

There were traces of me all over. When we got to the dishes, we found a tea pot with a chipped rim, and for a few moments we lost ourselves in reminiscence.

"You broke this," I said. "Remember?"

"You're the one who broke that."

"Look at this sloppy repair job! This is obviously your handiwork."

"But I didn't break it! I glued the piece back, badly, it's true. But you broke it when you banged it on a cup. That was *you*."

"Are you sure?"

"Absolutely. You don't remember? You were so upset you were about to cry."

As the room emptied, the scent of Masao's body, and of mine, faded. By going through our possessions, we were also working through our memories. It occurred to me that this was how a couple breaking up might feel. We weren't going to be breaking up, but I felt bad anyway.

Masao was probably feeling a little of the same, because all day he was much more considerate than usual, and never so much as made an unpleasant expression. The sunlight was gentle and our conversation pleasant, so we should have been in the best of moods; but since each of us was making a conscious effort not to displease the other, a sadness hovered over us. I couldn't imagine how I'd feel if I did break up with Masao. How would I live the rest of my life if we didn't get married in two years? I had no idea. Because now I didn't have Yoko.

The windows were open wide, and we could hear the guy playing the piano next door. This guy was versatile; he could play classical, jazz, blues, and he was good at all of them. Right now he was doing a jazz riff on "My Favorite Things."

"Once he starts with that song, he can't stop," Masao said, as he taped up a cardboard box. "He goes on and on. But the bastard can really play. If I had money, I'd hire him to be my own personal musician."

I smiled, pleased to hear something besides the usual curses.

Masao set down the tape, rose to his feet, and held out his hand to me. "Let's dance," he said.

Two hands together, one on top of the other, arms around each other's waist. My only experience with this kind of dancing was in gym class, but I managed, if inexpertly. There were objects all over the floor, our kneecaps kept colliding, and our heels and toes kept bumping into things. After a little while we gave up, and as the pianist continued to play, we stood in one spot, gently rocking our bodies together.

There were beads of sweat on Masao's forehead, but his body odor wasn't disagreeable. I laid my forehead on his shoulder, and he wrapped his arms around my back. And though I no longer took any pleasure in these embraces, I felt comforted. Deep down inside, though, the little waves of loneliness continued to churn. To deal with the ache, I started goofing around. I shook my hips, adding a comical spice to our dance. Masao stumbled, then bumped me back with his stomach. Our mutual pushing and bumping grew more excited until we were practically wrestling.

"Okay, I give up," Masao said, panting.

Having taken a head butt in the chest, he plopped down on the floor, pulling me down into his arms. By then I was sweating, too, and we took a moment to catch our breath. The pianist was still playing "My Favorite Things." Because we had the melody in our ears, the feeling we'd had when we were dancing—or rather, wrestling—stayed with us. This made me feel bold, and I yelled out toward the window, "How about 'After Hours'?"

Masao hissed at me to be quiet. But to our surprise, the neighbor immediately dove into a rendition of "After Hours."

We lay on the floor while the piano played, our arms and legs stretched out, relaxing. When the song ended, we returned to packing.

We managed to keep the peace until that night. But by the time I came back to the apartment after going shopping for dinner, we were tired of being considerate.

"I'll be moving into a dorm full of guys. What a bummer," Masao moaned. Sitting on his bed with his back against the wall, one hand fiddling with the can of beer I'd bought him, Masao grumbled about the place that would be his home starting the following evening—a dorm for single employees of the company. "After a nine-to-five day, I'll go home and be surrounded by the stench of all those guys."

"It's cheap, and you get meals."

"What crap. I don't want to sacrifice my whole life to a company."

"Oh, please. You'll be an elite salaryman."

"A student like you can't understand this depression."

I was getting pretty tired of listening to Masao's complaints, and without meaning to, I adopted a curt tone. "I've worked in a company myself, don't forget."

"Yeah, sure, the sex business. It's practically a game."

"It wouldn't have done so well if it were just a game."

"You only did well because you were selling women. You expect anyone to take a business like that seriously?"

I didn't reply to this.

Without turning to look at me, Masao mumbled, "Women have it easy. Just being female gives them value."

I wasn't in the mood for this. "Great," I snapped, "maybe you should become one."

Masao looked at me, a sullen expression on his face. After a few moments, he twisted his lips into a sardonic smile. "Easy for you to say. After all, you became a man."

I no longer tried to restrain myself. "If I'm a man, what does that make you for sleeping with me?"

"Sorry. I should have said you're not *even* a man."

Masao had never been so nasty. "Why are you being like this?" I asked, my voice a little softer.

Masao hung his head, saying nothing. His face still wore the same sullen expression. He's such a child, I thought. He's old enough to take care of himself, but inside he's a spoiled brat who's only satisfied when he can be comforted, "deeply loved," and have sex, all at the same time. The thought struck me that since we had come this far, I might as well say something that I had never been able to say before, because I hadn't had the courage. My lips trembled as I spoke. "Have you stopped loving me," I asked, "because I'm 'not even a man'?"

Masao's expression changed. "Of course I haven't stopped loving you," he said, suddenly softening his tone. "You're an unfortunate girl, and I feel sorry for you. Come on, don't look so sad."

Once more, I found myself seized with anger. Because when Masao said he felt sorry for me, I detected a profound arrogance. "It seems to me," I said, "that you should have asked me how I feel before making up your mind to pity me. And I suspect the reason you didn't is that you pity yourself even more for being unable to ditch me, since I'm in such a sorry state. I bet you're feeling pretty pleased with yourself."

"You have some nerve, talking like that." Masao sat up, lifting his back from the wall. "As if you had any idea how I felt when I saw your toe-penis."

"You thought it was dirty, right? You thought it was ugly, right? You've got one just like it, they're exactly the same, but you only care about your own. Who cares about me, anyhow? As far as you're concerned, I'm just a tool that comes in handy when you want to give your penis some love, right?"

Masao sprang wildly off the bed. I shrank back reflexively where I was sitting on the floor. But he sailed on past me. Dashing over to the pile of boxes, he grabbed a box cutter.

"You've been getting weird on me ever since you acquired that freaky thing of yours." Masao ratcheted the blade out about two inches. "It doesn't make you feel good either, does it, having a thing like that stuck on you?" Masao glared down at me; his eyes were gleaming, but the rest of his face was deathly pale. "I'm going to cut it off for you," he said quietly, his lips twitching.

Masao bent down as I started to stand, and I rammed my head as hard as I could into his jaw. He let out a groan and fell backward, clutching his chin with both hands. I dashed out the door while he was still sitting there, not stopping to put on my shoes. Behind me, I heard Masao scream out my name: "Kazumi!"

I was sure that if he chased me, he'd catch me. So the moment I got outside, I ducked around the side of the building, watching as Masao burst out the door and kept running straight. My heart was pounding. As if I'd even consider letting someone cut off my toe-penis! Over my dead body! Masao had lost his mind. And I was absolutely terrified.

I went through the courtyard of the building and made my way around to the back. The window to Masao's apartment was lit up brightly. I'd hide here and leave only after Masao got back. Then it occurred to me that my bag with my wallet was still in the apartment. Where had I left it? By the window. Which meant I should be able to reach it from outside. I padded across the cold earth until I was beneath the window, reached in over the windowsill as far as I could go and felt around for my bag. Got it! I thought of going around and getting my shoes, too, but decided that would be too dangerous.

As I backed away from the window, I got a glimpse of the light-filled room I'd run from. I had been there countless times, but now it looked like it belonged to a stranger. I felt a terrible loneliness. I crouched down, my arms around my belly. I wanted the evening to be over.

Just then, I heard the door to the house on the other side of the fence open. It was the pianist's house. Someone stepped outside, walking light-ly. I held my breath. I could see, in the gap between the ground and the bottom of the wood fence, a pair of legs dressed in bold striped pants moving toward where I cowered.

The legs stopped right next to me. The person rapped softly on the fence, as if checking whether anyone was there. And then, in a gentle, sweet voice—the sort that could only have belonged to a boy in his early teens—the person spoke, obviously to me.

"Over here! Come on!"

Chapter 3

"Over here! Come on!"

There was a warmth in his tone that kept me from becoming alarmed. Still, this was a complete surprise, and I took a few moments to respond. He knocked on the fence again, then crouched down and stuck his hands through the gap at the bottom. "You're hiding, aren't you? Come on," he said, "I'll hide you."

He beckoned with his hands like he was calling a dog. I was struck by the slenderness of his fingers and the smooth look of his skin—his hands were just like his voice. I guessed that this was the pianist who had obligingly accommodated my request for "After Hours." I stepped toward the fence and squatted down.

"Do you know me?" I asked.

"Sure. And you know me, right?"

"The piano guy, right?"

"That's right."

Our upper bodies were hidden by the fence, and the guy made no attempt to look at me from under it. After this brief conversation, it wasn't like we weren't acquainted, but I hadn't seen his face, however trusting and open he sounded. Unsure how to proceed, I stared blankly at his hands.

"Are you still there?" he asked, and then stretched his hand under the fence toward me, bumping against my left arm. The movement was easy and unhurried, like some exotic dance, and when his fingers grasped the sleeve of my sweater, I thought something no less peculiar: this was like a little bird picking up fabric in its beak. Without any forethought, I reached out and pinched his fingers.

This was the first time I had ever touched the hand of a man I didn't really know at all, and I was taken aback at my own boldness; the pianist didn't seem surprised, however, and simply gave the hand I'd pinched a little shake.

"C'mon, hurry up," he said.

"Why do you want to help me?"

"Why shouldn't I? I know you."

Before I had a chance to dispute that, the pianist gestured at the space between the ground and the bottom of the fence. "Is it too narrow? Can you squeeze through?"

I knew no more about this man than he knew about me, but I decided to go ahead and do it. I wasn't thrilled by the thought of wriggling snake-like on my belly, but how could I be finicky about dirt now? I would have swum across a cesspool rather than face Masao gone berserk.

As I inched, head first, onto the other side of the fence, the pianist grabbed hold of me and pulled. His grip was strong, nothing like the bird-like peck, and in a few seconds I had been dragged under the fence onto the neighboring property. I had scraped the back of my head and was in a little pain.

"Sorry, was I too rough?" the pianist said, relaxing his grip. "Can you stand up?" He tried to give me a hand.

"It's all right. I can get up."

I put my hands on the ground and got to my feet unassisted. The effort made it seem like I was trying to shake his hand off me, but he left it where it was, not removing it even as I brushed dirt from my clothes. Was he being friendly? Or did he enjoy this sort of physical contact? I wasn't sure, but his touch wasn't offensive or sexual, it was frank and open, and I wasn't annoyed. He did seem to be a rather unusual person, though—that much was clear.

After I straightened up my rumpled clothes, the pianist finally withdrew his hand, then turned and walked toward the house I had looked at many times from Masao's apartment. It struck me, glancing at his back, that he was fairly small for a man. He wasn't much taller than me, and I'm only five foot two. I had been too distracted to look into his face, but judging from his voice and the childlike slimness of his body, he must still have been in his teens. A boy. Maybe his youth was responsible for his unguarded friendliness.

The pianist walked slowly forward, as if pausing with each step to feel the earth beneath his feet, in the same way he had when he first came outside; perhaps this was habit. When we reached the door, he beckoned to me. "Come on in," he said.

The lights were off. Relying on the faint illumination from the windows, and on the density of the air, I was able to get some sense of the space: a single room about the size of eight tatami mats, and with all sorts of things scattered on the floor. In front of me, the pianist agilely picked his way through the darkness, heading toward the back of the room, clearly accustomed to the path. I tried to follow after brushing the mud from my socks, but after a few steps my foot got tangled in what apparently was an electric cord. I stumbled, and something toppled against me. I grabbed hold of it, and found my hand around the neck of an electric guitar.

"Oh, sorry. You can't see, can you?" the pianist called out. "Hold on a second, I'll turn on the light." A bulb-shaped lamp on the bedside table came on, brightening and darkening and brightening and darkening. The pianist was fiddling with the dimmer switch. "Is this bright enough?" he asked.

Now that the room was lit, if not quite brightly, I could see it was a mess. There was an upright piano, a synthesizer, an electric guitar, musical instruments the names of which I didn't know, an impressive stereo system with large speakers, and a weight-training machine with barbells . . . So much had been crammed into the space that it looked like storage.

"The only place to sit is on the bed," he said, having already taken up residence there, legs crossed, hugging a cushion. For a fraction of a second I thought, what a sleazy way to get me in bed, but the way he was holding the cushion certainly didn't suggest that was on his mind. It also seemed possible, given his overall manner, that he was so young as to have not yet discovered sex. I went over to the bed, maneuvering through the debris.

"What's wrong? You can't walk even with the light on?" he said, his face now buried in the cushion. "Do you have bad eyesight?"

"You've got so much stuff in here," I said, sitting down on the edge of the bed.

"Oh. So your eyes are okay," said the boy, his face still in the cushion. "I'm blind."

He lifted his head and turned toward me. His face had a comical, child-ish look: cheeks that bulged slightly at the jaw; a round nose with a sharp bridge; smooth skin. His eyes were sunken, a little more than average. I had been puzzled by his cautious steps, the way he touched me by the fence, and his utter lack of interest in my face . . . Now I understood.

"What do you think of my face?" he asked, sticking his face toward me. "Do I look kind of funny?" He grinned, stroking his cheeks and nose. "Everyone says I'm adorable."

He seemed to mean this as a joke, but I couldn't manage a laugh. "Who's everyone?" I asked.

"Chisato, for instance, and people I meet through work."

Obviously, I had no idea who Chisato was. "What sort of work do you do?"

"I'm a composer."

Ah. Things began to make sense. The room was filled with musi-cal instruments—the tools of his trade. And apparently he could afford them—not like M., the novelist, who couldn't afford a computer.

"By the way, thanks for playing my request this afternoon."

"You mean 'After Hours'? My pleasure."

"I didn't think you'd hear me."

"As long as both our windows are open, I can hear a lot."

"So you heard that commotion earlier?" I asked, the image of Masao holding the box cutter rising before me.

"Not all of it," he replied, tossing the cushion into the air and catching it as it fell. "I can hear women's voices pretty well. I knew your voice from before."

"From before? Since this house was built, you mean?"

"Earlier than that, when I was living in the main house. Sometimes at night I used to go into the garden to listen."

I blushed, pleased that he couldn't see. Masao and I had generally left the windows of his apartment open during the summer. The students in the adjacent apartments went back home in the summer months, so we thought we didn't need to worry about anyone hearing what we were doing. I was so embarrassed I couldn't speak, but the pianist just went on squeezing then punching his cushion, his expression nonchalant. His brazenness was beyond comprehension.

"Why would you want to listen?"

"Because you have a beautiful voice."

He said that completely innocently; I was astonished.

"When I hear a woman's voice, I feel like someone's tickling my ears, and it's a really, really nice feeling. But your voice is unlike anyone else's. It's like my ears are filling with cotton candy or something, and I wish I could keep listening forever."

"Huh," I said, aware that I was being drawn in by his childish tone. "No one has ever said my voice was special before."

"Really? I love it. I was always hoping you would want to come over. That's why I played 'After Hours' earlier."

I certainly didn't find these compliments unpleasant. But the truth was, *his* voice was much nicer than mine—it had the sweetness and gentleness of a prepubescent boy whose voice was changing. I could relax and be open with him, a total stranger of the opposite sex, because his voice made me so comfortable. As soon as I realized this, my own ears felt like they were being tickled, too.

The pianist stopped fiddling with the cushion. He tilted his head, apparently listening to something, then whispered, "I think he's come back."

I started, turning my head toward the window facing Masao's apartment. *Bang*, the window was slammed violently shut, unnerving me. I was about to leap to my feet and go when the pianist pushed my arm with the cushion.

"Don't worry. He won't find you here," he said.

My heart was pounding—from a mix of terror and sadness. The pianist let go of the cushion, which was squashed against me. It was my turn to hug it.

"You don't want to go back there, do you?"

"No! Absolutely not!" My tone was so vehement that it surprised me.

After a brief pause, the pianist smiled. "Wow, so you have a voice like that in you, too!"

This eased the tension I had been feeling, and I smiled back. "You liked that voice?"

"I liked it. It was like mint sherbet. I bet you have all sorts of other voices, too. I hope I'll get to hear them."

I was captivated by this unusual young man's frankness. "So what's your name?"

"Kendo Shunji." He was still smiling.

I couldn't help smiling, too, now.

"How do you write it?" I asked.

"My family name is the characters for 'dog' and then *warabe*, as in 'child'; my given name is the characters for 'spring' and 'aspiration.' That's how my teachers at the School for the Blind first explained it to me. I knew what 'dog' and 'child' and 'spring' meant, but I wasn't so sure about 'aspiration.' Anyway, I can write my own name! Let me show you. Give me your hand."

He took my wrist and rested it on his knee, which made me have to lean over and move closer to him. Holding my wrist with his left hand, Shunji began tracing out the characters on my palm using the index finger of his right hand. He only got as far as "dog," however, when I jerked my hand away, laughing; it was too ticklish.

"Ah, that voice," Shunji sighed. "It's wonderful, it really is."

This struck me as funny, so I kept laughing.

"Don't laugh too loud, or that guy will know you're here," Shunji said seriously.

He held my hand still again, attempting this time to write "child." But once something feels ticklish, it goes on feeling ticklish, and I ended up yanking my hand away again.

"Hey, stop it! How am I going to write my name if you keep doing that!"

Even as he spoke, Shunji was narrowing his eyes, relishing the sound of my laughter. Each time my giggling stopped he would reach for my hand again, insisting that I let him finish writing his name. I kept him from doing this by grabbing his hand, pressing our palms together.

"Get a pen and write it on paper, please!"

"I don't have any paper. Except for tissues."

Of course. A blind person wouldn't be in the habit of writing things down. How could I have said something so stupid. Then Shunji started tickling my palm with the thumb of the hand that I had grabbed. We tried a variety of offensive and defensive maneuvers, shoving and tugging and twisting each other's arms. I couldn't contain my delight. In the pauses between laughs, I wondered how I could be playing so intimately with someone I had just met, but it felt perfectly natural, so I decided not to worry about it.

At some point we had taken hold of each other's hands. Shunji's face was directly in front of mine. The broadness of his grin showed the fun he was having. The more he grinned, the more innocent his childlike face looked.

"How old are you?" I asked, trying to catch my breath.

"Nineteen."

"Really?" I looked again at the face before me. "I'd have guessed sixteen or seventeen."

"I grow slowly. I don't have much of a beard yet. How old are you?"

"Twenty-two."

"One year younger than Chisato." Once more he mentioned this stranger's name. Then, as if the thought had just occurred to him, "That guy called you Kazumi. Is that your real name?"

"Of course. What else would it be?"

"Chisato's real name is Satoko. She doesn't like her real name, so she has me call her Chisato. That's the name on her business card, too."

Was she was his manager? I was about to ask, but Shunji asked faster, "What's your family name?"

"Mano. Mano Kazumi. *Ma* is the character for 'truth,' *no* is the character for 'field'—"

"It doesn't mean anything to me even if you tell me," Shunji said, giving our linked hands a shake. "I only know the characters for my name."

69

Once again you've said something stupid, I thought, annoyed with myself. But Shunji didn't seem at all bothered. He launched cheerfully into a new topic.

"Shall we play a game? Do you want me to play something for you?"

I was in as good spirits as he was. Since I'd come into his room, I had completely forgotten the time—and the significant problem of how I was going to get home. It had to be about ten now. Masao was probably still packing, wrestling with his fierce emotions. It should be safe to go outside.

"Could you lend me some sandals or something, if you have any? I'll return them in a few days. I ran out without putting on my shoes."

"You're leaving? Why don't you stay over?"

I stared at Shunji, stunned at how casually he said this.

"Do you let everyone sleep over this soon?"

"If they come at night, sure."

Attractive as I found Shunji's personality, I couldn't say yes right away. He looked younger than his age, but he was still a nineteen-year-old man, and perhaps his boyish innocence allowed him to make sexual advances in an innocent, lighthearted way. That was possible. On the other hand, nothing in the touch of his hands, which I had been holding for some time now, suggested sexual interest. Of course, acting innocent might just be a ploy to get a foot in the door.

As I turned these thoughts over in my mind, something altogether different occurred to me: How would it feel to have sex with this young man? I didn't like the idea of getting involved with someone on the very night I had fled in fear from my fiancé. But there was something very attractive about it, too—perhaps because Shunji was so unlike Masao, or Haruhiko, or any other man I knew.

"Your silence means you want to go?"

Shunji's question rescued me from my bewilderment. I sighed. Then, the very next instant, Shunji's timing so exquisite he could have planned the whole thing from the start, he pressed the back of my hand to his cheek. He did this nonchalantly and naturally. I wasn't even fully aware of this, not until I felt the warmth of his skin on my hand. This action didn't appear to mean so much to Shunji either, as he started talking again, still holding my hand.

"I've got a one o'clock appointment in Aoyama tomorrow, so I could take you in the car."

"That won't work. Masao is moving tomorrow, so he'll be going in and out of the apartment all day."

"He's leaving?"

A door banged shut in the direction of the main house. I hardly had time to listen to the footsteps coming in our direction when the door to Shunji's apartment flew open. The overhead light came on. A woman of twenty-three or -four, her hair bobbed, appeared in the glow.

Shunji lowered my hand from his cheek, but didn't release it. After a few seconds of silence, during which the woman raised her thick black eyebrows, looking as if she couldn't believe what she was seeing, she cried out, "Who are you?!"

Out of habit, I changed my sitting position, which happened to be on the bed, by sliding my feet under me so that I was more proper. "I'm Mano Kazumi. I don't think we've met."

"That's not what I'm asking." The woman turned to Shunji. "Why is this girl here?"

"I'm hiding her," Shunji said, perfectly calm. "Keep your voice down. There's a demon out there who wants to find her and eat her up."

The woman pulled the door shut and strode over to the bed, her skirt swishing back and forth. "It looks to me like you're the one trying to make a meal of her." Having delivered her message, she turned back to me. "Are you all right? He hasn't done anything to you, I hope?"

Her expression and tone were both very mild, completely different from a moment before. Her breathing had evened out, too, but the harsh gleam in her eyes had not changed. She must be very proud. She didn't want me to see her lose her composure.

"Give me a break, Chisato," Shunji said. "I haven't done anything."

"Just holding hands like the good friends you are?"

"So you're Satoko?" I said, hoping to change the tone of the situation. "Shunji was telling me about you."

My words had the opposite effect. Chisato, or Satoko, or whatever her name was, glowered at me. Maybe she was annoyed that I called her Satoko? My only reason for doing that was because it might be presumptuous to call her by a nickname.

"You fly off the handle too easily, Chisato," said Shunji.

"Oh no, no, I'm not angry!" Chisato or Satoko or whatever said, dripping saccharine, the anger in her expression giving off steam.

"Hey!" Shunji clapped his hands together. "This is perfect! Do me a favor and get the Pajero out, will you? We can go for a little spin and take Kazumi home at the same time."

Chisato glanced back and forth between Shunji and me.

"No," I said. "Thank you, but I can take the train."

"I would be glad to drive you home," murmured Satoko gravely, "but the Pajero has been acting up lately."

"Then how are we going to get to Aoyama tomorrow?"

"We'll take a cab."

"I don't want to take a cab. The Pajero will be okay, won't it?"

I put my bag under my arm, indicating that I was serious about leaving. "Don't worry, really. I'll take the train. But I'd be grateful if you could lend me a pair of sandals or something to put on my feet."

Chisato folded her arms. "Sandals, huh? I wonder if we even have any."

"There are tons in the main house, and you know it," Shunji said.

Before Chisato's expression could turn more menacing, I practically yelled out, "Anything will be fine, flip-flops or slippers or whatever, as long as I can put them on my feet!"

"Hold on. I'll be right back."

Chisato plodded out of the room with heavy steps. I mopped my brow with my handkerchief. Shunji hugged his knees to his chest.

"Today's Sunday, right?"

"Yeah."

"Chisato isn't even supposed to come today."

"How is she related to you, anyway?"

"She's my cousin."

We were still talking when Chisato showed up at the door and pointed down at the vestibule floor where she'd placed some footwear. "These were all I could find. We were going to throw them out anyway, so don't bother to return them."

They were brilliant red plastic slippers, with w.c. printed in white on them. A thin smile played on Chisato's lips as I slid my feet into them.

"Sorry to put you to so much trouble, Chisato."

"My name is Satoko."

"No, it's not. It's Chisato," said Shunji.

Such a charming young man.

Shunji tried to go out and see me to the gate, but Chisato pushed him back.

"I'll show her out. You go to bed."

Frowning, Shunji was about to say something, but I stopped him.

"It's fine, really. Thanks so much for everything."

Shunji didn't look happy, and didn't respond. I knew how he felt. I would have preferred to tell him in private how appreciative I was. I didn't want to make his cousin angry and have her take it out on him later, so I had no choice but to give up on that idea. She closed the door in his face.

We headed into the narrow alley beside the main house.

"You wouldn't guess it from looking at him," the woman whispered, "but he doesn't waste any time with women. I bet he asked you to stay over, didn't he?"

"No, he didn't," I said, not for Shunji's sake, but because I didn't like women who said nasty things about cousins behind their back.

"You don't need to come back and thank me," she said sharply when we reached the gate. "Goodbye."

I bowed in return. "Please give my best to your cousin," I said.

"He's not my cousin." The woman smirked. "He's my husband."

♥ ♥ ♥

Noncombustible trash was collected on Saturdays, so I had to look at that pair of red toilet slippers, lying where I had kicked them off in a corner of my vestibule, every time I went in or out for the next five days. And as much as I would have liked to forget her, I couldn't help remembering the smirky, boxy jaw of the woman who had given them to me. At the same time, the image of Shunji—who had been so kind I couldn't believe he and that woman were actually married, as she had said, or even cousins—kept rising up before me.

Of course, I didn't spend those five days doing nothing. It was April, the start of a new school year, and I was going back to college after two years off. I got my books out of storage and attended guidance sessions on campus. I have to admit that I thought about Masao, who would have started work by then, but with each day that passed, my thoughts turned with increasing frequency to the blind Shunji.

If that woman hadn't burst in, our encounter might have made only a faint mark on my memory, just another of the happy events that pop up in a person's life. I had wondered what sex with Shunji would be like, true, but I wasn't sure whether he had any interest in sex; if that were all there was, that would be all there was.

But instead, a could-be cousin, as nasty as the "bad girl" in girls' comics, claimed that Shunji was her husband. Which suggested sex, which made me very curious about Shunji. I doubted they could be married. If they were, they'd be living under the same roof, not just meeting on scheduled days. They might be sexually involved, but if so, she must have instigated it—she was the one talking about marriage, not him. And when she saw us holding hands, she got jealous, so she was mean to me to get me to stay away.

Well, it wasn't going to work. I recalled the touch of Shunji's hand. He was enjoying the physical contact with another human being, like a child holding hands with a classmate. Could the boy even feel sexual desire? And, say the right person came along and he did feel desire, how would he express it? My curiosity knew no end; never before had I been so interested in a member of the opposite sex. Once sex with Masao stopped being any good, I had imagined making love to another man, but Shunji had really got my imagination going.

After I put the slippers into the garbage on Saturday, I decided to go visit Shunji. After all, I did want to thank him for his kindness. His cousin wouldn't be very happy if she found me there, but so what? I bought some handmade cheese crackers to take as a gift. But as I was leaving the shop, which Yoko had introduced me to, I mused that Yoko would have gone one step further and given *the cousin* the crackers—the triumph of sarcasm!

The next day I went to Shunji's. His cousin didn't come on Sundays, he'd said, and anyway, a woman her age, in the most freewheeling stage of her social life, wasn't likely to be sitting at home during the day. As I passed Masao's old apartment, I remembered the awfulness of a week ago, and I wondered why I was here at all. I hesitated, but kept going.

There were two nameplates on the gatepost: EGUCHI and KENDO. The gate was closed, but I had no problem slipping my hand through the bars and unlatching it. The main house was quiet; no one seemed to be home. I proceeded nervously to Shunji's house in the back and knocked.

There was no response. Shunji's quarters were as quiet as the main house. Suddenly he started playing the piano. The song was "After Hours." I banged harder on the door, sort of in time with the pounding of my heart. The piano playing stopped abruptly. A few seconds later, the door flew open, and Shunji came crashing into me.

"Hey! You came!" he exclaimed, gripping my arms, without me having said a word.

He must have been exercising when I first knocked, because he was wearing a tank top and shorts and his body shone with sweat. Shunji's greeting made me pleased to see him, so I gave him a little hug.

"Hello," I said.

"That's the voice!" Shunji gave his head a shake. "I knew it!"

Twining his arm around mine and pulling me inside, Shunji began walking, with no hesitation, toward the bed.

"I brought you some crackers."

"Wow, great!"

Shunji wasn't really interested in the crackers, however. He tumbled onto the bed, his arm still locked in mine, and rolled me on top of him, which made me drop my purse and the bag of crackers. The extravagance of his welcome was overwhelming, but my previous visit had taught me that if I just went along with him, adapting to his pace, I'd be able, strangely, to relax. I made myself comfortable lying on top of his body. His physique was not too different from mine.

"I've thought about you constantly," he began. "I kept wondering how I could see you again."

"Me, too. We didn't really say goodbye last time."

"I had some crazy ideas. Like you moving into that apartment next door."

I was rather taken aback by this. "You wanted to see me that badly?"

"Ah, your voice—it makes me feel so good! How do you do it?"

Shunji stroked my back with the same earnestness he invested in his words. His touch was a straightforward expression of the sort of intimacy and tenderness one might feel toward an animal or small child. Sometimes you come across women who touch their women friends that way, but not many men can do it. I was right: Shunji wasn't interested in sex, or at least not in sex with me. The slight bit of nervousness I'd been feeling drained from my body.

"How'd you know it was me?"

"Not many people come by on Sundays. Why did you?"

"To say . . ." I'd had a prepared answer—that I wanted to thank him—but now I felt embarrassed to say it. Why was I trying to act so cool? Tell him the truth: "Because I really had a lot of fun the other night."

As soon as I'd said it, Shunji hugged me tightly. For someone so small, he had surprising strength, and I couldn't breathe. What he did next was surprising, too: he slipped his hands under my blouse.

"What do you think you're doing!" I cried.

"C'mon, let's be friends!" said Shunji, with all the calm in the world.

Sitting up abruptly, I pinned his arms to the bed. That was when I discovered that he had pretty big biceps. Big enough to shake me off, but instead he just lay there docilely, looking puzzled.

"What's wrong? Don't you want to be friends?"

"What exactly do you mean by being friends?" I had to catch my breath before I could answer.

"What do you mean, what do I mean? Everyone does it, right?"

"You mean, try to feel up their friends?"

"They don't? But don't friends touch each other?" His expression was so ingenuous, it was disarming.

"You have a pretty odd idea of what it means to be friends," I began earnestly. "People don't have to touch each other to be friends. I mean, men don't touch their men friends, do they? And women don't touch their women friends. Well, I guess there are some who do, but apart from them."

"Hmm . . ."

Shunji allowed his hands to fall onto the bed. I released my hold on his upper arms but couldn't decide if I should stop sitting on him, too. I didn't want to overreact to his wandering hand when a second before I was perfectly at ease lying on him. Of course, if he had been some other nonlover who suddenly put the moves on me, I would've been off him in a flash. But with Shunji, whose physicality was unique, communicative, soothing, a different response seemed called for. As I straddled him, I peered at the boyish face that was wreaking havoc with my intuitions.

"But . . . ," he began, folding his hands, his tone meditative.

"But what?"

"I've been touched by lots of men. Men I meet through my work. It's not so unusual."

Without meaning to, I put my hands on either side of his face.

"You let them touch you?"

"I'm glad I can be friends with them."

I was dumbstruck, but Shunji went on, matter of fact as ever. "To tell the truth, I don't have much fun playing around with men. They're only interested in my penis. Women are more fun. They do more stuff, you know, they touch me all over—they touch my whole body. And they have such nice voices."

"Hold on. You're nineteen?"

"That's right. I told you before."

"And how many people are you so friendly with?"

"Hmm. Six or seven, maybe. But Chisato is my only long-term friend."

"What about the rest?"

"We don't get together once we finish the job we're doing."

"But they must call you up and stuff, right?"

"No, not really."

I climbed off Shunji and sat a bit away from him on the bed.

"Why did you move away?" he asked.

I could only sigh. I was dismayed and depressed.

And stunned. For some reason I'd thought he was sexually innocent, when in fact he had plenty of sexual experience, even with other men. I could accept that, but what really shocked me was that more than just a few people had toyed with his body, even though he was still a boy, without any love for him. And Shunji had no idea these people were treating him like a plaything—on the contrary, he was glad they could get "friendly"! But the worst thing was that this naïve young man now equated having sex with being friends! Shunji was totally oblivious to the fact they were victimizing him. It made my heart ache.

"Did you say something? I didn't hear you. Is something wrong?" Shunji said, reaching his hands out toward me. I could easily have taken them in my own, but after the painful things he had told me, I didn't want to be so casual about touching him. I was disgusted with myself; I'd taken his tenderness and warmth and wondered, if only for a moment, what it would be like to make love to him.

Unable to find me with his hands, Shunji sat up. He leaned forward; his hands came closer. I leaned back. His hands waved through the air, seeking me out.

"I can't tell if you're there if you don't speak."

Eyebrows pinched, Shunji flung his hands down in exasperation. One hand landed directly on the big toe of my right foot. I groaned.

"There you are!" Shunji cried gleefully. "I didn't hurt you, did I?"

He felt my toe, patted it gently, then taking it between the palms of his hands, cradled it like a baby. His touch sparked a tremor of sensation that radiated up almost to my waist. My toe started getting erect. Horrified, I tried to pull my foot away, but Shunji was too fast: he was already gripping my toe-penis firmly.

"What's this? Why do you have this bulge in your sock here?"

My toe-penis, readily growing in size, was trapped in my sock; it was bending over double, and I was in pain. "Let go, please!" I pleaded.

"C'mon, what is it?" Shunji held on determinedly. "People don't usually have these things, do they? What's it called?"

"Please, Shunji! Let go!"

"I will. But it's funny, you know—it feels like a penis."

Finally, unable to bear the pain any longer, I shouted, "It is a penis! It's stuck at the end of my sock, and it hurts!"

Shunji went into action immediately. He bent his head over my foot and bit down a few times on the stocking, tearing a hole large enough for the head of my toe-penis to slip through. The moment my toe-penis was freed, Shunji, without giving me a choice in the matter, popped it into his mouth.

The surprise and pleasure I immediately felt shoved all thought of resisting from my mind. My toe-penis had never been inside another person's mouth, and the experience was profoundly moving. All the more so because Shunji knew exactly what he was doing. He slid it in almost to the back of his throat, then back out, seeming to locate the most sensitive areas, then skillfully sucked and licked, using his tongue to poke, prod, and stroke. The pleasure grew more intense, then more mild—the sensations changed constantly. Unlike when I'd done it to myself, I had no idea what the next bit of stimulation would be. In a matter of moments I had given myself entirely over to Shunji; my whole being was concentrated on the pleasure he was giving me.

He started using his hands as well, increasing the intensity of the stimulation little by little. The motions became grander, more animated. A gush of pleasure surged through me, and I gasped. I climaxed. I heaved a tremendous sigh.

"Wow, you sure gave me a surprise," said Shunji, sitting up, though it seemed a bit late for him to be commenting on it now. "A woman with a penis! Wow!"

The sight of him wiping spit from his mouth with the back of his hand shocked me. I looked away in embarrassment.

Shunji, unable to see me, had to ask, "How was it? Did I do a good job?"

I felt too shy to respond, and simply smiled silently. Shunji seriously wanted an answer, and he placed his hands on my knee and asked again, "Tell me, did it feel good?"

I took his hand and held it to my cheek so that he could feel my smile. "No one has ever done that to me before," I said.

"Really?" Shunji exclaimed, genuinely surprised. "But why not? That guy you were with didn't do it?"

"Masao thought it was gross. He wouldn't even touch it."

"What's gross about it? He has one just like it, doesn't he?"

This struck a chord in me. After the loneliness and the sense of injustice I'd known with Masao, I felt vindicated. "He tried to cut it off," I said.

"What? But that's crazy!" Shunji's lips started twisting, and his hands began feeling down along my right leg. I realized where they were headed and hurriedly stopped them.

"What's wrong? I thought I'd do it again."

I almost cried when Shunji said that. I was bursting with gratitude and affection. I threw my arms around him. At first he seemed unsure how to react, but then, very gently, he wrapped his arms around me.

"Do you think we can be friends?" he asked, a change from his earlier brazen tone.

Earlier Shunji had said, "C'mon, let's be friends." This time it was gentle, warm. He hadn't been hungry just for sex, after all. Maybe for him being friends and having sex *were* the same thing, but the urge to be friends came first. That's why his physicality didn't feel sexual, and why it was so soothing; that was what made him so kind and gentle. It was such a simple thing, why hadn't I seen it earlier?

Shunji was a bit odd, no doubt about it, but what about Masao, with his hatred of all penises other than his own? Which of these men was more normal, more grounded? I didn't care if Shunji was odd. I wanted to be friends with this wonderful young man. That was the whole reason I came to see him in the first place.

I pressed my lips to Shunji's. He responded with a few deft movements of his tongue. Then, as soon as we drew apart, he said blandly, "You brought something to eat, didn't you?"

♥ ♥ ♥

The feel of Shunji's mouth on my toe-penis was so deep in my conscious-ness that for several days my cheeks grew warm when I thought about it. On the Sunday I had been with him, I went home utterly flustered. I left as soon as we had eaten the crackers I'd brought, staying only long enough to exchange phone numbers. That night, for the first time since my toe-penis appeared, my imagination kicked in as I masturbated. Masao was right—there was a pleasure in this that I wouldn't want to go without. I had new discoveries. The fact, for instance, that as you approach orgasm, your consciousness dissipates and you almost go blind, only to have the object of your fantasy come pirouetting back into your mind when the climax crests, suddenly making you want to call out the person's name.

The addition of this new pastime to my evenings wasn't the only change in my life. My thoughts started, without my noticing, turning to Shunji—as I was walking down the street, sitting in boring classes, or chatting with classmates in a café. Suddenly a scene in which he figured, one that had no connection with whatever was going on, would bob up in my mind. Shunji getting up to make tea after declining my offer to make it, pressing the button on the hot-water dispenser, warming the teapot and cups before putting in the leaves and water. Shunji taking his first bite of a cracker, murmuring "It's an interesting flavor," then flicking a crumb from his lip. Over and over again, the images kept coming to me. These Shunji moments came over me so frequently that I lost track of time and sank into a dreamlike daze.

In short, I was atwitter about Shunji. As a child I used to be so thrilled I couldn't sleep when my family went on a trip or I learned a new game, but I had never been this excited about a person. Even in the early days of my relationship with Masao, I would knock off as soon as my head hit the pillow. And there was something that left me stunned the first time it occurred to me: Shunji had only performed fellatio on me once, but that single experience was enough to make all the pleasure I had shared with Masao seem hardly worth the bother.

Shunji's attentions had also done a terrific job of undoing the emotional damage I'd suffered as a result of Masao's rejection of my toe-penis. Now I could hardly believe that I was so anxious about it, and it no longer hurt so much to remember my days with Masao. I realized, looking at things objectively, that his attempt to cut off my toe-penis had probably been a fit of temporary madness spurred by his anxiety about the job he was starting. I didn't even feel angry about that outburst now.

One Friday night, the phone rang. I assumed it was Shunji, so I grabbed the receiver and answered with a single word, "Yes!"

"Uh, hi. It's me," Masao said. Even though he no longer haunted my thoughts, sweat broke out on my palms at the sound of his voice. "You must be pretty mad at me."

"No, not anymore."

"Well, not mad then . . . You must hate me."

Unsure how to respond, I said nothing. After a brief silence during which he seemed to be waiting for me to say something, he spoke, his voice hoarse: "I know it's no good trying to make excuses—you won't let me get away with that. I really feel awful about what happened. I don't know what I was thinking, trying to hurt you like that. I'm very ashamed, and I hope you'll forgive me. But at the time, it didn't occur to me that your toe-penis was part of your body. I saw it as something separate, so I didn't think it would hurt when I cut it off."

"It's okay," I said, genuinely meaning it. "After all, you didn't do it."

"Still the same cool, gentle Kazumi," Masao said with a chuckle. "I wish I was born with a personality like yours."

"Don't be sarcastic."

"I didn't mean it that way."

The roar of a passing motorcycle interrupted the conversation—apparently he was calling from a payphone. Masao waited until it was quiet again, then continued, "I thought we were going to get married."

"It seemed that way, didn't it?"

"I really wanted to marry you."

"I wanted to marry you, too."

It hurt to speak those words. For a moment, I remembered the sense

of peace I had felt when things were going well. But I knew, without having to stop and think, that while I could recall that feeling, it was history.
Never again. The receiver felt heavy in my hand.

"You don't want me to return your shoes, do you? The shoes you left in
my apartment. Would you mind if I keep them?"

"No, I'd like you to send them back."

"Sorry. Actually, I threw them away." Masao chuckled again. "I couldn't
bear to see them. It hurt too much."

"Don't worry about it."

There was a lull in the conversation.

"Guess I have to hang up now, huh?"

"Yeah," I said.

"I'm glad we were able to talk."

A second wave of sentiment washed over me. I rode it out. "Thanks."

I replaced the receiver and just sat there for a moment, unable to look
up. I felt grateful to Masao for having the decency to make this last call.
As that feeling drained away, the image of Masao in my mind's eye began
to fade; eventually his face dissolved into darkness.

Chapter 4

The second time Shunji and I kissed, I wondered if this was the sort of kiss people describe as "sweet." Our first kiss had been so hurried it was hardly more than a superficial exchange of courtesies; when we took our time and kissed *seriously*, Shunji's character came through. He didn't suck or lick or do anything fancy, he simply caressed my tongue with his, the way he stroked my arms and back with his hands. That was his style. His tongue was tender and somehow coaxing; the way it moved in my mouth was as light and marvelous as the beating of wings.

Masao's kisses hadn't been like this at all. His tongue was bold, bordering on rough. He whirled it around in my mouth as if he wanted to scrape something off, and things always got so wild I thought he was trying to swallow me whole. Before Masao, I had only been kissed by my high school boyfriend, who never did anything more than mash his lips against mine, so it never even occurred to me that there were other ways of doing it. Now, in comparison to Masao's aggressive technique, Shunji's sweet kisses actually left me feeling a little dissatisfied.

During our third time, however, I realized that Shunji's tongue danced lightly in my mouth because he was so delicately attentive to me, leaving himself plenty of room to maneuver as I responded. His tongue answered each of my forays, going along with the course I had set, then stepping in and executing perfectly what I'd attempted but couldn't, for lack of experience, really manage. If there are expert and nonexpert kissers, Shunji was assuredly an expert. French-kissing Shunji became an addiction.

By now I was going to Shunji's house regularly, mostly on Sundays, when I could be sure Chisato wouldn't be around.

Shunji confirmed my suspicion that he and Chisato were not husband and wife. They were cousins. Chisato's parents were his guardians, having taken him in after his mother ran away from home and his father died in an automobile accident. He lived in the dormitory at the School for the Blind until he was fifteen, then moved in with the Eguchis. His music teacher introduced him to people in the music industry, and he started writing jingles for commercials and video games. Shunji had talent, and he got so much work that he had this house built in the back garden. The Eguchis were delighted with Shunji's success, Chisato especially. She'd gotten a job after graduating from junior college, but now she was thinking about quitting to become Shunji's manager. Not that Shunji needed a manager: he just needed someone to do the bookkeeping and drive him to appointments in town.

Chisato wanted to marry Shunji, an idea her parents didn't much like. They were cousins, after all. But Chisato wouldn't give up, and even became hysterical on one occasion, which caused her father to slap her across the face. She had been less adamant lately, and the marriage issue had been left hanging. Her parents didn't seem to mind her spending time at Shunji's house.

The way Shunji talked about this, you wouldn't have thought he was involved at all. So I had to ask: "Do *you* want to marry Chisato?"

"Oh, I don't really care either way."

"You don't care?"

"I mean, I don't really understand marriage. Does it change things?"

"Well, it makes it official that you'll be together your whole lives."

"That's what Chisato says. She'll take care of me for the rest of my life, she says. So marrying her is the best thing for me. I'm not sure, though. I don't really need much taking care of. I learned just about everything I need at school."

"So you wouldn't mind if she married someone else?"

"No. We'd still be able to meet, wouldn't we?"

Despite their sexual involvement, Shunji seemed rather indifferent to Chisato; the feelings he had for her didn't have much to do with love. He had known her longer than any of his other partners, but sexually she was just one of the many who had come on to him. For that matter, maybe I was no more special than she was. I didn't care; I was thrilled to know him and have him as a friend. I didn't hope for more. Chisato's presence didn't concern me.

Besides, I thought her vaguely hilarious. Her attempt at being nasty, giving me toilet slippers instead of shoes, was like a cliché; her obvious jealousy at me holding hands with Shunji was pitiful; and that stupendous lie about Shunji being her husband . . . She was so transparent she might have been in a soap opera.

After our second kiss, Shunji put his hands on my face and asked, "What sort of face do you have?"

First he felt my bones; then he checked the width of my forehead, cheeks, and chin; and last he traced the outlines of my eyes, nose, and mouth. When the examination was over, he said, very deliberately, "I take it you're not beautiful." His tone was like a doctor giving a diagnosis.

"I'm not the sort of woman who's always being told how beautiful she is, no. But what gives you that impression?"

"Your bones don't stick out enough. Beautiful women have prominent noses and chins and stuff, don't they?"

"I guess that's true. Who told you that anyway?"

"Chisato. She had me touch her face. See, she said, I've got a sharply ridged nose and my face has a clearly defined bone structure. That tells you I'm beautiful, because beautiful women have distinct features."

I couldn't keep myself from laughing. The bridge of Chisato's nose was very high, it was true, and her eyes weren't too narrow, which gave her face a Caucasian look, but the corners of her eyes slanted up funny and she had pointy cheekbones and a sharp, boxy jaw . . . All in all, her face was rather severe. The nicest thing one could say about her was that she had a face like a model from the early seventies.

"Why are you laughing?"

"Chisato isn't exactly what you'd call a beauty."

"People I work with are always saying how pretty she is."

Ah, I suddenly remembered: Masao talking about the pianist's woman— her heavy makeup, her being good to fool around with.

"Well, she's not so ugly that any praise you gave her would be taken for sarcasm."

I didn't want to insist that Chisato wasn't beautiful; Shunji might think I was jealous. I knew that, but I still couldn't stop laughing.

"So you don't think Chisato is beautiful?"

"Sorry."

"So it's not that clear. She's pretty pleased with herself, though."

That made me laugh even harder.

Shunji loved the sound of my laughter. He would tell me funny stories just so he could hear it. He looked so happy when I laughed.

"In elementary school, I was chosen to play the piano at a school recital. Guess what they made me wear? A polyester shirt with frills all over the front. The sleeves were so wide both my arms would've fit in one of them. I had on these velvet shorts that ended at my kneecaps; they were so big I had to hold them up with suspenders. And they made me wear this bow tie that was so huge it almost covered my chin. The teachers dressing me kept saying, you're so adorable, you're so adorable. When I started playing, the bow tie kept rubbing my chin, and it got so itchy that I clamped down on it with my teeth and that's how I played the piano, with my bow tie in my mouth. I didn't understand why the teachers didn't say anything nice to me afterwards."

Hearing me burst into peals of laughter, Shunji murmured contentedly, "That story makes everyone laugh."

I laughed a lot around Shunji. Ordinarily I'm not an especially merry person, but when I was with Shunji the tiniest things could set me off. I was so relaxed when we were together.

Shunji had a habit of nodding or shaking his head exaggeratedly when he was talking to people. It really was adorable. Once, when he was stretched out on his bed, he answered a question by rolling his head back and forth on the mattress. It cracked me up.

"Why are you laughing?"

"Because you're like a kid, shaking your head so hard."

"Oh, there's a reason for that. When I first started school, I used to get scolded all the time because I zoned out and didn't really give an answer when the teacher asked me something. 'If you want to say yes, nod so I can see it. If you want to say no, shake your head.' He used to hold my jaw and make me nod and shake my head, over and over. His grip was so strong I thought he was going to dislocate my jaw. So I've been nodding and shaking like that ever since."

By then my laughter had stopped. "They were strict, huh?"

"Yeah. I don't like teachers. They're scary."

It couldn't have been easy, and imagining all he went through to learn what sighted people just assume, I felt bad about laughing at him. But the next moment, Shunji broke into a wide mischievous grin and added, "He got on my nerves, so once when he was holding my chin, I spat on his hand. Boy, did I get yelled at."

At times like this, overwhelmed by an emotion that wasn't quite admiration and wasn't quite sentimentality, I feel like crushing my body against Shunji. I want to be warmed by the brightness of his personality, and to rock him with my laughter. He folds me lightly in his arms and cocks an ear near my lips, sort of drinking in the sound of my laugh. Sometimes I press my lips to his and try to blow my giggles straight into his mouth. We can't kiss then, because when I laugh, my tongue pulls back. Shunji wishes we could—laugh and kiss at the same time.

Kissing, it turned out, wasn't necessarily a prelude to sex. After a kissing session, we would sometimes stretch out on the bed and lie there holding hands or stroking each other's hair or arms, and most often that would lead to quiet, relaxed conversation. He might get tired of lying in bed and announce that he was thirsty, or jump up all of a sudden and go over to his weight-training machine and start doing bench presses. When we weren't touching each other, he would toy with the pillows and blankets.

All this made me wonder if maybe he really didn't have sexual desire, that for him my kisses and caresses were just another way of passing the time. He wasn't indifferent to sex, but he didn't seem to get aroused—not by me anyway.

"I don't get hard that easily," he said. "When we lay on the bed together the second time you visited, I didn't get an erection either. But if you rub my penis, I get hard right away. I've heard that most guys have erections automatically, without being touched. Is that right?"

Masao had always been ready for action by the time he got naked.

"How is it with yours?" Shunji asked, reaching for my toe-penis.

"It doesn't get hard until it's touched," I answered, bending my foot under my leg to get it away from him.

"Let me touch it."

"But it'll get hard."

"Oh." Shunji smiled. "That's okay. Let it get hard."

Shunji slipped his hand under my leg, seized my ankle, and began rubbing my toe-penis. He squeezed harder and softer, moved his fingers in different ways; he used techniques that I had never attempted—either on myself or on Masao. And he hummed as I dashed up the steps of pleasure.

"I've never encountered such an inexperienced penis," he said, as I was gasping in climax, then fell back into bed. He didn't demand that I pleasure him, now that I'd had my fun. Doing things to his partner didn't appear to get him excited.

"Why do guys get hard automatically, do you think? The only time that happens to me is in the mornings, when I wake up. Why is that?"

"I don't really know, but I guess if they're embracing and fondling someone, they must get excited, right?"

"Excited? But don't people feel *relaxed* when they embrace?"

"That's what I'd think, too."

"If a guy got aroused every time he had his arms around someone, he'd never be able to relax. That would be exhausting."

"I'm not sure people do that stuff to relax, actually."

"You think it's like a sport or something?"

"No, I don't think it's like that either."

It seemed crazy that I was having to explain male sexual desire to a man. There were plenty of things I would have liked to have explained to me, not the other way around. But the way Shunji approached the topic, he didn't seem to be viewing me as a woman, or himself as a man.

In the beginning, I didn't know what to make of Shunji's style of initiating sex. He went about it abruptly, in more or less the same manner he had the second time we met, when he suddenly put his hand under my blouse. Once we kissed and talked and fondled, he would, seemingly on a whim, stick his hand up under my clothes. Because I'd be feeling very easy and comfortable, this sudden change of gears would cause me to pull back in surprise. Now it was Shunji's turn to be startled.

"What's wrong? You don't want to?"

"It's not that. You just leapt from one step to another so fast. When did you have time to get excited?"

"What do you mean, when did I have time?"

"You're not even hard."

I placed my hand on Shunji's limp penis. He seemed to be noticing this fact for the first time, and lapsed into thought.

"You weren't exactly dying to do it, were you?"

"*Dying* to do it? No . . . I mean, I never feel that way."

"So why did you try to initiate things just now?"

"I don't know, I just felt like it."

"Is that usual with you? You start when you feel like it?"

"No. My partners always take the lead. I'm never the one to start it. And you? You don't usually initiate things?"

"No, Masao always started things."

"So what's the problem?"

"But it's not supposed to be this way. Usually I'd realize that Masao had gotten into the mood, and that would get me excited."

"Yeah, I'm the same way."

Shunji seemed a bit perplexed at having run up against a person so unlike his previous partners. Our muddled back-and-forth began to seem a bit ridiculous.

"Well," Shunji said, "let's do it. If it's not too much trouble."

We got naked and hugged each other tightly. His embraces were half tender, half almost desperate. He wasn't overbearing at all. Once we got started, I found myself getting naturally into the mood. The thing I'd been most afraid of was that I wouldn't feel anything with Shunji, since I had stopped feeling anything with Masao; but the moment we folded our arms around each other a sense of well-being washed over my body.

One hand twined around my body, Shunji kissed me, brushed his cheek against mine, fondled me. He didn't hurry. Every so often he would lay his head on my body. Sometimes he would let his fingers play across my skin, the way a bored child fiddles with whatever is at hand. He didn't need to prove what hot stuff he was, so I didn't have to be anxious about touching him. I wasn't abandoning myself to him, and I wasn't having my way with him; our sex play was much easier than that. We kept playing for a long time. Often a hand that had wandered toward our genitals would find its way heading back up and resting by our faces. There were even moments when it slipped my mind that we were having sex.

As we made love, I ended up lying on part of my blouse, and when Shunji felt this, he changed position.

"You've got a button mark on your hip. Does it hurt?"

"Not a bit."

"I hate having to button and unbutton clothes. Whenever I'm at home, I never wear clothes with buttons. I only wear T-shirts and sweatshirts. When I go out, though, Chisato always makes me wear a button-down shirt, because they look neater with a jacket."

"I think a T-shirt and jacket can be nice."

"You're okay talking at times like this?"

"Why wouldn't I be? I like talking with you."

"Most women aren't interested in talking in the middle of sex. They say it ruins the mood. I like to listen to their voices, but they seem to find it a bother to have to speak."

"What about men?"

"There was one guy who kept panting, 'Is it good? Is it good?'"

I burst out laughing.

"So it's okay for me to talk with you? I'm glad."

Shunji rested his head on my shoulder. I don't think I'm so unusual, but it made me happy that Shunji saw something special in me.

The next time we made love, as we were getting started, Shunji was struggling to unbutton my blouse. I intervened and told him I could do it.

"Really!" he said, evidently deeply moved. "It'd be such a help if you could! It's so hard for me, you know. Chisato would never dream of undressing herself. She says women prefer to have men undress them."

Masao didn't like me undressing myself either. Let a man have his fun, he'd say. But having my clothes taken off for me made me feel like a child. "*Some* women do, I'm sure, but I wouldn't say all."

"She also says sighted men like to undress women."

"*Some* men do, I'm sure, but I wouldn't say all."

I wasn't interested in other men's tastes. I was happy with Shunji's.

Shunji seemed to feel the same way about me.

"Making love to you is nice and easy," he said, "because you don't keep telling me to do things."

"Does Chisato tell you what to do?"

"Oh, all the time. She was worse in the beginning. She kept telling me I had to learn to make a woman feel good. Bite my nipple, moisten it with your spit, things like that."

"Huh . . . so that's what she likes?"

"Yeah. With other women I tried to do everything that Chisato taught me, but they said to stop, it hurt. So whenever I do it with other women, I don't do any of the things she told me."

"You've got a good head on your shoulders, Shunji."

"Some people say so, yes."

Much as I liked Shunji's style, that didn't automatically translate into great pleasure when we made love. I tended not to get very excited, no doubt because I felt so utterly at ease. Sometimes I even fell asleep while he was touching me. I'd wake up and realize with horror I'd fallen asleep, and get all panicked at the thought of how offended Shunji would be, only to discover that he was fast asleep himself, his breathing deep and slow. So we only actually arrived at sexual intercourse when one of us managed to maintain the desire until the end, actively touching the other person's genitals.

I didn't mind putting Shunji's penis in my mouth. I did the same things to his penis that he had done to my toe-penis. But he wasn't interested in my drawing out the pleasures of fellatio; before long, he would push my head away and climb on top of me. He wasn't hung up on oral sex the way Masao had been, and he had no desire to ejaculate in my mouth.

Shunji's penis tended to go limp almost as soon as stimulation ended, so successful intercourse could only be achieved if I refrained from touching him until I was near climax, or if we kept fondling each other throughout. Over time, the latter became the routine, although Shunji would often get distracted midway and start fooling around.

"Which do you want me to touch?" he'd ask. "The toe-penis?"

If neither of us was set on achieving intercourse, I was content however things went. It was great massaging each other's penises, and it wasn't bad if one of us worked on both of them. It could be tiring to use both hands at once, and it was hard to make us feel good equally—if I concentrated on his penis, my own pleasure diminished, and vice versa—but I loved the intimacy that came from experiencing the same delight. I wished I could have experienced this with Masao.

I had a hard time deciding who was the better kisser, Shunji or Masao, but the difference was starkly apparent when it came to coital technique. Shunji was well seasoned; Masao was green. I was amazed by the things Shunji could do, absolutely amazed, and I'd often lie there with my eyes open, watching in awe as he executed different thrusts.

"Let me hear your voice," he'd whisper. "I like hearing you at times like this."

His thrusts grew more forceful when I cried out. I moaned between breaths. Shunji rolled his head from side to side, as if to show me the pleasure his ears were feeling. Soon I couldn't tell whether I was crying out in response to his thrusts or he was thrusting in response to my cries. I would climax, sigh deeply, then pull Shunji's sweaty hip into me.

Once, after we had made love a few times, Shunji cocked his head in a gesture of puzzlement and said, "It's funny—for some reason it feels good with you."

"Better than with other people?"

"The sound of your voice makes me feel more. Not just my ears— my penis, too. I've never experienced anything like this before." Shunji paused, then continued, almost pensively, "I always thought it would feel the same no matter who my partner was."

The joy that I felt hearing this came as a total surprise to me. I couldn't recall ever being so happy to hear another person say, for whatever reason, that I was special. And I felt so good because Shunji had said it. I felt the same way about him, too: no one else had ever been as special to me as he was.

The emotion that hit me next left me completely bewildered. Because it was fear—a terrible fear like when you accidentally swallow an ice cube whole, and it's going slowly down your throat.

♥ ♥ ♥

I tried asking myself the same question Yoko and many of my women friends asked when I was dating Masao. Was I in love with him? I'd been satisfied with our relationship during the three years it lasted, I never thought of breaking up, and I never checked out other men. But none of that was proof that I had loved him. I thought I loved him, yes, but I didn't really. If Yoko could hear me from the next world, she would sneer . . . I saw now that I hadn't *selected* Masao, believing he was the one for me. No, he was just a likable young man I happened to get to know, an acceptable partner whom I'd gotten used to.

I thought I loved my old boyfriend, but I was wrong. This time my love is real . . . If that was the way I saw things, I was no different from the flaky young women who had given Yoko the idea for LOVESHIP. I hadn't gone with Shunji because he was richer, and Masao and I split up because that's the direction things were heading, not because I dumped him. But looking back, seeing how oblivious I was to the shallowness of my feelings for Masao, I couldn't help feeling embarrassed. I'd had no idea what it meant to fall in love with a man, which meant there was hardly any difference between my feelings for Masao and my feelings for Yoko and other female friends. In the end, the only thing that distinguished these relationships was sex.

You always act so indifferent, Masao had said, *so I had the feeling maybe you didn't really like me that much.* I had failed to understand what he was saying, and I was ashamed. It was awful to have believed I loved him enough. I didn't fall in love with a man until I was twenty-two . . . a late bloomer if there ever was one. My slowness must have kept me from realizing all kinds of things—that was why Yoko was always getting after me for being so dull.

And now that I thought about it, maybe Masao wasn't the only one I had treated badly. At this point, I was ready to bang my head against the wall. I hadn't chosen Masao from among the men I knew, and neither had I even *selected* a friend from the people I knew. You don't make love to friends of the same sex, so I was fine with anyone, as long as they weren't overly unpleasant. That about summed up my friendship with Yoko: we became intimate because she came to me, not the other way around. And she had been dissatisfied with our relationship, too, just like Masao, because I didn't seem to care. Had I been awful to her, too?

Yoko always chose things very carefully. She disliked having things thrust upon her, she wanted to make the decisions in her life, she wanted to be in control. She was very strict in selecting friends, and in making choices relating to her lifestyle. She was passionate about the things she chose, and never cast even a backward glance at the things she didn't choose—it was like they didn't exist. Since she made choices for herself, she must have wanted to be chosen by people in return. Of course, she wanted us to be friends like that: two people who had chosen each other.

I admired Yoko's decisiveness, but the coldness of her decision-making scared me. "Do you have to be such a perfectionist every time you're faced with a choice? Can't you leave a little room for play?" I once asked.

"There *is* no room for play if I have to choose."

"Yes, but if you keep eliminating options at this rate, you won't have anything left at the end, will you?"

I had made this remark casually, but Yoko's expression told me she had been caught off guard, and suddenly she looked deeply lonely. Ultimately Yoko had chosen death. So in the end, nothing was left.

But when Yoko killed herself, I learned how irreplaceable she was to me. She had initiated our friendship, consciously chosen me, but unconsciously I had selected her, too. In my own way I had valued her friendship, so very much, and I was filled with remorse at having failed to convey that feeling to her. How *could* I have made her understand? I felt frustration and sadness welling up inside me.

Guilt about Yoko and Masao was only the beginning of my troubles. I was anxious about the future before me, now that I was beginning to learn about choosing. I wasn't suicidal, like Yoko. But each time you select one thing, you have to give up something. Now that I had chosen Shunji, my interest in other people was weakening. But what would life be like if Shunji ever lost interest in *me*? It was too awful to imagine—just the thought was enough to make the world go dark. Making choices meant painting yourself into a corner. Why had I allowed myself to do something like that?

As long as things were good with Shunji, though, all my fears and anxieties were blown to smithereens, replaced by rising waves of happiness and rapture. Seconds after he'd call to invite me over, I'd be bounding out the door. Recently we had started getting together whenever Chisato wasn't around, not just on Sundays.

One Wednesday I went over because Chisato was going shopping in the afternoon and had an aerobics class or something in the evening; when I got there, I could hear someone moving about in the main house. Shunji's aunt must be home, I thought, as I padded quietly around back.

Shunji was playing the piano. He came over to the door when I called. We hugged. I was so happy to be with him, I twined one of my legs around him.

"What's with the leg?"

"I'm hugging you with it."

"You're weird."

We sat down and kissed.

"I think your aunt may have seen me."

"You didn't talk to her?"

"Of course not! What would I say?"

"Just say hi."

"You think hi is enough?"

"Sure. My aunt is nice."

"She may be nice, but she'll still tell Chisato about us."

"I doubt it. My aunt and Chisato don't get along."

"They're still mother and daughter."

"That doesn't mean much, not to me anyway."

That's right. His mother had abandoned him, and his father was dead.

"They really don't like each other," he said. "They hardly even speak."

"But in a pinch, your aunt is bound to take her daughter's side. I could be chased out of here."

"Who would do that?"

"Chisato."

"Oh." Shunji's forehead clouded. "Chisato is too much, really. She's friendly with other guys. I don't know why she needs me."

I couldn't believe my ears. "She's told you she's seeing other men?"

"No, but I can hear them. Sometimes after we finish a job, Chisato and I and the person I'm working with at the company go out drinking. In the taxi on the way back, I can hear their lips smacking and clothes rubbing up against each other. It's pretty obvious."

"But Chisato thinks you can't hear?"

"I don't know. Sometimes she's holding my hand while it's happening."

I'd figured out from what Shunji told me that Chisato was a sensual type. Now I learned that she liked to play around and was a little . . . adventurous. She might want to marry Shunji, but her love didn't appear to be exclusive.

"You don't say anything?"

"I just listen. Chisato has a nice voice, too."

Shunji grinned, amused, and my body went limp. I was stunned by what he had told me, but strangely enough the sight of Shunji's smile made me feel that everything was fine in the world, and there wasn't a hint of abnormality anywhere.

Smiling seemed to have made Shunji forget the tiresome situation we had been discussing. All of a sudden, he said cheerily, "Next month, my old classmate is coming to Tokyo!"

Somewhere in the back of my mind, the specter of Chisato continued to trouble me. I hated worrying about her every time I came over. I had dismissed her as any kind of threat, but as I began feeling closer to Shunji, wanting to stay with him for the long run, her presence loomed large and troubling. But Shunji just kept chatting about his friend, utterly uncon-cerned.

"His mom will be coming with him. I haven't seen them for ages. Why don't you come over and visit us? Chisato will be in Bali, so we won't have to worry about her."

"I won't be intruding?"

"Not a bit. Kensuke is really a load of fun. He's a masseuse in Tochigi. I'm going to get a massage when he comes."

A worry of a different nature sliced into a corner of my heart.

"Were you friendly with this friend of yours?"

"Of course."

"I mean, were you *friendly*? Like, did you kiss, and—"

"Ah, I see. No, I don't guess we ever did. But we are very good friends."

I was annoyed with myself for having sunk so low. But after dropping his casual response, he trotted off to his piano.

"A piece by Chopin, whose music I played at school until I grew to hate him," he announced.

He started playing a nocturne, but then, little by little, the rhythm shifted, and the piece was transformed into one of his boogie-woogie arrangements. "This is my favorite rhythm of all!"

As Shunji played, I went over and sat on the bench of his training machine.

"Did I ever tell you about the time some people tried to set me up as the Japanese Stevie Wonder?"

Leaving the boogie-woogie nocturne behind, Shunji launched into "Uptight (Everything's Alright)." He started singing, the sweetness of his speaking voice transforming to rich, husky tones. But he didn't sound like Stevie Wonder at all. He was more like Smokey Robinson when he was a teenager. If I closed my eyes, I wouldn't have thought this was Shunji. When I realized this, my heart started to pound.

After a couple of stanzas, Shunji stopped abruptly. "But the plan fell through. Someone decided it wasn't right for the times. When I told Ken-suke I wasn't going to be the Japanese Stevie Wonder after all, guess what he said?"

"What?"

"He said, 'That's great—because Stevie Wonder swings his head back and forth when he sings, and if you start doing that you'll end up even more of a dumbass than you are now!' That Kensuke—such a cheeky bastard!"

With that interlude, Shunji was back pounding out a boogie-woogie. He was fascinating to watch, the way he tapped out the beat, looking like the pleasure of the music was going right to the core of his body. He was totally relaxed, humming along, even with one leg crossing the other. I had seen someone play like this before. Who was it . . . Glenn Gould? . . . No, no, it had been Yoko, doing an imitation of Glenn Gould, whom she really loved, at somebody's house, I forget whose. She wasn't good at the piano, but she had looked good doing it. I felt a wave of nostalgia wash over me, along with some guilt . . .

"Tell me about your friends," Shunji said out of the blue. "Tell me about someone you're real friendly with."

The request was so perfectly timed, it was like he'd seen straight into my heart. I was stunned. He didn't wait for me to answer, but instead started playing something else, no longer boogie-woogie, maybe ragtime.

"She died."

"She died?" Shunji lifted up his hands from the piano. "That's too bad." Then he swung a hand in a huge arc and brought it down onto one black key. The sound of that single key reverberated in the room. My hands were wrapped around my knees, and I squeezed them tightly together.

"Tell me about a friend who's alive."

I was dismayed to find that no one came to mind. I'd thought I had plenty of friends, but since Yoko's death, they all seemed to have blurred. I felt no delight or pleasure when any of these blurs got in touch. What was wrong with me? Or were those people really just sort of blurs after all?

"The one who died was my closest friend."

"You must be awfully lonely, then," Shunji said. And then he said something unbelievable: "I guess I'm the only one you get to kiss now."

I was flabbergasted. "She was a woman! Why would I want to kiss her?"

"You didn't?"

"I told you I don't touch other women like that. I'm not like you!"

"Your voice sounded strange when you said that."

"Yes, because you seem to think I get friendly with anyone."

"Isn't it good to be friendly with everyone?"

"Don't talk like a schoolteacher."

Shunji spun around on the piano stool. "You don't like teachers? We're the same!"

It was impossible to argue with Shunji.

"Yes, I'm like you in that respect."

"Oh, I get it. When you said you're not like me a second ago, you mean it's your policy not to touch people of the same sex? Is that it?" Shunji was as lighthearted as ever.

"It's not my policy, I just don't want to."

"But you *do* want to touch men?"

"No, as a matter of fact I don't want to touch men in general either."

"You don't want to kiss men simply because they're men. So doesn't it seem funny that you wouldn't want to kiss women simply because they're women?"

"Your logic is nuts," I said.

"Besides, with your body you could even have sex with a woman."

His words, which I would rather not have heard, hit my ears like a slap. All I could do was mutter, "I don't think this tool of mine is meant for women."

"Mine doesn't have to be either." Shunji grinned. "I think people are happy when someone makes them feel good, no matter who it is. Don't you?"

"It only feels good with the right partner."

Yoko used to criticize me for being able to become friends with anyone. This wasn't the same thing as what we were talking about now, since she meant "friends" in the usual sense of the word, not sexually. But, still, here I was insisting that I wasn't the kind of person who wanted to get friendly with just anyone and condemning Shunji for doing precisely that. The way I was talking, I might have been Yoko.

I held a fist to my forehead, trying to calm down. I'm not interested in having sex with anyone but Shunji, man or a woman. But Shunji is probably still involved with Chisato, and if someone else comes on to him at some point in the future, he's almost certain to respond, without hesitation. And it won't matter whether it's a man or woman. I've selected him, but while he likes me, he hasn't actually made a choice. This made me very lonely. I was jealous of Chisato, I was jealous of the unknown women or men he might have sex with later, I was jealous period.

It pained me that even when the two of us were alone, as we were now, I couldn't help feeling emotions I didn't want. Had Yoko felt the same way with me? If so, she must have hurt terribly. My pain doubled.

"I'm going home."

Shunji said nothing for a moment, looking suspicious. "You just got here."

"There are some things I want to think over alone."

"Can't you think here? I won't disturb you."

"No, that won't work."

Standing in front of me, Shunji explored my face with his hands. The meltingly pleasurable touch of his fingers on my cheeks made me sad. I wanted to flee from this sadness.

"This is no good," Shunji said, his hands moving over my face. "The muscles are dead. Maybe it's best for you to go home."

"Yes."

"You don't sound too good."

Shunji wrapped his arms around my neck and kissed me tenderly on the cheek. The subtle emotion that his body expressed was incredible. He had probably hugged me on a whim, hardly intending anything by what he was doing, but in this gesture I felt a trace of something special. This led me now to envy Chisato, who was sure to have this sort of contact with Shunji all the time.

After summoning up enough energy to return Shunji's kiss, directing mine at his ear, I headed for the door.

Shunji's voice came chasing after me.

"Kudzu water is great for a cold!"

♥ ♥ ♥

I had told Shunji I wanted to be alone to think, but my solitary rumina-
tions didn't produce any major breakthroughs.

The fact that Shunji hadn't really *chosen* me as his one and only partner left me somewhat dissatisfied, but I wasn't sure how to set about
making him choose me. I found myself recalling headlines from women's
magazines—"How to Become His Necessary Evil," that sort of thing—but
I wasn't convinced that attending to the petty details of his day-to-day life
or honing my sexual technique would make me stand out in his eyes as
utterly unique.

Shunji wasn't deeply attached to Chisato, though they had been involved for ages. And he didn't appear to mind when he fell out of touch
with people he had been involved with in the past. He seemed completely
uninterested in trying to find one special person who would cherish and
be cherished by him; apparently he was content to have fun while it lasted.
"People are happy when someone else makes them feel good, no matter
who it is," he had said. Maybe he assumed new people would keep appearing to make him feel good, one after another, so there was no need to
give anyone preferential treatment. He was attractive, after all, and considering the life he had lived to date, it made sense for him to think that
way. How, then, could I get him to choose me over everyone else?

At the same time these thoughts were running through my head, I was
also feeling frustrated with myself for having, without realizing it, become
so needy. Until now, I had never cared to be the most important person
in anyone's life, and jealousy had played no part in my relationships. Even
where Yoko and Masao were concerned, all I had wanted was a vague
sense that they were fond of me; I was happy with our relationships as
they were, so I never demanded anything more. Why was that? Because I
had never considered them special, the way I did Shunji? I hadn't believed
anyone in this world was so unmistakably unique that I would have to set
them apart from others in my mind—and that went for me, too. Yoko's
friends all agreed that she was unusual, but I didn't necessarily see it that

way. So I interacted with her as I would with anyone else, and didn't give any extra thought to our relationship.

Now I understood better the essence of strong individuals. Shunji was one; Yoko had been another. It was too late with Yoko. Why hadn't I realized sooner how special she was? Had I been too childish, self-concerned, dense? No . . . that wasn't it. Because I was hardly what you would call observant now. Had I been blind? And I didn't only have this problem with Yoko. I was always lacking in curiosity. I never actively got interested in anything—not in things, not in people. I never tried to find something to be interested in. I wasn't bored, so I didn't see. So . . . was I bored now? Had the need arrived? Was that why I was seeing what I never had before?

There was no doubt that I needed to look harder. When my relationship with Masao soured, I experienced for the first time what it was like to fail at working things out with someone. After agonizing over our breakup, asking myself why it had happened and how we might have fixed it, I began to wonder if I could have been happier with another man. And that was when I began searching, unconsciously, for a man who could accept me for what I had become—a ridiculous woman with a penis on her toe. All this introspection and observation had been set in motion by the appearance of that organ.

I resented my toe-penis. My interpersonal relations were so much smoother without it, and I had been happy then. But I had to admit that, while I was satisfied with my life and uninterested in others, the people who cared the most for me suffered for it. Should I be grateful to my toe-penis for giving me an opportunity to change?

How ironic—the person I meet, the man willing to accept the new me I had become since my toe-penis appeared, had even less need than I used to have of a one and only. Given all who I used to be and all who he was still, there was nothing to be done, really.

The moment I reached this conclusion, the phone rang. "Do you have a driver's license?" were the first words out of Shunji's mouth. All I could say was yes. So, could I drive him and his old classmate Kensuke around on June 3? Sure, I said.

When I showed up that afternoon, the synthesizer was being pounded on, and the two men were talking, practically shouting in order to be heard over the music. They barely noticed my presence. I stood watching them for a bit, waiting for a chance to break into the conversation.

Kensuke was rather large, just the opposite of Shunji, with pudgy arms sticking out of his short-sleeve shirt. His hair was cut short, giving him the air, at first glance, of a jock. I couldn't see much of his face because of his sunglasses, but he had a delightful smile that revealed pretty teeth, small and pearly white.

The two friends were sitting side by side at the synthesizer, taking turns doing imitations of Stevie Wonder. When one sang, the other would put his hand on the singer's head, checking the movements of his neck and appraising the style of the swing and its resemblance to the real thing. Needless to say, neither had ever seen Stevie Wonder perform, so someone must have given them lessons. Each insisted his own style was correct.

I put my hand on Shunji's shoulder.

"Hey, it's Kazumi!" Shunji shouted, resting his hand on mine. "Did you see us doing Stevie just now? Which of us looks more like him?"

"Neither of you looks at all like him."

"Really? Hear that, Kensuke? She says we don't look like him."

"Who is *she*?" said Kensuke. "Introduce me, man."

"Kazumi, of course!"

I told Kensuke it was nice to meet him, and he suavely held out his large hand for me to shake.

"So this is Kazumi, huh?" Kensuke said to Shunji. "Getting a bit above yourself, aren't you? Having a lady friend."

"You ought to try it yourself sometime."

"Oh, how I wish I could."

"Did you bring your license?" Shunji asked me.

"I did. Where do you want to go?"

"Where's good?"

"I want to go to a restaurant with a nice view of the ocean," Kensuke said.

"Since when can you see the ocean?"

"It's always there before me when I close my eyes."

"You better not drown."

Their conversation had a rhythm of its own, and I found it difficult to share in it. But it was fun listening.

Shunji patted Kensuke's arm. "You wouldn't know it to look at him, but this guy always had the best grades in our class."

"You wouldn't know it to look at me? And how do I look?"

"Fat."

"Makes me easy to spot. You're such a shrimp, I bet even sighted people step on you by mistake."

We were all laughing when the door opened, giving me a start, causing me to straighten up. A woman of about fifty, dressed plainly, stepped in. She didn't resemble Shunji or Chisato, but I assumed she was Shunji's aunt.

"Kensuke," called the auntlike woman, "your mother wants to know what time you'll be back tonight."

Shunji's aunt might have been a bit surprised to see me here, but only a bit. When she spoke to Kensuke, she didn't look at me, which made me feel relieved.

"We'll be back by evening," Shunji said.

"You're welcome to stay over if you'll be late," the aunt said.

"Thank you very much," Kensuke said politely.

"Will your guest be driving?" The aunt now turned her gaze on me. But it was informational, not prying, not even asking for an introduction. I simply nodded a hello, and she bowed her head in response.

"We won't go too far," Shunji said.

"Thanks for entertaining my mother," Kensuke added.

"Be careful, all right?"

With this, Shunji's aunt vanished through the door. The aura of plainness she had brought with her lingered in the room a few moments after she left.

"See, she was fine, right?" Shunji whispered to me.

"She's not at all like Chisato."

"That's why they don't get along. Well, let's go! How about we go to the Tama River?"

Kensuke, constantly ready for banter, came back instantly with, "Tama River? Is that where the young and hip hang out these days? I hope you're not dressed like a dope, Shunji."

"All my clothes are cool. Here, I'll show you." Shunji poked me. "Hey, do me a favor and get out my best shirt and hat from the closet. And can you get my sunglasses from the drawer?"

"I've got my own personal stylist. I've got tons of clothes," Shunji added.

Presumably the "stylist" was Chisato. She had to choose his outfits for him since he couldn't do it himself. I was curious to see what her taste was like, but when I opened the closet door, I was dumbstruck: it was mostly empty. There were hangers and there were dresses, which were probably Chisato's, but no more than five shirts, including one that was purple and one garish pink thing.

"Which one do you want?" I asked.

"So many you don't even know where to begin?"

He wasn't being ironic. Did he not know?

"Something silk, maybe. I like how it feels."

There was no silk shirt.

"Don't you think cotton would be better, if we're going to the river?"

"Yeah, that's true. Anything is fine."

Of the three shirts that I thought even wearable, I selected one with a deep blue batik print; then I reached down and picked up a blue tulip hat lying on the floor. Now the sunglasses. The drawer was packed with a whole bunch of them, every one with a designer label. Shunji wore sunglasses to conceal his eyes, not to keep out the sun, so less expensive sunglasses should have been fine. Some of the pairs in the drawer were so faintly tinted they wouldn't hide his eyes at all. What was Chisato thinking?

I kept quiet about this, and handed Shunji the things I'd chosen.

He started changing.

"This shirt isn't cotton. It's rayon."

"Don't whine." This was Kensuke.

106

Very casually, I asked, "You can wear women-sized shirts, too?"

"Yup. Chisato borrows my clothes a lot. She said she was taking some on her trip."

"Hmm. Sure she's not picking things for herself and letting you wear some?"

Good old Kensuke, no need to mince words; he'd said exactly what I'd been thinking. Maybe that assortment of expensive sunglasses was for her to wear and for Shunji to borrow. All with Shunji's money!

"I don't know," Shunji replied when he finished buttoning his shirt. "I never thought about it."

"Yeah, you're way too lax, man. You have to watch out, or some sneaky broad will come along and take for you for all you're worth."

Shunji, showing no interest, said nothing. He put his hat on and pulled the rim down low over his eyes. Then, grabbing Kensuke's hands, Shunji wrapped Kensuke's fingers around the brim of his hat and yanked down until the hat was down to his nose. "What are you doing!" Shunji shouted. "I can't see!"

Kensuke laughed. "You're such a baby."

In the Pajero, Japan's answer to the jeep, Shunji and Kensuke kept goofing around in the back seat. "So how do you like the car?" he asked me. "The suspension is nice and high, so you have a great view, don't you think?"

"Is that why you chose a Pajero?"

"No, Chisato chose it. Because it's big enough to carry my instruments."

"Such a competent manager," Kensuke said.

I wasn't sure if there was any sarcasm in Kensuke's comment. I wasn't an impartial judge to begin with, and my head was reeling with suspicions. Did Chisato want to marry Shunji for his income and his indifference to her friendships with other men? Were my suspicions coming from my jealousy? I needed to butt out. Maybe Shunji didn't mind shelling out to keep her in fancy clothes. Maybe it was just fine . . . I couldn't keep from thinking while trying to concentrate on driving the Pajero, which was a big car and not so easy to steer. It didn't help that it was the first time I was driving in the area.

"How about some speed?" Shunji said. "I like the feel of the wind on my cheeks."

"We're still in a residential area, aren't we?" replied Kensuke.

"Chisato drives *really* fast."

Kensuke give Shunji a swat. "Chisato this, Chisato that. Give me a break already. You don't want to marry her anyway. I thought you were more interested in this babe who's driving."

"What are you talking about?" I shrieked.

"You mean he hasn't told you?" Kensuke asked, seeming quite surprised. "What the hell are you thinking, man? You've gotta tell her how you feel!"

"I didn't know what she'd say."

"Go for broke, Shunji man. Love is blind. And so are we."

This threw me off totally. My eyesight clouded. And as I took the next curve I failed to turn the wheel far enough and had to slam on the brakes as the Pajero swerved and screeched and rammed into the guardrail.

Chapter 5

Fortunately we weren't going fast, and no one was injured. I apologized profusely, but Kensuke said, nah, it was his fault for dropping such a bomb like that. Then, bending his head down, he started to pretend he was in pain from whiplash.

The drive home was without incident; I shook hands with Kensuke and said goodbye.

Shunji didn't care in the least about the damage to the Pajero. He ran his hand along the long scrape on the fender. "This scar will be a reminder of going for a drive with you today," he said.

"But how will you explain it to Chisato?"

"I'll tell her it was a friend of Kensuke's."

"But your aunt knows it was me."

"My aunt isn't a snitch."

Assuming that she wasn't, was Chisato going to buy it? Women have these instincts, even if I don't. Before leaving Shunji's house each time, I was careful to clean up in the kitchen and around the bed, but Chisato probably suspected something was going on anyway. Sooner or later I would have to tell her about our relationship. It would be terrible if she found out about us first, when I wasn't around, leaving Shunji to face her music. But for now, Shunji insisted there was no need to worry.

Only after I got back home did it come to me: I'd forgotten to ask Shunji about what Kensuke was saying just before the accident.

When I went over the next day, Shunji was very cheerful.

"At breakfast," he said, "my aunt asked if I was planning to marry you."

"And what did you tell her?"

"I said that if I'm going to marry anyone, I want it to be you."

"Really! You said that?" I was tickled to hear Shunji express himself so directly. In fact, I was thrilled, but the excitement in my chest was so great that I could only giggle as I offered this fatuous response.

"What are you laughing at?"

Incapable of speaking coherently, I just sat on the bed, giggling and hugging my knees tightly to my chest. My arms felt like they were wrapped around the reality of my future with Shunji.

Shunji reached out to touch me. "You feel feverish. Are you sick?"

"No, that's not it at all! I'm blushing!"

"You're embarrassed?"

"I'm embarrassed and happy."

"Oh." Shunji pressed up against me, putting his arms around me. "When we met, I thought you were . . . sort of . . . adorable. I never felt that way about a person before. Only about dogs and cats. I never understood what people meant when they said I was adorable. Now I know." Shunji hugged me harder. "I want to do things for you, all kinds of things. Not just because I want to make *you* happy, but because it makes *me* happy. I feel so nice when you're with me. I want to be with you all the time, for a long time. I was thinking that because we're not related, we can't be together, and you'll marry somebody else and I'll have to say goodbye, and then I thought we need to get related and that's when it hit me that all we had to do was get married."

Yes! I thought. When two people get married, they create a bond that's as good as blood. I'd almost forgotten. But Shunji hadn't.

"I think that's a wonderful idea."

"You think so? I'm glad."

Shunji let go of me, tumbled back onto the bed, then rolled over on his side and punched the mattress. This, rather than a deeply felt kiss, was how he expressed his emotions. He really wasn't like other people. He was unique—wonderfully unique. I wanted to go on watching him be unique for the rest of my life.

"Hey, I want to go to your apartment," Shunji exclaimed suddenly. "Can we?" He had one fun idea after the next.

"Of course! Do I have to drive?"

"Nah," he said, sparing me. "I haven't been on the train in a long time, so why don't we do that. You'll stay by my side, right?"

The thought of walking in public with our arms locked together made my heart leap. Each little thing we did together was fresh, enjoyable. I was happy.

"What should I wear?" he asked, jumping up from the bed.

"You're all right as you are. You look good in a T-shirt."

"I don't look like a slob? Chisato always makes me change when I go into town."

"You look fine," I said. "But if you feel uneasy, why don't you change?"

"Okay. How about that silk shirt I didn't get to wear yesterday?"

This gave me a flash of inspiration. "Why don't you go choose what you want to wear by touch?"

"That's a pretty crazy way to choose," he said, walking over to the closet.

Would he be shocked to find the closet mostly empty? I watched as his hand found the closet door, opened it, felt around inside.

"Huh?" Shunji cried, as hangers clattered together and one fell to the floor.

My heart ached.

"Why are there so few clothes in here?"

"That's all there was yesterday."

"How come? I should have six or seven things just for spring and summer. I wonder if Chisato borrowed some."

"Wouldn't she tell you?"

"No. She doesn't tell me everything she does."

"You usually have more?"

"I think so. Chisato says she always has to buy new things for me."

I felt myself growing sadder by the second. "But you're not sure?"

"No. Chisato always chooses what I wear. I never go out without her." He continued to feel around the closet. "My silk shirt isn't here."

"Chisato must have borrowed it."

"I can't believe it." Shunji sank down to the floor. "Why do I have clothes if I can't wear them when I want to?"

I had to ask, "Why do you have her buy all these things?"

"She says I need them! She says people look down on you if you're not well dressed."

"Does she really buy a lot?"

"I don't know. I think so."

"You know, Shunji, two or three pairs of sunglasses ought to be enough. There's more than ten pairs in the drawer, and they all look very expensive . . ."

"I never thought about it."

Shunji sat without speaking, then stood up and grabbed a shirt at random. It was the purple one.

"I wouldn't wear that if I were you. It'd be kind of weird for a man."

"What's the shirt doing in there, then?" Shunji was getting flustered. He threw the shirt on the floor. "Forget it, I'm not going to change."

I scooped up the shirt and hung it back in the closet. I wasn't going to say anything more. Shunji would decide for himself whether Chisato was only pretending to buy him clothes he needed when she was really buying clothes she wanted. He stood motionless, dazed. Maybe he was in shock.

Finally Shunji looked up. "Okay, let's go!"

He must have forced himself into a different frame of mind, because his voice was bright, and he put his arm around my shoulder. I felt cheered, too.

After we put our shoes on, Shunji pulled a white cane from the umbrella stand and whipped it up before him like a fencer. "Behold, my wand!" he shouted. "When I walk down the street with this, the crowds part before me."

The moment we stepped outside the front gate, he slipped his arm through mine, making me lead the way. I didn't mind him clinging to my arm, but our positions made me look like I was dragging him behind me, almost like a detective bringing in a criminal. I felt better after I adjusted my arm so that I was holding onto him, not vice versa, steering him by pushing lightly with my upper arm. He swept his cane back and forth across the sidewalk in front of him, whistling. I glanced at our reflection in the shop windows, pleased to see that we looked kind of cute together. We made a nice young couple.

Shunji had forgotten his handicap pass, so I bought two tickets. But as we were going through the wicket, the station manager waved me off and refunded the price of Shunji's fare. On the platform, Shunji complained that it stank and buried his nose under my arm. I pushed his head away, afraid that people might see, but he kept clowning around, even on the train, rubbing his body against mine, which made people smile.

As soon as we were inside my apartment, Shunji paced off the interior to familiarize himself with his surroundings. We took a shower together, washed each other, and then, steam still rising from our bodies, went out on the veranda and drank a beer. We played around in bed after that, and then I made dinner. Shunji offered no unwarranted praise for the meal. Instead, he said, "I can make a perfect medium-rare steak just by the sound and smell. I'll do that for you sometime."

By the time we stretched out in bed, after sunset, I was filled with a deep sense of contentment. I was beginning to feel as though Shunji and I had been a couple since before we were born. The thought that he and I would be together like this from now on made me feel peaceful, but also a little excited. I no longer felt the compunctions of a week earlier. I laid my fingers on the palm of Shunji's hand.

"My uncle says," Shunji said solemnly, "that I need to make something clear if I'm going to marry you."

"Oh?"

"That I'm going to cause you more trouble than I realize."

"You don't cause me trouble. I love you."

"He says a young lady who's never known hard times could easily get swept up in passion and decide to get married without really thinking about what she's doing. So a man needs to be conscious of his responsibilities when he proposes."

I couldn't see Shunji's expression because the lights were off. "I wouldn't say I'm going into this without thinking," I said.

"Yeah, I know that. But my uncle worries that I'm too laid back, that sometimes I make people suffer without realizing it. He says even though

---

I feel grateful when someone helps me, I don't have the imagination to understand how much trouble it took."

"That's fine. I don't need you to understand that."

"He says only a young person who has never experienced hardship would say that. Marriage is not all fun and laughter. That's what my uncle said, but that's his opinion."

In the face of such a rebuke, I could only be silent. Was his uncle saying he was against our marriage? I started feeling discouraged, but then bucked up: if my marriage with Shunji was going to be so difficult, getting upset about something like this wasn't going to help.

"All right, then," I said. "In full consciousness of the responsibilities I'm taking on, I hereby propose marriage to you."

Shunji's calm demeanor did not change. "My uncle said that if you said something like that, I should say yes. Only I should expect to be henpecked."

"What?" I cried. "Your uncle taught you how to make me propose to you?"

"Hmm. Maybe."

I lowered my head back onto the pillow, and the peacefulness of being together in the dark returned.

"Your uncle is a good man."

"Yeah," Shunji said, pleased. "I didn't know that at first, though. After my father died, when I started spending vacations with him and my aunt, he never talked to me. My aunt always took care of me, and for a long time I thought my uncle didn't care about me because we weren't related by blood. Chisato hated me, too, and—"

"Chisato *hated* you?" I asked.

"We were kids, and she was always angry at me. We don't need someone like him in our house, she'd scream, and my aunt would scold her and make her stop. So when we were alone, she would hit me and pinch me and stuff. She terrified me."

When Shunji said "she terrified me," his body seemed to shrink. Which made me want to shrink, too.

"I didn't know what to think when she started being nice to me in junior high," Shunji went on quietly.

He could jump from one emotion to the next very quickly. He'd gone from being terrified to being bewildered. But there wasn't any resentment. My heart beat wildly as I listened.

"My uncle knew Chisato was bullying me, though." In the darkness, Shunji sighed, or maybe he was laughing.

"I must have been in third grade when it happened. My aunt had gone somewhere and Chisato was outside playing, and my uncle and I were in the house. I was on the floor, just sort of lazing on the tatami, doing nothing, wishing my aunt would hurry up and come home. My uncle was sitting in the same room, not moving, maybe reading, and then suddenly he got up and came over to where I was. I was rolling around and bumped into his leg, which sort of surprised me, so I stayed still. Then he bent down, put his arm around me sort of hesitantly, and hugged me. I remember feeling how big his bones were." Shunji wrapped his own arms around his body. "It made me real happy. No one has ever hugged me that way again."

I was touched by this story, but at the same time I felt a little lonely. I could never hug Shunji the way his uncle had, not with these scrawny arms of mine. And I'd never be able to make him feel the way his uncle had, no matter how much of my heart I put into an embrace. So there were some things Shunji wanted that I wouldn't be able to give him. If there was anything that would cause problems, this was probably it. Shunji needed other people, not just me.

I put my mouth near Shunji's ear.

"Do you want to be hugged that way again? The way your uncle did?"

"No. I want to be the one hugging. I want to hug you that way."

Ever so slowly, Shunji moved on top of me. His arms weren't particularly large, and there was nothing hesitant about the way he hugged me, but the wave of emotion that I felt in my heart had to have been at least as strong as what he had felt with his uncle, long ago.

"I really love you, you know," I said.

"Me, too. I love you."

After this mutual expression of love, our kisses were deep. We began to touch each other, and it felt utterly natural. It wasn't the mild pleasure we knew, like being washed by warm water; there was electricity in it, a heat that emanated from the core of our bodies. Each time I touched Shunji, or was touched by him, the words "I love you" echoed in my head. As our touching grew more vigorous my body suddenly began to feel hotter and more sensual. A sense of urgency came over us. We rubbed our bodies together; our genitals joined, as if there were some force drawing them together. I experienced the most amazing orgasm ever.

After the echoes of that feeling faded, a feeling that had radiated all the way to my fingertips, Shunji stirred and said quietly, "Are you okay?"

"I still feel it."

Shunji had one of his hands between my legs.

"Why?"

"I don't know."

He nudged my hip with his still-hard penis.

"This little guy keeps moaning—I love you, I love you."

"I know. I hear him."

I embraced Shunji. He wrapped his legs around mine. Our toes touched.

"Yours is hard, too," Shunji said quietly.

I bent my leg and reached down to touch it. My toe-penis was becoming a bit more savvy these days, no longer responding to the merest stimulation, but now it was almost fully erect.

"What's it doing?" I said.

"Don't ask me. It's your penis."

"But you're a man. You should know."

"No. You're a woman, after all."

I sat up and turned on the bedside lamp. My toe-penis was standing up, very straight. It was kind of cute.

"This *thing* of mine seems to be pretty crazy about you, too."

Shunji took my right foot in his hand and placed it on his thigh. Our two erect penises were now lined up. They looked like two elementary school students standing and talking. I burst out laughing.

"Are you having fun?" Shunji asked, sounding amused.

I gave his hand a squeeze. The shadows our two penises cast on the wall were so sweet. I was sorry Shunji couldn't see them himself.

Shunji stayed over that night.

♥ ♥ ♥

Loving and being loved makes sexual pleasure more intense. Is this, I wondered, common knowledge? Now that I had learned this, I couldn't even imagine having sex with a man I disliked—not even just for fun. People who sleep around suffer from impotence of the heart. I doubted they felt much pleasure either. Or is their passion something else? I couldn't imagine it.

After my class let out, I went from my college to Shunji's house. I hadn't seen him for three days. By now, Chisato would be back from Bali. Would she have noticed the damage to the Pajero? Shunji hadn't called, so I wasn't too worried.

I no longer envied Chisato. It wasn't that I felt more secure now that Shunji and I were engaged; it was because of what Shunji had said the other day about her bullying him as a child. It was rotten of her, but it was also understandable: of course an only child would view another child who suddenly barged into her life as a nuisance, even if he was a cousin, or blind. Until Shunji turned up, she got all her parents' attention; then she was deprived of that privileged position. In the beginning I thought her behavior was outrageous. Now I saw that she was normal, human, as easily hurt as anyone, and I started feeling a kind of sympathy for her.

Breaking the news about Shunji and me might prove tricky, but if I spoke from the heart she would listen. I would wait for the right moment. I would talk things over with Shunji first. There was no rush. And so, having arrived at this conclusion—or maybe it was because we were eager to recreate the incredible sex we'd had the other day—Shunji and I put all conversation on hold for a while when I arrived at his house.

When Shunji did speak as we lay naked in bed, I was floored. "Hey," he said, "I told Chisato I wouldn't be needing any more new clothes for a while."

"You did! Why?" I squeaked.

"What happened to your voice?"

"Your timing was terrible. What did she say?"

"She said it was kind of sudden. She sounded sort of grouchy."

"And what did you say?"

"I said I was afraid if I got any more, the closet might burst."

I clutched my head. "I had no idea you could be so sarcastic."

"That's what Chisato said. 'Where did you learn sarcasm like that?' she said. Does it sound that sarcastic? I thought it was a pretty clever excuse."

"I bet she was livid."

"She was quiet for a little bit, then she apologized for borrowing clothes without asking, and then she left. She hasn't returned the clothes, though."

"Yeah, she was mad. Did she notice the damage to the car?"

"I told her that it was Kensuke's friend. She didn't say anything."

I sighed. "So she knows it was me, huh?"

"No, she doesn't!"

"I think she does. The car's scraped, you've noticed the closet is empty, you're putting an end to the shopping, and you've learned to be sarcastic. She's bound to think there's a woman pulling the strings in the shadows."

"Why couldn't it be a man?"

"A man, a woman—it doesn't matter. Either way, she knows there's someone else. Where did she go today?"

"She went to a party. She said she'll be late."

Very suspicious. She'll probably come back early. She could be listening under the window right this moment. I better not stay long.

Shunji, who didn't find Chisato's behavior odd, was grumbling. "She's greedy, you know? I pay her a manager's salary, and she still takes twenty thousand yen from what I give to my aunt and uncle for room and board."

"And you don't say anything?"

"Even kids in elementary school know stealing is wrong. It's hard to tell a twenty-three-year-old woman she shouldn't do something like that."

I took Shunji's face in my hands. "You said Chisato takes care of your accounting and income taxes and all that, didn't you?"

"That's right."

"Don't you think it'd be wise to check them sometime?"

"Yes, now that you mention it."

A sense of exhaustion seized me, and I let my head sink into the pillow. There was no telling how much Chisato had exploited Shunji's indifference to money matters. A second ago I felt close to her, now I couldn't believe her balls. Will I be able to take her on when the time comes? Even together, Shunji and I might not be strong enough to fight her.

Suddenly Shunji, who was lying quietly beside me, gave me a poke with his elbow. "I hear footsteps," he whispered. "It's Chisato!"

I could hear them, too. A figure darted past the window. In a panic, I gathered up my clothes.

"Hurry! Hide!"

The nearly empty closet came in handy. I sprang inside, and the next moment, the front door opened. Shunji couldn't have had enough time to get his clothes on.

"Were you asleep?" Chisato asked, trying to sound like she was in a good mood.

"Yeah, I'm really tired," Shunji said.

"Are you sick? Want me to take your temperature?" Her voice was as gooey as corn syrup.

"That's okay. I thought you were going to a party."

"My friend decided not to go, so I didn't either. Aren't you hot with that blanket on?"

"No."

"You must have a fever then."

That woman wouldn't give up! Shunji probably didn't know she was playing this game. I peered through the crack of the closet door and saw Chisato's back as she stood by the bed. She had on a tight, black miniskirt. The skirt was rather racy, but it made her firm buttocks look good.

"No, I don't have a fever. What do you want?"

"I came to return the clothes I borrowed. I'll just put them back in the closet."

Chisato's butt twitched. I plastered myself to the wall of the closet. But there was nothing I could do. Chisato was heading my way.

"Can you go get a cockroach trap?" Shunji's tone was earnest. "I've been hearing rustling noises in the closet."

"I'll do it later." Chisato's voice was directly in front of me. "If I see a cockroach, I'll kill it."

She pulled the closet door open wide, and the world came to a standstill. I stood there, hiding my nakedness with the clothes in my hands, looking miserable.

"There is a cockroach, after all," she said, and leered at me. She was suntanned, and her hair had been permed into tight little curls.

Shunji dashed over, wearing nothing but a pair of boxers. "That's my fiancée!"

Without a glance at Shunji, Chisato said to me, "Have we met?"

"Yes," I replied, "although it's been a while."

In a flash, Chisato's smirk vanished. "That's right! You're the insolent—" She sized up my body. "What are you doing in there? You like dark, narrow places?"

"No, no. I was just hiding."

"So it's a game? Well, I've found you, haven't I?"

It occurred to me at that moment that Chisato was the devil. And suddenly her entire appearance began to look devilish, which made me smile.

"Is there something funny?" she said sharply.

Smiling gave me confidence. "I wonder if you'd be so kind as to let me get dressed? We can talk after—"

"Talk?"

"Yes, let's talk!" Shunji seized Chisato's arm. "I'll make tea for three!"

Chisato allowed Shunji to lead her away, but her eyes bored into me.

"I'm sorry," I said, stepping out of the closet, "but would you mind just looking the other way for a moment, please?"

Chisato leered at me some more, ogling me. My body was mostly covered by the clothes I was bunching in my hands over me, so my scrawniness couldn't be so easily compared to her glamorous figure—she had just the sort of body men go for. It was her contempt that made me want to turn away. But by then, Chisato's eyes were glued on my toes.

"What is that!" Chisato shrieked. "Shunji, you've been taken in by a freak!"

"Don't call her a freak!" Shunji barked back.

"That's what she is. Is she a man? A woman?"

"A woman. Isn't it obvious?"

"Hardly."

Chisato mashed a red-lace stockinged foot down on my right foot, then yanked Shunji's hand down to it.

"Feel this thing here! What kind of *tool* do you think this is!"

"What? That's her toe-penis. I know about it."

Chisato stared at Shunji. I slipped my foot out from under Chisato's heel and frantically threw on my clothes.

"You're telling me," Chisato said to Shunji, "that you're able to get along with a person like this?"

"A person like what? I don't understand what you mean."

"Oh my god! What sorts of obscene things have the two of you been doing?" She no longer sounded angry, but rather curious.

Shunji also sensed this, judging from the question he popped next, his manner perfectly composed: "You wanna see?"

"Don't be stupid."

I finished dressing, and could now meet Chisato's gaze calmly. The sight of my toe-penis seemed to have given her quite a shock, because her eyes weren't as hostile as they'd been a moment earlier.

Chisato walked to the bed and sank down onto it. "Of all things," she said out loud, "to be cuckolded by a woman with a dick."

Depending on one's interpretation, this could have been taken as an admission of defeat. Shunji and I didn't say a thing.

"Why don't you two say something? Huh?" Chisato said. "So you're engaged? I guess you must be in love."

There was no way to respond to this either.

Chisato flew into a rage. "What's up with you two! You aren't just playing house, are you? It's not that kind of an engagement, right? Do you know what it means to get engaged? You don't just decide to get married because you have good sex!"

In the space of a few seconds, Chisato had gone from playing a defeated lover to a high and mighty parent, handing down pronouncements.

"We know that," Shunji muttered.

"Do you? Where will you live once you're married?"

"Here."

"This place is too small; there's not enough room for two."

"We'll rent an apartment."

"Can you find a place? Can you handle the contract?"

"I can, yes," I interjected.

"Really? You're in college, right? Have you ever filed income taxes? Do you know how to write the rent off as a business expense?"

"I do." Chisato's tone was getting on my nerves. "I've done all that at work."

"Yes, Kazumi was one of the heads of LOVESHIP."

Chisato's expression changed dramatically.

"LOVESHIP? The love-distributor? Are you serious?"

"Yes," I said. "My friend founded it."

For the first time, Chisato looked at me as an equal. Her lips moved silently, as if she was itching to ask something, but—maybe because she didn't know how to frame the question—she didn't speak. Her expression was now overflowing with curiosity.

Deciding to give her another little dig, I said: "At LOVESHIP, I also learned about how people cook the books and embezzle funds."

Chisato's cheeks went scarlet. I'd hit where it hurt. She looked back and forth between Shunji and me, clenching her teeth. "You're more mature than you look," she said in a low, trembling voice. "I can rest easy leaving Shunji in the hands of such a capable woman." Chisato stood and came over to where I stood. "I'm glad Shunji has found such a wonderful match. Take good care of him, okay?"

Suddenly she was the cousin thinking solely of Shunji's welfare. I couldn't help but marvel at her transformations. I shook the hand she held out to me. Her fleshy palm was clammy.

Next, Chisato put her arm around Shunji's shoulder. "Congratulations, Shunji. I hope you'll let me use the Pajero sometimes."

With that, Chisato headed for the door, her hips swaying gracefully. As she slipped on her shoes, I could see that her face was still flushed. She turned and waved, a smile on her lips, before closing the door. I wasn't able to smile back.

Alone again, I leaned against Shunji. "I'm exhausted," I said.

Shunji put his arm around me. "But everything's solved."

"You really think everything is okay?"

"Sure, everything's fine."

Leaning on each other, we slid down to the floor.

♥ ♥ ♥

Once she had acknowledged our engagement, Chisato became weirdly friendly. Whenever I went to Shunji's, she would come over with sweets, beaming. She would stay for ten minutes or so, talking and laughing, then say that I should feel free to use the bathroom in the main house if I wanted, or encourage me to spend the night. When Shunji came to my apartment, she would drive him over in the Pajero, then pick him up the next day. Of course, she had her own plans on these occasions: instead of returning home she would park the car by my apartment and spend the night somewhere in town.

Chisato's familiarity was rather unsettling. Generally speaking, women like her are liked by men and reviled by women—they only bond with women like them, who dress in the same slutty way. Someone like her ordinarily wouldn't deign to wipe her snot on a plain jane like me. Sometimes when she came to fetch Shunji, she would take a nap in my bed, saying she hadn't slept the night before; my apartment turned into a convenient pit stop for her.

On the other hand, she always wanted to hear more about LOVE-SHIP. She wanted to know how much profit we made, what kinds of men signed up, what Yoko had been like. She'd even wanted to register with LOVESHIP herself, she said, but decided against it out of fairness to Shunji. What a brazen liar, she who had no qualms about making out with another guy in Shunji's presence.

When I told Shunji how disconcerting I found Chisato's buddy-buddy-ness, he responded, "There's no harm in it. Don't let it bother you." He had a point. And after we were married, Chisato would be my cousin, so it was a good idea to keep our relationship on a good footing. I made up my mind just to accept her sudden friendship.

So when Chisato called one night to ask me to have drinks with her at a Roppongi club, it was impossible for me to refuse, even though I had a paper due in a few days.

"We should talk sometime without Shunji around, don't you think— just you and me?" she had said. "Besides, I want to introduce you to my new boyfriend."

The club seemed nice enough. At nine on a Thursday night, a significant proportion of the customers were yuppie businessmen in suits. Chisato was sitting at the bar, sipping a gin fizz. She had straightened her hair, getting rid of the little curls, and was playing the part of a quiet, well-bred young woman.

"He isn't here yet," Chisato said.

"Is he a businessman?"

"Yes. At a trading company. He just started a couple months ago."

"So he's younger than you?"

"No, we're the same age. He took a year off to prepare for his college entrance exams. He's not the sort of guy I can blow off easily, though. I've never met a man like him before. I have trouble pulling his strings—he rolls right over me." Chisato seemed very taken with her new lover: her eyes had a far-off look, and she couldn't stop smiling.

"When you meet him, you'll see it's true. He was eager to meet you, too, when I told him about you."

"Oh? What exactly did you tell him?"

"You've got all sorts of interesting stories, no?"

A smile that could hardly have been described as delicate played across Chisato's lips. She wasn't directing it at me—it was more of a self-satisfied smirk. But I didn't want her to think I was around for her amusement. I washed down my discomfort with a large gulp of dry sherry.

"I'm so happy I had an opportunity, by whatever mysterious workings of fate, to get to know a person like you. It's great . . . I brag about you to all my friends."

Now I was suspicious. And I didn't like the way she leaned close to me when she talked, speaking in a hushed tones. She must have learned this from flirting with so many men. I took another gulp of my sherry.

"Hey!" came a voice from behind. Chisato swung her head up and around. "So you made it! Finally!"

"Sorry, I had a lot of work to do, and it took a while to get out of the office."

"Kazumi, my boyfriend has arrived!"

The young man, dressed in a navy-blue suit, sat down beside Chisato. I gasped as he began to pull his business card from his coat pocket. Chisato's new boyfriend was none other than Iwai Haruhiko, Masao's former best friend.

"Well, well—it's you!" Haruhiko said, raising his eyebrows.

"You two know each other?" Chisato's eyes widened.

"Been acquainted for years. Not too intimately, though."

His tone was as obnoxious as ever. I hadn't seen him since that March night when he was drunk and burst into Masao's apartment. He didn't seem to have changed a bit, despite the suit. The card he handed me bore the name of a prestigious trading firm.

"I hear you and Masao broke up?"

"Who told you?"

"Masao."

I leaned forward. "You're in touch with him, then?"

"Sure. Things may come between us, but we never separate for good."

Was it possible for a friendship to endure so bad a falling out as theirs?

Haruhiko launched into an explanation, taking the tone of a teacher lecturing an ignorant pupil. "The truth is, your suspicions were correct. Emotionally, Masao and I are gay. The bond between us only grows stronger every time we go through hard times together. He and I will never break up for good. I doubt Masao thinks of himself as emotionally gay. It's funny, though, because he's the one who needs me, not the other way around."

"What's going on here?" Chisato said. "The moment you see Kazumi you start talking about being gay? Were you and her and this Masao guy involved in a three-way affair or something?"

"Hardly." Haruhiko gestured to the waiter. "Dry martini, please."

"No? No love affair with three penises?"

Haruhiko swiveled his head around and peered into my eyes. "So you're the girl with the penis on her big toe?"

My face reddened. Had Chisato been telling everyone about my toe-penis? Was that what she was bragging about me for?

Haruhiko pursed his lips. "Funny, Masao never said anything about it."

That was one thing I could be grateful to Masao for. I swallowed the rest of my sherry. Haruhiko ordered me a Kahlúa milk and then moved on to his next question: "Did you two break up because of it?"

"I'd rather not talk about it."

"I see. He must have hated it."

I stared at Haruhiko.

"Masao is like that, you know. He's even more hung up on his penis than I am. He views all penises but his own as the enemy."

"You're not like that?"

"I'd have no problem kissing your penis."

"That's enough!" Chisato said, slapping Haruhiko's arm.

Haruhiko ignored her. "I'm not at all uptight about sex. I'm all for omni-directional diplomacy, polymorphous perversity, and all that. You could also say I just sleep around. I put my penis anywhere if it looks like fun."

"Haruhiko!" Chisato screeched. "Have you really had sex with men?" Her face was scarlet, and she was drunk.

Haruhiko blocked Chisato's mouth with a kiss. She immediately let her eyelids droop and responded. Not knowing where to look, I turned to my Kahlúa for help. Haruhiko had spoken of his omnidimensional diplomacy, but this was a kind of predation, dark and foul. He was not like Shunji at all.

As he removed his lips from Chisato's, Haruhiko winked at me. Chisato leaned her body against his.

"I do anything, you see. I love sex. Guys I know used to bully women into fucking them, in the name of liberation, but they were too uptight when it came to men. When I tell them about the things I've done, they get this look on their face that's half inferiority complex and half longing."

"So you've really had sex with men?" Chisato asked again, sleepily.

"In high school, a cute classmate came on to me. I gave him what he wanted—hemorrhoids," he said with a thin, cruel smile.

"So do you like men? Or hate them?" I asked, full of revulsion.

"I like them."

"Are you sure?" I stared at him.

Haruhiko narrowed his eyes in response. "I like men and I like women. I admit, however, that deep inside I feel a very powerful hatred for everyone. It's not directed at either men or women."

"And how about yourself? Is it directed at yourself?"

"Maybe, maybe," Haruhiko replied, without batting an eye.

This man's heart was as cold as ice. I couldn't stand to be around him. Chisato was slumped against him, limp—maybe asleep. I paid for my drinks, and without saying another word, headed for the exit. But Haruhiko caught up with me and blocked my path.

"I hear you got a big cock, bigger than the average cock in Tokyo," he whispered, his mouth right up against my ear. "Chisato is wildly curious."

The bastard was taunting me. I didn't need it. I smiled thinly and walked off.

The rainy season wasn't quite over, and the air outside was heavy with humidity. But Haruhiko's noxiousness left me feeling more soiled and slimy than the night. I wanted so badly to see Shunji. But I had that paper to work on. I hurried toward the subway station.

I got home, immediately took a bath, and right away my doorbell rang. It was Chisato. It was like she'd chased me home. "Hey, it's me, it's me," she pleaded from the other side of the door. "Let me in!" I worried Haruhiko was with her, but no, she was alone. I opened the door, and she tumbled in, reeking of alcohol, her eyes bloodshot.

She threw her arms around me. "Why didn't you tell me you were leaving?" she slurred. "Haruhiko, that son of a bitch. Was he rude to you? Did he piss you off? Is that why you left?"

"Oh, it was nothing, really," I said. Then out of politeness, I offered her coffee.

"Who would have guessed you two knew each other!" Chisato said, hardly touching the coffee. "He's such a pig, but I think he's great. Below the belt, he can be a bad boy, but really, he wants to believe in people so much, he doesn't know what to do with himself. We're a lot alike."

The description of Haruhiko sounded like the sort of thing any woman who had fallen for him might say, but she was right about one thing—they *were* alike. And while this may sound corny, I felt a sliver of pity for her. That was why, when she asked if she could spend the night, I agreed, even though I didn't want her anywhere near me.

I prepared a futon for her and then fell into my bed.

Chisato, even after a shower, kept talking to herself. "I'm a slut and I lie and I'm beautiful and I'm lonely, I'm so lonely . . . That's what Haruhiko says . . . I'm so lonely."

I was too tired to listen anymore and knocked off. Next thing, Yoko and I were sipping champagne . . . in the early afternoon . . . on a spring day . . . in a field of lotus blossoms. I felt an incomparable sense of calm. The sun sank so fast it was like watching it on fast-forward, and the tints of the blossoms were dissolving into the beautiful twilight, but we still felt cheerful. Yoko raised her glass, smiling more happily than I'd ever seen her in real life, and the thought occurred to me, in a dim sort of way, that I didn't want this moment to end, I wished we could stay like this forever . . . And then suddenly I realized that I was supposed to go see Shunji . . .

There was a break in the dream. The next scene was Shunji and me in bed, kissing and embracing. The image segued into sensation, the pure physical sensation of pleasure, pleasure centered around my toe-penis. Someone . . . was sucking on it . . . someone who wasn't as good at it as Shunji . . . but wasn't so bad at it either. Then this person was replaced by someone else who was better . . . whose mouth was tighter, and warmer . . . and it felt so good I could hardly breathe . . .

The pleasure was so good, I couldn't keep from opening my eyes. Which was when I realized: This is *not* a dream! My eyes drifted toward my lower body.

The sight of a disheveled Chisato straddling my foot stunned me. My toe-penis was up her vagina.

Chapter 6

In the faint early morning light, Chisato's immaculate white stomach and tanned, muscular thighs hovered in midair, solemn forms detached from everything around them. I felt the warm flesh of her thighs on either side of my right foot. My toe-penis was enveloped by the pleasure of warmth and moisture, but as soon as I realized this came from Chisato's vagina, it all turned to revulsion.

Chisato was clenching her thigh muscles, getting ready to raise and lower her hips. Uttering a voiceless scream, I tried to yank my right foot from between her legs. But since I was lying on my back, my heel got stuck in the mattress and I couldn't bend my knee. When I rolled over on my side and wriggled my foot out of her, I felt my toe-penis jabbing into a soft wall; an anguished cry escaped from Chisato's lips, and her body shook. Finally, I managed to slide my toe-penis out.

"What the hell do think you're doing?" I cried as I sat up.

Chisato returned my gaze, an insolent gleam in her eyes, then coolly rearranged her legs and adjusted the hem of her nightgown to hide her genitals. I was reeling from shock and couldn't think what to say, what words to throw in her face. The toes of my right foot, liberated from the disagreeable warmth of her thighs, now felt a little bit chilly. I wrapped my hand around them, only to find them coated in sticky strings of mucus. I shuddered, and wiped it on the sheet. By now my toe-penis was completely limp.

"There's no need to be upset," Chisato said. "I just thought we could have a little fun together, and you respond by getting frightened. You'd think I'm some sort of monster or something, the way you react."

"You . . . you . . . thought we could have . . . fun . . . *together?*" I had a hard time speaking. "I was asleep! How was I supposed to—"

"People relax when they go to sleep, so it's a good time to set things in motion. Sometimes men without much experience get nervous if you start something when they're awake, and then they have problems, you know?"

"Who are you calling a man?"

"Well, it's true, you're not a *real* man."

"No, because I'm a woman."

Chisato burst out laughing. "Your foot marks you as a man."

I wanted to intimidate her physically as I argued back, but my body refused to move. Chisato's inability to see anything wrong with the unspeakable act she had just performed on me was worse than perverted, it was repugnant. I despised her.

"This may *look* like a male sexual organ, but it is *not* one," I said, my voice quavering.

"Let's not split hairs. If that isn't a penis, what is it?"

She was treating me like a fool. This was her technique for worming out of tight spots: even if she was obviously wrong and standing on shaky ground, she tried to turn the tables by going on the offensive, thus evading the issue. I wasn't going to fall into her trap. I was going to be a little creative myself.

"Do you use anything that looks like a penis as a penis?" I said.

Once more Chisato burst out laughing. "Don't turn the conversation somewhere else. Even if that isn't a male organ, you can't deny it's an organ meant for pleasure. So enjoy it."

I wanted to tear out my hair. "You have no problem enjoying yourself with another woman?"

"I'm not a dyke, if that's what you're asking. I'm not interested in lesbianism. But you're a hermaphrodite. This is different."

This made me extremely annoyed, which was a bit of a surprise to me. *I'm not interested in lesbianism,* she'd said. That got on my nerves. I myself had no interest in that sort of thing, but for her to say that after impaling herself on me, a woman like herself, the same in all respects but one . . . "So you're only interested in my big toe. You don't care about the rest of me, which is female?"

"Of course."

"You ignored most of me, taking just the toe?"

"That's right."

"Quite adept, aren't you, to be able to isolate such a little part."

Chisato stared at me, puzzled by my anger. "What are you trying to say? You're like me; you're repulsed by the idea of doing things with another woman, right? I mean, by using parts other than your toe?"

I couldn't stand it anymore. "I don't want to use my toe to do things with another woman either!" I said, raising my voice.

Chisato's eyes widened, and her jaw dropped. It occurred to me that I'd seen this expression before—in one of Masao's porn magazines. I'd seen it in an ad for a life-size plastic sex doll. Spiteful of me, but it was her fault. She wanted to have sex with my toe. She wasn't interested in any other part of me, let alone *me*! Talk about sexual objectification! My big toe–penis was not a vibrator.

It didn't take Chisato long to get over her surprise. "You have no idea how that *thing* of yours is meant to be used, do you?" she said, almost haughtily. She cast a sideways glance at me—maybe this was what people mean by "making eyes."

A chill ran down my spine.

"You're a virgin," she went on, smug, "so you're suppressing the desire your penis feels." She leaned forward, like she was going to start creeping toward me.

"Chisato!" I cried. "I'm a woman!"

She paid no heed. "You're a prisoner to how you used to feel when you were still a woman. Now that you've got a penis, you have to think differently. Don't you understand? Penises are made to go into places they fit. A hand, a mouth, it's not enough. You're cruel, not giving your penis an appropriate outlet for satisfaction."

Chisato stretched out a hand toward me—like some dissolute lecherous guy trying to seduce a young man who wouldn't be able to resist. But I wasn't a young man. And her cloying tone and full body made me disgusted, unpleasantly hot, frantic to get away. I knocked Chisato's hand away and leaped back.

"You're stubborn, aren't you?" Chisato said. "Do you really dislike me that much?" She actually seemed sad; what an actress. "I think you're marvelous. It hurts that you hate me so."

First she's holier-than-thou, trying to provoke me; then she tries to win my sympathy; and now, an instant later, she's praising me, acting like a supplicant. Was this how women who actively went after guys managed to get laid? I was kind of impressed, to tell the truth, but I couldn't stomach the theater.

"I don't hate you," I said. "You've got to understand, this *thing* of mine isn't a male sexual organ, so there's no reason to put it into a female sexual organ."

Chisato narrowed her eyes. "Male sexual organ, female sexual organ—whatever. Let's not get hung up on terminology, okay? The point is, you put your 'surplus' into where I've got a 'deficit,' as they say, and you and I can share the pleasure."

The conversation was going in circles. Why couldn't I make it clear that I wasn't interested? Was I stupid? That's how it was beginning to look. "I already told you," I said, "I don't enjoy sex with just body parts!"

"No sex without love. Is that it?"

"Yes."

A cold, condescending smirk hovered on Chisato's lips. "Ah yes, the disease of modernity. Could there be anything more unnatural than not having sex without love? Isn't it *really* much more unhealthy to wrap love and sex up in a package and then suppress your desire?"

"I'm not suppressing anything. I don't have the slightest desire for you."

There, I'd said it. I hadn't wanted to offend her, so she wasn't getting the message. Now I'd finally said it, and it was like throwing a bucket of water at the ugly smile in front of me. But the smile didn't go away; it got even broader.

"I've already proved that's a lie," she said.

Now it was my turn to burst into laughter. "That was just a reflex. My toe was just responding to stimulation."

"But I was the stimulation."

"I had no idea what the stimulation was because I was asleep."

And it was true. The moment I realized it was Chisato, the pleasure was gone and my toe-penis went limp. It wasn't so innocent as in the early days, so I'm sure it wouldn't have gotten hard if I knew it was Chisato touching it. No matter how good she was at it, I'd only feel disgusted.

Blunt as I'd been already, I still had to soften the message. "And I was dreaming of Shunji, you see."

"The implication being," Chisato said, narrowing her eyes, "you wouldn't have responded in that way if you knew it was me? I *can't believe* you have the nerve to say something so awful to me. Am I that ugly?"

"No, no, it has nothing to do with being—"

"I've never felt so miserable in my life. Why are you so prejudiced against me?"

"It's not *prejudice*. I just make a distinction between you and him."

"Why? We're both human."

I said nothing. I'd had enough of Chisato's make-it-up-as-you-go-along-ing. Chisato, too, was quiet, and sullen. The only sound to be heard as the morning light crept into the room was the chirping of the birds outside. I was in a daze.

Chisato jerked her chin up. "Then let's have a test," she said. "Let's see if I can make that *thing* of yours get hard."

This girl just wasn't giving up! She was wearing me down, and I actually began to wonder, why not? Why not, if it would shut her up, just close my eyes and let her do what she wanted with my toe-penis. I could always imagine she was Shunji. Fortunately, I pulled myself together.

"You have Haruhiko. You must like doing it with him best, right?"

"Neither of us is a devotee of the monogamous way."

Listening to Chisato's wooden words, I finally got it. Chisato, who worked so hard to fan the flames of her own desire—she was the one, not me, who was unnatural and unhealthy. "Understood," I said. "That's fine. Just leave me out of your policy."

Chisato leaned forward. And then, with no warning, like lightning, she slapped me across the face. I sat there, shocked, and then she started screaming. "Who the hell do you think you are! As if you're so lofty and pure! You think you're such hot stuff? The truth is you're stingy and a coward and immature, you're prejudiced, you've got this sickness of modernity, and it's not even clear whether you're a man or a woman, because you're a freak!"

"This is all a misunderstanding."

Chisato raised her arm to slap me again. I ducked, shielding my face with my hands, and her blow landed on my forehead.

"I hate how you play innocent. Acting cool, making a fool of me," she spat.

And she kept hitting me as I covered my face. I had no choice but to take it. I didn't know what I'd done to deserve this. Then the attack seemed to end, and I peeked timidly out between my fingers. Chisato had thrown off the nightgown I'd lent her and was putting on her clothes.

Dressed, she picked up her handbag and looked up at the clock. Six-thirty. She headed for the door without looking at me. I was too scared to say anything.

Halfway out the door, Chisato stopped in her tracks and turned around. "Just to be perfectly clear," she began, her eyes sparkling, "you can try and act as though you're nice and pure, but your penis went all the way inside me. You and I, we've had *relations*. I've sullied you." With that, she sashayed off, leaving behind a smug cackle as a souvenir.

Her parting words had their intended effect. The moment I heard the door click shut, I flew into the bathroom. I turned on the faucet and scrubbed not only my toe-penis, but each toe on my right foot.

♥ ♥ ♥

More than a week later, the feeling of Chisato's vagina still seized my toe-penis from time to time, the sensation alarmingly real, as though it had been pasted to the surface of my skin. As a result, all the papers I turned in at school were complete crap. I was very angry.

Shunji didn't seem to find Chisato's behavior at all eccentric. I'd waited until nine o'clock that morning to call him; his reaction left a lot to be desired.

"So that's why she asked all those questions about your penis—she wanted to have sex with you! I had to put up with a lot of interrogating, you know. How long does it get, and how thick—all kinds of things."

"And you told her?"

"Sure."

So that's how word got out. Haruhiko said he'd heard my penis was bigger than average. He must have heard from Chisato, who must have gotten it from Shunji.

Shunji didn't sound apologetic either. Of course, Chisato was the villain. I couldn't blame Shunji for answering her questions, but I was disappointed he had no sympathy about the calamity that had befallen me. His voice was quite mellow.

"Funny, I didn't realize Chisato liked you so much," he said.

"But she doesn't like me! She was just curious about my toe-penis. She said she wasn't interested in any other part of me."

"Huh? If someone has that kind of curiosity about somebody else, even if it's only the toe, it means she likes her. You don't you think so?"

For a moment the brightness of Shunji's statement made me feel like the scales had fallen from my eyes. I was not, however, entirely satisfied.

"There's no pleasure in having someone like just one part of me."

"Oh, so you want to be liked a whole lot. You're right, it's better to be liked a whole bunch than just a little."

"I don't really want to be liked a whole bunch by Chisato."

"You dislike her that much?"

Asked this in such an innocent tone, I began to feel that maybe I was just a curmudgeon, coldheartedly disliking someone. And this made me timid. "She's fine to talk to, but . . . I don't want to have sex with her."

"Why not?"

"It's gross!"

"Really? Chisato never made me feel gross." He and Chisato had slept together—countless times. He had no problem with the gooey clinginess of her vagina.

"Yes, but Chisato and I are the same sex."

"Oh, yeah—you don't touch other women."

Shunji had experienced homosexual sex, so he didn't understand the instinctual revulsion I felt about doing things with other women. He just didn't get how I felt about what happened between Chisato and me, that it was a calamity. And indeed, far from sympathizing with me, the words he murmured next came from an entirely different angle.

"It must hurt to have someone tell you to keep your hands off because she thinks you're gross."

I was shocked. "You think I should have accepted her advances?"

"No. But I bet Chisato was pretty startled when you turned her down."

Seems Shunji had a better understanding of Chisato's feelings than he did of mine. This wasn't because he had known her longer than me; it was because his sexual life, until now, had been more like hers than mine.

"I was pretty startled, too, when she started slapping me," I said.

Shunji groaned. "Yes, Chisato lets her anger get the best of her."

I no longer had the energy to talk. Maybe Shunji got the hint, because for a few moments he seemed to be casting in different directions. Then, sounding as if he had been struck by inspiration, he blurted out, "I know! You just shouldn't have woken up! If you went on dreaming that you were doing it with me, you and Chisato would both have been happy."

I gave up. It had been a mistake to hope for any sympathy from Shunji. But after hanging up the phone, I was even more bewildered. In part, this was because Shunji had empathized with Chisato, and that left me feeling as though people who saw things the way I did were a minority in this world. Which left me feeling chaotic inside. I needed to find someone who could see my side of things, or there would be no quelling the turmoil in my heart. So I rang M., the novelist, who already knew about my toe-penis.

When M. heard my voice, she cried out with glee, "Mano Kazumi! How've you been? How's the Big Toe P doing?"

Smiling wryly to myself, I started down the list of the various things that had happened.

M. sighed. "All that in such a short time."

"You bet," I said, having angled for this opening. "In fact, I've even had sex with a vagina."

"With a vagina! So you've converted?"

I hung my head at this, bumping my chin on the receiver. When I told M. that I hadn't sought out the vagina, she changed her attitude.

"You were raped, in other words."

"Raped?"

"Officially it might be quasi rape. I believe that according to the legal definition, quasi rape is when a person takes advantage of another person's inability even to try to resist fornication."

"It counts as rape even when a woman attacks a man? Or rather, when female sexual organs attack male sexual organs?"

"There's no precedent for that in Japan, but in the U.S. there have been rulings against women accused of rape for doing things to boys that they shouldn't have."

"So I'm a victim of quasi rape!" This gave me deep satisfaction: my anger at Chisato wasn't unwarranted. But at the same time I sort of had the feeling that calling it quasi rape was too strong.

"Are you going to press charges?"

"No," I replied. "To tell the truth, I don't really feel that what happened was horrible enough to qualify as rape. It was unpleasant, sure, but if you ask me if this has ruined my life, I'd have to say—"

"Of course, it's bound to be different from when a woman is raped by a man." Her voice sounded muffled.

"M., are you laughing?"

"I'm sorry!" M. now laughed out loud, as if she simply couldn't hold it back any longer. "I'd never dream of laughing about a woman raped by a man, but the image of one woman climbing on top of another . . . You know that I'm not laughing at you, right?"

Calling up the image of Chisato astride my foot with M.'s laughter ringing in my ear, I had to admit that, as nauseating as it had seemed, it was pretty funny. Chisato had walked out with a sneer on her lips, but she was the one who had disgraced herself, not me. All at once I felt like laughing, too.

"I guess I'm with you there. I never would imagine a woman trying to rape another woman."

"I do feel sorry for you, though, from the bottom of my heart," M. said, reining in her hilarity. "You should have just smacked her up a bit and chased her out of your room. She's a woman, too, after all."

"Chisato's stronger than I am."

"She's still a woman. There can't be that much of a difference."

M. was right, but at the time I'd been so shocked and creeped out, I just wanted to get away. It hadn't occurred to me to switch tactics and start attacking. On the other hand, maybe I just wasn't all that concerned. On some level I knew there couldn't be much of a difference between my attacker and me in terms of strength because she was a woman like me, so there was no fear I'd be forcibly taken. Deep down in my heart, maybe I knew I had room to maneuver. There was a fundamental difference between what had happened to me and what happens when the rapist is a man. Compared to the anxiety and nervousness I felt early on in my relationship with Masao, when I had no idea when he might try to start something sexual, the intimidation I experienced with Chisato was hardly worth making a fuss about.

"Did it hurt?" M. asked.

"No."

"It hurts plenty when a woman's genitals are violated. If you think about it like that, the rape of the penis by the vagina doesn't seem so bad."

"It's definitely unpleasant, though, being used as a vibrator."

"Oh, absolutely. Man or woman, I'm sure anyone would be angry about being used sexually while asleep, without consent. Even if the person who did it was a lover, you'd feel you were toyed with."

"Chisato was so furious you'd think she was the victim."

"You don't think she was just disgruntled that she couldn't have her way with you? The vaginas of women like this Chisato are just inverted penises, you see. I'm sure if she had a toe-penis, she'd rape someone with it."

What a horrible thought. I didn't even want to think about Chisato anymore.

"At any rate, what happened allowed me to confirm once again that I have no leanings whatsoever toward homosexuality."

M. thought about this for a few moments, then asked, "All right. So I take it the answer to the question I asked you before is, you wouldn't?"

What would you do, M. had asked, if Yoko were still alive, and she asked you to put your toe-penis in her? That was the question. I was about to reply that I'd already told her I couldn't answer that question, but I stopped. If Yoko were my partner, I doubted I would feel as grossed out as I had with Chisato. I was extremely fond of Yoko. She didn't have that steamy air of Chisato's—looking at her made me feel good. Chisato was simply the sort of woman I didn't get along with; I wouldn't have liked her even if I were a man.

Could it be that the disgust Chisato inspired in me had been due not to the fact that we were both women but to the fact that I didn't like the kind of person she was? There were plenty of men I wouldn't want to have sex with—guys who just weren't my type. On the other hand, the realization that I didn't after all feel a deep, instinctual disgust toward certain members of my own sex was a surprise. This was a brand new discovery for me. Of course, it didn't follow automatically that I could have had sexual relations with Yoko. That wasn't how it worked. Even now, that wasn't a question I could consider.

After promising to introduce M. to Shunji, I ended our conversation.

Talking with M. left me feeling better. By the time my memory of the feeling of Chisato's vagina began to fade, I had come to view the incident as outrageous but also funny, and my fear of Chisato vanished. I was now composed enough to tell myself that if I ever saw her again, I would be bold, and not let her see any sign of trepidation.

Though I wasn't really mad at Shunji, he seemed troubled by his inability to understand my agitation. When we talked on the phone, he would mention that Chisato hadn't been home for a while, then add that not having her around made life easier for him, too. I was pleased to see that he was trying, in his own way, to adjust to my feelings.

Once midterms at school were over, I went over to Shunji's. I hadn't been there in ages. His aunt and uncle had gone to the hot springs in Izu for a few days, and Chisato had gone out in the morning, taking her bag with her. Shunji was thrilled at the prospect of cooking for himself for two days. Going into the kitchen of the main house, I found dishes and spices, labeled with braille stickers, placed where it would be easy for Shunji to reach.

That evening, Shunji cooked us those medium-rare steaks—which he was so proud of. I was impressed that they were actually medium rare. We ate at the dining room table in the main house, sitting across from each other. It felt odd to be eating with a man I'd only been dating four months in a room steeped in such history—the dining room with its slightly sooty walls, the vinyl tablecloth with its out-of-date floral pattern, the ancient wooden chairs.

We talked about the sort of house we wanted to live in once we were married. Shunji wanted a room with thick, wall-to-wall carpeting. We wouldn't put any furniture in there, only blankets, which we would leave piled up against one wall. He wanted to be able to roll around naked on the carpet. He said he and I would have fun rolling around together, and then when we got tired we could fall asleep and cover up with the blankets. I wanted a room we would never go into. I didn't really have any reason for wanting it. I just figured it might be fun to have a room that was shrouded in mystery.

The living room was fairly small, with ochre sofas and a low table, a twenty-two-inch television and a large vase. Hanging on the wall, side by side, were framed photographs: in one a girl in a tutu with one leg swung high in the air, and in the other a boy in a frilly shirt standing beside a piano. Chisato and Shunji as children.

It was a little after ten when we heard the sound of the front door opening. Was it someone breaking in? No, it was simply Chisato, with Haruhiko in tow. Chisato showed no surprise when she discovered me sitting in the living room; she just stared down at me in silence. Despite my resolution not to get jittery when I met her, I couldn't think of anything to say by way of a greeting, so I just stared back up at her, silent, too.

"We've come here to attack you," Chisato said expressionlessly.

Haruhiko tapped her shoulder. "Stop it. You came here to apologize."

Chisato's expression softened. Haruhiko walked over toward Shunji, crouched down, and took hold of his hand. "You must be Shunji?"

Shunji nodded, looking confused, his hand in Haruhiko's.

Chisato and Haruhiko then sat down on the sofa opposite us. Haruhiko stretched his arms out along the top of the sofa and crossed his legs, making himself at home.

"We had a feeling you'd both be here. Chisato said she wanted to apologize to Kazumi, so I came along for the ride."

Chisato didn't speak; Haruhiko did the talking.

"I feel awful about the trouble Chisato caused you."

I was confused. "There's no need for *you* to—"

"There is. I couldn't convince her you wouldn't accept her advances."

I looked Haruhiko in the eye. "You're telling me that before she made a pass at me she discussed the idea with you?"

"Yeah. She asked if I thought she could have sex with you. I told her I doubted it, but she wouldn't listen."

"And you didn't stop her? Tell her not to fool around on the side?"

"I'm not a devotee of the monogamous way."

He used the same words as Chisato. Judging from the false sound of Chisato's recitation of the line and the fluency of Haruhiko's, she'd gotten it from him.

"I mean, I realize that there's logic to monogamy. If I were confident that I'm the best guy in the world, I'd come right out and boldly tell my woman not to sleep with other men, but as it is, when the world is clearly teeming with better men, I can't order a woman not to fool around and to make do with me."

Haruhiko's reasoning was surprisingly self-effacing, considering how much he prided himself on his ability to make women fall down at his feet. Seeing him sitting there after the conclusion of his speech, a weak smile at the edge of his mouth, I had the sense of a tolerably intelligent young man who had resigned himself, with a touch of wistfulness, to the fact that he was not as great as he wished he was. For a moment I found myself wondering if I'd had the wrong idea about him all along, if the impression I had of him as a cheeky bastard was a misunderstanding.

But at the same time, I also suspected that his modest manner of speech, which hinted at a gap between his rough exterior and his soft interior, might just be his way of getting women interested in him.

"Then, too, I don't want to invest sex with more meaning than it deserves. Why can't we just view it as something that feels good? The idea that one shouldn't have sex without love—that, I'd say, is the disease of modernity."

Once again he used the same line Chisato had. It looked like Chisato was gazing at him in rapture, though I might have been reading more into her expression than was really there. At any rate, Haruhiko seemed to have been the one to put those ideas about sex into Chisato's head. I knew she was head over heels in love with him, but to go this far, taking his opinions as her own, was more embarrassing than endearing.

Still I had my doubts about what he was saying. "But doesn't sex feel better the more you love your partner?"

"That's true, yes," replied Haruhiko, "but it feels good even if you don't."

"I'm sure it can feel reasonably good, but do you really want to go through all the hassle of sleeping with someone you don't really like when the emotion you feel isn't going to be very deep?"

Haruhiko grinned, evidently amused, then uncrossed his legs and sat up. "So you'll never do it with someone you're not crazy about?"

"No."

"For instance, let's suppose you have an acquaintance—someone you don't like in a sexual way but who likes you a lot. Say he's in a terribly lonely, painful situation, and all it would take for you to save the guy is to let him cling to you for support for just a little while. You wouldn't share your bed with him?"

I thought his question was ridiculous. Presumably the "support" he mentioned would be given through sex. Why should sex be the only thing you cling to for support? Why did he assume having sexual relations would save this man from his lonely, painful situation? I was processing his so-called logic when, apparently interpreting my silence as vacillation, he made a final push.

"Personally, I wouldn't be so heartless as to reject him," he volunteered.

Chisato, sitting beside him, nodded in agreement. I wasn't a fan of the spiritual solidarity between these two, and I didn't I like the way Haruhiko tried to rig the argument by tossing out a word like "heartless." So I decided to take a firm stand.

"I wouldn't do it."

"That's what she's like," Chisato boomed, "stingy and cold and—"

Haruhiko held up a hand to silence her. "Why not?"

"Because I can't believe a person's really hurting if sex will save him."

"Life isn't so sweet, in other words, that mere sex can offer salvation. But let's suppose, taking an optimistic point of view, that this guy is the sort sex *can* save?"

"He won't be saved! Even if I were to let him 'cling to me,' as you put it, I suspect he would only feel miserable afterward."

Haruhiko fell silent. Chisato glared at me, eyes brimming with anger.

"It's impossible," she said to Haruhiko, "to have a conversation with this woman. She's frigid and impotent too."

"Stop that. You came here to apologize."

"I don't feel like it anymore."

"That's no good. Having differences of opinion is a good thing."

Shunji, who had been silent all along, poked me with his elbow.

"All this is over my head," he whispered. "What are they arguing about?"

"They're not arguing."

Having calmed Chisato down, Haruhiko turned to me. "I understand your point of view. Your perspective is refreshingly open, and I envy you for it. Because for me, sex is like an obsession—it never leaves my mind. And I think most people in this modern age are the same way."

Chisato butted in, annoyed. "So you'll suck up to any woman."

"Will you shut up?"

Chisato sulked. An uncomfortable silence brewed. Shunji yawned. Haruhiko glanced down at his watch, then bowed his head lightly at me.

"We only came here today to apologize," he said. "Last night Chisato told me how bad she was feeling, and—"

"Hah!" Chisato snapped. "So you're the good guy in this?"

Haruhiko looked aghast. "You know, I guess the only time you're pleasant is just after sex."

"Because during sex is the only time you're faithful to me."

Haruhiko smiled sardonically. "I have no more desire to be your servant when we're not having sex than I do when we are."

Chisato leaped furiously to her feet. I clutched Shunji's arm.

"Fine, maybe we'd be better off just having sex?"

"That'd be great."

Chisato swung her right hand up overhead. Just as I was wondering whether she hit men as well, Haruhiko swiftly stood and confronted her. There was about an eight-inch difference in their heights. With Haruhiko towering over her, Chisato lost her nerve, and her hand stopped in mid-swing.

"You think I'd let you hit me?" Haruhiko said.

What a slimy way to threaten her. He was like a cat cruelly toying with a mouse. Haruhiko's chest was right in front of Chisato's eyes; she twisted her face into a humiliated grimace.

"Go home," she spat.

As she spun around, Haruhiko grabbed her arm. She struggled, trying to get away, but Haruhiko's grip was firm. They knocked against the table as they tussled. Shunji held his breath, squeezing my hand in his. Chisato was on the verge of screaming out, but Haruhiko shoved her face up against his chest. She began sobbing. Haruhiko rubbed her back.

"You're so silly. I would have let you hit me."

His tone of voice made me feel queasy. Satisfied at having completely crushed Chisato with his superior strength and build, Haruhiko now was making a display of his calm. He was so unruffled that he could favor Chisato with these generous words. For Chisato, this was a double humiliation. I felt mortified just watching. Chisato had picked the fight, but my sympathy lay with her, and I even found myself thinking there was no point being angry with her anymore, since the quasi rape I had experienced at her hands didn't even come close to being a real injury.

Chisato, however, reacted differently to the situation. She writhed for a time, struggling to free herself from Haruhiko's embrace, but then her sobbing turned to a sensuous nasal purring, and her unclenched hands twined themselves around Haruhiko's back. No trace remained of the ferocious antagonism that had hung in the air between them a moment before; Chisato was simply cuddling up to the man she adored.

I gaped, utterly at a loss for words, at the two lovers.

♥ ♥ ♥

Stepping onto the concrete path around the pool, Shunji took a deep breath of the wind carrying the scent of water. His face took on a contented look.

"It feels very spacious here. Is it a park?"

"It's a garden. Beyond the pool, it's all garden."

The pool at this hilltop hotel looked out over a Japanese garden that each spring seemed to be dyed by the pale pink of cherry blossoms.

Shunji said he had never gone swimming in his life, so I'd been wanting to take him to a pool. The ocean and public pools were crowded, and they were also too deep. The only sort of pool that seemed right—small and shallow, intended more for a quick dip and sunbathing than real swimming, and with few people—was a hotel pool. We had been staying at this hotel in the city since yesterday.

I had to bandage up my toe-penis, hide it from view, before I could go into the pool; but it took Shunji a while to get ready, too. We couldn't wander around the hotel in our swimsuits, of course, so we had to change in the changing room; but as I couldn't accompany Shunji into the men's room, we decided to wear our bathing suits under our clothes.

No one was in the pool, which was shaped like a cloud. A few foreign tourists were sunning themselves on chaise longues, eyes closed. They must have been able to hear us talking, but no one moved a finger. We put our belongings down, and I led Shunji to the pool.

He shivered when we immersed ourselves in the little antibacterial pool; then, up to his waist in the large pool, he called out to me, "I'm telling you, it's cold in here."

"You'll get used to it."

Before long, as the rays of the midsummer sun beat down, Shunji was sweating. He was pale and slightly built, but all the weight training he had done at home had put muscle where it was needed, so he didn't look spindly. I wrapped my arm around his shoulder, which was about as high as my own, and we waded around the edge of the pool. At first he seemed to have difficulty maneuvering, but then he got interested in the sensation of being in water, and began moving forward on his own. A short while later, he was kicking and splashing.

"Water's heavy, huh? You can't tell in a bath."

Laughter spilled from Shunji's lips. It was dazzling to watch him with the sun behind him. As he played with the water, scooping it up, one of the sparkling drops got into my eyes, and for a fraction of a second his brilliant smile blurred. I leaned against him. He embraced me, bent backward, and lifted me up.

"Hey! You're so light! Oh, I see—it's because the water's heavier than us."

Still holding me in his arms, Shunji rotated unsteadily on his feet. The green of the garden and the white walls of the hotel streaked through my field of vision. The blue of the sky touched the corner of my eye. I asked Shunji to put me down, then dumped water over his head, which was warm from the sun.

"Try floating," I said.

"How do I do that?"

I helped Shunji lie on his back on the water, arms at his neck and waist.

"Let the water hold your body up. Relax. Don't tense up."

"I've never been tense in my life."

It was true. I slowly released my hands, and he was afloat.

"Try moving your legs up and down."

Shunji raised them both at once, and his body sank. I quickly stuck my arms under him. "One leg at a time," I said.

This time things went better; Shunji glided slowly across the surface of the water. "There, you're swimming!" I said, applauding.

"What—it's this easy?"

His legs stopped moving, and Shunji began to float quietly. His skin shone in the sunlight penetrating the water. He looked very sexy.

"You'll drown if you fall asleep, you know."

"I won't go to sleep."

He must have tensed up when he said this, because the moment he spoke his body started to sink. I dove under and lifted him back up.

We then got out of the pool, wrapped ourselves in our towels, and sat down on our chaise longues. The humid Tokyo wind felt good on our still-wet skin. Drops of lukewarm water trickled down onto our faces. "It's neat," Shunji murmured, "I feel cool and warm at the same time." His hands were crossed over his stomach, and he was smiling dreamily.

A white man who had gotten into the water just as we were climbing out was doing an energetic crawl from one end of the pool to the other. The sound of his splashing only continued a short while, as after a couple laps, he climbed out and headed off toward the changing room. The ripples subsided, leaving nothing but sunlight glinting on the water's surface. The other hotel guests lay motionless, like those dolls whose eyes snap shut when you lay them on their backs. Beyond us, in the garden, no one walked along the paths. It was like we were relaxing in a landscape painting.

Shunji turned on his Walkman. I started thinking about Haruhiko.

No matter how bizarre Chisato and Haruhiko might seem as a couple, people have their own ways of loving, and I didn't in any way find fault with them. But seeing them go out of their way to create opportunities for their egos to clash, bringing emotions other than love into play in order to make their relationship more tense and heighten their pleasure . . . I had no interest in that kind of thing. Was that the only way they could enjoy themselves? Their desire was boundless.

Haruhiko did have a certain crude charm, I had to admit. From a distance, people whose hearts have smoldered with hatred—the object of which was not entirely clear—often seem to have a rich emotional life, and that can be appealing. But when you see a person like that make a pass at a friend's girlfriend, or suck up to his friend after being told their relationship is over, or use his superior strength to overpower his girl-friend . . . scenes like that make you wonder if maybe he's simply unable to socialize the way other people do.

I didn't want to become intimate with Haruhiko, and I doubted he felt much interest in me, but for some reason he always seemed to pop up just when I was starting to forget him. He had done this again just two or three days ago, when he called me up out of the blue.

"Sorry you had to see us in such a state the other day. Somehow you always encounter me in these peculiar situations."

I half-suspected it had been less an "encounter" than a scene Haruhiko staged, and it was all I could do to groan vaguely in reply. Haruhiko let a few moments pass, as if to confirm my chilly response, then launched into an explanation of the reason for his unexpected call.

"Have you ever heard of the Flower Show?"

"A botanical exhibition?"

"Yeah, I didn't think you'd know about it."

This got me a bit annoyed. "Would you mind telling me what you're talking about?"

"There's a troupe called the Flower Show. They take their show on tour across the country, but only a few people are even aware of their exis-tence. They've never once been taken up by the media. Needless to say, they aren't ever listed in any weekly guides."

"And they're able to keep their show going?"

"Absolutely. Because—and this isn't something you want to say in too loud a voice—most of the people who pay to see it are bigwigs in politics and finance. Ordinary folks like you and me can't attend."

He seemed to be talking about some underground theater, but I failed to see what connection this had to me.

"The troupe is made up of very special members. I'm not really clear on the details, but from what I gather the special thing about them is their sexual organs—that's the characteristic that links them together. I'm sure you can imagine what sort of show people like that would put on."

I was starting to get wary and didn't say a word.

"Evidently you make a lot of money touring with them. I suppose for people who aren't able to have a normal sexual life, the troupe must be a kind of salvation."

"And how did you learn about it?"

"A friend of mine saw the show. It was that guy I told you about, the classmate I had sex with in high school. He's completely homosexual, and his lover is the president of a big entertainment company. They saw the show at some classy Japanese restaurant. He told me about it."

"I see." This bland response was all I could manage.

"And here's the point. It seems the troupe is in Tokyo right now. And they're interested in you."

"In me? Why?"

Haruhiko chuckled at my surprise. "What do you mean, why? You're qualified to join, aren't you?"

"How did they find out about me?"

"Oh, yeah—I'm afraid I told my old classmate about you. Seems he told his lover, the company president; the president told a politician he's close to; and then the politician told a Flower Show representative. The troupe wants to get in touch with you. They asked me to talk to you."

"You're knocking on the wrong door." I was satisfied with my life as it was; I had no need to join a show.

"Doesn't sound like a bad deal, though, does it? You just let people look at you—you don't have to prostitute yourself. And you get to know people who are suffering from the same cause."

"My toe-penis has never caused me any suffering."

"Yes, you've got Shunji. But consider the future—don't you think it might be worth giving it a thought? For Shunji's sake, as well as your own?"

"What do you mean?"

"You'll have to feed him when he stops getting work as a composer."

"When Shunji stops getting work . . ."

"I wouldn't be too optimistic if I were you, you know. He writes music for TV commercials and video games and stuff, right? There's got to be a limit to how far he can go working on music that's so intimately con-nected to visual elements when he isn't able to see himself."

His argument was persuasive. Shunji had once expressed similar apprehensions himself.

"I'm not trying to push you into anything. It's not like I'll be getting a broker's fee if you join the troupe or anything. I'll give you their contact information just in case, all right? Why not wait until you feel in the mood and then at least talk to them, hear what they have to say? They'll be in Tokyo until after the Festival of the Dead."

Haruhiko gave me the phone number, which, without particularly thinking about it, I wrote down.

I now regretted that I had let Haruhiko cajole me into even doing that. Because even at a time like this—enjoying a peaceful midsummer afternoon by the pool—that phone number, which I had ended up memorizing in the course of staring repeatedly at it, rained down through the darkness behind my closed eyelids. I had to admit that, over the last few days, I had gotten more and more curious about the Flower Show.

What are these people like, I wondered, who go around making a display of their abnormalities? The fact that Haruhiko was the middleman had put me on my guard, making me think that the Flower Show members had to be as shady as he was. But then I thought it might be nice to meet people who were in a situation similar to mine.

I didn't want to go on tour with them. I was eager to graduate from college as soon as I could, and above all I had no desire to live apart from Shunji. If he did stop getting music work at some point, it'd be okay. I'd have to work hard at some job, but I didn't need to live lavishly. Who cared if we wouldn't be able to unwind at a hotel pool, as we were today? And Shunji said he felt the same way. Last night, as he deftly used his knife and fork at the French restaurant in the hotel, I casually asked him, "Do you want to do things like this more often?" And he replied, "Oh, I could take it or leave it. It's not like this is the only enjoyable thing in the world."

I hadn't told Shunji about the Flower Show. M. had agreed to come see us at the hotel, so I planned to let him hear the story when I discussed it with her. For a while now, Shunji had been fingering the strings of an imaginary guitar, playing along with the music coming through his headphones. I checked what time it was. We still had a little while before M. would be coming. I placed my hand on Shunji's arm and invited him to come play in the water again.

M. arrived at the hotel at four. After taking a step into our room, she cried out in admiration. "This is three times the size of my apartment!"

She dashed from the living room into the bedroom at the far end of the suite, peeked into the bathroom, and then dashed back out into the living room. She had a lot more energy than her anemic appearance would have led one to expect. She kept taking in her surroundings, until her gaze fell on Shunji, who was sitting on the living room sofa. I introduced them. He stood up and held out his hand.

"You have an odd voice," he said.

"I know. I sound like a cow, don't I?"

"I bet you're a surprisingly good mezzo-soprano."

"Such acuity."

"Sechekewity? What's that?"

Shunji's manner was strikingly different from the time when he first met Haruhiko: he started chatting amiably almost immediately. I got the feeling he found it easier to talk with women. While the two of them chatted, I called room service for coffee. By the time I took my seat next to Shunji, he and M. were talking up a storm, completely at ease with each other.

"Sometimes people forget I'm blind the first time we meet, and without thinking they hold out a business card. It hits them when they see I'm not taking it, and then they start to withdraw the card, but I sense that, so I hold out my hand and take it, and then I lift up my sunglasses and act like I'm reading it."

"Stevie Wonder does the same thing, you know. When he gave an award at the Tokyo Music Festival, he raised his sunglasses and acted like he was scrutinizing the prize he was going to give out. The whole house was laughing."

"They laughed for Stevie, huh? I can't always get people to laugh. Some people just gasp, like they don't know how to react."

M. looked at me. "Your face has changed, hasn't it?" she asked.

"Oh? In what way?"

"You look a little more mature, maybe—more like a normal person."

"Implying that I didn't look normal before?"

"You used to seem more above it all. Like a princess born to a mad king and queen, someone who miraculously reached adulthood untouched by the world as a result of having her every wish granted."

That wasn't a very pleasant thing to say, but then there was a hint of regret in M.'s tone, so maybe she meant this as a compliment.

"Setting that aside . . . tell me, M., have you heard of something called the Flower Show?"

"The three-woman comic group active ages ago in the Kansai region?"

I'd never heard of these people. When I explained further, M. grew animated.

"I have the feeling I've heard of it," she said. "A long time ago—I must have been twenty-three or twenty-four—a man who claimed to be in the CIA invited me to go with him to what he called a very interesting show. That must have been it."

"Was he really a CIA agent?" I asked, dumbfounded.

"He said that he was, but who knows whether he was lying or not. Back in those days, all the hot spots were crawling with people stuck on themselves, and every so often people would hint at something shady in their background. This guy from the CIA, or PTA, or whatever, told me you almost never had a chance to see this sort of show, a "live-action sterile sex show," and that it would be a big plus for me as a novelist to see it. I turned him down. I'm so bad at arithmetic I didn't know what the big plus was. I also didn't like his arrogance. So I never saw the show."

"Anyway, the Flower Show really exists?"

"I'd say so, yes."

Room service arrived. We put a hold on the conversation until the coffee was served and the waiter got my signature and left.

"Are you being scouted?" M. asked.

"What do you think?"

"Sounds like it to me. Why don't you at least go meet them?" M. said, as if it was no big deal.

Still, I was intimidated by the idea of CIA agents and bigwigs in politics and finance.

"Who knows," M. went on, "maybe there'll be someone else with a penis on her toe?"

"For all I know, mine could disappear tomorrow."

"Or maybe you'll grow another one! The big toe on your left foot could sprout one, too. And then your thumbs . . . You could end up with a penis on all your fingers and toes!"

"Stop!" I said.

M. went on undeterred. "What if it doesn't stop with your fingers and toes—what if you start sprouting penises all over your body? Don't you think it'd be a good idea to exchange information?"

M. was acting as if this was funny, but it hit close to home, and my mouth went dry. I took a gulp of coffee. Shunji put his hand around my waist.

"I'd kill myself if anything like that happened," I said.

"Or you could join the Flower Show."

"You think that would save me?"

"Maybe not, but you'd make a heap of money."

"But would that heap of money make me feel better?"

"Some would say it's better to live and have fun spending money than to kill yourself, yes."

"Do you think that's how members of the troupe see it?"

"You'll find out if you meet them."

I was beginning to be convinced, and felt more and more inclined to go see them. Even if nobody in the troupe had a toe-turned-penis, someone might have experienced a similar calamity. I wouldn't feel like such a freak. I'd have someone to talk to. "But," I said, "you don't think it's dangerous?"

"You mean, like, it's run by yakuza, and you'll be kidnapped and forced into servitude? Nah," M. said offhandedly, then got serious. "You designate a place to meet. Choose a spot that's busy. Bring someone with you. When you get there, look around; if there's anybody who looks suspicious, if you smell something funny, get the hell out. And when you leave, make sure that you aren't being followed. Don't go anywhere where there aren't other people, and return home while it's still light out. Just go prepared."

Shunji listened in silence, no special expression on his face. So I asked, "What do you think, Shunji?"

"About the Flower Show, you mean? Let's go see them!"

I had to smile at his assumption that, of course, he'd go along.

"I agree with M.," he said. "It'd be good for you to meet them."

I had no way of knowing how deeply Shunji had considered the matter. But it was settled. I would call the number Haruhiko had given me—maybe even that very night. I made up my mind not to worry, and put my hand on the arm Shunji had wrapped around my waist.

Chapter 7

Shunji and I sat across from two members of the Flower Show: a man and a woman, both in their late twenties. The man had the unremarkable, tidy features of a typical Japanese man, with a longish face and narrow eyes. The unaffected style of his slightly overlong hair, which hung over his forehead, and his casual dress—a short olive-green jacket over a cream-colored shirt—gave him the air of a student. The woman seemed to be the younger of the two, and was so dazzlingly attractive she could have been a TV star, but there was nothing flaky about her—on the contrary, she seemed kind of rigid. The man, who introduced himself as Suwa Shigeki, did most of the talking.

"I'm sure most people would be on their guard if they were meeting people from our troupe. I remember I was a bit alarmed myself when someone first suggested I join the Flower Show—I thought I was about to enter some ghastly, nightmarish world. I don't think I would have taken the plunge if I hadn't been so disgusted with my life."

We were seated in a ridiculously spacious café in Ginza, bustling with businessmen and women toting department store shopping bags. The room hummed with the drone of voices, punctuated with the clinking of cups and saucers, and yet, due to some marvel of acoustic design, I could hear Shigeki's mild baritone voice perfectly clearly. It was obvious why I suggested such a busy place and brought Shunji along, but the two Flower Show members didn't seem bothered at all.

"Supposedly, the history of the Flower Show dates back to the prewar period. As the story goes, a certain decadent marquis, weary of all the money and free time at his disposal, rounded up all the deformed people in Japan he could find, and invited them to live at his manor. When he gave parties for his aristocratic friends and zaibatsu buddies, these deformed people would put on sex shows. After the war, the marquis's family fell on hard times and the marquis died; the members of the group were about to disperse when a few regulars at the marquis's parties worked things out so that the group could take the show on the road. They used the marquis's old connections, got bookings around the country, and started to earn a living. This, we're told, is how the Flower Show got its start."

The young woman next to Shigeki, who had introduced herself as Sakurai Aiko, listened in silence until the story was finished, but now she gave a merry laugh. The solemn expression on Shigeki's face melted into a smile.

"It's just a story that troupe members have been passing down through the generations. To tell the truth, we think it's baloney."

Aiko grinned. "Of course, no one in our troupe is descended from the legendary original group this marquis or whatever put together. In fact, no one even claims to have met an original member . . ."

"But imagine if the farts who come to see us perform turned out to be descended from the marquis! Our whole world would be turned upside down . . . It would be like suddenly losing the ability to distinguish between toads and butterflies!" Shigeki exclaimed.

The way Shigeki and Aiko were going on, smiling and laughing, they seemed like two ordinary, bright young people. I relaxed a bit, and started to wonder what their sexual organs were like. But it wasn't yet time to ask.

A subtle smile hovering on her lips, Aiko tried to explain what Shigeki was saying. "Occasionally people in politics or finance sponsor performances, but when we go into the countryside, our patrons tend to be more lowbrow. We do shows for executives of local companies, but they're not all like that—we get bookings from real-estate sharks, people who suddenly got rich selling land . . . Once we did a show for a mayoral candidate."

"We were the attraction at a banquet held to drum up votes."

"Didn't the guy have us perform in an old storehouse?"

"That's right—by the light of paper lanterns. God, was that awful." Shigeki cast a glance in my direction. "It's not all fun and games, you see."

Aiko nodded. "The people who pay for the performances rarely contact the Flower Show directly. Usually our instructions come from a middleman—we're told to be at a certain location at a certain time. Often we don't know who's sponsoring the gig, an individual or an organization. Once, we arrived at the site and discovered it was a banquet for a fourth-generation yakuza boss."

"They didn't give us any trouble, but we were too scared to perform at our best." Shigeki kept his tone cool, like an experienced businessman.

"Is the Flower Show independent?" I asked. "Or does some organization own it?"

"We're independent," Shigeki replied without hesitation. "I mean, I'm sure the middlemen we rely on belong to organizations, or are at least influential in a certain community, but our interactions with them are strictly limited to business. We have no knowledge of their organizations or their positions, and we don't need to. We're just a crowd-pleaser."

"And there's no link between your sponsors?"

"Not organizationally. Life in the Flower Show is much more humdrum than you'd expect—no excitement at all. Some people actually feel a bit let down when they join; their hopes were so high."

"If there is a link," Aiko interjected, "it's the network of men with dirty minds and a taste for the perverse. In fact, it's this network that gets us our customers. We never advertise in the media."

"That's true," Shigeki said. "At first I didn't know how the Flower Show could make it without media, but grassroots networking is all we need. Word of mouth is pretty powerful, I have to say."

"As is the power of dirty minds," said Aiko with a cynical grin. "I don't know where they get the energy to keep searching for below-the-belt stimulation." She must have remembered something unpleasant as she was talking, because her tone turned a little harsh midsentence.

"Enough. No need to bad-mouth our customers."

Having said that, Shigeki was ready for my next question. Aiko still had the irritated look on her face.

"How do you find people to join the troupe?" I asked.

"The network gives us inside information. The same way we learned about you—information travels along the grapevine. In Aiko's case, it was the doctor at the hospital where she went for help."

Aiko's face brightened at this, and laughing, she launched into her story merrily. "It was awful! I go to the hospital needing help, and the doctor tells me, 'You know, I really don't think there's anything we can do, so instead of me trying something that's not going to work, why don't you consider putting your condition to use?' And then he suggests the Flower Show."

"We get lots of introductions from doctors. Because when there's something peculiar about a person's body, the first thing he or she will do is go to a doctor, at least once. I never went to a doctor, though."

"So how'd you find out about . . . ?"

"The president of a company that makes porn for the black market put me in touch. Before I joined the Flower Show, I used to work in porn."

Shigeki's answer was short and to the point, utterly matter-of-fact. I had a hard time bridging the gap between the nice-looking young man opposite me and my image of a porn star. Without meaning to, I let my gaze freeze on Shigeki's face.

He laughed shyly. "I used to be involved in some pretty unsavory stuff. I guess I still am."

I couldn't let it go. "So . . . did you do the same sort of thing actors usually do in adult videos?"

Shigeki seemed to have read more into my question than I had intended. He looked me straight in the eye for a few seconds, then began speaking. "I know your big toe is a penis, so it's only fair for me to tell you about myself. I've got an unusual protuberance on my penis. It's on the top side, I guess you'd say, the part I see first when I look down, slightly beneath the head, as it's called—toward the base. It looks like a little branch, kind of like this."

He crossed the thumb of his right hand and the pinky of his left. Aiko burst out laughing, and Shigeki jabbed her with his elbow. Then he continued: "Sometime in junior high school, I started thinking that the shape of my thing was weird. It was still covered by the foreskin then, so I couldn't be sure, but when I touched it, I got a very strange feeling. I wasn't in any pain or anything, so for the time being I just let it be, and I never asked anyone about it. As I got older, the shape of this protuberance became more pronounced . . . It was in high school that I first realized my penis wasn't normal; I was staring at it when it got completely erect, and it was so bizarre I almost fainted." Shigeki's eyelids drooped, as if he were think-ing back nostalgically to those boyhood days. "I laugh about it now, but it was agony then. After all, I didn't know a thing about how the vagina works, and I had no idea how women think. All I could think was, no girl will want to have anything to do with a guy who has a creepy thing like this. Even if some eccentric girl did take a liking to me, the moment she set eyes on *the thing*, she'd run screaming from my bed. And even if she *didn't* bolt for the door, I highly doubted I'd be able to fit my unit inside her vagina—if the girl let me try and force it in, she'd be ruined. So I'll never be able to have sex! Never! That's what I thought. It was pretty bleak."

"And yet," Aiko said, "you had no problem masturbating, right?"

"Right," he answered without embarrassment. "It functioned perfectly fine. You'd think, since that was the case, I would have assumed sex was possible; but it never occurred to me that the vagina could expand and contract. So I just masturbated all the time, and never even tried to meet girls. But I really wanted to be normal, so when I was in college, I decided to have the extra bit of thing surgically removed. I started looking around for a part-time job to pay for the operation, and an upperclassman asked if I'd be willing to help out behind the scenes making black-market porn videos."

Shigeki's saga continued. At first, the thought of actually *acting* in porn never crossed his mind—he worked as a prop man. One day, the actor who was supposed to star in one of the movies was sick, and Shigeki was asked, right on the spot, to fill in. He declined, but then the actress in the movie chimed in saying she wanted him to do it, so he had no choice but to reveal the secret of his penis and say he was incapable of having sex. By the time he had finished his explanation, every single member of the crew wanted to see his penis, and they basically forced him to show it to them.

"When they saw it, they laughed, they laughed uproariously. A little protuberance like this won't keep you from having sex, they said—girls will love it because the bit that sticks out will touch the most sensitive part of the vagina. It's an exquisite instrument, I wish I had one like it myself, you lucky bastard—things like that. So I had my first sexual experience in a room with a dozen people watching, and the whole thing was filmed for commercial release. There was even a close-up of me after it was over, with tears in my eyes. The video went on the market as a real-life record of the first sexual experience of a man with a deformed penis. It made a huge splash."

Having instantly become a big name in porn, Shigeki went on to star or make cameo appearances in dozens of videos. He made enough money to pay for his operation, but by then what was the point? His penis was hot stuff. Women were constantly turning up, eager to experience his "exquisite instrument," and he had as many sexual partners as he could ever want; it would have been pure idiocy to demote the "exquisite" to the "ordinary." He lost himself in easy pleasures, and fell into a dissolute life.

"After a couple of years of all the sex I could ever want, I began to realize, if only in a very hazy sort of way, that I was intrinsically unsuited to that lifestyle. That came as something of a surprise, actually. I realized that the women who came on to me had this mixture of selfish calculation and primitive desire—and they weren't seeing me as a human being. I suppose a lot of men could say to themselves, *I can be as cool about it as they are, I can use them for sex just like they use me.* But I started getting fed up with the emptiness of it all. Except that I couldn't immediately give up my way of life, and I wasted a lot of time making the same stupid mistake, over and over."

There was no way Shigeki could avoid making himself more miserable, and as a result, his face began to acquire an aggressive look. Around this time, there was a party for people in the industry, and the president of a company—a man Shigeki knew by sight—called him over and suggested he think about joining the Flower Show. Ultimately this gave him the opportunity to wash his hands of the morally bankrupt life he had been leading. That was, Shigeki said, four years ago.

"And since then, I have to say, emotionally speaking, I feel much more stable."

"Not all our members will tell you they found peace of mind when they joined the troupe," Aiko said, never failing to add her two cents.

At the very least, these two seemed honest to me. I could trust them.

"At any rate," Shigeki said, sitting up straight, "we would really like it if you would be willing to join our group."

Aiko, too, looked straight at me. "Of course, it's only natural that people are suited to some sorts of work and not others, so if you feel unable to participate in the sexual performances, you can just tell us. We'll understand."

"What do you want me to do?" I asked. I seemed to have been a bit too abrupt, because both Shigeki and Aiko looked puzzled, not immediately grasping my question. "In other words . . . I'm engaged, you see . . ." I glanced over at Shunji. "I can't do anything that my fiancé would find offensive."

"Ah, I see what you mean," Shigeki replied, his manner sympathetic. "In your case, since the special feature is on your foot, that's the only part you would need to show. There's no need for you to actually do things with anyone else—it will be enough to let people watch you masturbate. Do you ejaculate?"

"No."

I could keep my poise when I was listening to other people's stories, but my cheeks grew hot when the conversation turned to my own situation.

"You don't? That's too bad. That money shot would really hit the audience with force," Shigeki observed, serenely as ever. "Anyway, you can even keep your clothes on if you want."

"You mean I don't have to get naked?"

"Not if you don't want to, no. You're a rookie, right? And we haven't happened across anyone qualified to join the troupe in quite a while. If you do agree to participate, we'll only ask you to do the bare minimum."

This led to the original reason I was willing to meet them. "I guess," I started, "from what you've said, none of the other members have penises on their toes, do they?"

"No."

"There's no one with similar symptoms?"

"Afraid not. Are you looking for someone like that?"

I answered honestly, "Yes." I told them I had been hoping for a chance to meet someone like myself, a chance to sit down and discuss the whole nine yards, the practical stuff, the stuff that might come later, the stuff that goes on outside and in, mentally and emotionally.

"In other words, you want a friend who's in the same boat that you're in?" Aiko said with an intelligent gleam in her eyes.

"Exactly." I hadn't been thinking in terms as clear as "friend," but put that way, yes, what I wanted was a friend. Someone who would understand me, and whom I could understand.

"In that case, I think you'll do just fine. The particular forms of our abnormalities are different from yours, but we've all found ourselves in unusual situations, just like you. I think we'll make great friends. Don't you agree, Shigeki?"

Shigeki answered Aiko's prompt with the nicest smile ever. I had a hunch, too, that I could be friends with them. If they had been trying to recruit me for a more ordinary club activity, rather than the Flower Show, I wouldn't have hesitated an instant.

But I couldn't see myself performing. "I can't even masturbate in front of anyone."

"You'll get used to it."

This was Aiko. I hadn't the slightest idea what she did in the show, but when a woman who looked, on the face of it, perfectly normal gave a response like that, it was hard not to take her word for it. And the two of them then set about trying to convince me.

"Your classes are out now, right? Why don't you come around with us during the break, just to see what it's like? We travel by minibus, so you won't have to worry about travel expenses, and we'll cover the cost of the hotels."

"Please, do come! You'll see for yourself, and then you can make up your mind."

"You can always refuse then, if you want."

"But I'm . . . ," I mumbled.

"Can I come, too?" Shunji suddenly piped up.

I was flabbergasted at Shunji's complete lack of common sense, but Shigeki replied as though it were nothing at all. "Sure, partners are welcome."

I was distraught, even if no one else was. "Shunji," I said, "what about your work?"

"I'll take a portable synthesizer with me on the road. I've got an answering machine that I can check, so clients should have no trouble getting in touch."

"You're a musician?" Shigeki leaned forward. "In that case, how would you feel about doing live background music for the show? Until now, we've always used a tape. We'd pay you to be our troupe musician."

"I can do that, sure," Shunji replied, much too casually.

I tugged his arm. "Shunji, I haven't even said whether or not I'm going!"

Shunji wrapped the arm I'd seized around my waist. "C'mon, let's do it! Don't you think it sounds like fun? I've always wanted to travel."

Shigeki and Aiko exchanged sunny smiles. Now that things had taken this turn, I could think of no reason to refuse. In my heart, I saw no problem traveling with the troupe under the conditions they had proposed. The only thing that troubled me was the inordinate generosity of those conditions: I felt as if I was taking advantage of the Flower Show.

"Don't you think," Aiko said to Shigeki with a faint suggestion of excitement in her tone, "we ought to ask for a demonstration? I'd love to hear Shunji play."

"Yes," Shigeki said, nodding, then turned to Shunji and me. "Why don't you two come back to the apartment? There's a digital piano, though it's only for decoration. No one plays it."

"We'd be happy to!" Once again, Shunji answered before I could speak.

Shigeki grabbed the bill and stood up. Aiko followed suit. Finally, urged on by Shunji, I got to my feet. Things were moving so fast I hardly knew what to think.

Where, I wondered, was my toe-penis taking me?

♥ ♥ ♥

I parked the Pajero a short distance from the garish neon lights of the Akasaka entertainment district. There were several other cars parked nearby, so I decided we probably wouldn't be towed. Having flicked on the overhead light, I began studying the map that Shunji had been holding. It was a five-minute walk to the expensive Japanese restaurant where the Flower Show would be performing that evening. Clear on where we were headed, I opened up the hatch and got Shunji's synthesizer and chair.

This evening was to be his debut with the Flower Show. He said he was so used to appearing in stiff, formal attire at the School for the Blind that it was impossible for him to perform in anything else, so he had on a tuxedo and a bow tie. He wore the tuxedo well, with an artless, boyish flair, but with his sunglasses, and the synthesizer slung over his shoulders, he had the air of a cabaret band member.

A week earlier, when he gave Shigeki and Aiko a taste of his piano wizardry, effortlessly playing everything from boogie-woogie to jazz and classical, they had been knocked out. They said it would be a shame to limit him to mere background music—they wanted him to open the show with a solo. Shunji was thrilled, and the very next day he started rehearsing in earnest. He said that while synthesizers could produce notes that sounded almost exactly like a real piano's, there were differences in the tone, the feel of the keys, and the acoustics, so it was necessary to select songs that would work well on a synthesizer and perform them appropriately.

Listening to him play, I sometimes couldn't tell if he was seriously practicing or simply fooling around. Sometimes he repeated the same piece several times in a row, experimenting with different arrangements, and sometimes he rewrote sections of songs originally meant for the piano with its sixty-one keys; but then he would pick out fragments of melodies as they occurred to him, or suddenly stop playing, and put on a braille-labeled cassette from his rack of recordings and play along, or begin talking, rap-style, while he played. I had no idea, for that matter, what sort of music he was thinking of performing for his opening night.

I came away from that week of rehearsal, however, with a vivid impression of the depth of Shunji's love of music. After a session, he would fling himself on the bed and lie with the half-intoxicated look of a man who has just eaten a full-course meal consisting of all the pleasures in the world, spiritual and physical. His cheeks were flushed; his lips were parted, and they curved into a gentle smile. His arms and legs lay sunk in the mattress, unmoving, spread out around him, and when I brought a towel to wipe away his sweat, I couldn't tell whether he noticed the touch of the cloth. Perhaps for Shunji, music provided a more intense pleasure than sex. During that week, Shunji never once so much as snuggled up to me. He seemed to have forgotten sex altogether.

My right arm holding the chair, my left arm around Shunji, I walked along a street that I had never been on before. It was lined with the imposing entrances to restaurants that looked as if they had a distinguished history. Passersby stared at us. Once we were beyond the neon stretch, the street became surprisingly dark and quiet. We walked slowly, and then I caught sight of Aiko under the next streetlight, waving to us.

"I didn't want you to get lost, so I came out to wait," she said, greeting us. She had worn her hair down the week before; tonight she had it neatly done up to reveal the nape of her neck. She looked so beautiful that she took my breath away. She offered to carry the chair, but of course I wouldn't let her take it, dressed as she was in her gorgeous dress.

We came to a gate bearing the name of the restaurant that was our venue for the night, but Aiko passed right by it, entering through the service gate on the side. Of course, in our current roles, we were hardly entitled to go in through the front. We walked a short way down a dreary path between the restaurant and a wooden fence, our footsteps illuminated only by the dim glow coming through the paper-paneled sliding screens. The service entrance was clean enough, with a floor of packed gravel that had recently been splashed with water. Once inside, we went down a hall that smelled of tempura, and then to a sliding door that Aiko opened.

"You made it!" Shigeki said, rising from where the group was seated and coming over to us. As he took our things and set them aside, he whispered to Shunji amiably, "I wasn't sure you'd come. I told our sponsor we'd be adding a new segment tonight. We're looking forward to hearing you, Shunji."

Shunji, who was already at ease with Shigeki, grinned.

"And you're in a tuxedo! You look great!" Shigeki said, adjusting his shoulders and collar. I was happy seeing him being so good to Shunji.

Besides Shigeki and Aiko, there were five others. A man and woman about my age were leaning against the wall side by side, but apart from them everyone sat alone, relaxing. It was a small room, about the size of six mats, and I could feel powerful waves of personality emanating from different points in it. But there seemed to be a disappointing absence of atmosphere, a lack of the intimacy you might expect in a group of people who traveled together.

Shigeki, who seemed to be the only cheerful one in the room, spoke up. "This is Mano Kazumi, whose reputation precedes her. This young man with her is her fiancé, Kendo Shunji, who will be the troupe's pianist this summer. As for the members of the troupe, there are seven of us—"

"Don't you mean eight?"

This came from the young man sitting with the woman against the wall.

"Sorry. Eight."

Despite Shigeki's correction, I could see only seven of them. Was the last member late?

"I'd like to introduce the cast," Shigeki went on, "but since Shunji is blind and will have to tell us apart by our voices, let's go around the room and each of you can introduce yourselves. So . . . let's go by . . . umm, how about age?"

There was a burst of laughter, like a folding fan whipping through dry air. It wasn't clear who had laughed, but it was certainly not an outburst of merriment. Someone cleared her throat. A woman sitting with her elbow propped on the low table lifted her head. Her hair was dyed brown, but judging from her skin, she must have been about fifty.

"Kinoda Yukie," she said curtly.

There was a pause, then a hoarse voice called out, "I'm Ayase Masami." This speaker had long hair, styled in a slightly old-fashioned, wavy perm, which spilled down over the shoulders of a deep-red blazer the exact shade of his lipstick. It was tempting to think this person's sex was uncertain, but his sturdy build and roughly chiseled features made it obvious that he was a man. That said, he was enough of a beauty that he could reasonably be compared to Chisato. But since he wasn't wearing a skirt, I couldn't tell if he meant to be taken for a woman.

"I'm Tanabe Yohei." This third person to introduce himself was the most eye-catching of the men in the room. He had the sort of looks that would be etched indelibly in your memory after a single glimpse—in a word, outlandish. His head, covered in little shiny black ringlets that looked as hard as plastic, was too big for his bony frame; his cheeks were so abundantly fleshy that the word "plump" didn't apply. They were like two swollen lumps, dangling on either side of his face. The sagging skin of these cheeks tugged on the corners of his thick lips, causing them to droop slightly. He had huge, bulging eyeballs, but his flaccid eyelids hung down so far that they covered almost a third of the irises. I feel bad saying this, but he reminded me of a Neapolitan Mastiff.

The last two members of the troupe, the young man and woman against the wall, were whispering and poking each other, evidently having a little argument about who should go first. The man, visibly irritated, punched the woman's knee.

She turned to face us. "I'm Mio Eiko," she said.

She was the only one to have given even the slightest of smiles.

Behind her, the man peered out. "I'm Kodama Tamotsu," he said. He had a bit of a potbelly and spoke in a unique style, each syllable clinging to the next. "My kid brother's name is Shin."

So his brother was the missing eighth member of the troupe.

"You'll have a chance to see Shin soon enough," he added.

Introductions over, Shigeki announced to the group, "We'll be moving to the performance space in ten minutes, so it's time to get ready." He put a hand on Shunji's shoulder. "Just to confirm, your opening solo should last about ten minutes. Try to build up the atmosphere for us, okay? Let us know your solo has ended by pausing for five seconds. Once you give us this cue, we'll start going out on stage, doing one segment at a time, and you'll give us background music. Is everything clear? All right, then, give 'em all you've got."

"Sure thing."

Shigeki now put his hand on my shoulder. "As for you, just sit back and enjoy the show."

As soon as Shigeki had moved away, Shunji put his mouth to my ear. "I've got stage fright," he whispered.

"Wow, you mean even *you* get nervous?"

"I haven't performed live in a long time."

"What do you do to get over it?"

"Nothing."

Shunji took a handkerchief from the inside pocket of his jacket and wiped his palms. I took his wrist in my hand. His pulse was faster than usual.

"This will all be over in two hours. Then you can relax."

"Yep, I just have to keep that in mind and try to stay calm."

Aiko came over carrying a bottle of juice.

"You look nervous. Don't worry, it's hardly an audience to get jittery about."

Aiko gave Shunji a cup of juice, which he immediately gulped down half of.

"You may have more fun looking at the faces in the audience than watching us," Aiko told me, then walked over to where Shigeki was sitting. Here and there, people started murmuring to one another. Maybe the Flower Show was just a moneymaking organization, and its members had no sense of a shared fate. That might make life easier, but it might make it kind of lonely, too.

After a bit, Shigeki announced that it was time, got to his feet, and then turned to Shunji. "Stay right behind me, okay?"

He stepped out into the hallway, carrying Shunji's chair. I followed with Shunji, who had hoisted the synthesizer up on his shoulder. We walked a long way, through a rather intricate sequence of hallways. We emerged into a courtyard alive with the gurgle of falling water.

The slope of a small, sculpted hill rose before us in the darkness. The light that fell across its surface came from a detached, elegant structure that stood unobtrusively in the courtyard—though on closer inspection it was so large it could have been an establishment of its own. The artificial hill was intended, no doubt, to conceal this second building from the eyes of the restaurant's ordinary customers. The stepping stones led to the back door of this detached structure. Here, too, we would enter by the service entrance.

Shigeki went in first, by himself, to let the audience know we had arrived. While we were waiting, my ankle started to itch. A mosquito bite. The itching got worse, and I bent down to scratch the itchy spot.

"What's wrong?" Shunji asked.

"Mosquitoes. They're not biting you?"

"No."

I seemed to have been bitten in three or four places, including on my arm. As I fidgeted, a hand holding a bottle of anti-itch lotion appeared in front of my nose. Looking up, I saw Mio Eiko, the young woman who had been sitting next to Kodama Tamotsu earlier.

"Want to use this?" Eiko asked.

I decided to accept her offer, and took the lotion.

"Mosquitoes," Eiko grumbled, "prefer women."

"Yes," I said, "if a woman and a man take a walk in the park, the woman is always the one to get bitten."

Just then, Aiko came over, scratching her elbow. "You can say that again. When I'm going crazy from the itchiness and the guy is looking cool, I start thinking that I'm his bug repellent."

For some reason, people really seemed to be getting into the conversation.

"Why is that? The mosquitoes that come after us are female, so why don't they go for the men?"

"They go for the scent of female hormones."

"On the other hand," said Aiko with a smile, "I don't get bitten when I'm with other women. The mosquitoes always pick my friends over me. I guess I'm not feminine enough, though I must count as a woman on some level because I get bitten when I'm with men."

The women were having fun, getting involved in our mosquito talk.

Then Kodama Tamotsu joined in. "So I guess if you're not sure what sex *someone* is, all you have to do is take that person where there's a lot of mosquitoes."

Everyone turned to look at Ayase Masami, with his shoulder-length hair. He raised his eyebrows and let his jaw drop exaggeratedly.

"Is that *really* true? That women are more easily bitten than *men*?"

His speech was feminine. Was he a transvestite?

"I'm afraid the simple fact that you don't know proves you're not a woman," Aiko replied.

For a moment Masami looked chagrinned; then he adopted a different attitude, starting to rattle on in precisely the style transsexuals use on television talk shows: "Well that's just *fine* with me, darling, because I don't need a little mosquito to show *me* I'm a woman. No—my *man* makes that clear *all* the time."

"The mosquitoes might be more reliable, though," Eiko said.

"Personally, I don't even *feel* the *prick* of a mosquito."

Masami boldly took the argument in a completely different direction. This sort of conversation hijacking was what Chisato was best at. Masami's looks reminded me of Chisato, and now I was getting the feeling that the inside of his head resembled hers as well. Except that Masami could make people laugh. Everyone had chuckled at that line of his, and with that, the debate was over. Admittedly, the tone of the laughter did carry a suggestion of stunned disbelief.

I passed the anti-itch lotion back to Eiko, enjoying the sense of ease that came over me now that I had broken the ice with the group. That's when Shigeki opened the door and beckoned to us.

He stepped into the hallway and opened a sliding door, revealing a four-mat room. One side was lined with sliding doors, three panels in all, the middle of which was partly open. The interior of the next room looked quite dim, seeming to be lit by only a single small bulb.

"This is the dressing room; the next room is our stage," Shigeki explained, speaking very quietly. "You'll be best off watching from a corner in there, the room where we do the show."

At Shigeki's urging, I took a peek into that room. It was relatively spacious, wider than it was deep; a futon, covered with a white sheet, had been spread out to the left. The lights were just like Shunji's, spherical bulbs hooked up to a dimmer, much brighter than the small one in the dressing room. The back wall was sliding doors, on the other side of which the audience for the evening's performance was waiting. When the show was ready to begin, the sliding doors would be opened.

When Shunji played, he would be seated behind the futon, facing the audience. I helped him remove the synthesizer from the case and set it up on its stand. I plugged in the electric cord, and Shunji fiddled with the switches, setting the sound on piano mode.

"How big is the room?" he asked Shigeki.

"About ten mats."

On the basis of that information, Shunji adjusted the volume; he made no further sound check. He stood up straight, then walked back to the side of the room, counting his steps. He took a deep breath. "Okay," he said. "I'm ready."

"All right, I'll open the doors."

As Shigeki began to slide the doors to the side, Shunji gave my hand a firm squeeze. The total darkness of the room beyond now came into view, and gradually I began to make out dim white forms of people who almost seemed to be levitating. I rested my hand gently on Shunji's shoulder. He squeezed it tightly, then strode over to the synthesizer. I held my breath and watched.

When he reached the instrument, Shunji bowed to the invisible audience. His demeanor left little doubt that he was a professional pianist, causing people in the audience to stir, baffled. Shunji paid this no attention and sat down, preparing to play.

"He's got guts," Shigeki whispered beside me. Other members of the troupe had come up behind us, waiting with bated breath for Shunji to begin.

Shunji raised his hands, then banged them down on the keyboard. It gave me a start. The volume was much louder than anyone had expected, and the hum in the audience stopped immediately. Shunji had launched into a Rachmaninoff prelude, and the shock of it banished all other thoughts from my mind. The synthesizer's sound was incredibly cheap and clunky, compared to what a real piano would have been like, but there was nothing cheap about Shunji's artistry. And I was hardly a classical music fan.

After about ten minutes, Shunji brought his little recital to a close. Sighs could be heard in the audience and from the members of the Flower Show standing beside me. Shunji rose briskly to his feet and bowed again. Hesitant applause broke out. I wanted to dash over to Shunji and hug him, and tell him how wonderfully he had played.

Shigeki's expression, however, showed more than admiration. "The music set too high a tone for a show like this," he said, perplexed. "I don't really feel like having sex anymore."

I couldn't help laughing. It was true, immersing oneself in a performance like Shunji's didn't put you in the mood, it took you out of it. In fact, listening to him play, I had almost forgotten what the occasion was. On the stage, Shunji paused for five seconds, but when nothing happened and no one from the troupe came out for the next act, he cocked his head, puzzled.

"Oh well, I guess we'd better do it," murmured Shigeki, turning toward Aiko.

Shunji, uncertain about this lull, started to play again. This time it was a simple ditty, the left hand keeping rhythm and the right hand laying a melody over it. He kept the volume low, creating a sensuousness in the syncopation.

A smile appeared on Shigeki's face, and he started unbuttoning his shirt. He took off his pants and socks, and strode out onto the would-be stage wearing nothing but his briefs. You could hear a shift in the breathing of the audience—very different from when Shunji had stepped out. The light over the futon grew brighter, affording me a view of a middle-aged man in a well-tailored suit and a woman of about thirty in the audience. Probably an extramarital affair.

Shigeki sat down on the futon and crossed his legs. He stretched out one hand. Still in her dress, Aiko whisked past me and onto the stage. No one wanted to see a man take off his clothes, but everyone wanted to see a man take the clothes off a woman. *That* was erotic. Aiko knelt down where Shigeki was seated, and he began to undo her zipper. The troupe members, who had seen this all before, trickled back to the dressing room. Shunji kept fingering the keyboard as calmly as ever.

From where I stood, I could see Shigeki's hands gently wandering up Aiko's arms. When he reached her shoulders, he quickly slipped her dress down, exposing her white back. Shigeki's arms circled that whiteness, as he pulled Aiko slowly toward him. After holding her for a few seconds, he got up on his knees and pressed his lips to hers.

The gradations of light and dark on their skin were so beautiful that I felt like I was watching a movie. But it wasn't sleazy or lewd, as one would expect. Shigeki was making love to Aiko, and it was full of feeling, and it was clear from their every movement that they were lovers.

The first time Shunji and I had met Shigeki and Aiko, they invited us to come back to the apartment, which it turned out they shared. "Are you two married?" I had asked; Shigeki had replied shyly, "We haven't done it officially, but . . ." They had a plain, undecorated one-bedroom apartment with windows that looked out over a park immediately below; there was a low sofa and a coffee table in the living room, and then there was the digital piano. The sight of them there made me think they were either content and living a quiet life, or very lonely.

Aiko's dress fluttered lightly to the floor. Her underwear followed. She undid her hair herself. Was it right for me to be seeing this? But I couldn't look away. Aiko's breasts were voluptuous, her body slender. Bending over, she lowered her face over Shigeki's crotch. So far, her body wasn't the least abnormal.

I recalled what Shigeki had told us that afternoon as we were having some wine in their apartment: "After all the time I spent having sex, wallowing in the pleasures of the flesh, I started to feel a deep spiritual aversion to women. Of course, the women I was sleeping with were all nasty, calculating types who only cared about sex. I could sleep with them, but I could never love any of them. Then I joined the Flower Show and met Aiko, and she was the opposite of every other woman I had ever had sex with. Most men might not want to have anything to do with someone with her condition, but Aiko's perfect for me."

Aiko raised her upper body. A frisson of excitement ran through the audience. Shigeki's penis, with its additional little branch, had hardened and was poking through the fly of his briefs. He stood up, struck a pose to emphasize his peculiar genitalia, and froze. I couldn't see much more from where I stood, but I could hear the audience stirring. Then Shigeki stripped off his briefs and spun around to face the audience full frontally. Aiko walked around behind him.

I looked at Shigeki standing there nude: he was so trim, without a hint of excess fat on his body, like a statue. He was holding the base of his penis with his left hand, perhaps to keep his erection from standing up too straight and preventing the audience from getting a good look at it. It was just as he had described it: the branchlike protuberance was about as big around as a pinky and a little more than an inch long. Reaching around from behind, Aiko began to fondle him. The protuberance was flexible; it could be held down so that it lay along the stalk of the penis, but when released, it bounced back up to its original position, sticking up at an angle of about twenty degrees. Sometimes Aiko would handle the penis somewhat roughly, showing that the protuberance wasn't just a fake piece stuck on to the penis.

After this little exhibition was over, Shigeki and Aiko lay down on the futon and started to make ordinary love. There was nothing unusual about a man caressing a woman, touching her body all over with his hands and lips, so I heaved a deep sigh, and rubbed my tired eyes, and kept on watching. Shigeki's motions remained gentle, but now he seemed to be thinking about the visual effect he was creating: his actions had an unnatural rhythm, an exaggeration, which made it easier for the audience to see what he was doing. Their lovemaking would have been more restrained in private. Okay, they're lovers, I thought, but this isn't real sex.

Suddenly I noticed something red, like a rash, on Aiko's thigh. The swelling of a mosquito bite? Then I could see the rashlike color breaking out all over the fair skin of her thighs. Cherry-blossom pink bumps appeared on her torso and arms. Where Shigeki had licked her, the color shone. I blanched.

Shigeki and Aiko began having genital intercourse. The sliding doors began to clatter from the vibrations. Shunji's musical accompaniment also became more forceful. Was it my imagination, or were rashes breaking out over Aiko's body? And they were turning a deeper red! The audience was getting fidgety, almost alarmed.

By the time Aiko changed positions, straddling Shigeki's reclining form, scarlet rashes had broken over her entire body. I couldn't tell whether they hurt or itched, but the moans issuing from her lips gave the impression that she was in pain. Even so, she kept moving her hips up and down in concert with Shigeki's thrusts. After a brief spell of yet more frenzied motion, Aiko lifted herself off Shigeki and fell backward, collapsing onto Shigeki's legs. Her face was scarlet, too.

Shunji switched to a different style of music, stringing the sounds together with only his left hand. The audience was totally silent. Aiko leapt lightly to her feet and came back toward me, her arms folded over her stomach, her eyes on the ground. I didn't know what to say, seeing her in this pitiful state. Eiko wrapped a bathrobe over her and said, "Good job." I followed them back into the dressing room.

In the dressing room, Aiko leaned against the wall and slid down to a sitting position. "Now you know what my condition is," she said. The redness of the rashes was more vivid close up. "It's a kind of allergy. I react to other people's body fluids."

"Does it hurt?" I asked.

"It feels kind of prickly. It's better than feeling itchy, because at least I don't have the urge to scratch." She smiled, pretty as ever, despite the rashes. "I've never once enjoyed sex, you know," she added, sighing.

She was so beautiful, and she couldn't enjoy sex! I couldn't believe it. My heart ached for her.

Tamotsu, who had been wandering aimlessly around the room with his hands stuffed in his pockets, spoke up. "Yeah, same here. I wish I could have one of these orgasms you hear about, just once in my life."

I felt a bit awkward hearing this. My big toe was a penis, true, but so what? I had no problem enjoying sex. On the other hand, maybe there was no need for me to feel guilty: judging from this exchange, not everyone in the Flower Show was unable to enjoy sex. I was still wondering about this when Tamotsu, gesturing at Eiko with his foot, confirmed my hunch.

"You have your fun, right? After all, you're normal."

Startled, I spun around to look at Eiko. She pushed Tamotsu's foot, which he was still pointing at her, away. Her face was flushed.

"I fail to see why you're bringing that up now."

"I'm just ever-so-casually introducing your profile to the new member, that's all," Tamotsu said with a snicker. "I thought that would be nice."

"How about trying to be nicer when you're nice?" Eiko said.

Tamotsu seemed to be bullying Eiko, so I spoke up. "Oh I'm fine, don't trouble yourself over me."

Tamotsu exploded into rude laughter. "Oh dear, we aren't to *trouble ourselves*! What wonderful manners!"

Aiko gestured for him to be quiet. "Don't laugh like that. They'll hear you."

"I know, I know." Swallowing his laughter, Tamotsu headed off toward the place where Masami and Tanabe Yohei were sitting.

Eiko smiled weakly at me. "My *body* is normal, you see."

I couldn't help noticing the emphasis she put on the word "body."

"What about you isn't normal, then?" I asked.

"Good question." Eiko glanced over at Tamotsu. "The fact that I've fallen for a spoiled brat like him, perhaps?"

Shigeki came into the room carrying Aiko's clothing. "Well, it's over for the night," he said, crouching in front of Aiko. His gaze was full of concern for his partner, who had endured the pain of the performance. Aiko smiled at him, tired. It was a touching moment between two lovers, but it was also a private moment, not for others. Eiko and I returned to the next room, where the show was taking place.

Kinoda Yukie's act was just getting under way. Shunji was playing a piece in his favorite boogie-woogie style, taking it nice and slow. The lower half of Yukie's body was naked, and she was sitting facing the audience with her legs apart.

"She used to be a stripper," Eiko whispered. "That was quite a while ago, though."

"Does she perform alone?"

"She will tonight. Sometimes she has a partner."

Yukie began peeling a banana she held in her hand, using her mouth. She was following the usual routine, pretending that the banana was a penis, making bawdy gestures and lewd expressions. Her other hand hovered between her legs, moving this way and that. She was a masterful performer, but since the sight of a nude woman didn't excite me, I found it boring.

"Who is her partner?"

"Tamotsu. Or rather, Shin."

Now that she mentioned it, Tamotsu's brother still hadn't shown up. I suppose that explained things. Yukie was performing alone this evening because Shin hadn't shown up.

Yukie placed the banana, now three-fourths peeled, into her crotch. This was entirely expected. She clenched the muscles of her abdomen. The brimming flesh of her thighs quivered, like plastic bags of water, creating little ripples. Yukie pulled out the banana and held it up for the audience to see. It looked like it had been chewed on!

"Yukie has teeth in her vagina," Eiko explained.

"Teeth?!" I was stunned.

"I've heard there've been similar cases since way back."

Yukie, holding the base of the banana, waved it in a circle and then reinserted it into her vagina. When she removed it, there were even more teeth marks in the flesh. She then tossed the abused banana into the audience. A woman screamed, evidently taking a direct hit, and a man let forth a lewd chuckle. Yukie smiled thinly. She was a very tough woman.

Yukie went through the same routine with a cucumber. She only pretended to throw the cucumber into the audience, although that was enough to cause several women to shriek. Instead, she thrust the vegetable into her mouth, took a bite, then loudly ate the whole thing. The audience burst into laughter.

The next object was a large, oddly shaped pear. This was worrisome, since there was no way it was going to fit it inside her, but it turned out to be a gag. Having given everyone a breather, Yukie next raised a long, thin metal file over her head, then turned toward Shunji and shouted, "Stop the music!"

Shunji, taken by surprise, stopped his hands in midair. Yukie slid the file into her vagina and started moving it in and out. In the silence, you could hear a faint grinding—the file was scraping against the teeth in her vagina. Listening closely, you could hear in the scraping the rhythm of a waltz! People started chuckling in the audience as they figured this out. A smile appeared on Shunji's lips as well.

"Music!" Yukie called out.

And immediately Shunji began playing a waltz of his own, with a charming melody, at the same tempo as Yukie's little solo. Once again laughter rippled through the audience.

"Fast thinking!" Eiko said. "They didn't plan this or anything!"

Yukie's last trick was with a balloon. She fit a tube into the balloon and blew through the tube to inflate the balloon. When the balloon had been inflated a little, she slipped it into her vagina and continued blowing into the tube. She huffed and puffed, and her face turned bright red. Nothing out of the ordinary happened, until there was a dull pop. Yukie removed the tube from her mouth, took a deep breath, and stood up. She left the stage to a chorus of cheers and applause. Obviously, the teeth in her vagina had popped the balloon.

"People only clap when she does her tricks alone," Eiko explained.

"I don't imagine most men could do it with her. I mean, how could they?"

"Most men couldn't, it's true." Eiko laughed. "There is one man in the troupe who can, though."

"Shin?"

"I mean, he's not really happy about it," Eiko mumbled. "He's forced."

"Who forces him?"

"Tamotsu."

He makes his kid brother do that?! I shuddered. "Why does Shin listen to his brother?"

"Because he can't resist."

"Why not?"

"You'll see soon enough."

Tanabe Yohei was now walking past us, carrying Ayase Masami in his arms like a husband carrying his bride over the threshold. The third act was about to begin.

Yohei had on only a pair of boxer shorts when he stepped up onto the futon; Masami was still wearing a blouse and a pair of pants. Yohei started to unbutton Masami's blouse, making his way down mechanically. There was no tenderness here, not like with Shigeki and Aiko. Masami must have had plastic surgery: as the front of his blouse fell open, the smooth curves of his breasts came into view.

"Is this a homosexual part of the show?" I asked Eiko.

"You figured it out already? That Masami is a man, I mean?" Eiko said, seeming impressed.

"Isn't it obvious?"

"Don't tell *him* it's obvious. He'll be hurt."

"Has he had a sex change?"

"He had the operation in New York."

Out on stage, a little tussle was being enacted in which Masami tried to pull his blouse together, hiding his breasts, while Yohei tried to keep him from covering them up. When Yohei ripped the blouse off and tossed it away, Masami buried his face in his hands. He must have meant this as a show of embarrassment, but it looked totally fake. Aiko, a real woman, hadn't shown any embarrassment—not that this comparison was necessary.

"Isn't it kind of boring if Masami is supposed to be a woman?" I asked Eiko. "That makes it common sex between a man and a woman, not between two men."

"Only halfway through."

Yohei removed Masami's final article of clothing, and Masami curled up into a ball, hiding his chest and crotch. Yohei went around back and pinioned Masami's arms, then wrapped his legs around Masami's. Unable to remain curled up, Masami sat up. He gave a little cry—it might have been a gasp or a sigh. Ever so slowly, Yohei pried Masami's legs apart with his own. Masami shook his head violently, and at the same time, he began to moan, sweetly. Clearly he was playing the role, well known in pornography, of the woman who struggles but ultimately gives into pleasure and becomes totally submissive to the violent man.

"Does he want to be a woman?"

"Yes," Eiko said, not at all annoyed by my continual questioning. "Got to wonder what he sees in it, huh?"

"And that's the type of woman he wants to be?"

"That's how men imagine us." Eiko replied matter-of-factly.

Finally, with his legs now fully pried apart, Masami stopped struggling; his body went limp, and his head sank onto Yohei's shoulder. Yohei picked up the lamp next to the futon and shone it at Masami's crotch. Shocked gasps could be heard in the audience. He had no penis.

"This is where they figure out he's an artificial woman," Eiko told me.

"He's had plastic surgery?"

"The thing is . . ." Even Eiko hesitated. "They didn't give him a clitoris."

The pornographic show continued. Fellatio, anal sex, vaginal intercourse with the artificial vagina—the two of them did it in every way and every position. I was dizzied by all the activity, but as their act had no emotion, no feeling, I was left somewhat bored. Masami continued whooping extravagantly.

"Dull, isn't it?" Eiko said.

"Yes, very."

"Things like this don't excite women at all, do they?"

"A real homosexual exhibition would probably be more fun."

"Exactly. But keep watching."

Yohei was on top, in the missionary position. As the couple fornicated, their hips shook violently. Yohei seemed to be in throes of excitement, his body drenched in sweat. Beads of sweat were pouring down his pendulum-like cheeks. But watching closely, I saw that the beads of sweat were spilling from his eyes each time he blinked—they weren't sweat, they were tears! With each thrust, Yohei bared his teeth, his thick lips rolled back, and his hanging saliva seemed to get thicker and longer. *Oh my god, this is not normal!* I thought.

Just then, Yohei pulled his penis out of Masami, and at exactly the same moment that the semen shot out, two white globes fell from his face. They seemed to dangle midair, swinging back and forth. The audience figured it out about the time I did: they were Yohei's eyeballs!

Perfectly composed, Yohei lifted his eyelids and returned his eyeballs to their proper places, one by one. Masami grinned wickedly and planted a kiss on his cheek.

"It's like a grade B horror movie," Eiko said.

I couldn't manage a response.

Shigeki came out of the dressing room as Yohei walked off stage and handed him a bath towel. Yohei vigorously scrubbed his face, which was covered in sweat, tears, and spit.

"Good job," Eiko said, looking up at him. I did the same.

He stopped for a moment and looked at me. His eyes were bloodshot, a brilliant red. "Just so you know, I'm not gay and I'm not a sadist."

"Are you being *sarcastic?*" Masami said right away. "But why not? Who cares? I'm just a *pervert*, right?"

Yohei, who didn't seem to be much of a conversationalist, simply walked back toward the dressing room, paying him no attention. Masami chased after him, waving his boxer shorts. I could hear Masami screaming, "You're such a *bore!*"

A moment later, Aiko came and tapped Eiko on the shoulder. "Tamotsu's calling you," she said. And when Eiko left, Aiko sat down beside me. "How's the show so far?" She smiled. "You look like you've had enough."

"That last act did get a bit dull after a while."

Shigeki, who was squatting beside Aiko, tried to explain. "With videos, you can do things to keep the boredom down. Put in close-ups or change the angle or cut from one shot to the next—things like that. Close-ups of the private parts can be pretty exciting, you know."

That wasn't what I meant. I was bored because this was a pornographic show aimed at male viewers. But I didn't say anything, and Shigeki went on talking. "It's no fun sitting around watching people have sex, right in front of you, if you can't participate yourself. Strip shows are different, because the audience does participate, sort of. And porn videos are fun because you can masturbate while you watch them at home. Our live sex show manages to hang on because we're abnormal. If we were normal, we'd be out of business. But to tell the truth, I don't know if the Flower Show can last another three years."

As we were talking, Eiko and Tamotsu made their appearance on stage. Eiko led Tamotsu by the hand, but rather than start out with the usual ritual disrobing of the woman by the man, Eiko removed her own clothes first. Tamotsu, standing opposite her in T-shirt and pants, didn't move. Eiko wrapped herself around his body and kissed him. Tamotsu remained as straight as a rod. Maybe their act was based on the theme of a woman's pursuit of a man?

Eiko knelt before Tamotsu and put her hand on his crotch. He had his back to me, but I assumed she had unzipped his pants, taken out his penis, and put it in her mouth. She then made Tamotsu lie on his back, still fully clothed, although his erect penis was now visible. But it was considerably smaller than Shigeki's or Yohei's, or Masao's and Shunji's. That wasn't the only thing that struck me as odd. The angle of the erection was off and the base of the penis seemed . . . incorrectly attached, somehow.

When Eiko was about to climb on top of Tamotsu, his penis wilted. Once more she took it in her mouth. The penis grew hard again, but when she started to straddle him, it went limp again. Tamotsu didn't seem to be in very good form this evening. Sitting down on his stomach, Eiko guided his hands to her breasts. He fondled them, then sat up and used his tongue between them. After a little while Eiko lifted her hips, but Tamotsu's penis had retreated into his pants.

"I wonder what's wrong," I said.

Aiko shook her head. "It's always like this."

Eiko pulled off Tamotsu's T-shirt. He had a drumlike bulge for a stomach, much too large for someone so young. He seemed pudgy, and yet his flesh looked tight—his bulge of a stomach didn't flop around. Next Eiko removed Tamotsu's pants, and I found myself staring. Where Tamotsu's legs connected to his torso there were two large, shiny scars with something like a small horn sticking out of each one. Eiko pulled off Tamotsu's underwear, and naked, Tamotsu stood up and faced the audience. He had no pubic hair. But most startling was the fact that his penis wasn't in his crotch. It stuck out from a point higher up on his body, near his pelvis. His body was covered with innumerable scars, whiter than his skin.

"That's Shin, Tamotsu's brother," Aiko whispered.

"What?!" My mouth was dry.

"Tamotsu and Shin are Siamese twins. The upper half of Shin's body is inside Tamotsu—only the lower half sticks out. The penis you see belongs to Shin. Shin is in the way, so only the tip of Tamotsu's comes out."

Aiko explained that the scars at the joints of Tamotsu's legs were where Shin's legs had been amputated. The hornlike bumps were his bones, which had kept growing even after the surgery. It was Tamotsu's body, but the penis was Shin's, so any excitement Tamotsu felt from looking at or touching a woman didn't reach the penis, and any excitement the penis felt being stimulated gave Tamotsu no pleasure.

Eiko said she had fallen for Tamotsu. But Tamotsu's own penis was almost entirely buried inside his body. She could let him put Shin's penis inside her, and she could imagine she was having sex with Tamotsu, but she would actually be having sex with another man—his brother. What kind of sex life could these two lovers ever have?

Having drawn himself up to his full height, Tamotsu was now rubbing *Shin's* penis, trying to get it hard. He handled it roughly, a cruel smile playing on his lips. Eiko looked on, her expression glum. Tamotsu turned the same cruel smile on her, and her face twisted in distress. Then he forced himself on top of her and began jerking Shin's penis. Without even realizing it, I shut my eyes.

I don't know how much time passed, but when I looked again, Tamotsu had gotten off Eiko. He knelt, clenched his hand into a fist, and started to punch himself. The dull sound of his fist hitting his flesh was horrible. Shin's penis had gone limp again inside Eiko, and Tamotsu was pounding it. Tamotsu himself would feel nothing, of course, but one could almost feel the pain Shin was feeling. Apparently sensing that something was amiss, Shunji stopped playing the synthesizer. The sound of the punching reverberated through the now quiet room. Eiko threw herself at Tamotsu, wrapping her arms around his torso. Tamotsu's arm was midair, and when it landed, it slammed squarely into her head.

Aiko cried out. Suddenly it became clear that the performance wasn't going according to plan.

Tamotsu stiffened, evidently brought back to his senses by the punch he had just landed on Eiko's head. Abruptly, he pushed her away from him and stormed off the stage, a nasty expression on his face. Eiko was left kneeling on the futon, stunned. Then hurriedly she gathered up their scattered clothes and chased after Tamotsu.

Aiko stared at Shigeki as he proceeded to close the sliding doors. A hum rose from the audience, and there was a smattering of applause.

Realizing that the show was now over, Shunji quickly played a short coda. This gave me a chance to recover from my shock. I stumbled over to him and threw my arms around his neck.

♥ ♥ ♥

"Tamotsu isn't professional," Aiko said.

We were walking down the hall toward the six-mat room in the main building. Shigeki had stayed behind to take care of business matters. Shunji and I had just finished packing up his things; the rest of the troupe seemed to have gone on ahead, but Aiko had waited for us.

"When Shin isn't having a good night," she continued, "he could just let people see that he's having problems, that would be fine, or he could take the act in some other direction . . . But instead he gets angry, for real, in the middle of the show. He's young, so when things don't go the way he wants them to, he just blows up. But he does have a lot of fans among our regulars—people love what he does and actually look forward to his number. They like it because he shows a slice of real life. He lets them see true emotions, not a staged performance."

"But," I said, "I had the feeling he was letting people see something he shouldn't be. It was like he was shoving his open diary in people's faces, even if no one wants to read it . . ."

"Except that the Flower Show is all about showing people things that aren't supposed to be put on display," Aiko said with a smile.

I regretted having said something so dumb.

"You'd be surprised at the number of people who get excited when they see things that people keep hidden—like sex and mental illness. That's how we earn our living." She paused, sighing. "But I feel so bad for Eiko."

"Are they lovers?" I remembered the cruel smile Tamotsu had directed at Eiko as he rubbed Shin's penis. Talk about a complex situation. A man who had no choice but to use another man's penis with a woman who loved him—no wonder it looked so warped and malicious. But he was supposed to love her. He looked more like he was full of scorn, like he hated her.

"Eiko doesn't seem to be able to leave Tamotsu," Aiko replied. "And Tamotsu . . . I guess he's just completely dependent on her."

"I think he's spoiled," said Shunji, suddenly breaking into the discussion. "I can tell from his speech. A mushy voice that sounds like he's squeezed it up from deep down in his throat, then sucked on it before letting it drool out. You know what I mean, right? I know a guy who talks exactly the same way. He wants people to do everything for him . . . Everyone used to say he had a mother complex."

Aiko stared at Shunji, her eyes sparkling. "You can tell all that from his voice? You're really brilliant."

Shunji grinned shyly. "I could be mistaken, though."

Aiko's whole face seemed to brighten. "I think you're great, Shunji." She beamed. "But I don't dislike Tamotsu. He's still a child, that's all. And the stupider kids are, the more you love them."

When we got back to the six-mat room, the "stupid kid" was back to pacing around slovenly, hands in his pockets. Eiko looked wiped out, but she smiled at Aiko as we walked in. The three other members of the troupe were sitting at the low table, picking at sushi.

"Help yourself, okay?" Aiko said.

Shunji seemed to have figured out from the smell what people were eating, and he sat down right away. "Is there any *uni*? How about *ikura*?"

I guided his hand to the spot where the *uni* were. Performing seemed to have left him hungry, and he gobbled down one piece after another.

I, on the other had, didn't feel like eating. Not anything raw. I love sushi, but after the show the mere thought of raw, fatty seafood oozing down my throat made me want to vomit. Like the first time I swallowed semen. Now why did that come to mind? Did watching people have sex make me nauseous? Whatever it was, I couldn't take the smell of raw fish.

Tamotsu, looking bored, came and stood over Shunji. "Hey," he said by way of greeting.

"Are you talking to me?" Shunji turned his head up.

"After throwing yourself into a performance like that," Tamotsu said, "don't you want to have sex? Like, really bad?"

I couldn't believe he was asking this, but Shunji wasn't at all flustered. "No," he replied, "not particularly."

"But don't musicians usually have sex after a show?"

"A lot of rock musicians do. Not me, though."

"You don't get turned on by the sounds you make?"

"When you play electric instruments with the volume really high, your body kind of goes numb, but I play the piano."

"Oh. I used to play electric guitar in a band when I was in high school, and when I really let go with it, Shin's thing would get hard. Even though he doesn't have any ears. Maybe he was feeling the sound waves."

"Who's Shin?" Shunji asked, stuffing a piece of *toro* into his mouth.

Tamotsu grabbed Shunji's hand and pressed it against his stomach. "This is Shin."

Shunji concentrated on what his hand was feeling, and even when Tamotsu let go of it, he kept it there where Tamotsu had placed it. "Your penis has a name?" he then asked.

Everyone in the room had been watching this, and they burst into laughter.

Tamotsu shouted, as if he had lost control, "No, it doesn't! It's the penis of my twin brother, this parasite inside my body!"

"Oh."

Apparently thinking the conversation was over, Shunji reached again for more sushi. But Tamotsu sat down next to him and wouldn't stop. "When do you get hard?"

"When someone licks me or rubs me or does stuff like that."

"What about other times, like when—"

"Can't you talk about something else?" Eiko cut him off. He'd been getting pretty weird.

"What's wrong? I like this topic," Tamotsu growled. "I want to hear what a man with a normal penis has to say about this stuff."

"Then why don't you ask me?" Yohei piped up from the side of the room. "You never ask me about those things. My face isn't normal, but the rest of me is."

Yohei's intrusion into the conversation seemed to surprise everyone. This caused Yukie to leap in with "Who knew you had a sense of humor—sort of?"

Tamotsu raised his voice, annoyed. "Look, what's your problem? I can ask anyone I want about whatever I want. Isn't that right?" He patted Shunji on the shoulder.

"Sure, it's fine with me," Shunji said, nodding his head.

"See?" Tamotsu puffed out his chest. Eiko, not pleased, looked down bitterly as Tamotsu inched closer to Shunji.

"Say someone has rubbed you, and you've gotten an erection . . . Does it ever go limp right away?"

"Not right away, no. But it gets small if it's left alone."

"Ah," Tamotsu exclaimed, turning his gaze on me. "It must stay hard longer because you have a good partner."

I felt myself blush. I tried to keep people from noticing this by joining the conversation. "No, I don't think that's it, actually."

Tamotsu ignored me and began muttering, "So all you need is a good partner and you have no problem getting it up. Guess I'll have to try and find Shin a better partner, huh?" This was a barb aimed at Eiko, and it hit its mark. Eiko blanched. But Tamotsu continued, not even glancing in her direction. "It's really a pain for me when I don't have a good partner, someone who can get Shin excited."

The atmosphere in the room grew tense. Tamotsu was leaning against the wall, his expression cool.

Eiko struggled to look cheerful. "It's true," she said. "If Shin had a good partner of his own, I wouldn't have to look after both him and you."

She was trying to smooth things over by intentionally misinterpreting Tamotsu's attack, but Tamotsu showed no mercy. "What are you talking about? You *are* Shin's partner!"

"But it's you I care about, Tamotsu," Eiko said quietly.

Tamotsu stared at her, and with his voice raised he spat out, "That's news to me. I thought you were in love with Shin."

"Why do you say things like that when you know they're not true?" Eiko was near tears.

"You only kiss me because you lust for Shin. I'm just an add-on. Isn't it my job to help Shin make you feel good? You think I like that? Do you have any idea how I feel when you kiss me?"

"What are you talking about? I keep telling you it doesn't matter, we don't need to have ordinary sex! You're the one who insists on using Shin!"

"And you love it when I do, don't you?"

This wasn't a conversation I wanted to hear.

"Cut it out, Tamotsu," Aiko said firmly, ending it.

But Tamotsu was agitated. "Aiko, this is a huge problem for the Flower Show, too! I need a partner who is appropriate for Shin so we don't have another failure like tonight."

"Tonight was fine."

"Yeah, well, unfortunately I'm a perfectionist! I won't be satisfied until I can give a perfect show, have perfect pleasure, a perfect body, perfect sex. Not to mention, of course, a perfect girlfriend . . ."

Aiko stepped forward and walloped Tamotsu on the head. The crisp smack echoed through the room. "Come back to us in your next life," she said.

I burst out laughing, though I was the only one who did.

Massaging his head where he had been slapped, Tamotsu tried wheedling. "I wish I had a girlfriend like you, Aiko."

"I don't like spoiled brats."

"Think up some other story line, Tamotsu," Masami suddenly butted into the conversation. "I'm sick of watching the same *dumb* routine."

This caused Eiko to frown, although she also seemed to be half laughing.

Whereupon Shigeki came into the room carrying a brown envelope. "Payday," he announced, and everyone cheered. He went around the room distributing the cash. Tamotsu, I noticed, got the same amount as everyone else.

Shigeki came over to Shunji and pressed bills into his hand as well. "Sorry it's so little," he said.

"You don't have to pay me!" Shunji said. "This isn't my real job."

"Just take it," Tamotsu said. "It's not like it'll be a nuisance, right?"

Shigeki turned to me. "Well? After tonight's performance, are you still interested in touring with us?"

I hadn't yet recovered from all I had seen and felt: I had been shocked to glimpse the depth of the love between Shigeki and Aiko, shocked to observe the warped ties that bound Tamotsu and Eiko. I hadn't had time to think calmly, sort through my impressions of the people or the show. But the excitement I felt, which wasn't sexual, was undeniable. Now that Shigeki had asked, I realized how deeply engaged I felt. Curiosity burned in my brain; I felt heat radiating through me. I couldn't predict whether I would grow to like them or hate them, but I wanted to be around these people. So I found myself blurting out impulsively—

"Yes, I'll do it."

Chapter 8

The Flower Show minibus is cream-colored and has flowers painted on it. On the front of it, smack in the center, is a reddish-purple hibiscus; on the back there is a bramble of red roses, stems craning upward; on either side, there is a tangle of magnolias, irises, lilies, and various other flowers. The brushwork is easy and elegant. This was the work of Tanabe Yohei, and I guess I wasn't surprised. He's an imperturbably calm guy, not much of a talker, the sort of person who seemed like he might have a special, highly developed talent. Unfortunately, I hadn't yet had a chance to tell him how much I liked his painting.

The Flower Show started its tour right around the time most people were winding up their vacations for the Festival of the Dead. We'd done two shows in Atami, one in Ito, and one in Hakone, and at some point around the fifth day, when we got to Nagoya, it occurred to me that for all the time we spent with each other, members of the group talked very little.

As soon as we arrived at our lodgings, we would all go off to our rooms. The pairings were always the same: Shigeki and Aiko, Tamotsu and Eiko, Yohei and Masami, and Shunji and I; Yukie had a single room. We were free to do as we liked between check-in and the time when we had agreed to gather, and we ate our meals when we wanted, where we wanted. Troupe members didn't try to keep their distance; if they happened to find themselves at the same restaurant they might share a table; but no one went out of her or his way to make dinner plans with anyone else.

We convened at showtime, and we put on our show. After that, during the hours traveling from one location to another, the troupe didn't talk a whole lot: Tamotsu played computer games; Yukie put on her glasses and knitted; everyone else either read or put on their headphones and listened to music. Everyone engaged in solitary diversions. For the most part, the only time anyone spoke was when someone finished a magazine and passed it on to the next person.

Maybe that's just how it is when a group spends a lot of time on the road. And I couldn't complain: this hint of coolness among everyone kept Shunji and me, the newcomers, from feeling isolated. We felt no pressure to try and fit in. This allowed us to sit back and take it easy without worrying about what the others might think.

Apart from the two seats up front, the minibus had three rows of seats, with three seats in each row. Shunji and I sat in the back row. Shunji, who was a master at taking things easy and not worrying, would have his headphones on and be getting into his music almost the second he sat down. I would sit looking out the window, or sometimes open a book. The first couple days, Shigeki came back and chatted with me when someone else took a turn at the wheel, but when he saw that Shunji and I were perfectly happy back here on our own he stopped coming unless he had a particular reason.

Though the troupe members respected each other's privacy, in the course of seeing them every day I gradually acquired a sense of their individual habits and personalities. I realized at some point, for instance, that the reason Yukie frequently pinched her eyebrows together, which made her look like she was frowning, was because she was astigmatic; and that when she peered at me as if she was curious about something, which she did from time to time, she was just looking, plain and simple.

I also realized that Tamotsu and Masami were inclined toward excitability: On the day we left Tokyo, Shunji commented on how comfortable the seats in the minibus were and how well they absorbed vibrations from the road. Aiko turned around to agree: "My lower back used to hurt before we got these new seats. All the women in the group had the same problem." Eiko, who was between Tamotsu and Aiko, turned around. "It was partly from the air-conditioning—we got too cold. How's the air-conditioning for you?" she asked me. "Do you get cold easily?" She and

Aiko were both wearing long-sleeved shirts and had blankets over their laps. "No, not especially," I said.

Tamotsu, apparently, could not resist: "So I guess not *all* women are as much of a pain as these two." Which caused Masami, in the front row, to cry out, "*Excuse me*, but *I'm* not a pain! *I* don't get cold, *I* don't get bitten by mosquitoes, *I* don't have a period, and there's no fear that *I'll* get pregnant!"

"Yeah, yeah, that's all wonderful!" shouted Tamotsu. "But you know, now that you've brought it up, why did you ask Aiko to give you some of that medicine she uses to delay her period when you don't even have one?"

"I put it in a little pouch for a charm."

"What, does the pouch have a period?"

That provoked some laughter, and Masami went into high gear: "What business is it of *yours* what I ask Aiko for! There's no chance that *I'll* get pregnant, but I still take my basal body temperature every morning! The first time I bought a BBT thermometer I had no idea where to put it, so I stuck it up my brand-new vagina!"

That particular exchange ended there, and silence fell again on the minibus. But that same evening, after the end of the first day's show, Tamotsu and Masami became embroiled in another scene that shattered the calm. Tamotsu and Eiko's (or, rather, Shin and Eiko's) number had gone relatively well—unlike the first performance I had witnessed. I figured this would put Tamotsu in a good mood. But on the way back to the hotel, he started grumbling to himself just as he had that first night.

"Shin's *thing* should be performing the way it did tonight all the time. I'm sick of constantly having to worry about whether or not he's going to be able to get it up. Isn't there some nice gal somewhere who can give him an erection every time, without ever messing things up?"

"Indeed there is, *darling*—and here I am!"

Masami, sitting in the first row, gave his hand a little flutter.

"Cut it out, will you? You're certainly not the one, Masami."

"Why not? After all, *mon cher*, I'm a *technician*."

"Technician or not, I don't want you."

"But why *not*? It's not like the two of *us* will be doing it. It'll just be Shin and me. Your tastes are irrelevant."

At first Tamotsu was at a loss for words; then he muttered, "I'm not sure I like the idea of pushing my little brother into your world of gay love."

"Oh? Why this sudden outpouring of brotherly tenderness? As if you weren't causing him excruciating pain all the time!"

"Shin doesn't have a brain! The question of whether or not he feels pain is—"

"Better not to bring *brains* into it, Tamotsu darling, since you clearly don't have much of one yourself. To think after all this time you *still* can't get it into your head that I'm a woman."

Tamotsu fell silent again. Later on, Aiko reported that there had been a sour smile on his lips.

Were Tamotsu and Masami the sort of friends who enjoyed teasing each other? Or were these interchanges simply a consequence of the fact that Tamotsu was spoiled and needed to feel loved, while Masami was chatty and eager to be the center of attention? Then, too, Masami might also have been stepping in to protect Eiko by drawing Tamotsu's fire.

Tamotsu was twenty—a year older than Shunji. Eiko was twenty-three, a few months older than me. They had been friends as children, before they became lovers. Tamotsu tended to take his anger out on Eiko, but they were as close as most couples.

And there was more to Tamotsu than the warped, unpleasant side of him that seemed to emerge so often; he could be very gentle, too. Toward evening on our day in Ito, when Shunji and I were sitting in the park outside the hotel, Eiko and Tamotsu happened by, Tamotsu cradling a cat in his arms.

"Hey Shunji, I bet you like cats, don't you?"

"Sure."

Tamotsu then pressed the cat against Shunji's chest. He had found it in the park. It didn't have a collar, but it was used to humans and allowed itself to be picked up. Shunji laid his palm gently on the cat's back and took it carefully in his arms.

"I love how cats feel. I like dogs, too, but cat fur is nicer."

"I had a feeling you would be a cat person!"

"I haven't touched a cat in a long time. Some day I'm going to get one of my own."

Tamotsu gazed down at Shunji, one corner of his mouth sagging in an off-kilter smile. He looked like the leader of a gang of little rascals, slightly embarrassed at his thoughtfulness. Eiko seemed to be relishing the pride she took in Tamotsu's nice side. The two ambled off, leaving the cat with us.

I enjoyed getting to know the members of the troupe a little better every day. Shigeki told us, "I can see you two are very adaptable. It's like you've been with the troupe for ages."

Speaking of adaptability . . . after four or five days I found myself getting used to Yohei's looks, bizarre as they were. At least I no longer caught my breath each time he appeared. Now when I saw him, before I noticed the peculiarity of his features, I would remember that he was the one who had painted those beautiful flowers. I saw his lovely flowers at the same moment I saw him.

♥ ♥ ♥

The Flower Show had made a guest appearance in a play the previous night. Needless to say, it wasn't open to the general public—it was a special, one-night-only performance held in a little private basement theater. The head of the company served as both the playwright and the director. His name, Utagawa Kin'ya, wasn't familiar to me, but I was told that after rocketing to prominence in the underground theater scene in the early 1970s and becoming the darling of a certain sector of the theater-going public, one of his plays had flopped miserably. He fled Japan, as if trying to escape his failure, and had been forgotten in his absence. A few years ago he returned and become an active member of the theater world again, this time in the Kansai region. The members of the audience were pretty much the usual suspects—rich-looking gentleman in suits and the women they had brought with them—but there was also a fair number of men and women in their forties whose long hair and tie-dyed jeans called up a tinge of nostalgia.

The content of the play wasn't the sort someone like me could expect to understand. Naked men came out with their faces painted blue-green, various oversize papier-mâché objects—slices of *kon'nyaku*, instant *ramen*, torn pillows leaking feathers—hanging between their legs, and proceeded to wander across the stage, screaming "Steal back the phallus!" After a while, men with papier-mâché jackknives and cat-o'-nine-tails hanging between *their* legs sprinted out from stage left and started sprinkling detergent on the men with the instant *ramen* between their legs, hollering "Dig mommy's ass!" A huge egg descended from the ceiling and broke cleanly in two, releasing blobs of the gooey toy known as "Slime." At this point, half-naked women wearing masks entered from stage right and started to whip the men, who in turn started whipping the women. The scene devolved into a full-scale S&M smorgasbord.

After helping Shunji to the only open seat in the theater, I had gone over to stand and watch from the back of the theater. Two men who looked to be in their late thirties and were wearing conventional jeans kept talking about the performance: "I hear those ladies getting their asses whipped are S&M queens, bona fide pros." "This guy's finished, huh. He's still hung up on stuff from twenty years ago." "I bet after being in the States for so long, he's made up his mind Japan is behind the times. That's the only excuse for this bullshit . . ."

Between this snideness and the endless stream of music blaring from the speakers, it was hard to follow the play. Presumably, since the men on stage were screaming "Steal back the phallus!" to each other, someone must have made off with their penises, replacing them with instant noodles and *kon'nyaku*. Maybe the bit about "Dig mommy's ass!" meant that if only the men could make up their minds to have anal sex with their mothers, the stolen penises would come back of their own accord . . . On the other hand, it could also express their desire to celebrate, after they took back their penises, by having anal sex with their mothers. I couldn't tell.

I had been expecting that the men would embark upon some mighty quest to recapture the penises that had been stolen from them, but after being sprinkled with detergent, blobbed with "Slime," and whipped by the women, they suddenly plucked off the papier-mâché objects hanging between their legs, and there were their penises. This, it seemed to me, was in conflict with the original premise of the play, since their penises hadn't been stolen at all, only hidden. There was also the obvious contradiction in the fact that, after being urged to "Dig mommy's ass," all that the men did once their penises were uncovered was to have S&M-ish sex with women who were much too young to be their mothers.

All right then, maybe the story was about a group of lying, flaky men who insisted their penises had been stolen when they had them all along, then went around mouthing off about how they were going to have anal sex with their mothers only to content themselves with other women, whom they whipped, got whipped by, and made love to? Or was it, rather, that the story was nothing more than window dressing, and the writer-director's real interest lay in putting on a porn show? Whatever the case, the slimy, obsessive mentality of the man came through very clearly, so I guess in the end the real theme was "self-expression."

The members of the Flower Show performed on a bed that had been set up where the actors shouted "Steal back the phallus!" during the first half of the play. I had been assuming that Tamotsu, who was incapable of having sex with his own penis, and Masami, who had intentionally disposed of his, would be used to lend greater depth to the idea of "steal back the phallus," but that turned out not to be the case. As far as I could tell, they were simply there to add color. Shigeki, Aiko, Tamotsu, Eiko, and Yukie were less enthusiastic than usual, and got through their scenes very quickly.

Only Yohei was given special treatment. He had lines to say. A spotlight picked him out where he knelt on the bed, his posture stiff and formal. "A woman!" he moaned woodenly from his sagging, down-turned lips. "A woman! A woman! A woman who will love me! Who won't fear me, or view me with scorn!" Masami came on stage and wrapped himself around Yohei. "I don't believe in equality," Yohei said, starting to get physical with Masami. Later, he spoke the line: "These women don't even notice my hatred."

Shigeki, who had come to stand next to me after his act was over, whispered, "He's got Yohei saying all these things, but Yohei has a partner. As a matter of fact, she's quite beautiful. She fell for him and moved right in with him without even asking how he felt about it. There's no need for the director to make him say all that garbage."

Shigeki was glaring at the stage, his forehead beaded with sweat. Up on stage, Yohei was prying apart Masami's legs. He shouted his next line: "Only she accepts my hatred!" The actors' chorus of "Steal back the phallus!" rose to an even higher pitch.

"People fall in love for all sorts of reasons," Shigeki went on, whispering. "The guy who wrote this play doesn't get that. He's convinced no woman could ever love Yohei unless she looked down on him or was ugly herself. You know why he wants to believe that? Because *he* needs someone to look down on."

I stood on tiptoes and said into Shigeki's ear, "I take it you didn't want to be in this play?"

"Of course not! It's idiotic."

Utagawa, the writer-director, was in his midforties, shaved head, booming voice, wearing a T-shirt that said I ♥ NEW YORK. I could hear him going on as we headed toward the dressing room after the play:

". . . I can stage this thing as many times as I want, you know. My sponsors say they'll pay. Next time I'm going to put more money into the show. I have a feeling I can get my sponsors to shell out some more. And I'll let you guys appear again. If only I could use you in the plays I do for the general public, too! Unfortunately, the time isn't yet ripe for that. But when the tide turns, I promise you, I'm going to make you guys my own exclusive actors. I'll pay you well, too. Because my sponsors think pretty highly of me, you know . . ."

Shigeki had gone in to collect the troupe's fee, but the writer-director couldn't stop talking. By the time Shigeki got out the door, Shunji and I were getting tired. Yohei came out next, the writer-director's thick arm draped over his shoulder.

"I hope you all aren't really leaving. You should come to the party! There'll be all sorts of people. I'll introduce you to everyone."

Shigeki smiled faultlessly, bowing his response to the writer-director, who was shorter than Shigeki and scowled up at him.

The writer-director then turned to Yohei, his arm still around him. "You can come, right, Tanabe?"

"My liver isn't doing well, I'm afraid . . . ," murmured Yohei.

The writer-director's swarthy face turned crimson. He swallowed, crushed the signs of his anger, and tried to act understanding, "I see. Maybe next time, huh?" Then he hugged Yohei, slapping him energetically on the back, and headed back into the dressing room.

When the door shut, Shigeki and Yohei turned to look at each other, smug grins on their faces.

"Man, what a pain in the ass," Shigeki said.

"Was he trying to keep you in the dressing room?" I asked Yohei as we climbed the stairs.

Shigeki answered for him. "The guy says he's crazy about Yohei. As an actor. He's always telling him, 'Put yourself in my hands, and I'll make a man out of you.'"

"I thought the line was, 'Put yourself in my hands, and I'll make a woman out of you,'" I said.

Yohei looked bemused by my comment, and Shigeki chuckled, "The old fart uses the same pick-up line with men *and* women. Except as far as we know, he only has sex with women." Then, turning to Yohei, Shigeki asked, "What do you think, should we stop doing these kind of gigs?"

"I'm fine either way," Yohei replied. "If we didn't meet jerks like him every so often, we might get confused and think we're living in paradise."

This brought on a bit of laughter, and then Shigeki and Yohei walked ahead of us toward the minibus, not saying anything more. As Shunji and I followed, I couldn't take my eyes off their backs. That brief exchange had shown me how deeply in tune the two men were, and the naturalness with which they adjusted to each other's pace hinted at the depth of their friendship. But somehow—maybe because we had just emerged from that raucous play, and escaped from that raucous writer-director—I saw a kind of frailty in them.

Not that I thought they were weak. Just that the energy between them was so hopelessly peaceful and mild in comparison with the obnoxious aggressiveness of the play and the playwright. If that playwright and his buddies ever ganged up on them, Shigeki and Yohei wouldn't have a chance. Which worried me.

I'd seen before, with Masao and Haruhiko and their buddies, how when a group of men band together, a sort of force field is created that does battle with the other force fields, or at least protects the men from other force fields. But in the case of Shigeki and Yohei, there was no such thing. They didn't make a display of their friendship, they didn't try to impress anyone, they just walked quietly away from other force fields. Maybe they didn't have that aggression most men have?

I prefer nonaggressive men. Aggressive men want to chop off my toe-penis. Shunji doesn't have an aggressive bone in his body. Shigeki, who serves so unobtrusively as the leader of the Flower Show, isn't aggressive in the usual way either. So it was with sadness and annoyance that, simply because Shigeki couldn't match the boorishness of the writer-director, I recognized that he didn't have as strong a presence.

By the same token, it upset me that Yohei had been forced to play the stupid, cookie-cutter role of a man who, because of his unusual physical characteristics, is unloved by any woman and is thus bitter toward all women. That wasn't who Yohei was at all. He was an individual who painted beautiful flowers and, according to Shigeki, had a beautiful girlfriend. The playwright had only paid attention to a tiny part of Yohei and pigeonholed him for this creepy play.

For this stop on our tour, the entire troupe was staying in a single apartment in Kobe. It was a luxurious place, on the fifth floor, intended for foreigners—it had two bathrooms!—that was being rented by one of the middlemen for the Flower Show. Or perhaps it was rented by the organization he belonged to, we weren't sure.

The first day Shunji and I set foot in the apartment, Shunji immediately smelled the lingering odor of marijuana. He had been exposed to it in the music industry, and it was true—you could tell the thick, pungent fragrance right off.

Tamotsu, inhaled deeply. "Ah, I'm starting to get high already," he said.

Eiko opened the window.

"Hey, you're wasting the smell!" Tamotsu said.

"It makes my throat hurt," Eiko replied, unwilling to be bullied by Tamotsu this time.

Shigeki and Aiko started opening a chest of drawers in the spacious living room. "Here's the source of the smell," Aiko called out, as Shigeki held out a tin crammed with leaves that looked, at first glance, like tea. There was more in the drawer than tins of marijuana: there were powders in paper packets, syringes, and the rubber tubing that's tied around your arm when you get your blood drawn.

She opened another drawer. It was filled with videocassettes, the covers of which told the story.

"Hardcore triple-X porn and some weird stuff," she explained, "mostly from the U.S. All illegal."

"I've acted in porn myself," Shigeki said, as he looked over the collection, "but the movies I was in were cartoons compared to these."

"I think we'd better not open any other drawers," Aiko said.

"The guy who rents this place has parties with this stuff."

"Is he a yakuza?" I asked.

Shigeki shook his head. "He may have ties, but he's not one himself. We don't need to know."

Shigeki locked the drawer, then handed the ring of keys to Aiko. She put them in her purse.

"Watch the movies if you're curious, but no drugs. They're dangerous," Shigeki said. "Do us a favor and don't tell Tamotsu where the key is, okay?"

Shigeki had said parties were held here, and I could see why: it had two bedrooms, as well as, in the large living room, three king-size sofa beds. At bedtime, the troupe split up into the same groups it did at hotels—four parties of two and Yukie on her own. Shunji and I slept on one of the sofa beds in the living room, Tamotsu with his forehead against Eiko's chest in another, and Shigeki and Aiko in the one near the chest of drawers.

Even though we were all in the same apartment, there was no deviation from the troupe's practice of trying to respect each others' private lives, and we didn't cook or eat together. Yohei and Yukie cooked for themselves because he didn't like going out and she was eager to save money, but everyone else ate out. Masami seemed to have a lot of friends in the area: every day, he would call someone up and make plans for lunch.

Still, because of our shared quarters, the troupe had more occasion to be friendly with one another. One night when we didn't have to perform, Tamotsu, Yukie, and Masami went to the pro wrestling matches in Kobe. I wanted to cook something for a change, but Shunji, who had become fascinated with the different rhythms and accents of speech in the Kansai region, and was always listening in on conversations on the streets, wanted to go to a restaurant. We decided on Italian.

It was around eight when we got back to the apartment. Yohei was stretched out on the sofa bed where Shunji and I slept, reading a book; Shigeki, Aiko, and Eiko were chatting in the corner near the chest of drawers. Shunji and I went over to join them.

"Hey, do you want to watch one of the movies?" Shigeki asked. "It'll be something to talk about. I don't think it will hurt to see what they're like."

I was curious, but I glanced at Shunji, who was sitting next to me. Shigeki immediately picked up on what I was thinking. "Oh, yeah. I guess Shunji would find that kind of boring, huh?"

"No, I won't," Shunji said. "Not if there are sounds and people speaking."

"Nothing too grotesque, though—" I said hurriedly. "I don't want to see anything that involves babies, or where a person really gets killed."

"Of course not. You want something soft, yet hard, right?" Shigeki stood up and walked over to the chest. "Don't worry—there are all sorts of weirdos in the U.S. We could start with a 'cat fight'—you know, two women tearing at each other. They don't get naked, and it doesn't turn into a lesbian scene or anything. Personally, I don't see how a movie like that manages to hold anyone's interest, but apparently it works for some people."

Shigeki was rummaging through the cassettes when Aiko called out, half teasingly, "You don't want to show her one of yours?"

"No," he replied, his tone serious. "I'd be too embarrassed."

I would have found it embarrassing, too. I saw him naked, having sex right in front of me, almost every day, but seeing him do it on video in a previous life would seem somehow like I was intruding.

"God, it's impossible to find anything in here," Shigeki grumbled, as he kept looking through the drawer. "They're not organized at all. And the titles have been abbreviated. Hold on . . . maybe this is one. It says 'cat' on it."

Shigeki pulled out the cassette and slipped it into the player. I had never watched an uncensored porn film before, and for some reason I found myself quite excited as I waited for the film to begin.

The very first thing to appear on the screen was an adorable kitten. No titles or credits. Was this a joke—because the film was in the "cat fight" genre? Maybe it's a fight between two real cats? I smiled to myself. The image was fairly grainy, and the camerawork completely amateurish and jerky.

The kitten paraded around on a carpet, then a man's hand came into the frame, scooped the kitten up, and set it on a table. The hand started gently caressing the kitten, which curled itself in a little ball. It seemed like an awfully long introduction, but the kitten was cute enough. The hand—you never saw the man's face—kept petting the cat, scratching its neck, patting its forehead. When the kitten got tired of being petted and started to wander off, the hand pulled it back and went on caressing it. The kitten meowed.

"Hey," Shunji said, poking me. "What's a kitten doing in a movie like this?"

"I don't know."

Right about this time, I began to sense that something strange was going on. There were no human bodies, even though it was supposed to be porn, and then this really peculiar petting of the kitten. There was something in the manner of the petting that did not suggest affection; it was teasing the kitten—toying with it. Clearly the kitten was now sick of being caressed. But the hand wouldn't let it alone.

As the group of us watched this, there was a shared anxiety.

On the screen, the man's hand had just grabbed the fleeing kitten by the scruff of its neck and was roughly dragging it back. The kitten began meowing insistently. As it squirmed, trying to escape, the man slapped its head. He then pinned the kitten down, rubbing its whole body so forcefully that the word "petting" didn't apply. He held it upside down and slapped its face again. The kitten bared its claws. The man grabbed its front legs and twisted them.

"What the hell is this?!" Shigeki said.

"It's an animal snuff film," replied Yohei, who had come over to where we were, book in his hands. "They torture young animals, puppies, kittens, and then they kill them."

"Are you serious? That's sick," Shigeki said. "Shall I stop it?"

None of the three women answered. We were too intent on what we were seeing. The bullying of the kitten on the screen was becoming more intense. It was horrible. I couldn't imagine anything more horrible; I couldn't believe what I was seeing. But I was so scared I couldn't move. I had no desire to watch, but I couldn't tear my eyes away. I was trapped in a nightmare.

Shigeki stood up. "I'm not watching this. I don't know how you three have the stomach for it."

Maybe he was right—maybe we did. But it wasn't that we didn't feel anything. My heart was pounding like crazy; greasy sweat was oozing out over my body. I felt total sympathy with the kitten. Had I seen something like this before—ages ago, when I was extremely young—seen a tiny, helpless creature tormented and killed just like this kitten? Or was it a dream I'd had? It didn't matter. My body was paralyzed by the distress and terror that came over me.

"What happened? Hey, what's going on!" Shunji shouted, shaking me.

But I couldn't speak. On screen, a scalpel gleamed. A moment later the scalpel glistened with blood.

Aiko got up and walked over to Yohei. "What's the point? Is the kitten a symbol for women?"

"No. He just likes killing the cat."

"He's crazy."

"Obviously."

The film continued for another ten minutes after the kitten stopped twitching. The man did things to the corpse; I can't bring myself to say what. It was a film of pure, unadulterated cruelty; there wasn't even a scene of the man masturbating. I could barely breathe when the screen went black. Eiko, who had also watched to the end of the movie, looked at me, her face pale, frozen.

Once again the screen brightened. This time it was a cute puppy. Eiko and I exchanged glances. "I've had enough," I said, Eiko nodded, and we turned off the player.

"You should skip the second part but watch the third," said Yohei. "In part 3 he kills a baby panda. But since you can't get your hands on a real baby panda, it's done as a cartoon. It's pretty funny. It's *so* terrible. What a bunch of idiots."

Eiko and I didn't have enough energy to laugh. Shigeki, who was sitting on the sofa bed, turned toward us. "You watched it even though you didn't want to? Why didn't you turn it off?"

"I don't know," Eiko said, almost whispering, then got up and walked shakily toward the bathroom.

I kept sitting there, dazed.

"I hate girls who start shrieking and blubbering when they see a movie like that," Yohei suddenly said, breaking the silence. "I like women who can keep their cool, even if it's only on the surface. Kazumi, I really think you're one hell of a woman."

I stared at him, rather stunned. I couldn't recall anyone ever telling me I was "one hell of a woman" before.

Yohei felt my eyes on him, and sighed. "But I guess it doesn't mean anything to be told that by a guy like me, huh?"

"Oh, it does! I'm thrilled!" I was thrown into such confusion that I nearly stuttered. "It's just that flattery like that doesn't often—"

"That was flattery?" Shunji interjected. "I don't think that was flattery. I mean, you've got one hell of a voice, right? Of course, I can't comment on your looks."

Being praised by my own fiancé in front of everyone made me more embarrassed. "I'm ugly!" I cried. "I am very ugly!"

"Oh, you're ugly?" Shunji, who had not picked up on my self-consciousness, turned toward Yohei and the others in the room. "Is that true? Is Kazumi ugly?"

"Would you stop it!" I said, wrapping my arms around Shunji's shoulders.

Aiko tried to stifle her laughter. "Kazumi isn't ugly—not by a long shot."

This generous evaluation did nothing to ease my embarrassment. Shunji seemed like he was about to say something ridiculous again, so I hugged him more tightly. Finding this funny, he tumbled onto the floor, taking me with him. He didn't mean any harm, but I find it even more mortifying when lovers horse around in public than when they talk baby talk. I tried to get up, but one of my arms was pinned under his body, making it impossible for me to move, so I had no choice but to give up trying to flee.

"I always wished I could fool around like that with a woman," Yohei said.

"Why don't you?" said Shigeki. "You have every opportunity, don't you, Yohei? You've got a girlfriend."

"I meant when I was young. By the time you turn thirty-three, you don't have the energy anymore, either physically or mentally, to fool around like a kid. And I never had a woman when I was young. You know that stupid monkey-play we did last night? I used to be like that. I really did hate young women."

"Because you didn't have a girlfriend?" Aiko asked.

"Yeah. Of course, now it seems like a joke. I'd wanted a woman really bad for a long time, and after all sorts of ordeals, when I finally managed to get close to a girl and we were spending our first night together, she was so shocked when she saw my physical condition that she suffered a seizure of the vagina. I could see how she could be shocked, but I despised her for it. She didn't have to act *that* horrified. I was really pissed off. So I started to go for older women who had been working in the baths, who had seen all different kinds of men's bodies and knew how to hide their surprise and disgust, and to hate girls who shrieked over the tiniest little thing. Of course, now I'm crazy about young women, too."

Shigeki and Aiko seemed unsure how to respond to Yohei's depressing story. Shunji, however, had no problem, singing out cheerfully from where he lay on the floor, "You should have had a blind girlfriend! She wouldn't have been shocked, because she wouldn't be able to see you."

My arm was stuck under Shunji, but I had stopped trying to yank it out. I wasn't sure how Yohei would respond to Shunji's blithe naïveté.

There were a few seconds of silence, and then he said simply, "You know, that never occurred to me." Then, his tone very gentle, he continued. "At the same time, I would kind have wanted her to see me. If she's going to be my girlfriend, I mean. You may not believe this, but I think that even more than a man who looks normal and has a normal body, I want people to see all of me—everything about me."

"All right," Shunji said, "then let me feel you."

Yohei took a breath, then replied, "Okay."

Shunji got up and crawled over toward Yohei. Yohei reached out and drew Shunji near. Shunji knelt in front of Yohei and began stroking his face, caressing the hanging folds of flesh. Yohei's eyelids drooped. Shunji ran his fingers across Yohei's skin, his touch as soft as if he were grooming an animal. Shigeki and Aiko watched, entranced.

When Shunji had felt his whole face, he said, "I understand."

And then, the very next moment, Shunji made one of those delicately expressive gestures that always touched me so profoundly. He took Yohei's face in between his hands and softly rubbed cheeks with him. Yohei peered over Shunji's shoulder at me, a look of bewilderment on his face. Then he closed his eyes and put his arms around Shunji. He was smiling.

We were sitting quietly like this when the door opened and Tamotsu hollered, "We're home!" It was the three of them, back from the wrestling matches. Tamotsu stormed into the living room, feet thumping across the floor, his gaze lighting on one person after another. When he got to me, sitting alone near the chest of drawers, he charged over, screaming "Steal back the phallus!" Then, pulling open a drawer, he withdrew something and shoved it in my face.

It was a dildo, which made me laugh out loud. Tamotsu's cheeks broke into a smile, too; he held the dildo up and made like he was jerking it off.

"Come to think of it, you don't need one of these," he said. "You've already got one!"

Eiko, emerging from the bathroom, glowered at Tamotsu. "What are you doing with that thing?"

"I just stole back the phallus."

"That awful Tamotsu tricked us!" Yukie was telling Aiko on the side. "I only went with them because he said we were going to see pro wrestling. Then we get there and find out that it's *women's* pro wrestling!"

"What's wrong with that!" Tamotsu shouted. "That's the good part!"

"I was looking forward to some hard, brawny male bodies."

This riposte caused Masami to sing out in a falsetto, "Oh, I must *say*— can an old lady like you *still* be interested in *men*? What a *lech* you are."

"And you? You enjoyed seeing those women's bodies?"

"Oh, yes, little *me*. I still have the tender heart of a little girl, you see. I get stars in my eyes when I see a charming lady—a lady I can look up to," he mocked, then threw himself down beside Yohei and opened the souvenir program he had brought back.

"Forty-one years old and you're a little girl?" Yukie said to his back, spitting out the words.

"Oh, I'm not *really* a little girl, no. More like a *young miss*," Masami replied, perfectly composed. "As a matter of fact, our *young miss* is very fond of one of these *young women* here in this program. If I were a little boy, I'm sure I'd want to make her my little 'cougar,' if that's the word. Oh *look*, here she *is*!"

Pointing at the open program, Masami gave Yohei a little poke. Yohei didn't seem interested, but he obligingly peered down at the page and said, in a bored tone, "Oh? Is that her?"

"Which one?" Tamotsu asked, standing up and walking over with the dildo still in his hand. I followed, too, curious to see what sort of woman was to Masami's taste. It was a woman wrestler with short hair and the face of a feisty, intrepid young boy.

"Too scrawny," Tamotsu said. "I like that heavyweight there."

"Well, *I* like this little girl. If I had someone as sweet as her, I might consider becoming a lesbian."

"I'd like to be crushed by the heavyweight," Tamotsu said, brandishing the dildo.

"Oh *my*, what a nice *thing* you have there," Masami said, noticing it for the first time.

"Put it away, will you?" Yohei swatted at it with one hand. "It's getting on my nerves."

"I go to all the trouble to steal it back, and you want me to put it away? Can it be!" Tamotsu went on in high camp. "Perhaps it gets on your nerves, Yohei, but I want a phallus of my own. No one here understands this deep desire of mine, I know. Masami willingly threw away the very thing I desperately crave, Kazumi has an extra one which she has no need for . . ."

"We get the point," Yohei said.

But Tamotsu didn't stop. "In my eyes, even a counterfeit like this is a treasure. After all, I've got to use one of these to make Eiko happy."

Oh boy, that's not a good thing to say, I worried, expecting discord. Eiko rushed over to Tamotsu, snatched the dildo out of this hand, and then smacked the head of the dildo against his forehead. My mouth fell open. Masami whistled. Aiko clapped. Tamotsu reeled, tottered, then collapsed on his butt and flopped down on his back. Eiko chucked the dildo into the drawer and slammed it shut.

Clutching his head, Tamotsu shouted, "Everyone, you have witnessed what just happened. You saw this woman's true colors? She acts meek in public, but in private she assaults me."

"Ah, so you're *m*?" Masami said. "I had no *idea.*"

"Who would have thought we'd still be watching pro wrestling when we got home." This came from Yukie.

Aiko: "Now I see. You pester us because you *want* to be hit."

Shunji, matter-of-factly: "Why do you want to be hit?"

Shigeki: "*That* (pause) is how some people love."

Tamotsu, now somewhat embarrassed, covered his face with his hands. Aiko had once said that he was cute, and she was right. He was very cute tonight. Maybe his sadistic and masochistic tendencies only surfaced when he became overly dependent on Eiko. Eiko, meanwhile, had retreated and was sitting morosely on the sofa bed. Babysitting Tamotsu must be quite a chore.

"That guy who wrote the play last night—" Tamotsu started, lifting his head, "he thinks I'm the bully. He thinks it's completely one-sided."

"Exactly. That's why he likes you," said Aiko coolly. "He loves that scenario: the woman who takes everything that a brutal man does to her, devoting herself wholeheartedly to him in return. That's why he hates me, a sentiment I reciprocate. He thinks I'm a cripple because I can't accept a man's advances."

"It's so depressing, talking about obnoxious people like that," Shigeki muttered.

I turned to Yohei, who was next to me. "That director guy's all wrong about you, too, right?"

Yohei looked up slowly. "That's okay, though. Let him be wrong."

"Doesn't it make you mad?" I said, with more feeling than I'd intended.

"Does it make *you* mad?" Yohei chuckled. "It's not that I don't think it's unfair . . . I have another reason for not telling him I have a girlfriend. It's because hearing the truth would be good for him. I don't want to do anything that might benefit him, so I just keep my mouth shut. I don't tell him anything, and I act as if I'm completely subservient—but at the same time I'm laughing up my sleeve. It's my way of having fun, you see."

I was stunned. "I didn't realize you were so . . . *devious*. I mean . . . don't take that the wrong way."

"I understand," Yohei laughed. "I think I have a pretty good idea of your personality."

I laughed, too.

"Yukie, Masami—aren't you getting hungry?" Tamotsu yelled out. "The fried noodles at the arena weren't enough. I'm starving."

"There's miso soup with pork and veggies in the pot," Yohei said. "Why don't you have the rest of that?"

"I think I will, thank you. You made it yourself?"

Masami leaped to his feet and ran into the kitchen. I heard the click of the stove being turned on. It was a late-night snack, and suddenly everyone seemed a bit tired, because they didn't speak much anymore. Maybe the Flower Show was back to normal—its usual cool relationships. I felt a bit sad that our little moment of togetherness had passed, but my heart still swelled from the fun we'd had.

As the scent of the hot soup came wafting into the room, I realized I was hungry, too. I decided to join the banquet. Masami and Eiko passed bowls and chopsticks around. Eiko served Tamotsu last. His lips twisted into his usual expression—the sheepish smile of the embarrassed leader of a gang of rascals. Eiko smiled faintly in return and nestled up to him.

The soup was delicious. "It's not only painting you're good at," I said to Yohei. He seemed perplexed, so I explained, "The soup is great, and I think the flowers on the bus are terrific, too."

Finally I had been able to tell him what I had been thinking since the first day of our trip.

Yohei glanced down shyly for a moment, then lifted his head, a happy, friendly look in his eyes.

Chapter 9

At some point during our week at the apartment in Kobe, I learned that Yukie had a boyfriend who was seven years her junior. Yukie was fifty-two, so he would be forty-five. At that age he should have been rising in his career, but the word was he had no steady job and squandered Yukie's earnings on pachinko, the horses, and the stock market. He was, it would seem, a sort of "pimp." Hard as it was to believe, considering that he was the lover of a woman with teeth in her vagina, he didn't have a steel penis; he was just a normally built man.

Almost every evening, Yukie called him. In Kobe, in the middle of a conversation she would get up suddenly, go over to the phone in the corner of the living room, and dial her number. One night her boyfriend wasn't answering, so she kept hanging up and then picking up and dialing, over and over, looking up at the clock on the wall.

"He's taking a shower!" Masami called out, teasing. He was playing on the excuse husbands always make in movies when they're having an affair and miss a call from the wife.

Yukie turned in Masami's direction, the usual dazzled expression on her face.

"Men," Masami sighed. His tone was listless, though there was a smile on his lips. "They're simply *hopeless*, aren't they? When the wives are away, they get so hung up on cleanliness."

"Why don't you put a phone in the bathroom?" suggested Tamotsu, not entirely seriously.

"He'd leave if you did something like that," Eiko said. "Even if his conscience is clear, it'd seem like you were monitoring him."

"That isn't all," said Masami. "If you *actually* put a phone in the bathroom and he stopped being able to use the shower excuse, it'd be just *awful* for the woman. You'd be afraid to call because you knew that if he didn't answer he *really* wasn't at home. Yes, *darling*, that's how we women work. Bless our tender little hearts."

"Read that in a magazine?" Tamotsu asked, a little sarcastically.

"Can it," barked Masami.

"On the other hand," I said, jumping into the conversation, "a man has an infinite number of excuses for not being at home. He could have stepped out for cigarettes or gone out for a drink."

Masami frowned. "My dear, you just don't get it. Really, you're as bad as Tamotsu! Haven't you ever thought your man was seeing someone else?"

Before I could tell him that I had, of course, Yukie interjected. "She's the type who wouldn't notice even if he were."

"Am I?" I was stupefied.

"You'd be so completely clueless, I bet the guy would have to start dropping hints, like 'What would you do if I had an affair?'"

Masami, Yohei, and Shigeki all chuckled. I didn't see what was so funny. Were they empathizing with the poor hypothetical man who was forced to clue me in about his affair? I found this terribly offensive. True, I wasn't the sort of person who'd get uptight just because my boyfriend was having a fling, but I wasn't so dopey as to have complete confidence in a man's faithfulness. All I cared about was our relationship, and if an affair didn't affect it, I wasn't going to worry, because once you start worrying about these little infidelities, there's no end to it.

That said, Yukie's critique wasn't completely off the mark: Masao had, in fact, once hinted that he was having an affair. This made it pretty hard for me to complain to the group. Besides, what was the point of arguing whether I was or was not the type to notice that my boyfriend was having an affair when I had so little experience being in love—and had no idea what it was like to agonize over a lover's faithlessness.

"Don't let it bother you," Masami said, stretching out an arm and patting my head.

Shocked that I was being treated like a child, I decided to drop the whole issue. And then Yukie left the apartment, wallet in hand.

Masami smirked. "She doesn't want us all to know he isn't picking up, so she's going to call him from a phone outside. She's such a *cutie-pie*, don't you think?"

"It's because you tease her so," Aiko sighed. "Poor thing."

The next day, in Hiroshima, we were back to our separate hotel lives, each of us keeping pretty much to his or her own. But to the extent that we felt closer to each other after a week together in the Kobe apartment, our travels had become more enjoyable.

Our days were always pretty wild, though, as Tamotsu started spending time with Shunji and me. He had more energy than his tantrums with Eiko and shouting matches with Masami could use up. He was an odd duck for sure.

One night, somewhere in Kyushu, we stayed at a hotel in an area famous for its hot springs. Each room had a private outdoor bath, so Shunji and I lost no time getting into the hot water after we got back from the show. The bath was at the base of a large rock formation that bordered our patio, and since there was nothing around but rocks and the mountain beyond, we didn't worry about being seen. Once Shunji had lowered himself into the hot water, he rested his cheek against the rough surface of the rock at the edge. Soaking in the water, I closed my eyes and inhaled the scent of the greenery and earth around us.

As we were relaxing in the bath, Tamotsu climbed over the rock formation from his and Eiko's room, which was next door. He was butt naked. I was used to seeing him without clothes, so I wasn't shocked, but I was struck speechless when he walked right over and jumped into our bath. It wasn't very large, so his legs knocked up against mine. I shrank back, crossing my arms over my breasts.

"You're embarrassed?" Tamotsu cried gleefully.

"Of course." I kept my gaze trained on his face.

He remained utterly blasé. "You're so unfair," he said, knocking my leg with his knee. "You see me naked all the time, but you hide your own body."

He had hit a sore spot. I was feeling odd traveling around with the

Flower Show without participating myself. I'd come to feel a bit closer to the troupe's members, but I was keenly aware of the fact that they didn't view me as a full-fledged member. Tamotsu was trying, in his own way, to narrow the gap between us. I understood that. I was glad that he had reached out to me, while everyone else maintained an adult reserve. Lowering my hands and uncovering my breasts, I let my body relax. My legs were squashed against Tamotsu's; the hair on his legs tickled my shins.

He turned his eyes away from me. "Hey, Shunji!" he said. "Are you embarrassed, too?"

"No, not really . . . ," Shunji murmured sleepily. "But I think it's kind of unfair of you looking at me naked when I can't see you."

"Good point. Very unfair." Tamotsu slid forward a step and a half, positioning himself directly in front of Shunji. "Here, give me a physical."

Now *this* was embarrassing. "You want to play doctor?" I asked.

"No," Tamotsu said, wheeling back around. "How else is he going to 'see' me?"

"You know, I've never really understood this business about being embarrassed or ashamed," Shunji announced, paying no attention to the exchange between Tamotsu and me. "My teacher at the School for the Blind tried to drum shame into us—it's shameful to be naked and all that—but he never explained why. It was just shameful, shameful, shameful. Of course, if somebody tells you something over and over, you start to think it's true. But what is it really like? What does it feel like, being embarrassed?"

Tamotsu's expression turned very serious, almost meditative. "When you're embarrassed," he said, "blood rushes to your face. That makes your blood vessels expand, and then your face gets itchy. You get flushed and your face starts to feel hot. And if you look in a mirror, your face is red."

Tamotsu's earnestness seemed kind of funny.

"I wonder if that's ever happened to me. When I was a kid, I thought the feeling I got when I wasn't wearing any clothes was embarrassment, because they told us that naked people got embarrassed. So for the longest time I thought when people got embarrassed they felt chilly."

Tamotsu and I laughed, our legs jostling together. Soaking in the bath and talking with these two guys, I completely forgot my embarrassment.

When I was a kid, when my uncles and aunts got together, I used to be put in the bath with other children, and this was kind of like that—Tamotsu, Shunji, and I were like kids who had been rounded up and tossed into the water by the adults. It used to thrill me, getting into the bath with my cousins; it was so much fun pouring water over each other's heads and making bubbles, playing as much as we wanted without picky, annoying adults around. I felt now just how I had back then.

Tamotsu groped along the bottom of the bath until he found the toes of my left foot. Startled, I pulled my foot away and stepped on his hand, pinning it down. "What are you doing?" I said.

"I thought I'd say hello to this famous toe-penis of yours."

"The penis is on my right foot. You've got the wrong one."

"Oops."

Tamotsu now started to reach down with his other hand. I twisted around and grabbed it. I wasn't exactly *embarrassed* at the thought of him feeling my toe-penis, but I felt an urge to protect it.

"What's wrong? I just want to touch it. Don't be such a prig."

Jerking his shoulders back and forth like a peevish child, Tamotsu pressed closer. I was amused by his use of "prig" and giggled. This seemed to encourage him, and he yanked his hand out from under my foot and started to reach for my right foot more boldly. We were tussling like this when, all of a sudden, Tamotsu shrieked and slapped the surface of the water. Shunji had reached out and grabbed his lower stomach.

"That hurts!" Tamotsu cried.

Shunji let go.

Tamotsu looked at me, hurt in his eyes. "He twisted my stomach skin!"

I must have been feeling manic, because the words "stomach skin" just made me laugh out loud.

"Sorry," Shunji said softly, sounding sincere. "I didn't mean to hurt you. You were moving."

"I won't move now. Go ahead and touch me," Tamotsu said, turning to Shunji.

Ever so slowly, Shunji moved his hand toward Tamotsu. "I touched Shin before, right?" he asked.

"Yeah. Here, this is mine."

I couldn't see what was going on because Tamotsu's thighs were in the way, but Tamotsu seemed to have guided Shunji's hand to his own penis. His penis . . . which I hadn't even gotten a good look at myself, which was evidently hidden down there in the shadow of Shin's, with only its tip protruding.

"You don't have any testicles?" Shunji said.

"They're inside my body," Tamotsu replied as he reached down and placed his hand on Shunji's crotch. Shunji paid no attention to this, and went on touching Tamotsu. Two naked men touching each other's genitals—it was odd to see, but there was nothing sexual about it, so I didn't feel like I had to look away. Tamotsu, who seemed to have no homosexual leanings at all, didn't remove his hand from Shunji's crotch, and turning toward me, he confided, "You know, I always dreamed about doing this. Guys in junior high and high school do this a lot—grab each other's things, just fooling around. But I never could. Sometimes a guy would make a grab for me, and I'd struggle to get away, frantic. If someone ever did touch me, they'd know I was a freak. I never went on any class trips or camping or anything either. All the boys bathe together, and I didn't want them to see me, so I never went. That's why sitting here in this bath with you two makes me so happy."

It was heartbreaking to hear this.

Suddenly Tamotsu grinned. "So you have to let me touch yours, too!" He sprang into action almost before he'd finished the sentence. A giant spray of water hit me in the face, and by the time I opened my eyes, the big toe on my right foot was cradled in the palm of Tamotsu's hand. "Fast, aren't I?" he said, and winked.

But then, his face lost its mischievous expression. His lips, which had curved up slyly, opened to form an o; he started to blink. My own expression must have changed as well. Tamotsu and I froze, face to face, grimacing. All was still, except for one part of my body.

"What the—" Tamotsu mumbled. "Did this happen because I touched it?"

"Not because *you* touched, no, it's just—"

I was so unnerved I didn't know what to say. True, in the early days, after it first appeared, my toe-penis would react to the slightest stimulation. But now that Shunji and I were together, it had matured. It wasn't supposed to get hard every time it was touched.

"Kazumi's thing gets turned on kind of easily," Shunji said.

Come to think of getting turned on, Shunji and I hadn't had sex in a while. We had been together every day since we started touring, but this new life and all the travel seemed to have pushed sex from our minds.

Tamotsu released my toe-penis, which continued to grow quietly larger, down at the bottom of the bath.

"Are you in the mood?" Shunji asked, reaching toward me.

I hurriedly held him off. I felt a flicker of desire, I had to admit, but I wasn't about to have sex in front of Tamotsu. There could be few things more "embarrassing" than that.

"Hey, go right ahead," Tamotsu piped up. "I don't mind."

"No thanks," I said.

"It's not healthy to suppress urges, you know."

"Just because I have an erection doesn't mean I want sex."

"Huh? It doesn't?" Tamotsu said, cocking his head. "Actually, I guess you're right. Sometimes Shin's thing goes limp right after it gets hard. I guess a penis can get hard if it's stimulated, but it won't stay that way unless its owner is turned on."

As Tamotsu waxed philosophical, my toe-penis was losing its erection, returning to normal. And when he pulled my leg up to see it, he moaned, "Oh no! What a waste!" Once again he grabbed hold of my toe-penis. He must have put more feeling into it, because I didn't have to see my member to know it wasn't drooping anymore. In fact, it was rising up rather vigorously. Before I could say anything, Tamotsu said, "Let me see it get really hard. That's what the guys did in junior high—show each their biggest hard-ons." Tamotsu seemed quite serious, no ulterior motives.

"Can you stop massaging it like that?" I asked. I didn't want to be drawn into an upsurge of desire.

Tamotsu loosened his grip until he was just holding my toe-penis. The feel of his hand there, gently touching me, was not unpleasant. A sense of comfort came over my toe-penis—nothing deep enough to keep me aroused, just enough that I could push it from my consciousness if I wanted to. We weren't doing anything sexual after all, only enjoying touching each other's skin, like two good friends holding hands. That's how it felt.

"Do you want to touch mine?" Tamotsu asked.

I wouldn't have, but I had started feeling like those guys in junior high. In some corner of my mind, I wondered whether women in general were in the habit of touching their male friends' genitals so easily, but in the world of the bath I was inhabiting—in the world of Tamotsu, Shunji, and me—this sort of physicality felt perfectly natural.

First I placed my hand on Shin's penis. It was small, the tip still hidden by the prepuce, as if not fully mature. Apparently it didn't ejaculate or urinate; its only function as an organ was to get hard.

"It's below that," Tamotsu said, taking my hand in his—the one that wasn't holding my toe-penis. As my fingers slid under the bottom of the fleshy bulge of Tamotsu's stomach, in which the upper half of Shin's body was buried, my fingertips brushed against something smooth that must have been the head of Tamotsu's penis. Moving my fingers up halfway along the head, I found the prepuce. The bulge was slightly more than an inch long. It seemed that little more than the head of the penis was outside his body. And Shin's body seemed to be pressing against it, because the head stuck out at a peculiar angle.

As we touched each other, Tamotsu got talkative. "It's strange," he began, "there's a part of me that doesn't want anyone to know I was born like this, but there's a part of me that, when I get to be really good friends with someone, wants them to know everything. It's not like I want people to understand—no, I don't need them to understand. I can't explain it, but somehow I hate always hiding it from people."

"Have you touched Shigeki and Yohei, too?" I asked.

"Nah. They're too . . ." Tamotsu smiled a little bitterly. "They're too . . . mature, stiff? I don't know, they kind of seem that way to me."

"The way they think, you mean?"

"Yeah, their minds. They're good guys, and I like them. But I don't feel like we can fool around with each other the way the three of us are now."

While we sat talking, Eiko could be heard calling for Tamotsu. She was standing on top of the rock formation that divided our bath from theirs, wearing a light cotton kimono provided by the hotel. Tamotsu arched his head back and waved energetically, beckoning her over. Lifting the hem of her kimono, Eiko picked her way down the rocks.

"So this is where you were!" she said to Tamotsu.

"Yep. Where were you?"

"Looking for you, obviously," Eiko answered tartly, but she seemed embarrassed, since Shunji and I were naked, and stared at her feet.

"Well, you sure took long enough to find me." Despite his recently acquired reputation as a closet masochist, Tamotsu could not bring himself to be pleasant to Eiko.

"Couldn't you have told me you were coming over here?"

"You would have stopped me if I had, right?"

"You shouldn't be pestering them."

Tamotsu looked at Shunji and me. "Was I pestering you?"

"No," Shunji and I said in unison, shaking our heads.

Tamotsu gave Eiko the thumbs up sign.

"But, Tamotsu, you shouldn't make Eiko worry," I added, throwing a lifeline to Eiko.

Tamotsu stood up and bowed. "I deeply apologize, Eiko. I shouldn't have left you alone like that. Here, come on in." He leaped out of the bath and tried to pull Eiko into the water.

She dug her feet into the ground and screamed, "What are you doing!"

"I feel bad about leaving you out of the group, so I thought I'd be nice and put you in!"

"Stop it!"

Dashing around Eiko as she tried to shake him off, Tamotsu shoved her toward the water. Eiko wasn't smiling. Personally, I thought it would be fun to have her join us—she was a woman, and it's perfectly natural for women to bathe together in hot springs. But when I saw her resisting, her face reddening, I called out to Tamotsu to stop. He didn't seem to hear, and the next moment he was dragging Eiko by her kimono into the bath.

Ultimately, Eiko ended up in the water still wearing her kimono. She sat there, water up to her shoulders, frowning.

"C'mon, take it off," Tamotsu said, tugging at the kimono.

"It doesn't matter. I'm wet now."

"You're not embarrassed being the only one in clothes?"

"Of course I'm embarrassed."

"Then take it off."

"You *want* to embarrass me, right? Shouldn't you just leave me alone?"

"Did you hear that! What can you do with such a stubborn person?" Tamotsu turned to Shunji and me. "You can guess what's going to happen later. She's going to smack me as soon as we're alone."

"I'll smack you right now, Tamotsu," Eiko said, and her hand caromed off Tamotsu's cheek. But because he was sitting next to her, she couldn't really slap him properly. Still, Tamotsu rubbed the place where she hit him as if it hurt.

"Wow, I just got Zamboni-ed."

Zamboni-ed? . . . Some kind of wrestling term, maybe?

Now that she had smacked Tamotsu, Eiko stood up, stripped off her kimono, and threw it onto the ground. She wasn't wearing underwear. She turned to me as she sat back down in the water, a shy smile on her face. "It's hard work being with a brat like this."

"I bet," I said.

"Terrible, terrible," Tamotsu grumbled, looking like he was having fun. "Kazumi showed me her toe-penis earlier, you know."

"Did she?" Eiko glanced at me, then asked hesitantly, "Can I see, too?"

How could I say no when I saw her naked and having sex all the time? I stuck out my toe-penis, which had gone back to its unerect form.

Maybe when people see something unusual they instinctively want to touch it. Because that's what Eiko did. It didn't occur to me that she would, though, so when she reached out her hand and touched it, I was startled. Needless to say, my toe began swelling.

Eiko showed no surprise. Instead, she murmured, "Oh my!" and smiled. She stroked the length of the stiffening organ, fondling it. I pulled my leg back, but the bath was narrow, and with the four of us in it I couldn't get it out of her reach. I panicked and tried to stand up, my hand on Shunji's shoulder. But by then it was too late: my toe-penis, numb with pleasure, was getting bigger and harder. Shunji supported me as I seemed to lose strength.

"Did I do something I shouldn't have?" Eiko asked, puzzled, not having meant any harm.

"Apparently her toe-penis is easily aroused," Tamotsu said.

"I don't think it's anything to be embarrassed about, do you?" Eiko said.

"I wish one of those would sprout on me somewhere," Tamotsu replied cheerily.

I found this jolly exchange between Tamotsu and Eiko at my expense irritating, but I was also struggling to repress the pleasure that had taken hold of me as a result of that little massage. But the more I struggled to repress it, the greater were the lingering waves of sensation. Unable to bear it any longer, I clutched Shunji's shoulder, and said, "Let's get out." I clambered to my feet.

"Hey," Tamotsu said, his eyes gleaming, "I just had a great idea."

He stood up, corralled Shunji and me, and sat us down at the edge of the bath. Then he grabbed my right foot, turned his back to us, and stuck my foot between his thighs. From the front of his body, you could see my erect toe-penis poking out, looking just like a normal penis. Tamotsu was in very high spirits now. "This is great!" he crowed. "Kazumi and I need to combine forces!"

"Stop it, Tamotsu," Eiko said.

I couldn't bear this any longer. I stood up on my left leg and tapped Tamotsu on the shoulder. "Don't use my body as a toy, please." I tried to pull my right leg out from between his thighs. But suddenly I felt dizzy, and everything became dim. I had gotten a bit lightheaded from being in the hot water so long, and now with blood flowing into my toe-penis, I seemed to be having an anemic attack. My hand slipped off Tamotsu's shoulder. Sensing that something was wrong, he released my foot, and I tried to steady myself. But my legs grew wobbly, and the next thing I knew I had fainted . . .

♥ ♥ ♥

Tamotsu would be fooling around one minute and then turn serious the next, and as soon as you had gotten used to his seriousness he would launch into some ridiculous game. He would tie you in knots if you tried to go along with every shift in his mood, and you would end up completely exhausted. The day after I fainted, he came to see me looking somewhat abashed, offering to let me use his treasured portable game system. Presumably this was his way of saying he was sorry, but when he saw I wasn't angry, he started teasing me. "Just so you know, I did you a favor and let your toe-penis have what it wanted while you were unconscious." He laughed hilariously when I took him seriously and flew into a tizzy. He also said: "Next time, let's *really* join forces and give Eiko a good time."

Eiko came to see me later, looking worried. "Do you hate Tamotsu now?" she asked.

"No. I've never really hated anyone," I said. "Not enough to not want to see them again, anyway."

"Yes, I can tell you're like that. Tamotsu's very smart that way; he detects goodness in people and takes advantage of it, makes himself dependent on them."

I couldn't suppress a smile. "Well, he's taking the most advantage of you, wouldn't you say?"

Eiko struck me as a pretty unusual woman, too. She seemed ordinary at first, but she had strong opinions and was pretty brassy. She seemed to have more common sense than Tamotsu, but there was a part of her that didn't let itself be held back by common sense, just like him. I was totally charmed by the fact that she got along so well with Tamotsu, difficult as he was, and that she even worried whether I might dislike him, and came by to ask. Her face, too, seemed ordinary at first glance, but turned out to be quite striking: there was a nice upward tilt at the edge of her eyes, and her lips were nicely shaped. I hadn't noticed either until our dip in the bath.

Tamotsu hadn't known about Eiko's private visit to me, and he must have been feeling a little insecure when he asked me one day in the bus, out of the blue, "Who do you like best in the Flower Show?"

Was there an answer he wanted to hear? Why should he even be thinking about something like that? "No one, really," I answered vaguely. "I like everyone."

Tamotsu shook his head at this. "Man, are you boring."

"Yes, aren't I?" I said with a snicker, mimicking Tamotsu.

At any rate, our travels continued, and I was having fun. We finished making the rounds of Kyushu and headed up northeast for our second visit to Hakone. By then it was September.

♥ ♥ ♥

One morning, as I woke up and flipped back the blanket to get out of bed, I noticed that Shunji's penis, inside his boxers, was erect. Shunji was breathing deeply, sound asleep. I had never seen his penis get hard on its own before, without being touched. In the light that pushed invasively through the weave of the curtain, this mark of Shunji's vigor seemed almost like a dream.

It wasn't until the night in the bath with Tamotsu that I realized that Shunji and I hadn't had sex once since we set out on this tour. That was several days ago, and we were still in this sexless state. The night of the bath there had been no question of having sex because I fainted, and the next few days Shunji had been so busy writing music for jobs he had gotten over the phone that once again we forgot about sex. So it was no surprise that Shunji should be having this unprompted erection.

After more than twenty days without any sex, I still didn't feel an urgent need for it. Shunji was always there beside me, and every day was a lot of fun, even if we weren't making love. Shunji didn't appear to be overwhelmed by desire either, since he hadn't initiated anything and seemed to be none the worse for it. Except that he was a man, of course, so it was probably about time for him to release some sperm.

Though I wasn't aching with desire, I did start looking back on the sexual act with nostalgia. I certainly wasn't averse to sex—maybe it would be nice to do it, at least a little. Now that I had started feeling the urge, I would have to act on it, or I would forget again. True, it wouldn't inconvenience me if I did forget, but it also seemed like a big waste to forget it so completely, for so long. Gradually, desire began to well up inside me.

I stretched my hand toward Shunji's crotch, but stopped myself. I recalled how awful it was when Chisato impaled herself on my toe-penis while I was asleep. I doubted Shunji would get mad at me for touching his penis while he slept, but the specter of Chisato stayed with me. I withdrew my hand. Shunji was fast asleep, ignorant of everything. I thought about waking him up, but I didn't want to rouse him from such a sound sleep.

Making use of someone's genitals when that person is asleep counted, I had been told, as quasi rape, but would it be okay if it were just a hand? I placed my hand over Shunji's, whose arm lay stretched out haphazardly on the bed. His hand didn't so much as twitch, and as I looked at it lying there utterly defenseless, at that same random angle, I began to see it as something pristine and vulnerable. I took my hand away. Maybe I wouldn't feel this tenderness for the sleeping Shunji if different parts of our bodies had come in contact—his foot and my face, for example. I went down to the bottom of the bed and tried aligning my face with the sole of his foot. This time I didn't feel like I was abusing him, but the bizarreness of the act made me feel dirty. I concluded that it was obscene to perform one-sided sexual acts with a sleeping person.

I would just have to wait for Shunji to wake up. I sat back up on the bed. His penis was still pointing at the ceiling. An erection was a cyclical biological phenomenon, true, but maybe this erection was accompanied by a sexual dream, or had been brought on by some other sort of stimulation. My toe-penis didn't ejaculate, so I had no knowledge of the mechanism that activates the penis. What was Shunji dreaming? Was he feeling pleasure in his sleep?

As I imagined the pleasure Shunji might be enjoying, I unconsciously wrapped my hand around my own penis. The sensation of holding my toe-penis merged with my memory of how Shunji's penis had felt in my hand. And an urge came over me to pleasure my toe-penis and his penis at the same time. My toe-penis and his penis had melded in my mind. So all I had to do to satisfy my rising desire was to stroke my toe-penis.

Presumably the desire I had felt earlier, when I started wanting sex, was that of a normal woman—the vagina's desire. At some point, without my knowing, that feeling had been replaced with my toe-penis's desire. This struck me as weird, but since I was a weird woman, I saw no need to get hung up on little logical niceties. I got off the bed and went into the bathroom; the shaking of the bed as I jerked off would surely wake Shunji up.

My toe-penis was already stiffening in anticipation of the pleasure it would soon feel. I sat down on the lid of the toilet and squeezed my toe-penis. An exhilarating shiver of pleasure ran through it. All I had to do now was move my fist mechanically up and down and abandon myself to the sensations . . . or so I thought, until something unexpected happened. As my toe-penis began responding to my touch, memories of that night in the outdoor bath bobbed up in my mind, making my toe-penis tingle sweetly. And at the center of that memory was the caress Eiko had given my penis.

Though I was surprised, I didn't stop my hand, because my yearning to feel this pleasure was more powerful than my confusion. As the feeling crested, I reflected hazily on Eiko's touch—it had felt good, no denying that, as good as this feeling right now. An image of Eiko's delicate, womanly hand came to mind. Then I found myself remembering other scenes with that same hand: Eiko seizing the dildo and whacking Tamotsu on his forehead, smacking Tamotsu's cheek in the hot spring, her hand wrapping itself around Shin's penis during the Flower Show . . . and the pleasure I felt rose to another level. By the time I started to wonder why I was calling up all these images, it was too late to stop. I had almost reached my peak.

Only after the excitement had subsided did it occur to me that I had engaged in an extremely perverted sort of masturbation. I couldn't believe I had found pleasure in imagining the hand of a woman touching me. Was it because the last time my toe-penis had been given any stimulation at all was in the bath that night? True, Eiko's caress of my toe-penis had been much more intense than Tamotsu's, so it made sense that she should play a role in my fantasies. But *everything* else about her? What was going on?

As far as I knew, I didn't have what it took to enjoy homosexual love. So why this? I saw Eiko naked all the time, and I never felt any sexual interest. Well, *that* was a relief. But the instant I imagined her hand, the same drunken thrill took hold of my chest—and caused my toe-penis to stir. Was I just turned on by Eiko's hand? Did that make me a homosexual fetishist?

The pleasure I had just experienced was so powerful that I worried it could become a habit, to touch myself while imagining it was Eiko's hand. Unless I was planning to turn myself into a dyke, I would have to stop masturbating until I had forgotten about Eiko's hand. This was the conclusion I came to. At the same time, I got to thinking maybe it wouldn't be so bad being a dyke, if it meant I could experience that pleasure again . . .

Without realizing it, I found myself reaching for my toe-penis again, but a sound in the next room brought me back to my senses: I've got Shunji. And since we're together, I *can't* become a dyke—in fact, there's no need for me to masturbate. Was I being unfaithful, masturbating without fantasizing about him? I needed to go fling myself on him.

But this impulse was quashed the moment I returned to the room. Shunji was awake now, masturbating with enough energy to rock the bed.

♥ ♥ ♥

Waking up, Shunji had realized that he was erect, and so he started masturbating. That's what he said. Apart from reflecting that it had been a while since he'd gotten hard in the morning, he hadn't been thinking of anything; he had simply reached down and put his hand on his penis. He wasn't thinking of having sex, he simply wanted to satisfy the urge his penis was feeling, so it didn't even occur to him to call me.

Because I was saddled with guilt when I was confronted with the sight of Shunji masturbating, I imagined he had intuited my betrayal of him as I jerked off in the bathroom, and had thus started doing the same thing himself. I knew this was ridiculous, but still found myself at a loss for words. Since I couldn't think of anything else, I called out, "Good morning!" Still stroking himself with his right hand, Shunji held his other hand out toward me. I ended up sitting and staring at the sperm spurting from the tip of his penis, with his left arm clutching me.

When he was through, Shunji hugged me. In his eyes, the impulse to masturbate and the desire to have sex were two entirely different things. I had just gratified myself, but as we hugged, I felt a new sense of longing. It wasn't sexual desire, it was the desire to kiss Shunji, to caress him, to "be friendly" with him from head to toe. Eiko's hand no longer haunted me. For the first time in quite a while, Shunji and I brought our genitals into contact, and I experienced a deep joy.

When one has sex after a long period of abstinence, the emotional impact and the physical act can both be almost violent. Toward sunset, I discovered that I was bleeding. The expected date for my period wasn't far off, so it didn't seem out of the ordinary, but I had a strong suspicion that our sexual intercourse that morning was the cause.

By the time Shunji and I returned to the hotel from the pharmacy, the group was leaving for the evening's performance, so I ended up taking the bag of sanitary supplies with us.

This was the final day the Flower Show had scheduled for this tour. We would check out of the hotel the next morning, return to Tokyo, and then have a week off. It was customary for Tamotsu and Yukie to perform together on the last day. I hadn't seen their act before, and I was somewhat nervous about it, afraid for Shin's penis, which was slated to be chewed by the teeth in Yukie's vagina. At the same time, I was interested to see how Tamotsu would handle it. I felt a vague discomfort.

The members of the troupe were gathered outside the minibus, enjoying the cool autumn air, waiting for Shigeki and Yohei. Tamotsu was unusually quiet; he was squatting down, lighting sparklers. Eiko stood with Aiko gazing down at the sparks, and her profile caught my eye. I felt awkward remembering her role in my morning masturbation; I had no problem looking at her face, but worried I might lose my cool if I saw her hand.

Aiko noticed the bag in my hand. "Your period?"

The sanitary supplies were packaged and in a bag, but a woman could guess. I nodded, which caused Aiko and Eiko to step away from me. "Don't come near—you'll give it to us!" they squealed.

Girls in all-female high schools play this game a lot. Sometimes even girls who aren't expecting their periods will start bleeding if they play sports or horse around too much with girls who have their periods, so when it gets out that someone has her period, the girls who don't will joke that she has to stay away.

"You two will probably get it tomorrow anyway, right?" I said, laughing.

The Flower Show organized its schedule around Aiko's and Eiko's periods. Occasionally, when there was a conflict, they would take a pill to delay the flow, but generally speaking, the week off started the day their periods were to begin. This week also gave Shin's penis a chance to heal.

Aiko laughed, too. "Still, I can't afford to get my period tonight. It doesn't matter for Eiko because she doesn't perform today."

"Well, just standing next to me won't give it to you."

"How is it supposed to get passed on anyway?" Eiko asked.

"Haven't you heard? From smelling the contaminated woman's sweat."

All of a sudden, Masami came running over and threw his arms around me. "*Please*, pass it on to *me*! I don't mind getting it!"

I screamed, dropping my bag on the ground.

"Oh, what a *lovely* voice!" Masami said, his arms still twined around me. "I'll bet when you were in primary school, little boys used to dump water on you and pull your hair and do all *kinds* of nasty things. You've got the voice to drive a man crazy—oh yes you do! *Ooo la la*, how I *envy* you."

I still wasn't sure what to make of Masami. He was always being campy, but I wondered how he felt when he overheard women discussing things that only women could really understand—about how we tended to be bitten more by mosquitoes, or how we got cold easily, or how we passed our periods on to one another. If he had a sex change because he actually wanted to be a woman, which was how it looked, it must pain him to be reminded that he wasn't born one.

"So," I said to Masami, "do you enjoy hugging women?"

After a slight pause, Masami stepped away from me. "Well, I'd *prefer* a man, of course."

No sooner had he spoken than he put his arms around Shunji, which caused Shunji to murmur, "Hmm?" without the slightest hint of tension in his voice. Tamotsu guffawed.

Shigeki and Yohei came out together, and the troupe boarded the mini-bus. I picked up the bag I had dropped on the ground, and as I was stand-ing back up, Masami whispered into my ear, "Actually, I don't *like* men."

Before I could say anything, he climbed into the vehicle. What did he like if not men? Maybe he didn't like anything? Why, in that case, had he gone to all the trouble of castrating himself and dressing like a woman?

♥ ♥ ♥

The minibus pulled into the parking lot of a plain-looking hotel of the sort used by companies for training sessions. As he got out, Shigeki glanced around, not knowing where to go. He had mentioned earlier that the sponsor of the evening's performance was new and that the venue was new, too, so he wasn't sure what to expect.

A thin man, who looked to be about thirty, emerged from the building and approached Shigeki. His complexion was peculiarly smooth and fair; he had a moustache and a beard about a sixteenth of an inch long. He was dressed in a style that wasn't quite up-to-date—a white polyester-blend shirt and brown pants, which contributed to a vague sense of his other-worldliness. As he explained, he was giving a seminar in Human Develop-ment, and he had engaged the Flower Show as instructional material. He would be lecturing between each segment of the performance, but asked that the performers not let it bother them, and just to do the same show as always.

We were shown into the building, and as we were walking down a hall, Shunji asked, "What's a seminar in Human Development?"

I told him what I had learned from the media. "They're training programs that try to help people break through their emotional shell and release their true nature, which is sealed inside them. Something like that."

"Their emotional shell? What's that?"

"The fetters we put on ourselves, maybe."

"Why would we put fetters on ourselves?"

"Afraid I can't answer that one."

Aiko came over to me and whispered, "That guy who's leading the seminar . . . does he seem kind of religious-cultish to you? Those eyes of his aren't looking at this world."

"I've read that these seminars aren't supposed to be religious."

"But I've also read that some rather suspicious seminars have been popping up lately. The guy's nametag says HIJIRINUMA TAKESHI. Seems kind of weird."

She was right. The characters he'd used for HIJIRINUMA meant "swamp of saints"; TAKESHI was written in hiragana.

The setup for us was a smallish room that functioned as one of the wings of the stage. To get up onto the stage, you had to climb a short flight of stairs. I could tell that there were a lot of people out there, but I couldn't see them unless I stood on tiptoes. Hijirinuma told the troupe members to come out in sequence when he raised his hand, then left, closing the door behind him. As we sat waiting for things to get underway, two young women, dressed in the bland style of female office workers, brought in an electric pot for hot water and the fixings for tea. Their nametags read HIJIRITANI KAORU and HIJIRISAWA YUKARI.

I went up onto the stage to set up the synthesizer. There were about thirty men and women in the audience, all gazing respectfully at the stage. Another ten men and women stood along the wall. Everyone looked calm, everyone wore nametags. No doubt all were in the saintly HIJIRI series: HIJIRIKAWA, HIJIRIUMI, etcetera. It was the sort of atmosphere that made me nervous. I located an electric outlet on the wall near the small room where the troupe was waiting, and positioned the synthesizer so that Shunji would be playing as far away from the audience as possible.

I helped Shunji to his seat and went back to the waiting room.

Yohei was talking when I entered. "I bet we're going be offered up as sacrifices."

Tamotsu unzipped his pants. "Shin's blood will be the sacrifice tonight," he said. Then seeing me, he added, "Kazumi, you're bleeding today, right? Want to pour it on the altar? Mix it with Shin's?"

"I'd be glad to mix it with yours," I answered casually.

But Tamotsu opened his eyes wide and stared at me. "Yeah, it's true . . . *I* don't shed any blood." His eyes didn't move. He had a can of beer in his hand. He continued, his voice more wheedling than usual, almost chanting a spell, "Except that *I'm* the one who takes the nutrients to make the blood, even the extra blood for Shin." He raised his voice another notch. "You hear me, Shin? You're stealing my blood, so you have no right to complain!"

I had no idea what I could do to calm Tamotsu down, but I started walking toward him.

Eiko pulled me back. "It's best to leave him alone," she whispered. "He's always like this on the days he has to hurt Shin."

The house lights went out. Only the stage remained bathed in brilliant light. A man, presumably Hijirinuma Takeshi, ran out in front of the stage. He spoke, using a cordless mike:

"At last, everyone, we have come to the final evening of our seminar. Having experienced a full eight days of sessions, four in Tokyo and then another four here in Hakone, all of you should be feeling, right now, the new self that you've become, a you that's different from the you you were before you participated in this seminar. The show that's about to get underway is my present to the new you, a touchstone that will allow you to confirm the change that has taken place in yourself, and the culmination of all the earlier sessions."

"This is quite a change," Masami muttered. "I don't get any dirty-mind vibes."

It was true, Hijirinuma Takeshi's speech sounded so sterile it was if his voice had been disinfected.

"The new yous you have all become ought not to be moved by what you see in tonight's performance. Not only will it not touch you, you'll be able to turn a cold, critical gaze on the scenes unfolding before your eyes, and I'm sure you will grasp even more firmly the true nature of that phenomenon we call sex, which formerly held you so firmly in its grip and caused you such terrible agony."

As Hijirinuma talked, a futon was carried out to the center of the stage. Shigeki, who would be performing first with Aiko, began unbuttoning his shirt; he seemed utterly at a loss. Aiko took his hand, and squeezed it between hers. Shigeki smiled, then his expression hardened. The voice coming over the speakers fell silent. Hijirinuma waved toward stage left, where we were.

The audience remained perfectly silent the whole time Shigeki and Aiko were performing—no one even stirred. Sensing something odd in the air, Shunji stuck to classical pieces, and played them quietly. Hijirinuma's expression was clearly visible from the wings, since he was standing in front of the stage. He gazed with the most unemotional, uninterested gaze imaginable—first at the performance that was taking place on stage, then at the faces in the audience. When rashes turned Aiko's entire body red, before she and Shigeki had a chance to leave the stage, he brought the mike to his mouth and resumed his lecture:

"How did you like the performance? There's no need to explain it to you, is there? We have learned, after eight days of sessions, that sex is violence inflicted by the strong upon the weak, an insult conferred upon the strong by the weak, an obscure battle, all too easily overlooked, enacted between two human beings, yes, and we have learned that this is true even when the two partners are in love. I believe this truth was clearly discernible in the sexual act we have all just witnessed."

Shigeki and Aiko, who had left the stage by now, stopped in their tracks and turned to look back at Hijirinuma as he went on.

"The man was equipped with a splendid sexual organ. The pleasure this organ induces is considerably more powerful than the agonies inflicted by the violence of sex—so much more powerful, indeed, that it causes us to forget that sex *is* violence. Perhaps by allowing the man's sexual organ to enter her, the woman did experience, in places, a deep pleasure. And yet her sensitive skin recognized the violence of the man's kisses and caresses. The rashes that appeared on her body are proof of this recognition."

"Huh?" Shigeki said.

"No matter how much pleasure the man gives the woman, he can never atone for the sin of the violence he has done her. Obviously it is not possible for *him* to claim that he is simply giving her pleasure, that this is not violence. In the woman's rashes, he is made to confront, inescapably, the sinfulness of what he has done. And the woman, confronting the man with these rashes, heaps scorn upon his deceit. Most of us are not men with special sexual organs or women who exhibit special bodily reactions, but while we may not be able to see what we do, the sexual act is the same one this couple just performed. Tell me, is this battle worthy of the name of love? If we truly love one another, how could we ever dream of having sex?"

The members of the Flower Show were stunned.

"He's twisting things," Shigeki said.

"Is this some kind of antisex religion?" Yohei asked.

"I think it's *very* interesting," Masami cried merrily. "I wonder what he'll say about *us*?"

The lecture appended to Yohei and Masami's performance was as follows:

"We are sick now, all of us, because we have partaken in the vile brutishness of sex. The artificial woman who took the stage in this act presents us simultaneously with two separate models: the man in agony, struggling to escape the violence of his own limitless desire, and the woman trying but ultimately failing to cast sex away from her. The man who performs with this artificial woman captures both halves of her—the traitorous male trying to break free from the circle of linked violence and sexual desire, and the rebellious female who yearns to be rid of sex, and attempts, through intimidation, to drag them back within the established order. And yet he, too, this man who stands on the side of order, is in the grips of the sickness, and is thus unable, at the moment of sexual climax, to remain in his normal form."

"C'mon, I'm not such a bad guy, am I?" Yohei grumbled.

"Listen, my friends! Over the course of eight days of sessions, we have closed in on the truth of sex, and we have seen how deeply diseased the order to which we are subject is. What, then, are we to do?" Hijirinuma paused theatrically. "We have no choice but to break away from the established order and create a new order of our own! A new order in which we will be liberated from sex! And what is this new order of which we dream? Here, my friends, is a hint."

Hijirinuma raised his hand, giving us the sign. But Yukie, who was supposed to go out next, was so bored she had fallen asleep. Aiko gave her shoulder a shake. She opened her eyes, then dashed out onto the stage with a cucumber, her file, a balloon, and a tube tucked under her arm.

Yukie's segment, which evoked laughter during most shows, didn't go over at all well with this evening's audience. There was no response even when she tossed out the chewed cucumber—just the sound of the vegetable hitting the floor.

"Did you see their faces, Shigeki?" Yohei said. "They're not human."

Shigeki, looking glum, replied with an "Mmm."

Tamotsu had been sitting with his head down, not saying a thing. Neither the back-and-forth among the members of the show nor Hijirinuma's lectures seemed to be registering. The empty beer can he had been fiddling with earlier, balancing it on his lap, was now crushed. He was so tense, you could see he would explode at the slightest provocation. Eiko must have found it too painful to look at him, for she had taken a seat a little distance away, and was staring at the floor, just like him.

When the balloon popped on stage, Tamotsu began ripping his clothes off with such violence it seemed his buttons would go flying. His face deathly pale, he wrapped his hand around Shin's penis and plodded slowly up the stairs. Eiko rose up from her chair and moved closer to the stage.

The audience remained enveloped in the same heavy atmosphere the whole time Tamotsu and Yukie were exchanging caresses, but there was a faint stir when people realized he was going to put the penis inside Yukie. Stroking Shin's penis, Tamotsu began leaning down toward Yukie, who was sticking her legs into the air, holding them wide apart. But the semi-impotent penis was having its problems today, too, and wilted when Tamotsu, preparing to insert it, stopped rubbing it with his hand. Time after time, Tamotsu lifted himself up again and started over. And then, growing frustrated, he began punching Shin's penis. The familiar, terrible sound reverberated through the theater.

Once he finally managed to push the penis inside her, his movements became brutal. I had no idea what was happening inside Yukie's vagina, but the slapping sound made by their flesh as their bodies collided was like a knife in my ears. My heartbeat quickened. Tamotsu thrashed his hips so wildly it seemed he'd lost his mind. And he kept giving his torso unnatural twists, moving in a way that plays no role in sexual encounters. He was trying to shred, to gouge out his twin brother's penis. That's what that movement was. The shining film of sweat that covered his back looked like transparent blood. *Tamotsu's body is smeared with blood,* I thought, horrified. And in that instant, I felt menstrual blood trickle from my vagina. I was ready to faint.

Tamotsu pulled the penis out. Groans rose from the audience.

As if this were the moment he had been waiting for, Hijirinuma began screaming: "Castration! Castration is the answer! Castration will liberate us from sex! I'm talking about both men *and* women! Let us all learn from this man's bravery! Sexual organs aren't worth a thing! Men must lop off their penises, women must sew up their vaginas! Not literally, but mentally, and completely. Let us be done with sex! We don't need to leave descendants. Humanity will perish, you say? No, no—no need to worry about that. Leave reproduction to the worldly masses!"

Tamotsu came stomping back. Shin's penis was covered in blood, but for some reason it was still hard.

"Castration will liberate us from sex, he says. Hah!" Tamotsu spat, a wild look on his face. "Are you kidding me? I was born castrated, but I want to have sex so bad I can't stand it!" His burning gaze fell on Eiko. "Lick me!" he commanded, his tone brooking no rejection.

Eiko balked.

"Lick me!" he commanded again. "C'mon, do it!"

Eiko's lips trembled. "That's not your penis," she said.

"It's mine. How is it different from mine?"

"Licking you won't make you feel good."

"It will. I'll feel good. I know you won't get this, but I can feel with this penis. The truth is, the pathetic little thing below is Shin's. This one is mine."

"Why tell a lie like—"

"Shut up! Are you going to lick me or not? Answer me!"

Tamotsu gave Eiko a shove, sending her flying toward the wall. Her body crashed into mine, throwing me off balance. Tamotsu came charging over as I struggled to keep from falling, and I tottered again. He no longer seemed conscious of what he was doing. He thrust me out of the way and stood before Eiko, penning her in against the wall. I wasn't angry about Tamotsu's rudeness, I was worried about Eiko. Her gaze was fixed on my hip. Glancing down, I saw that my skirt was smeared with Shin's blood.

With her eyes, she apologized, then she bent down and positioned her face in front of Tamotsu's lower stomach. I slumped onto a nearby chair, unable to bear the thought. Aiko checked on me, then went and got Shunji, who was still on stage. Puzzled that I hadn't gone to get him, he put his hand on my shoulder; all I could do was lean against him.

I kept thinking: How does Shin's blood taste as it spreads over Eiko's tongue? Only when Eiko stood up and I saw her hands and lips smeared with red did it occur to me that I could easily find out by licking the blood on my skirt.

Chapter 10

The members of the Flower Show parted at the west gate of Shinjuku Station.

As we were saying our goodbyes, Yohei and Eiko exchanged casual hugs with Aiko. It was rare for members of the troupe to express their affection so openly; I was staring at them when Tamotsu cut into my field of vision.

"Hey, hug me."

Ducking away as he stretched out his arms, I darted around behind Shunji.

"No thank you—not after the way you shoved me last night."

"I shoved you? When did I do that?" Tamotsu lowered his arms, eyes open wide. Apparently he wasn't even aware of my presence in the moments before he stuffed Shin's bloody penis into Eiko's mouth. "I don't remember . . . Was it after the show?"

I nodded across Shunji's shoulder. "I even have evidence."

Tamotsu scratched his head. "Don't hold it against me, please," he pleaded, his tone childlike. "I was in a state of diminished capacity, as the lawyers say." With that, he bounded forward, seized the hand I was resting on Shunji's shoulder, and embraced us both.

"Well, see you around. You, too, Shunji."

I couldn't help smiling when he spoke like that, but if he felt like showering Shunji and me with affection, he could be nicer to Eiko. I still felt pain in my chest when I thought of the searing red blood on her lips the night before.

I couldn't figure Tamotsu out. How could he force his lover to perform fellatio on a bloody penis that didn't even belong to him? Maybe he was kinder and gentler with her in private, but even so—didn't it occur to him that if he kept being so brutal in public, time after time, Eiko might eventually stop caring for him? Was he so confident she would never dump him?

When Shunji and I were having breakfast with Yohei the day we left Hakone, I had asked him, "How many years have Tamotsu and Eiko been like that?"

Yohei remained silent for a moment before replying. "I can imagine what you're feeling. It's hard to know what to do with Tamotsu, it really is. But you know, the thought of the enormous burden he has to bear makes it hard for me to be too critical."

"Doesn't Eiko's love lighten his burden?"

"Sometimes being loved makes a person even more twisted. Haven't you ever found yourself trying to confirm a man's feelings for you because you couldn't trust his professions of love?"

I turned to Shunji. "Have you ever felt that way about someone?"

"Nope."

"Me neither."

"Yeah, I guess not." Yohei smiled sadly. "You're the Emperor and Empress."

"What's that supposed to mean?"

"Oh, nothing. Those are the nicknames we came up with for you. Because you two look so perfect sitting there together, all prim and proper, like the Emperor and Empress dolls for the Dolls' Festival." Yohei's expression turned serious again. "Anyway, it's precisely the depth of their love that makes Tamotsu feel so hurt and frustrated at his inability to satisfy Eiko with his own body. That's why he acts in a manner so eccentric, at least from an outside perspective. Penis problems really take it out on a man."

"Even if he has a problem with his penis, I think he should just be happy that he has a woman who loves him! What more can he possibly need?" I may have gotten carried away.

Adopting a conciliatory tone, Yohei replied, "Tamotsu won't be this way forever. He'll settle down."

"And what if Eiko dumps him before then?"

"Oh, so that's what you're worried about." Yohei peered hard at me for a moment, then dropped his gaze. "You've got a point. I wonder what he'd do."

I was genuinely concerned about Tamotsu. Obviously he was dependent on Eiko, both mentally and physically. Putting myself in his place, imagining the scene when Eiko's patience ran out and she left him, I felt my heart tighten. Would Tamotsu ever be able to find someone to love him as deeply as Eiko does? He must know how unlikely that is. But then why was he backing himself into that corner?

There was no way a simple, uncomplicated person like me could get a grip on the psychology of such a complex individual. All I knew was that if I were him, I would treat Eiko better. Even in the unlikely event another woman fell in love with him, what a waste it would be to lose her!

Tamotsu and Eiko were still on my mind when I got to my apartment after taking Shunji home. Opening up my suitcase, I found my blood-stained skirt, and instantly the image of Eiko's lips, smeared with blood, was before me. The blood on my skirt had dried, turning a dark, murky red. I doubted the stain was ever going to come out, even if I took it to the dry cleaner's, so I tossed the skirt in the corner to be thrown out later. But each time I walked by it, I remembered Eiko's bloody lips.

It was probably only natural, in this strained state of mind, that I should be visited by bizarre dreams. About halfway through the weeklong vacation, I dreamed that I had a man's body, and that Eiko was fondling the penis between my legs. The pleasure was like silk, but as it was about to escalate to the next level, I abruptly woke up. Back in the real world, I broke out in a sweat. I tried to explain the dream away: It wasn't me Eiko was caressing just now. I was an onlooker, that's all, watching her have sex with some unknown, imaginary man. Of course it wasn't me! My penis is on my right foot, not between my legs . . .

The explanation wasn't entirely convincing, because a vague, silky pleasure still lingered in my limp body. The delicious sensations that took hold of my penis during the dream were, my waking self realized, pleasures that my female body was familiar with. I recalled something I had read once: apparently, all it took was a dose of male hormones and the crucial part of a female embryo would develop into a penis . . . Whatever, I couldn't have cared less.

The dream hadn't lasted long. It started with a pleasurable sensation that began spreading from the area around my abdomen and ended when my eyes landed on Eiko—who was starting to play with the penis between my legs, a rapt smile on her face. Because it was Eiko, I relaxed and gave myself over to her hands. I wasn't at all surprised this was happening, and I felt no reservations about what we were doing. And I felt even more drawn to Eiko than I did in real life.

I don't believe dreams are an expression of secret desires, as some suggest. I think they're just transformations of whatever little thoughts you happen to have on your mind when you go to sleep, no more. I had been thinking too much about Tamotsu and Eiko—I often put myself in Tamotsu's place, trying to imagine how he would see her. So I had a dream in which she and I were having sex, as if I were him.

It came as a blow, however, to have to accept that in my dream I quite enjoyed what Eiko and I were doing. That morning in Hakone, I was disgusted with myself for masturbating while fantasizing about Eiko's hand; I swore I would never again indulge in such perverted pleasures. And yet now, less than a week later, I had been swept up in a similarly sick dream. What was happening to me?

I shut my eyes and replayed the dream. Yes, it sure looked like I was enjoying myself. So maybe I should just go ahead and have fun, with no reservations? After my second lesbian experience, I no longer felt the same resistance to homosexuality. Why was I so against it anyway? If only I had realized sooner that I had the potential to enjoy this sort of love . . .

Realizing that my thoughts were barreling headlong in a totally crazy direction, I opened my eyes. No trace remained of my earlier languor. To think I'd come so close to losing my senses, giving in to a wild delusion that had seeped out beyond the borders of my dream, intruding into the real world. I went into the bathroom to wash off.

I had the sense, during the course of a somewhat cool shower, that the traces of pleasure were slowly ebbing from my body and my mind was clearing. Now that I had calmed down, I saw clearly where I stood. I would never have a penis between my legs in the real world, just as I would never feel any sexual interest in Eiko, so there was no point in letting my imagination wander the way it had. I felt I had wronged Eiko, making her play such an odd role, even if it was only in a dream. I felt I had wronged Tamotsu, too—he was her boyfriend, after all. And I felt I had wronged my own boyfriend, Shunji.

Writing off the dream as unreal had been my way of getting rid of it. But the despondency that washed over me the instant I realized I would never, in reality, taste the pleasure I'd savored in that dream suggested that the delusion was still there, stuck to the wall in some corner of my mind, like a stubborn stain. I might not care about having a penis between my legs, but there *was* something to my feelings for Eiko.

Whatever. There were other things to think about besides Tamotsu and Eiko. For one, although Shigeki hadn't yet asked me about my plans, I had to make up my mind whether I wanted to become a full member of the Flower Show.

At this point, the only thing I was sure of was that I did not want to break off my relationship with the troupe members. I was anxious about Tamotsu and Eiko, and I wanted to go on seeing Shigeki, Aiko, and Yohei. I felt comfortable with them. It wasn't just their personalities; I valued their style of friendship—the delicacy with which they handled the easily bruised areas of each other's hearts. I could only imagine the affection I felt for them growing deeper.

Originally, one of the things holding me back from joining the Flower Show was that it would prevent me from finishing college; but that no longer was a concern. After a phone call from a classmate informed me the spring semester had begun, I spent a day at school just to remind myself what it was like; class and campus life seemed duller and blander than they ever had before, only confirming for me how much I wanted to be with the Flower Show. There was no need to hurry to graduate; I could keep my place in the college for eight years, so taking another year off wouldn't be a problem.

My mind wasn't fully made up, though. If I joined the Flower Show, I would have to perform some kind of act involving my toe-penis before an audience. I didn't welcome that prospect. Shigeki had said I didn't need to take off my clothes; I just had to show my toe. I could force myself to do that, but there was something beyond embarrassment I had to face. What was I so afraid of? The clammy stares roaming over my body? The violence I'd be doing to my emotions? The thought of embarking on a path I had never imagined myself taking? Whatever the case, I was panicking. I tried to remind myself that Aiko and Eiko were doing the same thing, but I couldn't get over my dread.

Shunji, for his part, might as well have had no opinion at all.

"I'd like to travel with everyone again. But if you don't want to be in the show, I'm fine not going."

Shunji didn't understand how it felt to be exposed to other people's eyes—and to stares, moreover, dripping with curiosity and lust. If I had a sighted boyfriend, he would have hated my showing my toe-penis to total strangers, and opposed my joining the troupe in the first place; or perhaps he would have understood my terror and given some decent advice. Shunji, on the other hand, didn't seem to consider it a problem even if I had to get completely naked.

I was still agonizing over this when Shigeki called. "We've got a show the day after tomorrow in a suite in a hotel downtown. Do you think you and Shunji will be able to make it?" Not a word about my joining the troupe. Well, if he wasn't going to bring it up, I sure wasn't, so I just said we'd be there and that was that. When tomorrow arrived and Shunji and I set out for the hotel in Akasaka, I was feeling so hyper the Pajero almost seemed to drive itself; at the same time, I knew that if I didn't get a grip on myself I'd end up touring with the troupe, simply by inertia.

Shigeki and Aiko were waiting for us in the cocktail lounge. Aiko was, as always, gorgeous and beautifully dressed, but Shigeki looked especially good in a grayish-green suit; sitting together at a table, they looked like the ideal couple. They stood to welcome us, and my smile must have made it clear how thrilled I was to see them.

As Shunji and I found our own table, I glanced around the room, and my eyes were immediately drawn to a brilliant red mouth. The image of

Eiko's bloodstained lips popped into mind, causing me to do a double take. This mouth, I discovered, was painted red with lipstick, and it really did belong to Eiko. She was sitting with Tamotsu and Yukie at a table diagonally across from ours, daintily holding a sparerib between her fingers; her fingernails were the same brilliant red as her lips.

Seeing this, I felt the horror of our last night on tour seize my chest, but then I also felt the excitement of the sensuous dream I'd been trying to put out of mind. My breath grew labored. The suffocation I felt wasn't entirely unpleasant, so it never occurred to me to look away, but the moment Eiko turned in my direction I averted my gaze and lifted my glass of white wine to my lips.

Even though I had avoided making eye contact, Eiko got up and came over to us. I glanced up at her, trying not to let my shortness of breath get the better of me. Her red lips moved. "Did you get the blood out of your skirt?" they said.

"I figured it wouldn't come out, so I tossed it." Now that we were talking, the heaviness in my chest lightened.

Eiko's face clouded.

I smiled. "It's okay. It was on its last legs anyway"

"Really?" Eiko said. "I'm sorry."

"Tamotsu ought to be apologizing, not you."

Tamotsu, still sitting at their table, was sticking his tongue out at us.

"That kid . . . ," Eiko muttered, unable to believe her eyes. "He's incorrigible."

"It'd be nice if he were always so droll."

Eiko stared at me. I'd said too much. She didn't seem angry, though. "I had a feeling you two wouldn't be coming back," she said.

"Why?"

"I was afraid the atmosphere of the troupe might have put you off."

I burst out laughing. Far from being put off, I had spent the entire vacation yearning to see everyone. That Eiko hadn't realized this struck me as tremendously funny. With a hint of expectancy welling up inside me, I asked, "Are you glad we came?"

Eiko gave me a sunny smile. "Of course I am!"

Overjoyed, I turned to Shunji, who was drinking a Salty Dog. "Did you hear that, Shunji? Eiko says she's glad we came."

"Yep. So am I."

We were basking in our somewhat infantile delight when Tamotsu strode over, wagging his tongue, and then—for some utterly incomprehensible reason—wrapped his arm around Shunji's shoulder, pulled him over, and mashed his tongue against his cheek.

"Oh my god, what are you doing!" Eiko yelped, flabbergasted.

But Shunji was unfazed. "Hey, Tamotsu," he said, turning his face in his direction, "what's up?"

Tamotsu straightened his back and grinned, just the same as always. "I thought I'd let Shunji know I was sticking out my tongue."

"As if he'd want that sort of information!" Eiko said.

"Just saying hello—my way." Tamotsu looked down at Shunji. "Nothing ever surprises you, huh?"

"A little lick is hardly going to surprise me," Shunji replied calmly.

Eiko touched his hand. "But it felt gross, right?"

"Not at all. It was nice of him to come say hello."

Eiko's expression betrayed her puzzlement. That was understandable— she didn't know Shunji had had sex with men.

Tamotsu, delighted with the turn of things, tapped her arm. "Admit it, my tongue is magic. It can pleasure anyone."

"There are no limits to your idiocy," Eiko shot back and looked away.

We soon moved on to the luxury suite where we would be performing. In place of a dressing room, we would be using the bathroom, which was a little way in from the entrance, on the left. There were signs the bathroom had been used recently: strands of hair clung to the inside of the bathtub.

The troupe would be performing in tight quarters, so Shunji would have to play standing up this evening, his synthesizer on a desk. Since there was no futon, a mattress was laid out on the floor of the long sitting room. The Flower Show would perform with the audience looking down on them. There were about ten people, three of them women, sitting on the sofa and chairs around the room. They seemed to be in their late twenties—a bit younger than the usual crowd. The men looked like they worked in the entertainment industry.

"My, *my*, just look at these guys," Masami said, "developing a taste for these kinky games at such a tender age. If you ask *me*, middle age is quite soon enough to abandon yourself to sex."

"I wonder what kind of games they'll be playing with the three girls later on?" Tamotsu said. "I wish I could join them."

Masami snorted scornfully. "Even if you did, they wouldn't let you do much more than scamper around picking up their pubic hairs from the floor."

"That'd be fine with me. As long as I could be part of the group."

But when Tamotsu returned from his act, he was singing a different tune. "There was a guy who had his hand up a women's blouse the whole time I was fondling Eiko," he announced. "By the time I finished my number, he had his hands to himself—he was just sitting there, looking ill."

Tamotsu must have really beaten up on Shin's penis again tonight.

"I'll make all these lecherous bastards impotent," he said, venom in his voice.

I went out to get Shunji. He'd been on his feet all evening, so I thought I'd bring him back into the bathroom first and pack up the synthesizer later. I had just twined my arm around his when a man got up from the sofa and sauntered up to us.

"Hey, if it isn't Shunji!" he said. He wasn't very tall, but seemed solidly built.

Shunji stopped and cocked his head, indicating that he was listening.

The guy spoke again, "It's me, Oinuma!"

Shunji turned toward the voice. "Tama! My little buddy! Seriously?"

"That's me—your little buddy."

This man—Oinuma—wasn't the childlike, adorable sort of person you might expect to be called anybody's "little buddy." But his whole face was now lit up with an easy smile; he gave Shunji's chest a tender pat.

"I thought it was you playing, but the room was too dark for me to see your face."

"What are you doing here?"

Oinuma lowered his voice. "It's a party for this obnoxious little prince I work with. Going to see these idiotic shows with him is part of my job. Who would have guessed I'd run into you! Speaking of which, what the hell are *you* doing here? How'd you get mixed up in something like this?"

Shunji seemed unsure how to explain. He grabbed my hand before speaking. "I'm here with my fiancée."

"Your fiancée?"

For the first time, Oinuma turned in my direction. His eyes looked me up and down, inspecting everything from my hairstyle to my shoes. Then, very slowly, he grinned, "Nice to meet you. Shunji and I go way back."

I bowed a little, but by the time I raised my head he had already turned back to Shunji.

"You've put on some muscle," he was saying, running his hands over Shunji's shoulders and upper arms. "Have you been lifting weights?"

"Sure have. How about you?"

It was Shunji's turn to run his hands over Oinuma's chest. Oinuma smiled complacently, puffing up his chest; he held out his arms for Shunji to touch. I didn't know what to do with my hand now that Shunji had let go of it. As I stood there fidgeting, Oinuma put his hand on Shunji's shoulder and looked toward me.

"Would you mind if I talked to Shunji in private for five minutes? It's been a while."

I could think of no reason to refuse, and Oinuma led Shunji over to the window. I picked up the synthesizer and carried it into the bathroom, where the troupe was gathered, chatting.

"I hear there was some famous musician in the audience."

"Really? Who?"

"Sorry, can't say. I only know about three musicians in the whole country."

"Probably someone only people in the business know."

Drained of energy, I listlessly packed the synthesizer into its case. I felt queasy. That Oinuma guy had treated me so dismissively, barely concealing his scorn, and then brazenly made a show of his intimacy with Shunji—I bet he was gay. And the way he casually wrapped his arm around Shunji's waist, pulling him closer, as he led him over to the window, I was sure he'd slept with Shunji.

Right from the start, I'd had a bad impression of the men and women Shunji had been sexually intimate with in the past. Because listening to his stories, I realized that, with the exception of Chisato, none of his partners had ever bothered to call after an amount of time went by. These people felt no love or friendship for him; they had simply taken advantage of him sexually, exploiting his boyish innocence. How repugnant it was for a man like Oinuma to act as if they were the best of friends just because they happened to run into each other.

I didn't like to admit it, but waves of jealousy were churning in my breast. If Shunji hadn't responded to Oinuma with such friendliness, I might have been able to keep them apart. At the least, Shunji should have taken my feelings into consideration and told Oinuma he didn't have time to talk, or that they didn't need to go off alone, the three of us could talk together—yes, he could have asked me to come along, too. I started resenting Shunji. At the same time, I started feeling annoyed at my own pettiness.

I wondered if I was wrong to jump to the conclusion that Oinuma was gay. Some straight men enjoy that sort of physical male bonding. His short hair and muscularity fit my image of a certain buffed-up type of gay man, it was true, but that didn't necessarily mean he was gay. Perhaps I was being oversensitive, assuming he was giving me the cold shoulder just because I was a woman.

As I finished zipping up the carrying case, my eye landed on Masami's neatly shaven legs, extending from the edge of the bathtub, where he was perched. I thought I'd ask him. "Can you tell if a man is gay or straight just from looking?"

He had been humming a tune, and he let his answer ride the melody, as if it were part of the song. "I would have to say that there really is no way, whatever are you thinking, *you ass.*"

"There really isn't?"

"Oh, you notice when the man is *ogling* you, lust dripping from his eyes—that's true, darling. But there's no way anyone can tell whether some salaryman tossing down an energy drink on the train platform is gay. What's gotten into you, coming out with something so *silly* all of a sudden, my darling bozo?"

What Masami was saying made sense, but I clung to my hope. "Can you tell if the man standing with Shunji by the window is gay?"

"What! Is his *chastity* in *danger?*"

Sensing how earnest I was, Masami got up and went to check the man out. He came back to the bathroom a moment later, reporting that there was no one by the window.

A shiver ran down my spine. "What about Shunji? He isn't there either?"

"If you're looking for Shunji, he walked by a second ago on his way out," Yohei piped up, pointing a finger in the direction of the doorway. "There was a guy with him. Why, is something up?"

Masami peered into my face. "Did this man *seem* gay? Has he taken Shunji?"

"Hmm . . . I'm not sure that he actually took Shunji; Shunji might just have gone along."

"This is hardly the time for *objectivity!*" Masami shrieked. "That man waltzed off with Shunji without asking you! Get your *buns* on the move and run him down! Ball him out! Scream at his abductor! *Where are you taking my Shunji!*"

Masami grabbed my wrist and dragged me out of the suite. We dashed to the elevators, but all four were at the first floor. By the time one arrived and we got down to the lobby, there was no sign of Shunji or Oinuma anywhere. After checking to make sure they weren't waiting in the queue for a taxi, we went to the underground parking lot. It was deserted.

"Oh dear, we're too late." Masami gave his fingers a rueful snap.

The light in the lobby looked strangely white after the dim parking lot. The rest of the troupe had come down; they looked like paper dolls standing there in the faded light. In fact, the whole lobby seemed flimsy and unreliable, as if it were just painted on the walls and might peel off at any time, leaving me standing alone in the middle of a great void.

Yohei came over carrying the synthesizer, handing it to me. "Sorry," he said. "I should have said something when I saw him leave. I assumed you knew."

As I hoisted the instrument up onto my shoulder, my upper body rocked under its weight. "Are you okay?" Yohei asked, reaching out to support me, then took the synthesizer back from me. Aiko came and let me lean against her.

Masami reported to the troupe what I had told him in the elevator: "Evidently this guy who took Shunji may be *gay*, and they *may* once have been involved. The man said he wanted to talk with Shunji alone for five minutes and chased Kazumi away, and then made off with Shunji."

"And Shunji just went with him? Without saying anything?"

"So it seems. I'm sure that man must have sweet-talked him."

"He left his synthesizer behind?"

Each word spoken was a dagger into my heart. Oinuma might have been very clever in the way he lured Shunji out, but that didn't change the fact that Shunji had completely forgotten both me and the Flower Show. Aiko was holding my hand; I squeezed hers tightly. Images of Shunji touching Oinuma, and being touched by him in return, ballooned in my mind.

Shigeki, who had gone to use the phone at the front desk, returned with some information. "The man with Shunji doesn't officially belong to the musician's office. My contact said he has no idea where the guy could have gone, or if he'll be back, and since he doesn't have his address book with him, he can't give us his address or phone number."

I couldn't say a word.

After a moment's silence, Tamotsu spoke. "Look, maybe we don't need to worry. I kind of doubt the guy was planning to kidnap and murder him."

"I'm sure he's in no physical danger," Yukie added. "I thought the thing we're all worried about is that Kazumi's man has been stolen. Isn't that right?"

"Who cares if he's stolen for a night or two? The guy will bring him back."

"Ah, but who knows? Shunji might decide he doesn't *want* to come back. They say once you *get into* gay sex you can't *get out* again, you know."

"Don't be so gloomy, you old bag. I mean, we don't even know if that guy'll be able to lure Shunji into his bed, do we?"

"That's true." Shigeki placed a hand on my shoulder. "There's no point hanging around here. You should go wait at home. I'm sure Shunji will call."

I nodded. But my feet seemed disinclined to move, as if they had forgotten how to walk. I didn't even notice that I was still clutching Aiko's hand until she tugged on it. She was about to take hold of my arm when I saw the back of her hand, and I let out a gasp. My fingers had left brilliant, vivid red marks on her bluish-white skin.

"I'm so sorry, I . . . I didn't realize . . ."

"It's okay. Just the usual rashes."

The fresh burst of pain zigzagging through me brought my vision back to normal, and I regained some of my strength.

"I don't think you ought to be at the wheel right now. I'll drive you back to your apartment in your car, okay?" Shigeki said.

Together, he and Aiko and I went down to the parking lot, me walking between them. For some reason, Tamotsu and Eiko came along, too, and climbed into the jeep with us. As we started moving, Tamotsu shouted, "Shunji, you idiot!"

A flicker of warmth, ever so faint, spread through my cold heart.

♥ ♥ ♥

I didn't sleep a wink until dawn. Shunji never called. It was a long night. Try as I might not to think about them, I couldn't help imagining all the sex Shunji and Oinuma were having. My body was shivering; three blankets didn't make a difference. I knew about Shunji's sexual history; it was only too clear that if Oinuma came on to him, he would accept his advances. And then he would start responding actively himself, enjoying every minute.

What was Shunji thinking when he went with Oinuma? Didn't it ever occur to him that Oinuma might come on to him? No, no . . . I'm sure he was just happy to have run into an old friend, that's all—he wasn't thinking anything. For Shunji, sex isn't an act you perform when you have special feelings for a person, it's just a matter of "being friends," of responding to an advance. He had no reason to think anything else. It wouldn't even occur to him that he was being unfaithful to me by having sex with Oinuma.

And yet from my point of view, it was worse than a simple matter of infidelity. Shunji had left without saying anything. Was it so easy for him to forget me—was I no more to him? I thought I meant something special to him since he had chosen me to be his wife, but maybe I had just gotten carried away with my own conceit.

As much as I tried not to think about them, images of Shunji and Oinuma having sex kept filtering through my brain. They feel each other's muscles. They touch each other's arms and shoulders and chests; then they begin to stroke, to probe, to close their fingers around tendons. Soon they are fondling each other. Does Oinuma kiss Shunji? Will he fold Shunji in his arms, climb on top of him? Does Shunji, ever so naturally, take Oinuma's penis in his mouth?

I wasn't averse to homosexual fantasizing, but there was no pleasure in it when it was connected to real-life events like this. Shunji had said that he didn't have much fun touching men, he liked women better, but these words were little comfort now. My jealousy wasn't only inspired by the thought of them having sexual intercourse. The unbearable loneliness that coursed through me stemmed from the emotional intimacy I was sure they were sharing.

Even as I was being tormented, I struggled to turn my thoughts in another direction, telling myself that maybe Tamotsu was right—Oinuma and Shunji might just be talking, catching up, unlikely though that seemed. That's how I managed to survive the night.

When evening came and there was still no word from Shunji, I called his house. The answering machine picked up. Surely he'd be back tonight, so since I had to return the Pajero anyway, I decided to drive over.

I parked the jeep in front of Shunji's aunt's house, and walked around back to the little house where Shunji lived. The lights weren't on, which was not unusual, but the windows were closed and the air-conditioning wasn't running—he wasn't there. Still, I couldn't help knocking. The banging on the door of the empty house found an echo in my heart.

A window on the second floor of the main house opened, and I turned around. "Oh, it's you! What are you doing?" The voice was Chisato's.

Feeling like a drowning woman clinging to a straw, I called up to her, "Shunji hasn't come back yet, has he?"

"No. He isn't at your place?"

Seeing that I had no response, Chisato pulled her head back inside the window, and in a bit the sliding door rattled open. Chisato stepped out into the garden. When I saw her face at close range, I was shocked: the area around her left cheekbone was so terribly discolored I could make out the bluish-black bruise even in the faint evening light.

"Oh my god, what happened to you!" I asked, forgetting my own pain for the moment. "How did you get that?"

Chisato put a hand to her left cheek, as if she had only just remembered the bruise, and smiled thinly. "I think of it as a woman's badge of honor."

"Did Haruhiko hit you?" I asked, horrified. "How could he treat you like that! It's—"

"It's okay. Haruhiko loves me. He hits me to prove he isn't surrendering to his love. Those were his words. What I want to know is what's up with *you?*"

I explained the circumstances of Shunji's disappearance to her.

"Yeah, I know Oinuma," she said, grimacing. "He's gay to the gills."

My heart was thumping.

"He used to take Shunji to the gym a lot. And he'd shoo me off, telling me I wasn't necessary, even though I was Shunji's manager! Rude son of a bitch." Chisato lifted her jaw and gazed at me as I stood mute. "You sure are dumb, aren't you? Letting him lead Shunji off like that, right under your nose."

"Yes, I'm dumb."

"Sorry to say this, but I feel a teensy bit of glee."

"Yes, I can see that."

Perhaps my lack of fight touched her, because she softened her tone. "Shunji's gay streak just refuses to straighten out."

A "gay streak"? The way I saw it, Shunji simply didn't distinguish between homosexual and heterosexual love. All he needed was love. But I decided not to point this out.

"Well, at least it was a man, right?"

"Why is that good?"

"They say gay relationships don't last long."

So I could expect Shunji to return before too long? If only he would come back, I'd be able to forget this sadness, this loneliness. I wanted to shout, loud enough for my voice to reach his ears, *Shunji, I want you back!*

Instead of going back indoors, Chisato kept standing with her arms crossed, watching as I steered the Pajero into the garage. She didn't return my greeting when I nodded before leaving, but presumably she had stayed to see me off. When you're feeling miserable, even a minimal gesture of kindness makes you feel better. She'll be my relative when Shunji and I eventually get married, and when she is I won't forget her kindness today. Assuming, of course, that Shunji comes back.

Shunji didn't call that evening. Or the following day. I began to wonder if he was all right. He couldn't fail to think of me for three nights in a row—that simply wasn't possible. Perhaps he was confined in a room somewhere, and couldn't get to a phone? I was frantic, unable to concentrate, and so a little past noon on the fourth day of his absence, I called Shigeki. When I told him that Shunji hadn't even called, he moaned, his voice heavy.

"Do you think I should contact the police?" I asked.

"Well . . . how would you explain the situation?"

He had a point. The police couldn't know about the Flower Show.

"I did a little digging around myself, too," Shigeki said. "Apparently this man, Oinuma Tamayuki, works as a private manager for that musician guy—I think Kusakabe Shinobu was his name. He's been bobbing around as a free agent in the music industry for about a decade, finding ghostwriters for third-rate musicians and taking care of other business that goes on behind the scenes. But even if he's independent, we can still put pressure on him. I'll find some way to make him send Shunji back and—"

"No, no, you don't have to make him return Shunji," I said, cutting Shigeki off. "Shunji can decide for himself whether or not he wants to come back, so you don't need to pressure the guy. I just want to know that Shunji is all right, and I'd like to hear his voice, that's all . . ."

"Okay, I understand. I'll see what I can find out."

Around ten o'clock that night, Shunji called, totally unapologetic—*unaware!*—that he'd abandoned me, babbling on cheerily. "Tama found this really great job for me! He says I'm going to be the exclusive song-writer for Kusakabe Shinobu. I'll be a ghostwriter, so my name won't go on the songs, but I'll get a lot of money for it—in royalties. And I'll do studio work and tours with him as his keyboardist, too!"

Who did Shunji think he was talking to?

And after all that had happened, his voice, which should have sounded warm and familiar, making me want to see him, just seemed like noise. I had to struggle to keep my cool. "That sounds like a wonderful opportunity, Shunji, but what about the Flower Show?"

"Oh, yeah, I guess I won't be able to go. Tama says it's no help to my career to be on the road all the time. I need to be doing good work in a place where people can see me. You go on alone, okay? Tell me about it when we get together."

"When we get together . . . you mean we can see each other?"

"Sure. Boy, you say some strange things, don't you! Your voice sounds kind of weird, too, you know."

I couldn't take it any longer, and I blurted out: "What have you been doing these past three days? Why didn't you call me? I want to see you right now!"

For a few moments, silence. Then: "I've been with Tama the whole time. He says he's just fallen out of love, and he's so lonely he doesn't know what to do with himself."

"You made me worry, going off without saying anything like that."

"You were worried? Ah, I see—good point. Sorry about that."

His apology was nothing but a formality. He didn't have the slightest idea what it meant to be anxious about someone.

"Where are you now?" I asked. "Can't I see you?"

"Hold on a sec."

I listened as Shunji stepped away from the phone and then, faintly, the two men spoke. Their conversation dragged on for a bit. The fact that Shunji had to consult Oinuma about whether he could see me meant, obviously, that he himself didn't have any strong desire to. Struggling to keep from crying, I began to tremble. I was afraid my breathing would turn into a moan, so I clamped my hand over my mouth.

"Hey, Kazumi?" Shunji's tone was apologetic now. "Tama was drinking tonight so he can't drive me back, and he has to introduce me to all sorts of people tomorrow. He says I won't have any free time for a while."

I hadn't wanted to say anything too pathetic, but I couldn't control myself anymore. "You don't need me at all?"

"Oh, no, I'm totally fine. No need to worry."

His reply was bright and cheerful. He didn't mean to hurt me, he just was deaf to the emotion behind my question. I guess I could understand that, but I felt as if my heart had been ripped out of my body.

His jubilant voice sang out again. "I'll just have Tama look after me for the time being. Take care of yourself, okay? I'll call again soon."

I said goodbye, and Shunji hung up. I sat with the receiver pressed against my ear, unable to move.

I tried to take stock of the situation, thinking over everything that had happened. But no matter how exuberant and well Shunji had seemed, the content was still the same: he had said we wouldn't be seeing each other for a while. I had been "dumped." I dropped the receiver and buried my face in my hands.

♥ ♥ ♥

Shigeki and Aiko came by for a visit.

My hopes soared when the doorbell rang, because I thought maybe, just maybe, it was Shunji, deciding to come see me after all, but when I opened the door, it was Shigeki and Aiko, standing there very quietly. I would be lying if I said I wasn't disappointed, but the sight of them gave me relief.

"Were you able to talk to Shunji?" Shigeki asked once they were seated.

"Yes," I croaked. I hadn't spoken for days, and I hardly recognized my own voice.

"The day after you called, I reached Oinuma by phone. He said you and Shunji had come to an understanding, so there was no point in an outsider like me butting in. The guy sounded pretty sure of himself."

There was a brief silence before I realized Shigeki was waiting for me to respond. I cast around for something appropriate to say. "I suppose Oinuma feels he can take good care of Shunji."

"And that's okay with you? You're happy to leave Shunji in his hands?"

"It looks like Shunji would rather be with him right now." Even I noticed how listless and flat my tone was. "Forcing him to come back to me won't solve anything."

Shigeki exchanged a glance with Aiko, who then said, "If Shunji could see how pale you are right now—"

"He can't."

Shigeki swallowed uncomfortably.

"That's how Shunji is," I continued, "he never devotes himself to anything, so even if I explained how devoted I am to him, or how horrible and crushed I feel, he'd never understand. So it's really impossible for me to blame him."

Aiko exhaled.

"Shunji has gone away from me, but it's not like he died. We're both alive. We'll have chances to get together sometime." As I was talking, not really believing myself, I thought of something that brought a wry smile to my lips. "I was worried that Eiko might split up with Tamotsu, but Shunji ended up dumping me first."

"Have you been going to school these days?" Shigeki asked.

"No," I said. "I don't have the energy."

So, speaking cautiously and kindly, he broached the subject: "In that case, how do you feel about touring with us again? It'd be a lot better going around with us than just staying holed up in here."

"I can't convince myself to perform," I answered flatly.

"You don't have to."

"Then I'd be imposing."

Shigeki seemed to have anticipated this, because he launched into a speech that sounded as if he'd prepared it ahead of time: "Then how about this—you come along with us, thinking of it as a way to distract yourself. We'll look for the right moment to convince you to become a full-fledged member. Think of it as a game. If you haven't decided to join in the show by the end of the tour, you win. If we manage to talk you into joining, we win. Would you be willing to come along if you could look at it in that way?"

"Last time," Aiko continued, "we hadn't yet given any thought to what kind of performance we would ask you to do, so we weren't very dedicated in our efforts to persuade you. It was our fault for being so lazy. So as far as we're concerned, we're the ones who imposed on you by dragging you around pointlessly for three weeks."

"Don't be silly, I had fun!" I said, unable to restrain myself.

Aiko grinned as if she had been waiting for me to say this. "In that case, why not come? We want another chance to win you over."

The first point in the game went to Shigeki and Aiko. I nodded my agreement and shook hands with them.

Two days later, with my traveling bag slung over my arm, I set out for the west gate of Shinjuku Station, where the Flower Show minibus would be waiting. The troupe had been doing shows in Tokyo and the outlying areas while I was crying in my apartment; starting today, it would be making a tour of Hokuriku and Tohoku that would last approximately twenty days. Glancing in the mirror on my way out the door, I noticed that my face was looking less pallid. I was also looking forward to the company of my friends. My heart swelled when I caught sight of them.

Tamotsu started hooting the moment he saw me. "Yah! The jiltee!"

I laughed, since there was nothing else I could do, and then threw my bag at him. Tamotsu dodged it, leaving Eiko to catch it. She didn't speak; she just beamed at me. Masami sprinted over.

"So Shunji *dumped* you? To think he was so selfish—how like a *man!*"

"I don't know about selfish," Tamotsu said. "I mean, a kid like that, so totally lacking in social skills—"

"You're hardly one to speak," Eiko said.

"I've got more than Shunji, that's for sure."

"For sure?"

Masami sighed. "And you two were so *cute* as the Emperor and Empress."

Yukie sauntered over. "Yes," she said, "we're all human in the end— even the best of us."

"What a line. Heavy with the weight of years of experience . . ."

Paying no heed to Tamotsu's heckling, Yukie turned toward me. "You just have to keep going after men, you see—any man, not just Shunji."

"What do you mean?"

"You've got to make him believe no other woman could ever take your place."

"I think I'm aware of that, actually."

"No, actually you aren't," Yukie said. "Maybe it's not the right time to be saying this, but you left Shunji to his own devices much too much. I was watching the whole time, you know. During dinner, for instance. You didn't feed him, even though he's blind."

"But Shunji can eat just fine by himself, as long as he knows where the plates and bowls are."

"Whether or not he can eat isn't the issue. Men like to be pampered, and that's what draws them to a woman."

I knew people like to make these generalizations, but having the stereotype explained to me in such total seriousness left me at a loss. "Wouldn't a man feel that he's being treated like a baby, having someone help him when he doesn't need any help? I think he'd hate it," I said. "Personally, I think it's creepy when men pull out my chair for me at a restaurant, or jump out of the driver's seat and run around to open my door when we're getting out of the car. And I'm sure Shunji feels the same way."

Yukie's perpetual frown turned even more dour. "My, what a hard little head you have. You don't understand the games men and women play, do you? Not at all."

"I've read many arguments similar to yours," I replied. "Somehow it feels that they only apply in some other universe, not the one I live in. They are persuasive, to the extent that women and men, somewhere in this world, have fun pampering each other like that. But it doesn't feel real to me. And I suspect in real life that kind of thing hardly ever happens, or only happens in books. That's how it strikes me. It's like something in a fairy tale."

"You're the one who's living in a fairy tale," Yukie said quickly, seeming to have taken my comments badly. "I happen to have a handicap, so I can't be as blasé as you—I have to fight desperately to keep my man from abandoning me. I mean, can you even imagine how hard I struggle? Can you?"

"You call him every day." Tamotsu blurted. "I think we'd prefer not to hear anything more detailed."

Yukie glared at him.

"I'm just giving her a bit of advice. I wanted to help."

"Too late. Shunji's flown the coop."

Yukie still seemed inclined to speechify. "The point is, men and women have to negotiate, and—"

Shigeki tapped Yukie's shoulder from behind. "It's no use," he said. "Kazumi won't understand."

Aiko, who had one foot on the step of the minibus, threw in her two cents. "I don't understand either. Do you think it's a generation thing?"

"*I* understand you, darling," Masami muttered. "But I also know a woman whose husband ditched her because, as he said, her pandering wifeliness got on his nerves."

"Just goes to show you there are all kinds of couples in the world," Yohei said.

"Great, why don't we leave it at that," Shigeki said pleasantly, then wrapped his arm around Yukie's shoulder and helped her into the minibus. The rest of us followed.

Sitting in the very back seat, as I had last time, I was struck forcefully by Shunji's absence. A fresh wave of loneliness was about to crash over me when Aiko came and sat down beside me. Tamotsu, who had the seat in front of mine, turned around as well.

"Don't worry, I'll play with you."

I was about to thank him, but I changed my mind. "That sounds ominous," I said.

Aiko and Eiko burst out laughing.

"It's true, Kazumi. You'd better be careful."

"Sounds like you've got Tamotsu figured out."

He and I were still smiling at each other when the minibus lurched into traffic.

Chapter 11

The new job I was assigned, now that Shunji's absence had deprived me of my position as Assistant to the Troupe Pianist, was to facilitate the playing of the canned background music by pressing PLAY on the tape recorder.

No doubt Shigeki thought he was being helpful by giving me something to do, even if it was purely symbolic—he understood that I'd feel uncomfortable without some kind of role of my own. But the task was so mindless that a monkey could have done it, and repeating it, day in and day out, only made me feel more useless. I began to think about overcoming my qualms performing in the show.

Shigeki was going to try and win me over during this tour, but he had yet to make any direct overture. Maybe he was waiting for me to cheer up, since the pain of being dumped by Shunji was still fresh. I couldn't sleep nights, even now. I would climb alone into bed and struggle to empty my mind and not think of Shunji, but always my heart would start to ache and I'd end up lying awake there until the first rays of dawn. I must have looked worn out.

Tamotsu didn't let that worry him. Whenever he saw me, he'd cry, "Give masturbation a chance!" or "Hey, nothing cures a case of the blues like a good wank!" I paid him no attention because my heart was so heavy and I had no interest in bodily pleasure. But then, one sleepless night, having heard the word "masturbation" so many times, I thought, why not? Physical stimulation might at least make my body feel good, even if I wasn't in the mood.

But it turned out I was right after all: my toe-penis didn't respond, and neither did any other part of my body. The rubbing was painful, and my toe-penis—which had enlarged just a tad, as if out of politeness—began to look puffy, like it was having an allergic reaction. So things weren't looking good even in terms of my participating in the Flower Show. My spirits sank.

The next time Tamotsu trumpeted the benefits of masturbation, I protested. "It's no good. My body is half dead."

"Seriously? It didn't work?" He cocked his head, genuinely perplexed. "I wonder what's wrong."

"Would you be able to do it if your lover just left you?"

"Please." Tamotsu sniffed. "I can't *ever* do it. No masturbation. No sex."

Of course I assumed that was the case, his body being as it was, but he acted like such a true believer that I thought he had figured out a way. That was pretty dumb of me. "If you've never done it yourself, why'd you suggest it to me?"

Tamotsu scratched the side of his mouth, smiling thinly. "Well, it's pretty easy to imagine, right? The effect it'd have?"

"Your imagination is way off track."

"I don't know about that. You're probably just abnormal. I mean, don't most folks masturbate to cheer themselves up after the end of a relationship?"

"Some, maybe, but I suspect most people would find it impossible."

"Getting dumped really hurts that badly?" Tamotsu peered into my face. "I've never had that experience."

This was something of a surprise. I had just been given the heave-ho at the age of twenty-two for the first time in my life, but I was a late bloomer. Surely most people fall in love, and get dumped, sooner?

Tamotsu swiveled his head around toward Aiko, Eiko, and Shigeki, who were standing talking near us. "Hey, Aiko, you ever been jilted?"

"No," she replied. "Never dumped anyone, never been dumped."

"How about you, Shigeki?"

"I've loved in vain a few times, but I don't think I've ever had a woman I was going out with take a dislike to me or get bored when the feeling wasn't mutual, if that's what you mean."

How like Shigeki to be so specific about what it means to be jilted.

Without bothering to ask Eiko whether she'd ever been dumped, Tamotsu turned back to me and clapped his hands together. "All right then! I don't really understand what you're going through, but if you're feeling that down, I'll let you borrow my video games. Video games are *really* the best cure for the blues!"

The video game set Tamotsu handed me that evening wasn't the portable computer game he had lent me in the past; it was the kind you connect to a television screen. In my ignorance of such things, I had no idea how to hook it up. Tamotsu was incredulous—in this thoroughly video-gamed age!

He and Eiko accompanied me back to my room to set things up. Once done, Tamotsu seemed in no rush to leave. Seeing how inept I was with the joystick, he stretched out on the bed and started giving me instructions, punctuating them with curses. *How many times do I have to tell you to get the goddamn weapon there! . . . You're not doing dogshit! . . . No, NO, you can't jump over that monster! . . . Oh my god, why are you climbing on top of him? Get away! . . . You're gonna get fucked over . . .* Tamotsu's frustration must have peaked around the same time I'd had enough of his haranguing. Suddenly he grabbed the joystick and growled, "Let me show you how to do it!"

"How is your doing it going to help Kazumi?" Eiko called out from where she was sitting.

In the blink of an eye, Tamotsu had cleared level one and moved on to level two. "I'm just giving her a little demonstration, that's all," he replied, his eyes glued to the screen. "Here, look—if you jump, the shelter comes down . . ." A moment later, however, he was saying nothing. He was completely lost in the game.

Eiko turned to where I sat on the bed. "Hardly a night goes by when he doesn't play these games." She seemed to think Tamotsu was being rude.

I didn't. I didn't mind at all. I couldn't tear my eyes away from the brilliantly colored scenes unfurling on the screen, one after another, and I even felt comforted that Tamotsu and Eiko were spending the evening with me.

Only after Eiko had scolded him for the third time did Tamotsu relinquish the joystick. After they left, around midnight, I had a go at the game and actually got into it. It really was fun, and I didn't stop until dawn. It was a lot better than wallowing in my misery, unable to fall asleep. The next night, too, and the night after that, I saw in the new day playing video games. Before long, scenes from the games started rising up before me whenever I closed my eyes, even during the day.

Tamotsu was right about video games being the best cure for heartache. As long as I was playing, my mind was empty—I didn't even have to try to empty it. I was able to fend off the sadness, the loneliness. Video games have a special effect on people, something sports and other types of entertainment don't. Because no matter how wrapped up you get in other pastimes, you never completely forget the realities of life. With video games you lose yourself wholly in an alternate reality—it's as if you've been incorporated into the computer. You feel happy to be controlled by the machine, to hand yourself over to something mechanical. It wasn't sex, of course, but it was unmistakably erotic.

Needless to say, the second I finished a game, I would find myself back in the same old reality, and the pain would return. Video games might numb my feelings temporarily, but I knew the problem wouldn't be solved until I got over the hurt. I was whiling away my time on a mindless diversion, I knew that, but as long as the machine was in my room, I couldn't leave it alone.

Tamotsu chuckled when he saw my bloodshot eyes. "How's it going? Have you gotten any better?"

How could I *not* have? I invited Tamotsu and Eiko back to my room to show them. I tried playing against Tamotsu, even though I knew I wouldn't be any match for him, only to surprise us all by winning. Tamotsu took it very badly, and kept pestering me to play again and again until he won. Then he said he had an even better game back in his room and went and got it. That night they left at about three in the morning.

From then on, Tamotsu and Eiko came over every evening, and our game-playing continued until three or four. Eiko wasn't bad either. There was no three-player format, so while two of us were battling it out, the third would take a bath or flop down on the bed to wait their next turn.

Tamotsu really loved video games. For him, the intellectual pleasure of figuring out how each individual game could be won didn't seem to matter; no, it was the erotic bliss of becoming one with the machine. As I looked at him fiddling with the joystick, the thought crossed my mind that he, too, was playing to numb his emotions, just like me. Perhaps he, too, suffered unbearably every day.

Eiko wasn't committed to the game. Playing didn't bore her, and from time to time she would gasp and groan the way we did, but I got the sense she was playing mainly for Tamotsu's sake. She said she was grateful for the time we spent together because it cut down on her quarrels with him, but probably she'd have felt uncomfortable sending Tamotsu off to my room alone.

With their nightly visits, the three of us seemed to grow more intimate, and that was nice. My eyes got used to seeing them, and even a glimpse of them from afar helped me feel calmer. That's how one really becomes close. So little by little, my loneliness ebbed.

But after staying up late every night, the three of us slept all day in the bus. This did not go unnoticed by the others in the troupe, and at one point, Masami sidled over, his hips swaying, and said, "Tell me, my dear—I hear you're having video game threesomes every night. Those machines are so *frightening*! Before you know it, you'll be *impotent*."

"Kazumi's already impotent."

This statement of Tamotsu's, lobbed in from the side, came as a bit of a revelation. It gave a name to what I'd been feeling—a condition usually reserved for men.

"She and Shin are in the same boat now!" he added gleefully.

"Oh, you poor *thing*! You want a fixer-upper? I have a *special* technique!"

"You leave her alone. Shin likes having a pal. Don't steal her from him."

Shigeki, overhearing this, joined in the conversation. "Your toe-penis isn't well?" he asked, squinting anxiously at my foot. "I don't guess it's the same for a man, huh? You don't get an erection automatically when sperm accumulates?"

Shigeki was thinking of the show; there would be no point in my going on stage if the toe-penis didn't get hard. He looked at me like he was inspecting merchandise, his face showing no trace of his usual amiable smile. My sunny mood clouded, and I felt a burst of panic.

"I'm sure it's just temporary," Shigeki said calmly after a moment, his expression brightening. "You'll get better soon."

I had to get my toe-penis back into form. This thought hit me before I understood what it meant—that I was now willing to perform in the show. In part, this was due to my being sick of pressing PLAY on the tape recorder night after night, but it was also due to the fact that with Shunji gone from my life, the only place I wanted to be was with my friends in the Flower Show.

And if I wanted a place in the Flower Show, then I would have to get my toe-penis back in order. Would my toe-penis recover naturally, as Shigeki had predicted? How long would Shigeki be willing to wait? I couldn't take anything for granted. It wasn't like it was a real penis, after all. What if it remained incapable of getting erect, and then one day just vanished? . . .

I did *not* want to lose my toe-penis.

♥ ♥ ♥

That night, Tamotsu and Eiko had suggested that I join them in their room for a change. After my single, their double room seemed incredibly spacious. We video-gamed as usual, and after Tamotsu had pulverized me, he trotted off to take a bath. It was Eiko's turn to play me, but she begged off, wanting to trim her nails first.

She'd already taken her bath and was wearing polka-dot pajamas. A sheet of newspaper was spread on the bed, and under the light of the bedside lamp she proceeded now to clip her toenails. I flopped down on the next bed and gazed idly at her, my eye landing on the raised, bluish veins on the back of the hand. What with Shunji's leaving me, I'd forgotten: it was the touch of that hand that made my toe-penis get so hard. The memory of that pleasure was very deep.

I said nothing, watching Eiko clip the nails on her right foot, toe by toe. When she got to her little toe, it looked like she was going to clip the top of the toe instead of the nail. "Why are you doing that? You're going to hurt yourself," I said.

Eiko raised her head. "The nail is deformed. It doesn't grow out, it bulges."

This was the first time I'd ever heard of anything like that.

"The shape of my foot is a little unusual," she said. "I have a hard time finding shoes that fit, and it was worse before . . . The pointy ones I had to wear with my high school uniform were killers. I went on wearing them until the nail on this toe cracked.

"It split down to the base. The crack never really healed, and the nail got all bumpy, sort of yellow. I thought it was dead, but it keeps bulging back out, so I guess it's alive."

"Can I see?" I asked.

I went over to where she was on the bed, and she stuck out her foot. It was just as she had said. The toenail was thick and lumpy, like a little rock.

Strangely, I felt moved. There was such a contrast between the elegant firmness of her ankle and the unruly roughness of this toenail. Learning about this little peculiarity of hers, perched daintily at the very end of her body, I felt as if I had rediscovered Eiko.

"Don't stare like that. You make me feel embarrassed."

I burst out laughing. "Which is more embarrassing—a deformed nail on your little toe or a penis that's poking out on your big toe?"

Eiko laughed, too, then added, "But this toenail is gross and your toe-penis is cute."

"It's not gross." I put my hand on Eiko's toenail, touching it the way she had stroked my toe-penis in the outdoor bath.

She quickly pulled her foot away and sat on it.

"No fair! You touched mine!"

"It's too ticklish."

It was true: her body was quivering with laughter. I pretended to be taking aim at her armpits, and she squealed, scurrying away.

"The nail on my toe changed shape, too, when it became a penis, but—"

"Yes, but yours had a nice shape. Can I see it again?"

I sat down on the edge of the bed and stuck out my right foot. A gleaming, opalescent hemisphere about half an inch across sat decoratively on the tip of my freakish toe-penis. Eiko might think it was pretty, but it was bizarre. Eiko sighed, propping an elbow on the bed.

"Your nail doesn't grow?"

"No."

"It looks like you had it done. I wish my nail was like that."

"Oh?" I was about to tell her how nice I thought hers was, but I changed my mind. I wouldn't be able to explain why. Somehow, I felt like I would love to have a nail like hers on my foot, crushed beyond recognition. At the same time, Eiko's nail only seemed charming because it was part of *her* body.

I was about to ask to look at it again, at its deformity, when Tamotsu sprinted out of the bathroom, a towel wrapped around his waist. He rummaged through his duffle bag and pulled out a pair of brightly colored boxers.

"Wouldn't it be smarter to get your undies ready *before* you bathe?" Eiko said, still lying with her head propped on her arm.

"Mind your own business. I don't feel like I've had a bath unless I wrap a towel around me when I get out." With boxers in hand, he jumped up onto the bed with us.

"Oh my, it's the impotent toe-penis!" he cried. "Still can't get it up? Want a porn mag?"

"No thank you." I couldn't suppress a sniff at Tamotsu's complete predictability.

"Why not? You want porn aimed at women?"

"That's not the issue. Pornography is other people's fantasies. I don't see anything exciting in that."

"But you can find stuff in other people's fantasies that overlaps with yours," he said, pulling up his boxers. He sat on the bed and crossed his legs. "If you can't, that means you're immature. You haven't figured out what sort of pattern your sexual desires fall into."

"Is that what you call maturity? When your sexual desires conform to a pattern? That's just decadence."

"Yeah, maybe so. But you're bound to start repeating certain behaviors once you figure out that you like them, don't you think?"

"Why should you have to learn to like a fantasy?"

"You don't have to, you just do—that's how it happens. Normally."

"What do you mean, 'normally'? Who's your standard?

"You know . . . the majority of people."

"And you're one of the majority?"

Tamotsu had been speaking smoothly, but now his tongue began tripping. "Well . . . I'm different, it's true, but I know that's how the majority of people are. I'm so abnormal, I want to be 'normal,' so I make a point of studying the sexual desires of normal men."

"Using ridiculous magazine articles as your source, I bet."

"I don't know how ridiculous they are, but they're pretty convincing to me. I can imagine being like that, if I'd been born with a regular body."

"That just proves you've been poisoned by those magazines."

Tamotsu fell back onto the bed, his legs still crossed. He gazed up at the ceiling for a while, then dexterously sat up again without uncrossing his legs. There was a lively gleam in his eyes. "Can you show me what it's like, not being able to get it up?"

This was entirely unexpected. I didn't know how to respond.

"I've seen Shin have that sort of trouble," he went on, "but I've never seen anyone else. C'mon, let me see if you really can't get hard."

Tamotsu was asking me to masturbate in front of him! Until recently, this would have been shocking. But I felt perfectly at ease with Tamotsu and Eiko, and I knew the almost painful fascination Tamotsu had with penises. I was tempted to give him what he wanted. Besides, I smiled to myself, it could be like a dress rehearsal.

Sitting next to Eiko, I propped a pillow behind my back, then raised my right knee and began working my toe-penis. Tamotsu and Eiko watched intently. Their stares made me self-conscious, but the embarrassment and the exhibitionism were somehow titillating, and it occurred to me I might actually get an erection. I could feel my toe-penis responding, but not much. I felt no pleasure at all. The sound of flesh rubbing against flesh echoed forlornly through the silence.

Tamotsu planted his hands on the bed and began cheering my toe-penis on. "C'mon, stand tall!" When he saw that wasn't doing the trick, he said, "Just yanking on the thing isn't enough. You've got to think sexy thoughts, man!"

Tamotsu had wanted to see me impotent; now he was eager for an erection. I was trying my best to get it up, too. But nothing sexy came to mind.

"Think of the best sex you ever had with Shunji."

At the sound of Shunji's name, my hand stopped. I had grown used to his absence, but I was still a long way from being able to take pleasure in memories of him. I had slowly been getting over my depression, but now it returned, and my toe-penis, which had grown a size bigger, shriveled before our eyes.

"Tamotsu!" Eiko snapped. "You're so insensitive!"

"Gosh, I'm sorry." Tamotsu was both abashed and impressed. "It's true, huh? It really is a mental thing."

Lost in thought, he got up from the bed and put on a shirt. He came back with another plan: "Think about some really awesome sex you had with someone other than Shunji."

What made him think I had such a wealth of sexual experience? "I don't have any such memories," I said.

Tamotsu and Eiko gasped, flabbergasted.

"Are you serious? You're not just being stubborn?"

"You mean you never had sex with anyone but Shunji? Or that you did, but it wasn't very good?"

Wondering if it was common for lovers to have sex with other people, too, I explained how Masao had assiduously avoided my toe-penis and how Chisato had quasi raped me.

"So until now the only people who have touched your toe-penis, apart from Shunji and this Chisato person, are Tamotsu and me?"

"And you got hard when we touched you, didn't you!"

Tamotsu and Eiko exchanged glances.

Now that they had framed it for me in this way, I began to think the special bond among us might have been the critical thing. The next words out of Tamotsu's mouth didn't, then, come as a total surprise.

"Let me try, all right? Maybe you just need someone else to do it for you."

I have to admit I found the thought appealing, but his directness embarrassed me, and I felt my cheeks flush.

Tamotsu snickered. "Don't worry. I won't be stupid and conceited enough to think you're in love with me."

When he put it like that, I couldn't refuse. I nodded, grinning, and he stretched out a hand and wrapped it tightly around my toe-penis. I could feel the masculine force of his grip, and the sensation of actually being touched, skin on skin, brought on a wave of happiness inside me. Before the wave could crest, however, he started moving his hand and squeezing so hard that I found myself in dreadful pain. I pulled my foot away. "Ow! That hurts!" I cried.

Tamotsu looked puzzled. "But Shin doesn't get hard unless I squeeze like that."

"Different people feel things differently," Eiko said.

Tamotsu looked at her, then gestured to my toe-penis with his jaw. "All right, you try."

Eiko changed places with Tamotsu. She looked at me and smiled a little, as if she were simply saying hi. It was so natural that I forgot my embarrassment—as well as the discomfort I felt about homosexual sex. In fact, I found myself excited—as if some thrilling game were about to get underway. Looking at my toe-penis, Eiko caressed the tip of my foot lightly, as if she were patting a child on the head.

As I see it, there were two problems with Tamotsu's approach: his grip was too tight, and he was too mechanical, his touch lacking any emotion. Because that one caress from Eiko was enough to set the withered nerves of my toe-penis quivering. She folded her hand gently around my member. She let her fingers do the wandering. She didn't try to rush matters.

The things she was doing weren't themselves that exciting, and the test to get the toe-penis hard seemed to be forgotten; in fact, it had slipped my mind that my toe-penis was a sexual organ. I had the illusion Eiko was simply fondling my toe—an ordinary big toe, nothing remarkable about it. The tension drained from my body. The dance her fingers were performing looked so beautiful; I kept following the movements with my eyes, feeling perfectly relaxed. And when I noticed how wonderful what she was doing to me was, my toe began to feel more and more.

Suddenly she seized my toe-penis, squeezing it tightly. A shock of pleasure darted through my body. Eiko must have noticed how my foot quivered. The momentary surge of toe-penile pleasure subsided as she loosened her grip, but when she put her hand around my ankle to keep me from lifting my foot, I felt a tremendous pleasure in her touch, something that approached fulfillment. And then, as she began moving her right hand, my toe-penis began to stiffen.

"Hey, looking good!" Tamotsu clapped his hands. "Take it all the way!"

Holding my full erection, Eiko turned to me, a broad smile on her face. I was too surprised at the turn of events to smile back. She shifted to one side and lifted my right foot onto her knee. Now she was holding my ankle with one hand and my right heel was sandwiched between her thighs, fixed in place. The warmth of her skin began to seep into my heel, and the sense of comfort spread—it came to seem as if my entire foot, from the ankle on down, had metamorphosed into a giant toe-penis. Then, as the movements of her hand grew more rapid, the pleasure concentrated in the one organ.

I can't remember what I was looking at when the orgasm hit. But the sight that met my eyes afterward, as my breathing steadied, was Eiko's hand, gently stroking the top of my foot, which was still resting on her knee. The next instant all those enticing memories of the things her hand had done to me in the past came back to life inside me, vividly real, and I hurriedly pulled my foot away. I couldn't look at Eiko, because I was afraid I would get another erection.

"Congratulations on your recovery!" Tamotsu slapped my shoulder. "But what's the deal—how come Eiko can get you hard when I can't? I feel kind of insulted." He sounded a bit pouty, like when we were playing video games and he lost.

"You're too rough," Eiko said.

"Not having a working penis of my own makes it hard for me to know how to handle it, you know. I've never had sex with a guy either, so I don't know the best techniques."

I didn't think it was a matter of technique. It wasn't like Eiko had a secret recipe for erections. I suspected the reason my toe-penis had gotten hard was that she'd first gotten me relaxed, made me feel calm and

The Apprenticeship of Big Joe P

intimate, rather than just dragging me into an erotic impulse. Or maybe being gentle and intimate was her technique.

"Unlike you, huh, Eiko? You sure know how to handle a penis! I guess it makes sense, considering all the experience you've had."

I could feel the tenor of things suddenly changing. There was bitterness in Tamotsu's voice, anger at Eiko. That familiar grim smile appeared on his face.

"Remind me—how many dicks have you sucked?" His mood was turning ugly.

"I don't think this is the time to be talking like that, Tamotsu," Eiko replied, trying to keep calm.

"Yeah, I get it. You've had so much practice, you're good at getting guys hard. You have a right to brag. I mean, you've done it with . . . how many was it—five guys—right before my eyes!"

"What are you talking about! As if you didn't *make* me do it! You're the one who said you wanted to see how regular men and women . . ."

An unbearably painful scene rose before my eyes. Paralyzed by the image, I couldn't even intervene in their argument.

"Oh please, don't talk like I victimized you. You had your fun, too—or are you going to deny that?"

"You think I was having *fun*? God, you are so warped!"

"Ah, which is more warped, me or your lust? It made you excited that I was watching, didn't it? Oh sure, it must have felt a hell of a lot better than having me ram Shin's scrawny little dick into you. And the sight of me watching you, biting my fingers—that got you even more excited, didn't it? Didn't it!"

Eiko stood up. She put on her sweater and headed for the door, not looking back. Tamotsu hurriedly pulled on his pants. The click of the door closing behind Eiko reverberated through the room. Tamotsu ran after her.

"Don't you walk out on me! I'll *make* you listen, whether you like it or not!"

I could hear Tamotsu bellowing down the hallway until the door, which he had left open, eased shut on its own.

I was left alone in the spacious double room. I didn't know what to do. There were three little valleys on the bed, where the three of us had been sitting just a moment ago. The cord for the computer game was still plugged into the TV. The three cups we'd been drinking out of earlier were still sitting on the table. We had been having a great time, but that time was over. All at once the room began to feel cold.

I went back to my own room. The doors in this hotel locked automatically, so I went by the front desk and dropped off Tamotsu and Eiko's room key.

Something was up with my toe-penis. It seemed warm, and also kind of stiff. On the other hand, maybe it wasn't stiff at all—maybe it had contracted, shriveling into a little blob. I didn't think it came from the excitement I'd just experienced, for the first time in ages—it felt different from that. Each time I found myself recalling the awful things that Tamotsu had screamed at Eiko, worse than any I'd ever heard from him before, my heart ached and my toe-penis was overcome by a sort of tingly sensation that wasn't exactly painful but was far from pleasant. I was in shock at how outrageously twisted Tamotsu was, but would a shock like this really have such an effect on an organ so sensitive to pleasure?

I believed Eiko: she'd performed sexual acts with other men in Tamotsu's presence because Tamotsu asked her to. And the perversity behind his harassment of Eiko became a little understandable. The saddest thing was that every time he attacked her, he did it with stupid, cookie-cutter images of women in porn movies in mind: "The Woman Who Gets Excited Going to Bed With Other Men in Her Lover's Presence," "The Woman Who Wants Nothing But a Hard, Fast Cock," and so on. Tamotsu didn't actually know any women like that. He'd been taken in by a pornographic fantasy, and both he and Eiko were suffering for it.

A couple of hours passed as I tried unsuccessfully to fall asleep. There was a knock at the door. It was Eiko. Tamotsu was standing behind her, a distance back.

"Sorry to disturb you," Eiko said. "Do you have the key to our room?"

I told her I'd left it at the front desk, and she whipped around to face Tamotsu. "Did you hear her? The key's at the front desk. Go get it." Her words had not a trace of human warmth.

Tamotsu stood stock-still, his head down, peeking up at her.

"Don't just stand there!" she snapped. "Get moving! I don't even want to see your face."

She sounded like she meant it. Tamotsu clicked his tongue, then walked slowly off toward the elevators. He stopped once on the way and turned back to look at Eiko, who stood with her back to him. When he had gone, she apologized once more for waking me and started to close the door.

I held the door open. "What are you going to do?" I asked.

"Find some place to sleep."

"You'll catch cold!"

"That's better than having to be with Tamotsu."

I put my hand on Eiko's arm. "Do you want to stay here?"

Eiko looked at me, anger smoldering in her eyes; then her expression softened, and she stepped into my room. When we lay down next to each other, I sensed the October chill clinging to her body.

"Do you want to take a bath to warm up?" I asked.

"I'm all right. I'm so angry I feel hot."

I didn't want to press her.

"You think we're nuts, don't you?" she asked.

"Yes," I said.

"I think so myself. I mean, why should I have to sleep with men I'm not at all interested in for a loser like him? You wouldn't have done it, would you?"

"I don't know, I might have. If I were in your place."

I heard Eiko turning to face me in the dark, then a raspy laugh.

"Tell me . . . why do you think I haven't broken up with Tamotsu?"

"Because you're in love with him?"

"That's not the only reason. You know we grew up in the same neighborhood, and we've been friends ever since we were children, right?" Eiko's voice was tense. She paused for a moment, as if she were debating whether or not to go on, then continued. "Tamotsu is three years younger than me, you know, and he was a really nice, cute kid when he was small. Once, when I was ten and he was seven, we were in our shed, and I saw him. His body, I mean."

"You were playing doctor or something?"

"Hmm . . . I'm not sure I'd say that. Because I was the one making him take off his clothes—he wasn't doing it himself."

Eiko continued talking, speaking so quickly it was as if she was possessed. "Back then, Tamotsu wasn't aware yet that there was anything unusual about his body, so he was just giggling in this embarrassed kind of way. But I felt like I'd seen something I shouldn't have, and I got frightened. I sent him back home right away, and from then on I just kept praying he'd forget that I had seen him. But he didn't."

One day eight years later, Eiko came home from high school to find Tamotsu—who was in junior high school then, and had dyed his hair blond, trying to look tough—waiting for her in her yard. He shoved her into the shed where they had played their game those many years ago, and then, without any warning, he dropped his pants. "Remember this?" he shouted. "Of course, you're not likely to forget something this weird, huh?"

And so, on that very day, Tamotsu and Eiko became lovers.

"Even then I knew I didn't have to feel like I owed him anything just because I'd seen him when he was small. I went out with him for my own sentimental reasons. I had this idea we were destined to be together, and I felt kind of proud—I believed I was the only one who could accept him as he was, because I'd already seen him. The longer we went out, the stronger our emotional bond became, until I couldn't bear to be away from him."

"No matter what he says? No matter what he does?"

"Yes. Crazy, isn't it?"

"I don't know, but . . . haven't you ever fallen for anyone else?"

"Of course. I broke up with this college guy I'd been dating when Tamotsu and I started going out. I had to take all kinds of crap because of that, too, come to think of it. Maybe if Tamotsu had been my first boyfriend, he wouldn't always be comparing himself to men with normal bodies, and he wouldn't be so twisted."

Listening to her talk, I had the sense I understood, vaguely, why they didn't break up.

"Does Tamotsu love you?" I asked.

"I really can't say. I suppose so . . ." After a bit of hesitation, Eiko went on, "I've never had the experience of falling out of love, at least not like Shigeki describes it, but I think in a way I'm always in the process of falling out of love with Tamotsu, if you know what I mean."

I felt so bad for Eiko, tormented the way she was by Tamotsu, and I felt so sorry for Tamotsu, who was unable to accept Eiko's love for him, unable to stop tormenting her. What was he doing now, back in their room, alone? Lying in bed, staring into the darkness? Or playing computer games, trying to fend off his loneliness?

Eiko was lying quietly, facing the wall. Talking about these things didn't seem to have made her feel any better—quite the opposite. Reliving her past experiences must have set her mind racing, and she seemed restless. I wanted to stay awake until I heard her breathing slow and deepen, meaning she was asleep, but I drifted off to sleep first.

The angry flush still hadn't vanished from Eiko's face the next morning. As we stepped out of my room on our way to get breakfast, we ran into Yukie coming out of hers, which was directly across the hall. She gave us a funny look, and nodded perfunctorily when I said good morning. Only after we stepped into an elevator bound for the first floor did she raise her eyes and ask, "Where's Tamotsu?"

Eiko responded, without blinking, "I have no idea."

Tamotsu was already in the restaurant when we got there, sitting at a table with Masami, finishing his post-breakfast coffee. Catching sight of Eiko, he smiled sullenly, then looked away. Yukie went to sit with them, as Eiko and I found a table for ourselves. Masami turned around and regarded us suspiciously. Eiko just sat there, perfectly still, without a glance in Tamotsu's direction.

I did what I could to bear the awkwardness of the situation. I wanted them to hurry and make up. Shigeki and Aiko were sitting at another table nearby, chattering away cheerfully. I wished Tamotsu and Eiko could be on good terms the way they were.

As we started in on the toast and bacon and eggs, Tamotsu plodded over, looking like he had lost the battle of wills, and took a seat opposite

Eiko. I assumed he would apologize, but when he spoke it was clear he had no intention of doing anything of the sort.

"I bet you slept better without me around, huh? Maybe you ought to ask for a single room sometimes. Then you can masturbate all you like."

Eiko stopped moving her knife and fork, and responded without looking up. "Would you please leave? You're spoiling my meal."

Tamotsu's shoulders quivered. "Here, I'll flavor it for you," he said, then leaned forward and spat onto her plate.

Eiko threw down her silverware and stood up. Glowering at him, hatred oozing from every pore, she kicked her chair back and stormed out of the restaurant. Tamotsu ran mutely after her. Every eye in the restaurant had turned in their direction.

Aiko came and sat down across from me. My hand, holding a piece of toast, still hovered in midair.

"What's up with them?" she asked. "Did they fight last night?"

I nodded. I didn't know what to say.

Aiko chuckled. Naturally, they were all used to this. "And you couldn't do a thing, of course?"

I put my toast down on my plate and sighed. "You and Shigeki are lucky. You always seem so happy together."

"You think so?" Aiko replied, not quite enthusiastically.

"Well, aren't you?" I asked, glancing up from my plate.

Casting a glance toward Shigeki, she said quietly, "Yes, we're happy, but . . . You remember what happened that time you were squeezing my hand? When you saw how my hand had broken out in a rash, it made you feel kind of unpleasant, didn't it? As if you'd committed a crime—as if you were the cause of the disease?"

I didn't know what to say. I hadn't felt *unpleasant*, not exactly, but it was true that I'd felt dangerous, dirty, as if I had done something bad—at least as far as Aiko was concerned. Intellectually, I understood that it was an allergy, of course, but I had still felt bad.

"You think any man is tough enough to be with someone like me?"

"Yes, I do." I mean—Shigeki *was* that man, wasn't he? Tough and gentle, the perfect match for Aiko?

But Aiko shook her head. "No, even Shigeki . . . eventually he's bound to change his mind, decide he'd be better off with a normal woman. He's a normal man, after all, despite the wonderful thing he's got between his legs."

"I can't believe this."

"Our relationship is less warm than you think. We only make love when we have to, for the show. And we get sick of each other pretty regularly."

I lowered my eyes, disillusioned. Shigeki and Aiko had been my ideal couple. "The dream is shattered," I said. It came out a little ironic.

Aiko laughed and patted me on the head.

"My dream was, too. Who'd have thought the Emperor and Empress would part?"

I still couldn't believe what she'd told me. "If the two of you are bound to break up eventually, shouldn't Tamotsu and Eiko have broken up ages ago?"

"Those two are special. I mean, the whole nature of their relationship is totally different from ours. Keep watching, you'll understand soon enough," she said, starting to get up, only to freeze midway. "You shouldn't tell Shigeki what I just told you, obviously," she said.

Feeling my spine tense, I promised her I wouldn't.

♥ ♥ ♥

Eiko was still sulking when we checked out of the hotel and were getting ready to board the bus. Tamotsu looked as if he didn't know what to do, but he continued to be stubborn, making no effort to patch things up. Eiko sat down next to me on the bus, steering clear of Tamotsu. There were no further developments after the bus started moving, because all three of us soon fell asleep.

But that night, when I joined the group in the parking lot of our next hotel, from which we would be leaving for that night's show, Tamotsu was fooling around, sunny as ever, and Eiko was laughing and chatting with everyone. I strode over toward the group, relieved.

"I hear your toe-penis has recovered," Shigeki said to me.

My eyes turned automatically to Tamotsu, who looked back at me, utterly cool.

"Gotta broadcast the good news, you know," he said.

"Absolutely, it's terrific news!" Shigeki grinned. "No need to hold back now—we want you to perform in the show. We'll have to think about exactly what we want you to do. Tamotsu said Eiko's the one who managed to get you hard . . . Is that true?"

The thought that these intimate details were now common knowledge made me shrink. Eiko didn't seem embarrassed at all, and joined the rest of the troupe in the discussion.

"How long was her thing, completely erect?" Shigeki asked her.

"About six and a half inches, maybe seven."

The whole troupe tittered in awe. I shrank even more.

"Seven inches!" Yukie exclaimed. "*Gross.*"

"Don't be rude," Yohei said.

"No use, darling," Masami said. "Madame doesn't *like* penises."

"She likes men, though, doesn't she?" Tamotsu asked.

"Non *non*, no use trying. Madame has no *use* for a penis, you see."

"From a penis's point of view, her vagina's a pretty scary place, too."

"Thank you so much, all of you!" shouted Yukie, blushing a little. "If only you knew how many men's penises I've shriveled!"

Tamotsu chuckled. "You're an impotence factory!"

Shigeki, deep in thought, ignored the repartee. "Seven inches will have quite an impact, even if you don't do anything fancy. I think an exhibition of you masturbating will be fine. Do you think you'll be able to get it up every time?"

"I can't say for sure—"

"If you can't, Eiko can come out and give you a hand," Tamotsu said.

"Good idea. Gives the number a lesbian touch."

Now Eiko and I both were turning red, but Shigeki, in his role as producer, was all business.

"Is Eiko the only one who can get you hard?" Aiko asked.

"She sure didn't get cocky for me!" Tamotsu said.

"How like a penis to be choosy," said Yukie.

"You sure seem to resent the organ, huh, Yukie?" This was Yohei.

"I'm resentment through and through," she replied, twisting her lips.

"I can't hear myself think with all this racket," Shigeki muttered. "I'll think things over later tonight, and we'll talk about it when I've got a plan, okay, Kazumi?"

Since I was on the verge of stepping onto the stage myself, that night I watched the show seriously, paying attention to details. It was the first time I'd done that in a while. There was no mistaking the love in Shigeki's hands when he touched Aiko; I couldn't believe that their relationship was "less warm than you think," as Aiko had said.

Yohei and Masami's segment, and Yukie's, too, were the same as always.

Tamotsu was better behaved than usual with Eiko. She seemed to feel less tense with him when he was calm like this—she could relax and embrace him without fear. Shin had relatively little difficulty getting an erection. Moans that clearly weren't faked emerged from Eiko's lips as she lay under Tamotsu.

When Tamotsu walked off the stage, I thought I detected a touch of sadness in his expression, though I might have been imagining it. I was full of emotion, too. The two of them would, I hoped, spend a quiet, intimate night together at the hotel.

But as the three of us rode the elevator up, Tamotsu linked his arm with mine. "Come to our room again tonight, okay?"

Caught completely off guard, I turned to Eiko.

"Do come. Unless you're fed up with us," she said.

"Of course I'm not fed up with you, but maybe not tonight—"

"What's the big deal? We're family, you know."

I tried to leave the elevator at my floor, but Tamotsu wouldn't let me go. He was so forceful the thought crossed my mind that he intended to drag me into their room and beat me up.

Evidently he had no such plans. He and Eiko didn't seem to have anything in particular they wanted to talk about either. Tamotsu played computer games by himself; Eiko read magazines in bed. I lay in the second bed, doing nothing, wondering what was up.

"We're just like a family, don't you think?" Tamotsu said.

It was true. They sure weren't treating me like a guest. No one was worrying about social niceties. We were family. But was having me around really much fun for them? That was what was in my mind as I dozed off.

I don't know how much time had passed when I drifted back toward wakefulness. My toe-penis was feeling pretty nice. With a start, I realized I'd been in this situation before, and I popped my eyes open. Tamotsu, wearing nothing but a towel around his waist, was squatting over my right foot. Something was enveloping my toe-penis tightly. Tamotsu had no vagina, of course, so obviously the body part that was squeezing me was . . .

A split second before I let out a scream, Tamotsu raised his butt. He had soaped his hand, which he'd been massaging my toe-penis with.

"Hoohee! You fell for it, didn't you?" Tamotsu shrieked, gloating. "You thought it was my asshole, right?"

"God, what a moron," Eiko said from the next bed. "Sorry, Kazumi."

"But I was able to get you hard, too," Tamotsu chirped.

My jaw dropped and stayed that way.

Chapter 12

Tamotsu had come out of the bath and was just about to slip on his boxers when his eye landed on me, reclining on the bed; a second later he leaped up and straddled my right foot, wrapped his underwear around my toe-penis, and started jerking my organ off. I leaned over and whacked him on the head. I had meant to hit him with the flat of my hand, but somehow I ended up clenching my fist. There was a dull conk and Tamotsu teetered to the wall, clutching his skull.

"Tamotsu, what on earth are you doing?" Eiko asked. She'd been brushing her hair.

"I thought Kazumi would like the feel of my undies," Tamotsu said, picking them up where they'd fallen.

Lately I had been spending all my time with Tamotsu and Eiko, joining them in their room at each hotel we stayed in. Tamotsu kept insisting I come be with them, night after night, so it got to be something of a habit. He and Eiko had nothing to talk about anymore, he said; it got dull when it was just the two of them. They had been together for five years; did that mean they'd run out of things to talk about? Was that why married couples wanted a child—to keep them from being bored? Was that why Tamotsu and Eiko wanted to make me part of their family?

I took my bath at their place every evening, but I didn't spend the night, even though I could have: I went back to my own room to sleep. Because if I stayed, the second I drifted off, Tamotsu was sure to start diddling around with my toe-penis. He was brimming with curiosity about it, and was always coming over and fooling around with it. I could tolerate it when I was awake, because then at least he had my consent, and I didn't feel as though he was treating it as a plaything.

I now had no problem exposing my toe-penis in their presence, and after I emerged from the bath, I would simply lie there with my bare feet and no socks. I noticed, after I had to swat Tamotsu off me, that my toe-penis had grown a little. But the blood hadn't started to race in, so I figured it would settle down again before long.

"Has the poor thing been defiled by Tamotsu's underwear?" Eiko asked, walking over to me.

The next moment she was cradling it in her hands, as if to comfort it. The warmth she imparted caused a certain tightening in my chest at the same time it made my toe-penis start to perk up. This reaction no longer bewildered me the way it used to, because I knew it was brought on by the affectionate gentleness of her touch. Maybe it never occurred to Eiko to look for any significance in my toe-penis's erections. All she did was smile.

"Defiled?! Those undies are pure! They've just been washed!" Tamotsu said, but when he turned to look at me, his eyes widened. "Yow, she's hard again! What is it you do to her?"

One hand still wrapped around my toe-penis, Eiko glanced back at Tamotsu.

"Nothing particularly lewd, honest."

For some reason, I liked having Eiko handle my toe-penis like an object. Who cares, I thought, if this is a perverted pleasure? I surrendered myself to the sensation. It was too much, thinking about all these noxious questions. Recently I seemed to have turned into a perfect hedonist.

Tamotsu plopped himself down next to Eiko. He had on the T-shirt and sweatpants he wore instead of pajamas.

"Hey . . . how about putting on a show for me right now?"

Eiko started stroking my toe-penis, as if it were only natural that she should. This time she sat with her legs tucked under her, steadying my foot by clamping it between her kneecaps. The pleasure had been greater the time she held my ankle in her hand, but the newness of this method excited me. I climaxed, focusing on the movements of her hand.

"You come kind of quickly, don't you?" Tamotsu said, not allowing me a moment to savor the final wave of pleasure.

"What's wrong with being quick?"

"It's no fun for us if you end it too soon."

"I don't need it to be fun for you or for anyone else."

"What! You're thinking only of yourself?" Tamotsu hollered. "Man, talk about being self-centered! You have to make it fun for your partner!"

He made me sound like a guy who only cared about getting off himself and couldn't care less about the woman. This made me a bit flustered. "But . . . who'd want to have fun with a *thing* like this?" I asked.

"What about Shunji?"

"For your information, Shunji and I did *not* have anal sex."

"Really? Even though he's gay?"

Eiko seemed as skeptical as Tamotsu. I was racking my brain about how to respond—that Shunji was not homosexual, he was happy to "be friends" with anyone no matter what sex they were; or that maybe not all homosexual men had anal sex; or . . . —when Tamotsu moved the conversation forward.

"Well, even if you won't be doing it with Shunji, how about your next partner? Someone you'll have to make it fun for?"

The only person I could imagine wanting to make love to my toe-penis, either genitally or anally, was a sex-hungry, sexually indiscriminate woman like Chisato. Straight men would, I assumed, be as repulsed by someone else's penis as Masao had been. Shunji was a special case, that went without saying; and when Tamotsu touched my toe-penis, he thought of it the way boys in junior high do when they horse around, feeling each other up. He was just playing, that was all.

"Be hard to do it," Eiko said. "I mean, your penis being in such a weird place."

The sound of her voice drew my attention to her hand, which was resting in a quiet, relaxed sort of way on the top of my right foot.

"Yeah, you've got a point. She certainly can't do it in the normal position, and if she tried to do it standing on one foot she'd fall over. Doing it lying down would be difficult because—"

"I don't think the position's the issue—it's more that she'd have to move her foot with her knee. It'd get painful, and she wouldn't be able to move it very fast. Her partner would have to get up over her foot and do all the hip-shaking unassisted."

"You mean she'll just to have to lie there being totally passive the whole time? I guess this *thing* of hers isn't much use, huh?" Tamotsu jeered. "Sure doesn't live up to its impressive appearance." With that, he gave my toe-penis a vigorous slap.

Which caused me to groan. That hurt.

"Hey, be nice," Eiko said, continuing to stroke my toe-penis.

I went from painful numbness to pleasurable numbness. I got hard again.

Tamotsu guffawed. "I love it—the way this thing gets so big!" Once more Tamotsu's hand descended.

I jumped off the bed. "I'm not staying anywhere near you, Tamotsu," I said.

The rug felt good against my skin; I thought my toe-penis would get back to normal, but it kept its erection. Even I was astounded at how easily it gave itself over to its desires. I started for the bathroom, planning to splash some water on it, only to stub my toe-penis against the table leg. I wasn't paying attention to the fact that my foot was currently longer than usual. The pain took my breath away, and I crumpled to the floor.

"What a moron." Tamotsu was laughing. "Are you okay?"

Eiko rose from the bed, chuckling too, and crouched down beside me. "I'd say Tamotsu's the moron, wouldn't you?"

She rested her hand on the back of my head. The pain still hadn't receded, but I felt an unmistakable wave of good feeling emanating from her hand. It wasn't like the sexual pleasure of my toe-penis when she massaged it, but it soothed my heart and helped me to relax; I wanted her to keep touching me this way forever. What is it about her touch? Why does it make me so happy?

♥ ♥ ♥

"I'd like you to introduce your toe-penis to the group tonight," Shigeki said to me one morning. We were about two-thirds through our tour of Hokuriku and Tohoku, and we had no performance scheduled that evening. "We won't be able to work out the details until we've actually had a chance to see what you can do."

I had no objections.

The venue Shigeki had reserved for my debut was a suite in a hotel in Rikuchu, on the coast. I assured him there was no need to go to all the trouble of preparing a fancy room like that, and in fact I would rather he didn't; he replied that an ordinary room wouldn't fit all eight members of the troupe. And to help defray the costs, he asked that Tamotsu, Eiko, and I, the youngest members, share the suite for the night.

I was delighted to stay in the suite, but I felt bad about hogging it. "Wouldn't it be better to give the older members priority?"

"Perhaps. But Yukie insists on having her own room, and Yohei and I can't get comfortable in fancy rooms like that."

"Don't put yourself out. I'll take the fancy room," said Tamotsu, wrapping his arm around my neck from behind. And with that, our sleeping arrangements for the night were settled.

There were only two beds in the suite, but the sofa would do as a third. We passed the day luxuriously, relaxing and sipping tea on the terrace overlooking the ocean.

When the sun sank and the hour approached for the troupe to gather, I began to grow tense. As I sat on the sofa, I kept slipping off my right sock and pulling it back on again.

Eiko was sitting next to me. "You're nervous?" she said teasingly. "You're so fresh and innocent."

I felt too unsettled to make a retort. The fear that my toe-penis might not respond had undermined me. I peeled off my sock again.

"Man, I get irritated just watching you!" Tamotsu, sitting across from me, cried out. He then darted over to me and snatched the sock from my hand. "You wouldn't be so worried if you didn't keep it under cover." He balled up the sock and threw it into the air.

I looked down. Left foot socked, right foot bare. I felt half exposed. "Please give it back," I pleaded.

Tamotsu made as if he were going to pitch it at me. "Only if you catch it in your mouth!"

"You're crazy."

"All right, then, let's see what it smells like!" He started bringing the sock toward his nose. The only smell the sock would have was of detergent because I had just changed them and my feet never had any odor anyway, but the idea of him sniffing it like that hit a funny nerve. I leaped up and tried to grab it back. As we struggled, he stomped on my bare foot. I kicked him in the leg. We were back in elementary school, snatching the sock back and forth from each other.

"Just look at you two, playing so nicely together."

The troupe had just arrived, and we had to behave. Tamotsu gave me back my sock. I rejoined Eiko and plopped down, letting my body sink down into the soft sofa. Masami reached over the backrest and rested his hand on my shoulder.

"It isn't *fair*, you're always playing with Tamotsu—you ought to come frolic with us too, darling. What's up, have they *adopted* you?"

"Or have you taken on the role of Tamotsu's adoptive mother?" Yohei said. "Don't tell me: Tamotsu has gotten himself a second mother."

"Yeah, sure. What an original mind," Tamotsu said.

"I can't say this little pet here seems like much of a *mother*," Masami said, giving my shoulder a pat.

Personally, I didn't have any maternal feelings for Tamotsu. He and I did seem to have become family, though, since I didn't feel at all uncomfortable having physical contact with him. It was sort of like I had acquired a younger brother, half adorable and half annoying. That certainly didn't mean, however, that I was prepared to envelope him in warm sisterly or motherly love. I argued with him as an equal. And Tamotsu seemed to like that, too.

Eiko, who played the role of the calm spectator whenever Tamotsu and I had our little tussles, piped up next. "I think they're like fraternal twins."

"Triplets, including Shin." Masami peered into my face. "You *know*, I bet that toe-penis of yours was destined to be Tamotsu's spare. You must have stolen it from him in the womb!"

Now this was bordering on creepy. "I think you're getting a little too unscientific for—"

Masami ignored me and continued excitedly, "Oh, who *cares*. I'm only *playing*. So the three of you are triplets, and your toe-penis is Tamotsu's *external cock*."

"Bingo!" Tamotsu cried, delighted. "It belongs to me!"

"All right, enough talk," Shigeki said. "Let's see what you have."

The eight members of the troupe sat down in a circle on the floor. I stuck my right foot out into the center. The group focused its attention on my toes. I started touching my toe-penis. It squirmed. Apparently it was in good form. I heaved a sigh of relief, only to discover that it lost all its momentum the second I stopped moving my hand, wilting into a rather unimpressive slump.

"The dude just can't be trusted," Tamotsu chortled. "I guess he's just another Shin, after all."

"Don't let yourself tense up," Shigeki said. "You mustn't allow the audience to distract you. Try to lose yourself in a world of your own."

"And think of something *raunchy*," Masami added.

I kept moving my hand, hoping for nothing more than to maintain my erection. I knew perfectly well that simple mechanical stimulation wouldn't do the trick. But it was impossible to think of anything sexual. It was just like when I tried to masturbate in front of Tamotsu and Eiko. If I had a lover who was constantly doing things to excite me, I could have gotten myself aroused by replaying those sensuous moments in my mind, but with the chaste life I was living now, I had no well of desire to draw on.

Come to think of it, I didn't have much experience with masturbation either. Even before I got this toe-penis, masturbation had always been a way of reliving things that had happened to me in real life, and—with the exception of the first few days after the member appeared, when it was still totally new to me—masturbation for its own sake had never really interested me. So I was stunted in that way. But I would need little kernels of pleasure that could serve as material for masturbatory fantasies if I was going to perform in the show on a nightly basis. The mere thought of that sent tidal waves of exhaustion over me. My toe-penis remained limp.

"Just look at it," Eiko murmured. "The poor thing."

There was something marvelously gentle in her tone. I had forgotten about Eiko, sitting there next to me.

"You sure care a lot for penises, don't you?" Tamotsu said.

"It's not her penis I care about," Eiko shot back. "I'm thinking about Kazumi."

These few words reached deep into my heart—perhaps because I felt so alone at that moment, unable to rely on anyone but myself. But Eiko's words touched more than my heart: they had an effect on my body, too. All of a sudden, warmth rushed into my toe-penis. A new strength filled the hand I held it with. I'm not sure why I had forgotten Eiko, the pleasure she had given me, but now that I had stumbled upon an experience to relive, I began remembering: I called it all up, greedily, right down to the pressure of her hand on the back of my head. My toe-penis heaved itself up, so enormous you could hardly recognize it.

"Oh *my*, you did it!" Masami whistled. "What were you thinking of?"

Obviously that wasn't a question I could answer. I kept my eyes trained on my finger-wrapped toe-penis, pretending I hadn't heard. Luckily, the sight was so dazzling that Masami's question was forgotten by everyone.

"This is amazing!" Shigeki gasped. "It's huge! It'll be a sensation!"

"Men in the audience might get jealous," Yohei said.

"This would be normal for a foreigner, right?" Masami said.

Yukie glared at it out of the corner of her eye. "Just as I said, gross."

"Oh? So it's gross, huh?" Tamotsu grabbed my foot and thrust it at her. "Here, get a good look!"

Clamping my leg under his arm, he seized my toe-penis with his right hand and jerked it around right in front of Yukie's face. As he yanked me forward, I had to lean backward, putting my hands on the floor to support my upper body.

"Stop it, Tamotsu!" I said.

Yukie waved her hand in front of her as if she were shooing a fly. She didn't seem particularly disturbed by the toe-penis in front of her, considering how gross she'd said she found it. "I'm surprised at you—a man touching a penis" was all she could say.

"So what, it's a woman's penis."

"It's attached to a woman, sure, but a penis is the mark of a man."

"Bullshit. My penis is good for nothing, but I'm still a man. A penis isn't a mark."

"Yes, you're *so right*. I've lopped mine off, and *I'm* still a man."

The entire assembly whipped around at this statement of Masami's. He had never spoken of himself as a man before.

"But aren't you a woman?" Tamotsu asked somewhat sincerely.

Masami frowned, looking as if he had screwed up, then went on the offensive. "Well *obviously* I wanted to *become* one, and I *have*, but I'm quite aware that my chromosomes are still XY, thank you *very* much. I'm under no illusion that I'm a real, bona fide woman. I've got *that* much sense left, at least, despite appearances to the contrary."

"Huh? I thought your chromosomes were XXY."

I jerked my leg out from under Tamotsu's arm and sat down. My toe-penis was still looking very perky, just as erect as before. The excitement that had come over me when I recalled Eiko's touch hadn't faded either. If possible, I would have liked to go off by myself and keep savoring the pleasure. But for the time being I would have to rein in my desires.

Masami turned to me. "As far as *I'm* concerned, a penis is a *wonderful* thing, whether it's on a man or a woman."

"Then why did you have yours chopped off?" Tamotsu asked.

"Well, you see, I wanted to be a woman without a penis. But I just *love* the idea of a woman who *has* a penis. I can imagine myself being absolutely *smitten*."

"Why not go ahead and be smitten with Kazumi then?"

I looked up when Tamotsu said this. My eyes met Masami's. He gazed back at me expressionlessly.

"I'm not into *girlish* women like her," he said. "I like gals with more *spice*. And I must say, I'd prefer it if her penis were between her legs."

"I get such a headache listening to Masami yak about her tastes," Yukie sighed.

Shigeki and Aiko came and stood in front of me. Shigeki beamed. "We'll have you debut on the next tour!"

Pleased, I nodded vaguely. By now I knew what it took to have an erection. Every night, each time I performed, I'd have to imagine Eiko touching me. That's how it would be, because for the time being that was the only masturbatory aid I had to work with. But I couldn't help thinking things had turned out rather oddly.

Shigeki cast a fond glance at my toe-penis. "You'll realize this for yourself soon enough, but it's hard to perform every night. I hope you won't take this in the wrong way, but there are times when I really envy women, because they're always ready."

I was a bit annoyed to hear this tired, shopworn, blast-from-the-past male cliché coming from Shigeki, of all people, but Aiko did not hesitate to respond, "Yes, exactly. We're always ready, that's why we get raped." This caused Shigeki to raise his eyebrows. "On the other hand," Aiko continued, "maybe men think that women are always ready because they can be forced in a way men can't? Do you envy our potential to be forced?" Aiko had a smile on her face, but it wasn't exactly sweet.

"I said there are *times* when I envy women," Shigeki replied quickly, flustered. "I didn't say I envy everything."

"Oh yes, how silly of me."

Turning away from Shigeki, Aiko aimed a wiry smile at no one in particular. Something about her profile got me to thinking that maybe Aiko didn't like Shigeki. There seemed no doubt that Shigeki loved Aiko. So if their relationship was "less warm than you think," could it be that Aiko's heart had gone cold? Shigeki did seem a bit lonely. I was glad the other members of the troupe were caught up in their own conversations, and hadn't been party to this one.

Aiko was very adult, however. When she spoke again to Shigeki, her tone was professional. "What kind of performance do you have in mind for the toe-penis?"

"It's tricky," Shigeki said, relieved. "You have to shock the audience right off—that's how you get them hooked. Ideally, it'd be nice to begin with her touching herself through her sock, arranging it so that as it gets hard it pushes the sock up, until finally, just as the audience starts to won-der, she whips it off, revealing the toe-penis in all its vertical majesty. I suppose that might pose some technical difficulties, though."

Tamotsu, who had been horsing around with Masami and Yukie, caught wind of what we were talking about. "Great, let's have her do the impos-sible! And how about this! When she strips off the sock, a string of flags from all the nations of the world comes with it!"

Masami, unwilling to be beaten, offered his own ludicrous contribu-tion. "How about having her twirl a *ring* on her toe-penis, like the ones gymnasts use in the Olympics? She could keep upping the number of rings! Oh, what *fun*!"

"Maybe she could do the limbo under a burning rope?"

"Tamotsu, *darling*, be serious. I have a *much* better plan. She could pirouette on her toe-penis, like in *ballet*! How does that strike you?"

Shigeki shook his head. "Let's talk sometime soon," he said to me, "when we're alone."

The next instant, the room fell silent. Tamotsu, who had been talk-ing up a storm with Masami, had quieted, and the silence almost hurt. I turned to Tamotsu just as the mischievous grin faded from his face.

"To tell the truth," he said, his voice fuller than usual, "I think Kazumi and I should team up and do it with Eiko." He had practically rammed his words together in his hurry to say what was on his mind. And his tone was not suggestive, it was definitive.

I was speechless. I tried to catch Tamotsu's eye. But by then he was looking down as if he had forgotten what he had just said, toying aim-lessly with a button on his sleeve.

♥ ♥ ♥

Tamotsu made no effort to explain and no one pressed him to elaborate, so the discussion of how my toe-penis ought to be incorporated into the show simply stopped, abruptly and inconclusively, and my debut before the troupe never resumed. It was clear that Tamotsu had more on his mind than just the show when he broached his idea—that this was personal—but Shigeki and the others had no desire to go there. Tamotsu was trying to look blasé, but you could tell he was anything but.

This was offensive. It was selfish, and it was taking advantage of the goodwill of the troupe. And it was rude and presumptuous not to have said anything to Eiko or me first. After the group cleared out of our suite, he started playing his video games, as cool as could be.

To others, that night might have seemed no different from other nights. But tension hung in the air. Eiko tried to act as if everything was normal, but she was unusually quiet, and from the suggestive glances she cast in my direction I could tell that Tamotsu, sitting with his back to us, had her under his thumb. So this is the sort of relationship he had in mind when he said we were a family; I seethed with fury. Some family we are if we can't be frank with each other!

I wanted to ask Eiko what she made of Tamotsu's proposal, but I couldn't bring myself to do it in his presence. I also had to deal with the extreme shyness I felt at the prospect of talking in earnest with her, now that I had acknowledged the sexual thrill that came over me when we touched. Simply knowing she was nearby was enough, apparently, to set every nerve in my body trembling in anticipation of the pleasure she might bring. So, with everything else going on, I found myself struggling to divert myself from thinking what I was thinking.

But . . . did the fact that my body responded to her like this mean I "loved" her in a homosexual way? It was true I had developed an affection for her that surpassed friendship. I no longer harbored doubts about homosexual love, or felt uncomfortable with the idea; if this was the sort of thing people called by that name, that was fine with me, they could go right ahead and call it that. The thing was, even though I recognized that Eiko could give me sexual pleasure, I didn't really concern myself with the fact that it was same-sex pleasure. Intellectually I knew that she was a woman, but I didn't get hung up on that because for me, above all, she was someone who had the ability to make me feel absolutely wonderful. Shunji *never* paid any attention to the sex of his partners, that was simply his way; and now I seemed to be just the same, at least as far as Eiko was concerned.

It was also true that, for the time being, I was content with the level of physical contact we enjoyed in the course of our everyday lives; I had no deep urge to press my naked body against hers, or to have intercourse with her via my toe-penis. The thought never even crossed my mind that I might touch her in return. I just relished the caress of her hand—that was all. Desire like this, which took as its target only a particular, limited part of her body, was hardly serious enough to count as bona fide homosexual desire.

I asked myself whether I liked Eiko as I liked Shunji, but no clear answer was forthcoming. Shunji had surprised me in all kinds of ways early in our relationship, but Eiko wasn't easy to figure out either; she seemed more distant than Shunji, who had drawn me to him from the first, making it possible for me to feel at home with him almost immediately. All of this made me wonder if my toe-penis was leading the way, dragging my emotions behind in disarray.

If I didn't know how I felt about Eiko, I certainly couldn't "team up" with Tamotsu to have sex with her; that would only throw me into even greater confusion, mentally and physically. This made me furious with Tamotsu—what nerve he had, tossing out an idea like that without any regard for our feelings!

By the next morning, Tamotsu had emerged from his shell. I'd slept on the sofa in the sitting room and was awakened by the sound of Tamotsu and Eiko tittering merrily in the bathroom. Eiko had been tense the night before, unsmiling, but with Tamotsu in a good mood it seemed her spirits had improved. I couldn't shake off my own annoyance with Tamotsu so quickly, and the frustration I felt at his mood swings led to irritation with Eiko for being so easily swayed by his emotional ups and downs.

Tamotsu emerged first from the bathroom. Eiko followed, a smile on her lips. I didn't even say good morning—I had no intention of disguising the bad mood I was in. But Tamotsu either didn't notice or didn't let my sullenness trouble him. "So," he said, thrusting his hand under the covers, "do you get hard in the mornings?"

I kicked his hand away.

"C'mon, let me touch it!"

He kept grabbing, so I pulled my foot away. "I don't want you to," I snapped. "It's mine."

"Huh? I thought we decided yesterday that it's mine. My external cock?"

"Tell me," I said, practically strangling my voice in my throat, "do you *seriously* think that's what you want?"

The leer on Tamotsu's face froze, and he backed up a step. Eiko, who had been behind him, stopped in her tracks. But a moment later Tamotsu had recovered. "Sure, why not? It'd be handy to have a spare, and you're in a pretty sorry state right now, wouldn't you say? Having this great tool that you only use to jerk off?"

"You know, even if you did do it with my penis, you wouldn't feel anything."

The smile faded from Tamotsu's lips. I began to worry that he might get surly, and he himself pursed his lips as if making up his mind whether to or not. After a moment, he relaxed. "Ah, but it *will* feel good," he said, his expression serious.

Then, breaking into a somewhat sheepish smile, he continued. "Ain't the human mind amazing? You don't actually have to do something yourself—because as long as the image you call up is good enough, just imagining yourself doing it can make you feel like you really are. Like flying. If you try very hard to picture yourself flying, you can get a good taste of what it's like."

"Yes, but that's—"

"I know, I know—you're going to say it's not the same thing. But the pleasure you feel when you imagine something is legitimate. My penis is a dud, so I'll never know the pleasure of a working penis, but I *can* know the pleasure of an imaginary penis. I don't have any choice."

"Well, yes, but—"

Glancing back and forth between Tamotsu and me, Eiko cut across the room and took a seat across from me.

"But if you're always lost in these reveries," I went on, "eventually you'll lose track of which is dream and which is reality."

"That won't happen, don't worry. I'm not *that* stupid," Tamotsu said, laughing. "All I'm saying is, if you give me a chance to pretend that your penis is mine, I'll have a lot more imaginative room to maneuver in. It'll be great. I'll have a ball."

"That's great for you," I said, restraining my anger. "But what about me?"

"You can have fun, too," he said matter-of-factly.

I swallowed before speaking again. "By teaming up with you and doing it with Eiko?"

"You don't want to? But you don't dislike Eiko, do you?"

I was at a loss for words. Tamotsu probably didn't mean to insinuate anything by that, but since I was confused about how I really felt about Eiko, it came like a jab in a spot too tender to be touched. All he had asked was whether I disliked her, and I knew what the answer was. But my tongue had gone numb.

"You don't dislike *her*, do you, Eiko?" Tamotsu asked, whipping his head around in Eiko's direction.

"You make it sound like a threat, not a question," I said.

But Tamotsu kept his eyes trained on Eiko, waiting for her reply. I didn't have the guts to look at her. I sat, tensed up, as she spoke, her tone so lacking in feeling it almost sounded intentionally bland: "Oh, I'm okay with it."

Eiko was slumped in her seat, her expression as blank as her tone. Her disinterest gave me such a shock it almost sent me careening into despair. When she said she was "okay with it," that was exactly what she meant: she didn't actively desire to make love with me and she didn't feel repulsed by the idea; she just didn't care much one way or the other. If Tamotsu wanted to do it that way, she was willing. But she gave no clue to how she herself felt.

Didn't she find it frightening that the relationships among us—her, her lover, and her friend—might be thrown into disarray? Or did sex not mean very much to her? Had she made up her mind to tag along obediently no matter what schemes Tamotsu hatched, as a way to lessen his suffering? To make Tamotsu's hopes the first priority, because I, her friend, was just a supporting actress, and it didn't matter in the least what the results might be for me when I got entangled in their struggles? More and more, my anger built.

Ultimately, the fury I felt toward Eiko ended up merging with my anger at Tamotsu, filling my breast with a rage greater than any I had ever known. The rest of the day—during breakfast and on the bus and even during the show—I had trouble controlling my feelings. I couldn't meet their gaze for even two seconds, and I only talked to them when it was absolutely necessary. Needless to say, after the show, I rushed back to my own room and shut myself up.

Alone, I discovered that when one reaches the limit of one's anger, it becomes impossible to sleep. And that when you keep it bottled up inside rather than finding some way to blow off steam, it becomes even more concentrated, and you find yourself less and less able to think of anything else. After wasting a very long time lying there in bed, I decided I needed to distract myself, and switched on the bedside lamp.

I had no particular reason for doing this. But as I sat there staring into the air in front of me, it struck me that maybe masturbation could make me feel better. So I folded my legs and took hold, tentatively, of my toe-penis. No sooner had I done so than an image of Eiko rose in my mind. It irritated me that I should have to use the object of my anger to give myself pleasure. But I had no other material to work with—no other partner to call up. After some hesitation, I started jerking off. The promptness with which my toe-penis responded showed me quite clearly that, furious as I was with Eiko, I hadn't stopped liking her. Even so, I have to confess that part of me found it pathetic that my *thing* reacted in this way.

I was getting to the best part when, *knock knock knock,* someone was at the door. My hand froze. I had a pretty good idea who it was, so without even looking through the peephole, I put my hand on the knob and jerked the door open. All of a sudden, a cloud of searing pain exploded through the tip of my toe-penis. Once again I had forgotten that it was longer than usual. I stumbled backward a few steps, clinging to the wall, and collapsed.

"I seem to have caught you at a bad time."

The voice coming from above was Eiko's. Having her see me in this ridiculous state was more painful than the damage to my toe. I could think of nothing to say.

Eiko sat down on a chair while I plopped down on the bed. My toe-penis had shrunk to its usual size, but there was a red blotch where the door had banged into it. I rubbed it gently.

"Are you mad at me, by any chance?" Eiko asked.

I didn't feel like answering directly. So, with some trepidation, I struck at the heart of the matter. "Would you do anything Tamotsu told you to?"

My head was lowered, so I couldn't tell whether Eiko's expression had changed. But she had shifted position, and that was enough to tell me she was shaken.

After a few moments, she sighed and replied, "I can see it might look as though I would."

I immediately felt bad for having spoken as I did. I'd known I was going too far when I said "anything," that I was being too harsh, but I was too embarrassed to ask what I'd wanted to, which was whether or not she wanted to do it with me. I couldn't bring myself to ask that. Eiko didn't seem particularly put out, though.

"Are you mad because of what Tamotsu said?"

"I take it you aren't?" I said, looking up.

Eiko smiled, slowly. "It's been some time since you asked me how I felt."

Her smile had an air that some might describe as mature, but it made the same impression of listlessness on me as her response to Tamotsu that morning.

"Should I be angry?" Eiko dropped her gaze. "I'm so used to denying my own emotions that I can't tell anymore. Certain emotions, at least, having to do with a part of Tamotsu's body."

An aching pity flooded my heart. "You're Tamotsu's lover, right?" I said. "Not his toy?"

"Isn't a lover just a person you're willing to be a toy for?"

"No, that's not true."

There was a silence. Then Eiko whispered, "A refreshing viewpoint, that."

The only lights on in the room were the bedside light and the lamp next to the table; Eiko's figure was half cloaked in shadow. She looked so fragile as she sat there, perfectly still, that I wouldn't have been surprised if she vanished all of a sudden, swallowed by the darkness. I gazed at her, not speaking.

"Do you despise me?" she asked, ever so quietly.

"Of course not!" I said, taken aback.

"And Tamotsu?"

"Not at all. I get angry at him, but I can't help liking him."

A smile returned to Eiko's lips. This one was gentle, not limp. I interpreted it to mean that she was happy for Tamotsu's sake.

"I wish I had a toe-penis like you," Eiko said.

The thought that occurred to me first was that if she had a toe-penis of her own, Tamotsu would be able to fulfill his yearning for a penis through her, and there would be no need for a third party, someone like me, to intervene. But then if Eiko did have a toe-penis, Tamotsu wouldn't be able to use it as his "spare" to have sex with her, which was what he seemed to want. "Why?" I asked.

"I feel guilty for being normal when Tamotsu isn't."

"But there's no need for you to feel that way! Tamotsu is already making you stifle your emotions, at least in part—robbing you of a healthy mental life!"

I was probably saying too much, but I couldn't stop myself. After all, not only was Tamotsu bending Eiko completely to his own will, he was making her feel bad about herself. He was inconsiderate, he really was. Eiko, on the other hand, was extraordinarily giving. Only a truly giving person touches others so gently, bringing them happiness, leading them into rapture. Eiko must caress Tamotsu all the time; did it never occur to him to return her kindness?

Unconsciously, I shifted my gaze to Eiko's hand. She had her elbow propped on the arm of the chair, her chin in her hand. My eye landed on her index finger, which was slightly crooked; my heart throbbed with sadness and the memory of how she had touched me. I looked away. This time my gaze landed on her breasts. I saw her naked all the time, and yet I felt dazzled at the sight of their soft curves, rising and falling beneath the thin, soft material of her sweater. This response startled me. I ran my eyes down over her skirt, the tough-looking bumps of her kneecaps, then over her stockinged calves, which peeked out under the hem of her skirt. I felt as if I were seeing it all for the first time, and every part of her body seemed so *her*.

When at last my gaze settled on the tips of her shoes, I found myself thinking of that fascinatingly transformed nail on the pinky toe of her right foot. If my toe-penis counted as a deformity, surely that crushed nail did, too. What a splendid deformity! Compared to my toe-penis, which went around chug-a-lugging pleasure without a care in the world, that nail of hers was brimming with sorrow. Didn't Tamotsu feel any pity for it? Or was he so completely obsessed with his own body that he didn't notice her little deformity? If I were Tamotsu, that nail would have been enough to make me fold her in my arms and . . .

Unaware of my thoughts, Eiko sat up in her chair.

"It's late. I'd better go."

Why bother going back to Tamotsu—stay here with me. The words made it as far as the base of my throat, but I couldn't bring myself to speak them.

Eiko started to get up, then stopped, a look on her face as if she had just realized that she'd forgotten to say the most important thing.

"I'll tell Tamotsu, okay? That you don't like his idea of 'teaming up.'"

She stood and waited for my response. Thinking back over the exchange I'd had with Tamotsu that morning, I needed to tell her I didn't like the plan, but that didn't mean I didn't like her.

"It's just that I don't want to be used as a tool, for the sake of his fantasy."

"I know, me too. Frankly, if we were going to do it, I'd rather just . . ."

All at once Eiko stopped speaking, as if it suddenly hit her what she was saying. I stared at her, stunned. It was some time before I could look away. But Eiko said nothing more. She just opened the door and left.

♥ ♥ ♥

I passed the next few days in a giddy haze. I woke up the morning following my talk with Eiko, feeling wonderfully buoyant, both physically and mentally, and when I went down to the restaurant for breakfast and noticed Shigeki and Aiko sitting together, I felt a peculiar twinge of nostalgia, even though I saw them every day. I made a beeline for their table and sat down with them.

"You don't want to use Tamotsu's plan, do you, Shigeki?"

Shigeki glanced at me, a bit suspicious of my high spirits, before answering my smile with one of his own. "Not unless you and Eiko agree. You can't go along with every little whim of Tamotsu's, you know."

"You're right!" I said, as if he had given me just the answer I was angling for. "That porn-head and his crazy ideas!"

"*Porn-head?*" Aiko tittered. "What's up with you today, Kazumi?"

"Ah, the porn-head has arrived." Shigeki gestured with his chin. Tamotsu and Eiko were just walking into the restaurant.

Tamotsu came over to me. "So," he said, looking down, "I hear you can't help liking me?"

Relieved that he hadn't taken offense at my rejection of his big plan, I responded, in a tone as ponderous and arrogant as his, "Well, yes."

"Sheesh, that's a pretty stingy way to talk. Just be honest and say you love me, man!"

"Yes, Tamotsu, you big onanist, I love you!"

"Onanist? What the hell are you talking about?"

Tamotsu puffed out his chest, leaning forward; Eiko yanked him down into an empty seat. Our eyes met. She was grinning. Her smile had the same cheerfulness as the fresh slices of grapefruit on Shigeki's and Aiko's plates. Once again, my heart brimmed with a sense of newness. Eiko's presence made me feel absolutely exhilarated.

I'd had a premonition of this joy the previous night. For about ten minutes after Eiko left, my whole body had quivered with delight at her parting words: "If we were going to do it, I'd rather just . . ." I didn't even need to wonder what she would have said next. She had uttered, in a tone colored with a subtle hint of warmth, something important to both of us. I couldn't have been happier.

It goes without saying that I started my solitary masturbation session over from the beginning. My skin was twitching already, as if it were being touched by invisible hands, but I was burning to make it twitch more, to make my bursting, warm heart even warmer. Images of Eiko's hands and face, and of the parts of her body I felt I'd seen for the first time that evening—her breasts and kneecaps and calves—danced before my mind. Naturally, I recalled memories of her caresses, pushing myself to climax. As the undulating images faded and a burst of white blossomed across my mind, I began to feel that Eiko had wrapped herself around my body at the same time she filled me inside, and my toe-penis felt so good I thought the pleasure might set it on fire. As the heat overcame me, I had a vision of me taking the little toe of Eiko's right foot—capped with its rough, lumpy nail—between my lips.

It was the best masturbation I had ever experienced. Letting go of my toe-penis, I tumbled back onto the bed. I would have loved to dissolve, disintegrate, then and there. How beautiful it would have been to disappear like that, leaving in my stead nothing but Eiko's gorgeous toenail, faintly aglow, glistening with my saliva. This was a pretty bizarre idea, but that didn't bother me—I was tickled, that was all. By the same token, when I noticed that the area around my vagina had grown warm, too, I understood that a change had taken place in me, because until now my toe-penis hadn't been connected to the genitals I'd been born with; then, murmuring to myself that it didn't matter, who cared anyway, I let my head fall back onto the pillow.

As long as I could believe in the reality of the pleasure I felt, both physical and emotional, what need was there to try and puzzle these things out? I no longer tortured myself over the question of whether or not I was in love with Eiko. My love for Shunji and my love for Eiko weren't the same, but then neither were the ways in which I had come to know them both, or the events that had led me to become intimate with them. And of course they were different people—it was only natural that I should love them each differently. I came to the conclusion that people are able to love all kinds of people in all kinds of different ways, and that was enough for me.

Now that I was in this buoyant mood, feeling simultaneously relaxed and unusually turned on, just being in the same room as Eiko was enough to make me feel tipsy. I started going to Tamotsu and Eiko's room again. And while I might have been imagining it, I had the impression that Eiko was more open with me physically now. I couldn't tell if Tamotsu noticed the change that had taken place, but at the very least he didn't seem alienated, and tried to play on both our sympathies.

I had sat down on the bed one night when Tamotsu seized my right ankle and lifted my foot. "Too bad. I would have liked to have this as my own."

Mere regret didn't appear to be enough, because next he turned his back on me and sandwiched my foot between his thighs.

"See, it works great. Hey, Eiko. Give it a try, will you?"

Eiko, who had been sitting on the other bed, got up and knocked Tamotsu over. He landed on top of me, taking me down onto the bed with him. He rolled over onto his stomach, pinning me down.

"Damn it," he growled. "I'll get you!"

The thought of how Tamotsu must feel deep down inside injected a note of sadness into our play, but for the time being we just laughed it off. I wished these happy days could go on forever. But there was something I had forgotten: on the final day of every tour, Tamotsu performed with Yuki, not Eiko. And on that day, he was always in a terrible mood.

On this tour, Fukushima would be our last destination. Arriving at the hotel a little past noon, the three of us went into the café bar. Eiko and I ordered tea and cake; Tamotsu ordered gin with a twist of lime. When the waiter brought his drink, Tamotsu cradled the glass in his hands, bent his head down, and began muttering melodramatically to himself.

"So, Shin, tonight, at last, after a long month of anticipation, you have another adulterous tryst lined up. Are you happy, kid? Cheers!"

His speech was slow, but not the hand that raised his glass and poured half the gin onto his crotch. It happened in a flash. Apparently the waiter hadn't seen this mishap, because no one came to sop up the mess. Tamotsu held up the half-empty glass before him.

Not sure how to handle Tamotsu on his worst day of the month, I made the mistake of using my usual tone with him: "I guess it makes you feel better, doing things like that?"

Tamotsu glowered at me. "See for yourself if you're so interested," he said, and flicked the remainder of the gin onto my stomach. The possibility that he might turn his violence on me had never even occurred to me, and I was too flabbergasted to feel outraged.

Eiko put her hand on my shoulder. "You need something to wipe this . . . ," she said, shaken.

The waiter was hurrying our way with a cloth in his hand, but I was on my feet before he arrived. Tamotsu gazed up at me dully.

Back in my room, as I dabbed at the splotch of gin on my pants with a towel, I worried about the awful ordeal Eiko would have to endure again tonight. Couldn't it be stopped? Wasn't anyone able to stop Tamotsu? After Eiko, I was closest to him, and yet he had no problem dumping his gin on me. Obviously I had very little influence with him, and he would pay no attention if I tried to interfere. I feared what the night would bring.

Unsure what else to do, I went and knocked on Shigeki and Aiko's door. As soon as Aiko opened up, I stormed into the room, almost ramming into her. Yohei was there too, playing *shogi* with Shigeki at the table.

"What's wrong?" Aiko asked, softly touching my arm.

"Shigeki," I called out, "whose idea was it for Tamotsu to perform with Yukie? You think it's okay to make him do that? Isn't that what makes him so unstable?"

Shigeki and Yohei stared, unable to respond right off the bat. Aiko wrapped her arm around me and sat me down on the edge of the bed. Yohei poured some whiskey into a glass, added some water, and handed it to me. I took a sip.

Then Shigeki began, "Actually, that segment was Tamotsu's idea. He pressed us really hard to get it. He insisted we didn't need to worry—Shin wouldn't feel any pain because he doesn't have a brain." Shigeki broke off for a moment, glancing at me to see how I was reacting. "Naturally, we were against the idea, because it was so extreme. Maybe Shin wouldn't feel any pain, but it would hurt the rest of us just watching it happen. On the other hand, there was no denying that from a business point of view a performance like that had a lot going for it. Eventually we arrived at the conclusion that maybe if it served as a sort of therapy for Tamotsu, on balance it wouldn't be so bad."

"Therapy? But he's been doing it for years and he hasn't changed at all! He hasn't, has he?"

"We thought he would," Yohei said. "We only noticed recently that, far from functioning as a kind of therapy, that segment works on Tamotsu like bad liquor: it just gets him drunk and makes him violent."

"That portion of the show looks like pure masochism," Aiko added, "but the truth is we're only letting Tamotsu enjoy himself. Sometimes it feels good poking at a wound, you know, even though it hurts. But if you go on fiddling with a wound because you like how it feels, it never gets better."

"As if Tamotsu's wound could ever get better," Shigeki said, somberly. "Even being with Eiko hasn't helped. Love is supposed to heal all wounds, but it seems to me there are some even love can't do anything for."

Aiko plucked the glass of whiskey from my hand and took a gulp.

"I don't know, I still think that segment is . . . ," I began, but couldn't finish the sentence

"I understand. I won't ignore what you've said," Shigeki said.

Embarrassed at having become so emotional, I was about to leave when Yohei spoke. "You find it puzzling that Tamotsu doesn't improve at all, despite being with Eiko? Shigeki just said there are some wounds even love can't heal, but I have a different take on things. As I see it, Tamotsu has been stuck too close to Eiko for too long. He's been caught in an unchanging world with a population of two, and that's kept him from seeing what's really important to him. What he needs is a big change that will force him to open his eyes. Frankly, I think the best thing would be if Tamotsu were to fall in love with another woman."

"What would Eiko do then?"

"Problems arise the moment you take both of them into consideration," Yohei said with a dour smile. "Tamotsu either decides that Eiko is the only one for him and goes back to her, or the opposite . . . You just have to see how things turn out."

Trudging out of the room on Aiko's arm, I found Tamotsu and Eiko in the hallway. As soon as Tamotsu saw me, he dashed over and threw his arms around my body. "I'm really sorry, Kazumi! Don't be angry with me!"

"I'm not angry, I'm not angry," I said. Tamotsu seemed a bit insistent, more so than usual, and I couldn't help worrying about what would happen after the show.

No matter how scared you are, time marches on. That night's show was at a fancy Japanese restaurant; the sponsor was in real estate. A lanky older man in a tacky suit brought out a video camera when Shigeki and Aiko started performing. When Yohei called out to him, "Please refrain from filming the performance," he put down the video camera, only to pick up a still camera and start clicking away. Yohei had to call out again, "Please refrain from any photography."

"Stupid, lecherous old geezer. Shin will teach *you* a lesson," Tamotsu muttered backstage. He had a bottle of sake in his hand.

While Tamotsu was out on the futon that served as a stage, Eiko was sitting by the wall in the dressing room, hugging her knees to her chest. It was too painful for me to watch Tamotsu perform, or to see Eiko like that, so for the most part I kept my eyes focused on the buttons of the tape recorder in front of me. I could still hear what was happening, though, and that was painful enough.

Tamotsu plodded slowly back off the stage. Shin's penis, dripping blood, was precisely at my eye level. Tamotsu stopped and glanced around, then looked down at me with a grin. "You won't let me use your toe-penis, so Shin's all cut up," he said.

He turned his gaze away from me, and picked up the sake bottle from the tray. It was empty. He inverted it and shook a few drops onto the palm of his hand.

"This is all that's left?" He licked his hand. "How am I supposed to sterilize Shin's wounds with this? I guess I'll just have to have someone do it with her saliva instead."

Eiko raised her head, dreading it but prepared. But it was my hair Tamotsu grabbed.

"Maybe I'll ask you to do it this time," he said. Shin's half-erect penis approached my face. "If you feel any pity for Shin, do him a favor and lick him clean."

Fine, I thought, I'll do it. That, at least, will get us out of this hell. That, at least, will make Tamotsu happy for the moment, and give Eiko a way out of this mess. But Tamotsu let go of my hair.

"Nah, come to think of it, I'd better go with someone who's used to dealing with Shin." He turned to face Eiko. "I'd rather go with the woman who let me go out and do this awful job while she just sat here waiting, happy as a clam." He staggered over to Eiko. "Eiko . . . do Shin a favor, huh? Lick him." Tamotsu thrust out the sake bottle he held in his right hand. "I'll make you happy with this later in return."

I stood up. "Tamotsu," I said firmly.

He whipped around, irritated. I had no idea what more to say.

Tamotsu's expression grew vicious. "Don't call me unless you have something to say!" he shouted, and smashed the bottle against the wall.

The sound was terrible, shards flew everywhere. I felt a stab of pain in my foot, and discovered that a shard had pierced my stocking and lodged itself in my toe-penis. It hadn't penetrated deeply, and it was easy to remove. But there was blood on my gray stocking, and the stain was spreading.

Even Tamotsu seemed taken aback. But he quickly went back on the offensive, whipping around to face Eiko and growling, "You see what happens when you're slow! Hurry up and suck it!"

I hadn't been able to stop it. Once again, Tamotsu made Eiko taste Shin's blood.

♥ ♥ ♥

My heart was heavy when we arrived back at the hotel after the show. The other members of the troupe, who had witnessed the incident, seemed preoccupied with thoughts of their own, and the atmosphere on the bus ride back was full of gloom. Aiko sat beside me, absolutely still. Tamotsu was quiet, but he didn't yet seem to have calmed down, because he kept twitching and rocking back and forth.

Aiko and I parted outside the door to my room.

"How could Shunji have left someone like you?" she said, then bid me goodnight.

Alone, I stripped off my stockings. There was a cut on the head of my toe-penis, just above what remained of the nail. The blood had mostly dried, but when I pressed the area around the wound, fresh red beads oozed out. I washed it off, then went back to the bed and lay down. My heart ached terribly, hurting far worse than the minor pain of the wound. I was being buffeted by feelings of powerlessness, and of loneliness.

I thought there was a knock on the door but wasn't sure, so I went to peek through the peephole. Eiko was standing there, looking profoundly exhausted—or was it that *I* felt exhausted? In the distortion of the peep-hole, she seemed blurry around the edges, like a ghost.

I opened up. "Where's Tamotsu?"

"Oh, he's gone off somewhere. Drinking, probably. On days like this, he always comes back drunk."

Eiko had already washed off Shin's blood and she wasn't wearing any lipstick, but I couldn't bring myself to look directly at her lips.

"How's the cut?" she asked, once she had taken a seat.

"Oh, it's just a scratch."

I didn't have the energy to chat. I sat on the bed, slumped against the wall, and closed my eyes, my foot stretched out. Eiko came over to me, lifted my toe-penis and inspected the wound. My toe-penis, feeling the touch of her fingertips, grew slightly. I felt pinpricks of pain from the cut. Kneeling on the floor, she placed her fingers on either side of my toe-penis, careful not to touch the wound, and started fondling it.

My brain wasn't working well, and I didn't immediately realize what she was doing. The sides of the penis are relatively insensitive to pleasure, of course, and at first I was just watching her fingers move without feel-ing anything in particular; then I realized that she was trying to make me feel good, or rather that she was trying to show me that she cared, and this got me a tiny bit excited.

The pain that accompanied my erection wasn't bad enough to interfere with the mounting pleasure, and I made no attempt to say that it hurt.

When my toe-penis had become fully erect, Eiko wrapped her fist around it the way she always did and started stroking it, up and down between the base and the head. The pleasure wasn't as intense as peaceful; I closed my eyes. Just then, her fingers came into direct contact with my cut, and the pain was bad enough to make me jerk my foot away.

I wasn't worried about the pain, though. Eiko's expression had taken on an apologetic air, and so, before she had a chance to say she was sorry, I stretched out the foot I had just pulled away. My toe-penis did not, however, coordinate itself with my feelings; it was looking a little weaker than before. Eiko touched my toe-penis gingerly at first, then slid her hand down over the top of my foot. She lowered her head, enveloping my toe-penis in a gentle, wet warmth.

Maybe Eiko thought her tongue would put less stress on my cut, compared to her hand. Either way, her unexpected course of action startled me. As my surprise subsided, joy welled up inside me. And with the joy came a desire to accept everything, absolutely everything Eiko was trying to communicate to me. As her saliva entered into the cut, however, I found it impossible to remain still.

Picking up on my subtle response, Eiko raised her face from my toe-penis.

"It hurts, doesn't it?"

I nodded, regretting terribly that it was true. She gazed down sadly at my organ, which had shriveled to half its erect size; then she cradled my toe-penis between her hands and kissed the tip. I'm not sure if the delight I felt with this was sexual or spiritual, but the instant her lips touched my foot something deep inside me moved, causing me to shudder. At the same time, I was seized by a certain powerful impulse.

I stretched out a hand toward Eiko, whose head was tilted slightly downward, and wiggled my finger to catch her attention. She raised her eyes and peered into mine. I pulled my hand back and pointed at my lips. Eiko cocked her head slightly, and immediately understood. In the short time it took her to climb up on the bed and scoot over to where I was, my heart began to pound.

Eiko held my head in her hands and pressed her lips to mine. Pleasure and deep emotion coursed through my entire body. I couldn't stop trembling. It seemed strange that Eiko's lips, which had been dyed crimson with Shin's blood not long ago, and then been in contact with my own wounded toe-penis, were now kissing my lips, and yet there was no taste of blood. In fact, it was just the opposite: something very sweet, something very precious was rolling over my tongue, and I lost myself in its flavor. In the midst of my excitement, I felt without any doubt how dear Eiko herself was to me as a human being.

Eiko kept hugging me even after she took her lips away from mine. I had just been sitting there limply while she kissed me, but now I put my arms around her, too.

Then, all of a sudden, Eiko said, "Hey, how would you feel about eloping?"

"Eloping?"

It wasn't that I didn't understand what she was saying—that wasn't the reason I repeated the word. It was because it sounded so fresh, and so enticing. Naturally I found myself wondering where she was planning to go, and what we would do when we got there. But by the time these incidental thoughts arose, I had already answered.

"Okay."

Chapter 13

After making a few hurried arrangements, keeping discussion to a minimum, we set about "eloping." Eiko went to her room to get her luggage and to leave a note for Tamotsu, since it would be a pain if he came back late and woke up everyone else trying to find us. I slid a note under Shigeki and Aiko's door saying that we were going on ahead. Eiko and I went down to the front desk and asked for a taxi. And then we were off for Tokyo.

Eiko was calm.

"What did you write?" I asked. "To Tamotsu, I mean."

"I just wrote: I'm going."

She hadn't made up her mind to break up with Tamotsu. And it wasn't as if we were running off to some secret location; we were just going to hang out in my apartment, and it would be easy enough for him to find us. The troupe would be returning to Tokyo the next evening, so Tamotsu would probably show up sometime in the next few days, however he interpreted Eiko's cryptic note. When he did, the two of them could talk things over and decide on their next step.

We had called what we were doing "eloping," it was true, but I didn't really see it that way: my role seemed closer to that of a bystander—a passive partner. I couldn't believe I was important enough to Eiko that she would hesitate if she really had to choose between Tamotsu and me. I wasn't going to butt in with opinions on her relationship with Tamotsu. There were only two things on my mind: first, the fact that I liked Eiko and she appeared to like me; and second, that at the very least I would now be able to enjoy a few days alone with her.

In other words, I felt more or less the way I would have felt setting out on a picnic, and I hadn't given much thought to whether or not any serious sexual play was part of the picnic. I couldn't speak for Eiko, of course.

Arriving at my apartment near dawn, we showered, tumbled into bed, and fell asleep. I awoke around noon. Eiko was still asleep beside me. My gaze wandered around the room, and I realized that the MESSAGE light on the answering machine was blinking. I pressed PLAY.

"Hey, it's me, Shunji . . . I guess you're traveling now, huh? I'm on a trip myself actually. I'll call back."

I was shaken for a moment, then disappointed. I had called the apartment regularly to check my messages during the tour, and there had been nothing from Shunji. I was resigned to the fact that he'd dumped me. Why was he bothering to call now? What was the point?

"What a loser."

This was Eiko. Shunji's message had woken her up, and she was frowning.

"Something about this makes me angry," I said, unable to contain my emotions.

"Of course it does! How can he treat you so lightly!"

This confirmation of injustice made me feel free to let go, and another flash of anger exploded inside me. I was still sitting there silently, holding it in, when Eiko put her arm around my shoulder and kissed me on the cheek. This gave me the same feeling as the night before, as if something precious was raining down on me, and my fury was forgotten. Eiko smiled, looking a bit abashed. I moved my lips toward her face, as if her smile were drawing me in.

♥ ♥ ♥

As happy as I was the whole time we were kissing, I was puzzled. There was really nothing extraordinary about Eiko's kissing technique, beyond the gentleness and delicateness of her caresses and the way she used her tongue. How, then, was she able to make me feel so wonderful? Did her body contain a special pleasure-inducing substance? The more I savored my feelings, the clearer it became: the pleasure was less a matter of the warmth and texture of her skin, and less a matter of technique; it stemmed from the joy that swelled in my heart at the simple fact that I was embracing and kissing Eiko. Even the physical delight I felt—a sensuousness that blossomed everywhere on my body—seemed to be coming from my heart. And so I could only conclude, with yet another swelling of joy, that being with Eiko was what made me feel so good. No one else could possibly make me feel this way.

Naturally, I soon grew eager to cherish other parts of Eiko's body, beyond her lips and tongue, and so the orbit of my kisses and caresses widened; and then it struck me how *really* great it'd be to do this nude. I must have been half conscious when I'd believed myself free of any desire to be naked with her, skin against skin. Or maybe I had simply been incapable of imagining how good it would feel.

I started unbuttoning my pajamas, using only one hand. Eiko, seeing this, parted her lips uncertainly, then burst out laughing. This encouraged me and made me smile, and I gave the front of her pajamas a tug. Still chuckling, her face flushed, she started unbuttoning her own pajamas.

The emotions I felt embracing Eiko without any clothes on were . . . deeper than I'd expected. Once my arms were wrapped around her body, I was all but paralyzed. I was amazed at the naturalness of my desire to be naked with her, at how right it felt once we were naked. This wasn't the first time I had ever embraced another person in the buff, so it was puzzling that the emotion was so powerful. It had to be the fact that I was with Eiko.

But there were other things going on, too. Whenever things started getting sexual between me and Masao, my first lover, I always let him take the lead because he was more assertive. In retrospect, I could see that my affection for him hadn't really been love, and during the period when we were dating I seldom noticed myself feeling any sexual desire. In any case, he always stripped off my clothes so quickly I never had a chance to want to remove them myself. So I never experienced the urge to be naked with him, or the pleasure of acting upon that urge. Even the happiness I felt when we held each other, skin on skin, was the happiness of confirming the intimacy we shared, not the joy of feeling a desire fulfilled.

Sex with Shunji had been a tranquil game, an extension of more ordinary sorts of physical contact. One moment we'd be horsing around, sharing tenderness like little kids, and then suddenly I'd notice that we were naked—that's how it always was with him. We never took off our clothes *after* we had gotten ourselves excited. And in the company of someone as far removed from wild, passionate desire as Shunji was, I always ended up feeling extraordinarily relaxed, and never got into the state where sexual excitement took over.

I had fun making love with Masao and Shunji, it's true, and from time to time I'd have fresh discoveries and experience wonderful emotions, but now with Eiko was the first time I had ever wanted to get naked with someone and then actually gotten naked with that someone. This came as a shock to me—that in all the years I'd been sexually active I had never, until this moment, experienced something so fundamental to the act of lovemaking. What was making it possible for me to experience this pleasure now? Had the problem been Masao's and Shunji's sexual styles?

"Hey, are you alive?"

Eiko rocked my body in her arms—she must have found my stillness odd. The soft pressure of her breasts against mine was a reminder that we were both women, that I was engaging in an act that society at large considered abnormal. Even if we were only playing, what I was doing right now was homosexual lovemaking.

How much did it mean, though, to say that Eiko and I were the same sex? We both had XX chromosomes, we both had female genitals, and our bodies weren't different the way men's and women's were. But those commonalities seemed utterly insignificant compared to the fact that she and I were completely different individuals living different lives, with two separate physical bodies, and different sensibilities and ways of thinking. I put my hand on Eiko's breast, and sure enough, it was different from mine in volume and shape . . . Eiko didn't seem any more similar to me as a human being than Masao or Shunji.

Once I grew comfortable with the idea that it made no sense to set up distinctions based solely on how the sexes were paired in a couple—between homosexual love and heterosexual love—and that I had been rejecting same-sex love for no reason I could have articulated, everything became extremely, elegantly clear. And so I started looking for ways to feel even better. I had no idea what Eiko thought of lesbianism, but her approach to our lovemaking was relaxed from the start. Drunk on delight that welled up from deep inside and spread through my whole body, I realized that, making love, I had never before felt, with such heightened sensitivity, every little thing that was done to me. Obviously Eiko's technique alone wasn't responsible . . .

My fingers were lingering over Eiko's nipples, playing with them, when it suddenly hit me that I was doing something lewd. My happiness waned; I felt as if I'd strayed from the sexual path I'd been following. There was nothing unusual about fondling a nipple. It was an absolutely ordinary act in lovemaking. So why couldn't I enjoy it?

I didn't have to think too hard about it. The answer was crystal clear: I didn't really find breasts attractive. To be sure, vast numbers of humanity fondled breasts, but that didn't make it any less unnatural for me, because it wasn't something my desire prompted me to do. Yet I had to admit that, while I felt no particular excitement about a man's chest or a man's nipples, I never thought twice about running my fingers and tongue over Masao's or Shunji's.

When I had made love with Masao or Shunji, I had no problem accepting anything that was done to me, or that I myself did, as long as the action jibed with my idea of what sex ought generally to be like. In other words, as long as it seemed normal, I could accept that this is what sex is like. But compared to the unusually heightened sensitivity I was now feeling, that willingness to go along with anything seemed like dullness.

The truth was, when I had fooled around with Masao and Shunji, I had never really had the urge to savor, in a focused, conscious way, the basic acts of lovemaking. And the reason was, Masao and Shunji were men.

Before my first sexual experience, I'd had an intellectual understanding of what went on in the minds of men and women that led them to make love, of the caresses they exchanged, and of that most ecstatic of moments, when their sexual organs came together. I had pieced together this under-standing from tidbits from television, movies, and magazines, as well as from what friends told me. While the picture in my mind was sketchy in places, the impression was powerful enough, and deep enough, that the first time I made love, it reassured me that I was doing the right things.

When I began having sex regularly, I made little adjustments to my image of the sex act to bring it in line with my experience, but everything I did was in accordance with the model of normality in my mind. As long as I could tell myself that what I was doing was correct and normal, desire didn't have to be involved. I was so utterly dependent on this understand-ing of sex that I never felt the need to discover what I desired to do. And the same was true when I was having things done to me. Always I tried to feel the pleasures I was supposed to feel, reminding myself that when someone did *that* it was natural for me to feel *this*.

I gave my own emotional and physical sensitivities no free rein. Shunji was eccentric, even for a man, so my experiences with him often failed to conform to the understanding I had developed, and that allowed me to enjoy myself with a good deal more flexibility. Sex with Masao, however, had always fit the ready-made image perfectly. The reason that the sexual experience was much deeper with Eiko was, no doubt, that she was a woman, and being with her had freed me from the image of male-female sex in which I had gotten trapped. My feelings, both physical and emo-tional, had been stripped of their old conceptual clothing.

I was astonished at how supremely dumb I had been. And at the same time, I was thrilled that having conquered with Eiko my discomfort with homosexual love, I was finally in a position to enjoy sexual pleasure spon-taneously and fully.

I was lying there, reveling in this new understanding, when Eiko climbed on top of me and took my nipple between her lips. Unlike me, she seemed to feel no hesitation at all, and there was nothing lewd about the way she used her tongue. I just lay back and relished the marvelous sensations, completely giving myself up to them.

Now I began to realize how paranoid I had been earlier when I was touching Eiko's nipples and thought I was doing something lewd. Breasts are an erogenous zone. What's lewd about fondling your partner's breasts when you want to make her feel good? Even if you feel no particular desire to touch them yourself, there's nothing unnatural in the act of wanting to give pleasure to someone. This was obvious, of course, and on some level I'd known it all along; but now I was learning it anew, and in a way that really hit home. I was feeling it with my skin.

When Eiko got to a stopping place, I set about returning the favor, heart and soul. I kissed and licked her nipples, and I felt them get firm and stand up, which made me eager to give her even more pleasure. But in the act, I couldn't help noticing that my lips, tongue, and fingers weren't succumbing to the sort of trembling ecstasy I had anticipated. I remained calm, collected. My actions were being guided by reason, not erotic desire, so to some extent that made sense. Compared to the dizzying, shuddering instant of bliss I experienced when we first threw off our clothes and embraced, I got the feeling that I had wandered off the path I saw stretching before me when I first had the urge to get naked.

When I first kissed Eiko, and when I embraced her, I had felt one hundred percent fulfilled, in both mind and body—every part of me was enthralled. Right now, ninety percent of what I felt was emotional, and stemmed from my assumption that Eiko was enjoying herself; I was far from being in a state of absolute physical bliss. I now realized that while I had been in a heady state as she caressed me—drunk on the singularly focused joy of sexual stimulation, and on the gratitude I felt toward Eiko for being so generous, for making me feel so good—I hadn't, in all truth, felt completely fulfilled in mind and body.

Kissing and embracing were expressions of mutual affection, but the things we started doing next were aimed at eliciting pleasure from particular parts of the body—they were, in other words, more focused on physical than on emotional pleasure. So maybe it made sense that the rapture I was feeling tended in one direction more than another. Did I have anything like this in mind when we first started hugging? I didn't think so. But now that I'd let Eiko give me such pleasure, I had no choice but to give her pleasure in return.

I'm not saying I didn't want to. I wasn't indifferent to how she felt, now that I'd had my fun. Giving her pleasure made me happy, too. But when I started teasing one part of Eiko's body, I lost sight of the whole. All I could see was the one, isolated part—I no longer knew who I was trying to please. And that had no attraction for me at all. I wondered if she'd felt the same way. Or was it just me? Was I the only one who saw things this way?

I could try to tell myself that as long as Eiko was enjoying herself, it didn't matter—but that left me feeling uneasy, because I wondered if she really was. I tried to figure out her feelings from her movements, from her breathing. I tried doing different things to her, changing my approach depending on how she seemed to be reacting. And I felt encouraged when she responded positively. But before long, I began to feel that this whole process, trying one little trick after another in an effort to get a good response from the woman I loved, was no more than a kind of game. Yes, it was true . . . poking around, trying to find the most sensitive and responsive parts of a person's body was a lot like trying to figure out how a video game worked. There was some pleasure in this, to be sure, but that wasn't the sort of pleasure I'd been looking for when I initiated physical contact with Eiko.

I wanted to feel what she felt, to have direct access to her sensations. This wasn't a matter of erotic desire—it was more that the thought of treating her as some sort of "thing," like a computer game, freaked me out. My inability to meld with her in this way left me feeling frustrated and lonely. What inspired me to embark upon a course of action that would make me feel this frustration and loneliness, this uncertainty? I should have demurred when she lowered her head to my breast, but instead I let myself be carried away by the pleasure; I lay there passively, letting her do whatever she wanted with me. I had been shallow, shortsighted. But I couldn't have known this would happen. This was the first time I'd ever had sex like this—just letting myself enjoy the raw, naked sensations that washed over me.

Eiko took my head between her hands. I let her draw me toward her and found a kiss waiting for me. The ecstasy that had swept over me before hit once again. I caressed her, wherever my hands could reach, abandoning myself to the pleasure, and she did the same. There was nothing wrong now—I felt that we had gotten back on the proper path. But as far as Eiko was concerned, kissing was no more than an interlude.

When she sat up and placed her hand on my thigh, I made up my mind that this time I would definitely stop her and try to talk things over. But she seemed utterly confident in what she was doing, and I found myself being engulfed once more by the pleasure—even though I didn't think it measured up to kissing and hugging. I couldn't bring myself to give that up, even if the balance wasn't right. I felt as if my body were bounding off on its own in pursuit of erotic bliss, leaving behind my heart, which couldn't shake the suspicion that things weren't quite right.

From Eiko's perspective, from the moment I started peeling off my pajamas, it must have appeared a foregone conclusion that we would be pleasuring each other in this way. How could I explain that this wasn't what I had in mind? Now that things had gone this far, I had to swallow my discomfort and go with the flow. But before long, as I concentrated on the pleasure, I forgot my discomfort. And when Eiko began exploring my vagina with her fingers, I was helpless. This may seem debauched, but it's true.

My vagina was prepared to feel intense pleasure. The gentle movements of her fingers made me feel as if I were levitating. And as I began thinking about how I would reciprocate, her fingers moved out of my vagina and clammily wrapped themselves around my toe-penis.

Until that moment in our lovemaking, I had forgotten I had a toe-penis, and so it never even occurred to me that it should be a part of the pleasure we were having. Eiko straddled my shin, and no sooner were her fingers around my member than it was erect. A stab of pain zagged along the cut I'd gotten the night before, but today the excitement was greater than the pain, and my member held firm.

Eiko lifted her hips, and all at once, I understood what she had in mind. I wasn't surprised. By then I was willing to accept anything, and rather than being put off, I was tantalized: how would this feel?

She was ready. The head of my toe-penis seemed to cling to the mouth of her vagina as she gingerly lowered her hips, testing it. She must have been a little tense, as I was, because her vagina contracted, and my toe-penis was denied entrance. Changing the angle and breathing deeply, she tried again. This time the head of my toe-penis was completely enveloped, almost immediately, by the walls of her vagina. I'd scarcely had time to notice how narrow her vagina was before my toe-penis was entirely sucked inside, wrapped in its warmth.

I felt none of the disgust I had experienced when I was quasi raped by Chisato. The sensation of my toe-penis being grasped by an organ so soft and warm and all-encompassing certainly wasn't disagreeable, even though I wasn't sure whether or not I actually liked it. Nor did I have any particular reaction to the fact that my toe-penis and Eiko's vagina were now having intercourse. I experienced no sense of accomplishment, as if we had finally arrived at the place we were meant to be, and since the only part of me that was touching Eiko was my toe-penis, I didn't have the sense that we had become one.

All of a sudden, the soft fleshy walls encompassing my toe-penis tensed, and heat streamed over me. Eiko had clenched her vagina. She started raising and lowering her hips. The abrupt shift from squishiness to tension, warmth to heat, gentleness to vigor, clarified the feelings I was having.

The things Eiko's vagina did to my toe-penis felt quieter than when she used her hand and more dynamic than when she used her mouth. I was aroused, first and foremost, by the novelty of the sensation. The pleasure was surprisingly mild, compared to when she masturbated me, and I had the vague thought that, solely in terms of my own gratification, the vagina wasn't actually optimal. Assuming that my toe-penis experienced the same sensations as men's penises did, I failed to see what the big deal about a vagina was. Even men who cared only about themselves and didn't give a damn about a woman's pleasure were vagina-fixated. Why?

As Eiko increased the speed of her movements up and down, my pleasure increased more and more, despite my doubts. Perhaps I had been wrong to write off the vagina so quickly. I tried to clear my mind, to reconsider, but then the cut on my toe-penis began to smart. Not only was it being rubbed, Eiko's bodily fluids were oozing into it. The rest of my toe-penis was starting to feel quite nice, but the pain kept the pleasure from escalating very much.

Eiko had closed her eyes and was rocking back and forth, resting a hand on the wall to support her wobbling upper body; she seemed to have forgotten my wound. Eiko was a very considerate person, and if she was so engrossed in the moment that my cut slipped her mind, I wasn't going to stop her, even with the pain. Supposing she wasn't really enjoying herself, and was simply trying to make me enjoy myself, I still wasn't going to betray her generosity by putting an end to the proceedings. I would ignore my toe-penis's pain and focus on the pleasure.

Eiko writhed, rotating her hips. I knew myself that this felt better than straight up-and-down movements. As I imagined Eiko's pleasure, warmth began to radiate through my own vagina. I couldn't see Eiko's expression because her wildly disheveled hair had fallen over her face. I was entranced by the sight of her long hair whipping through the air, and by her dancing breasts. I tried moving my right foot myself as I gazed at her, and the pleasure I felt multiplied.

My toe-penis still hurt, though. It was an odd feeling, succumbing to both pain and pleasure at the same time. If it was impossible to ignore the pain, I thought, why not try and experience it as pleasure? To a certain extent, this aching and tingling resembled scratching an itchy insect bite. Scratching the itch felt good, but if I scratched too much, an element of pain was introduced. I could deceive myself only so much. At a certain point, I began wishing this would hurry up and end. Preferably while I still had my erection.

Eiko's vagina clenched ever more tightly around my toe-penis, and I felt a series of little peristaltic spasms. The heat surrounding my toe-penis dispersed, and Eiko came tumbling down on top of me. Her body was drenched in sweat, her heart was pounding wildly. I was relieved it was over; the pain had been worth it, because I had been able to give Eiko pleasure. Above all, I was happy that Eiko's body was back in my arms. The cut on my toe-penis was smarting, but that didn't matter.

Eiko now looked up at me. Her eyes were moist. She smiled. "Things headed in kind of a strange direction, didn't they?"

"A strange direction?" I knew Eiko didn't really think it strange, that was just her way of expressing the enormity of her emotion, but I couldn't resist needling her. "You think it's *strange* . . . it's just . . ."

Eiko fell silent, looking a bit perplexed. She kissed me on the cheek as if to say that she couldn't think of what to say, then gazed imploringly into my eyes, asking for help. But I myself couldn't say what had happened between the two of us. Shunji would have said we were "being friendly." But while it might seem that we had performed a single sequence of sexual acts, somewhere along the way the purpose of those acts, and the way they felt, had changed—had we performed not one sequence but two, purposefully blurring them? Had we succeeded in carrying out our desire to be friendly? Could what we had done together really be counted as being friends?

It seemed to me, furthermore, that while anyone watching would have thought Eiko and I were participating in one and the same act—and while our hearts had indeed seemed to beat as one while we were kissing and hugging—she and I had probably been thinking different things the whole time: you could say we were performing different acts. I began to feel somewhat down. Why was everything so complex now? Wasn't sex supposed to be fun? Was I making such a big deal of it because this was my first truly heartfelt sexual experience?

As I was turning these thoughts over in my mind, Eiko peered at me. Her brow clouded. She pressed her mouth to my ear and asked, "It didn't feel good?"

As I suspected, we'd been having completely different thoughts. That said, I couldn't dismiss the fantastic things she'd done to me just because she had her own ideas about what they meant. I shook my head vaguely, indicating that I hadn't felt much pleasure. Eiko's expression saddened.

"I've never done it with a woman before . . . It's weird. I mean, I think I'm pretty used to dealing with penises," Eiko said. She turned to look back at my foot, then froze. "You had a cut!"

I sat up, propping myself on my elbow. My toe-penis was still half erect. The cut was oozing blood; the rest of the organ was faintly coated with red.

Wrapping an arm around my head, Eiko said, "Oh, it must have hurt! Why didn't you say something?"

This made me burst into laughter. It had just occurred to me how hilarious it was that my toe-penis should bleed after its first real encounter with a female sex organ. "It's like the hymen has been broken—even though it's a penis!"

Eiko chuckled, too, but her expression quickly turned serious again. She scooted over toward my toe-penis on her knees and started lowering her head over it. I seized her arm, restraining her.

"I'm not Tamotsu, Eiko. I'm not going to make you lick off the blood."

Eiko hugged me tightly, then kissed me.

♥ ♥ ♥

Again and again, Eiko harped gleefully on the fact that I had taken off my pajamas because I wanted to be naked with her. "I mean, all of a sudden you just started stripping, without a word of explanation! I thought people usually took off their partner's clothes first."

"Do they?"

"Sure! That shows them you're in the mood."

"That never occurred to me."

"You really are kind of weird, aren't you? You're so fascinating."

I was glad she found me fascinating, but I didn't really see what was weird about deciding to get naked. I mean, when I started undressing, I wasn't in the "mood" that Eiko was referring to. But it didn't matter—Eiko seemed to have enjoyed having sex with me, and it would be crass to nitpick about the differences in our viewpoints at this stage in the game, so I dropped it.

"Actually," Eiko continued, "I was thinking about taking off *your* pajamas. I'm a go-getter, you know, so it never occurred to me to take my own clothes off."

"What made you hesitate?"

"Well, I didn't know if you wanted to go that far . . . and, in my mind, there's something a little lewd about taking off a person's clothes. Even if your partner doesn't mind, there's something sort of lonely about being stripped, no?" Eiko paused and shuddered. "I still feel ashamed of having done that to Tamotsu when he was just a boy." Then, shifting gears, she beamed. "So even though I was amused when you started tossing your own clothes off, I was happy. And of course you saved me the trouble of having to do it."

I had no problem returning her smile when she said that.

We kissed, as if to toast our love.

Eiko seemed to feel no resistance to homosexual love. This was the first time she had ever done it with a woman, she said, but not the first time she had ever *wanted* to.

"Then why didn't you do it?"

"Because I had my hands full with men. And I never met a woman I liked so much I couldn't get her out of my head—someone I just had to have. If I hadn't met you, I might not ever have had a homosexual experience."

"And you were content only going out with men?"

"Well, it's not like it would have killed me to do without a woman's love. But you can't get along in this society of ours unless you get in good with men, right? I've always been pretty calculating where things like that are concerned."

She was probably right. It is a challenge for a woman to make her way in the world without taking advantage of the economic and social power men command, and it was worse for lesbians. Maybe they had no choice but to keep quiet in the corner, as Eiko seemed to imply they should. To have to take such a cold, rational perspective, giving up on desire for other women, took a lot out of a woman. Even if she could do what she wanted with members of the opposite sex, her unfulfilled hunger for women was bound to intrude upon her consciousness—like a fishbone caught in her throat.

"What about you, Kazumi? Were you interested in other women?"

"Not before I acquired my toe-penis," I replied, then corrected myself. "Or rather, not until I met you."

Eiko seemed to take this as a compliment and smiled. "I feel like I should say I don't believe you, but I do. To tell the truth, the first time I saw you, I doubted you were sexually active at all."

"I certainly was!" I declared.

"I know that *now*, of course, but back then . . ."

I felt my face flush. Eiko reddened a little, too. After a bit, she asked,

"What was her name . . . Yoko? That friend of yours who killed herself? You didn't have anything going with her?"

"No!"

So Eiko had assumed the same thing about my relationship with Yoko as M., the novelist, and Shunji had! I was shocked.

"And she never came on to you?" Eiko asked suspiciously.

"If I say there was nothing between us, there was nothing between us. Why does everyone want to believe we were lovers?"

"Why not! Think about it—Yoko was fascinated with love and sex— enough to create a bank of available lovers; she put you on the board and allowed you to get rich even though you didn't really share her fascination; and then she arranged it so that you would discover her body when she killed herself. That hardly sounds like an ordinary friendship."

I was starting to feel deflated. "Would everyone see it that way, do you think?" I asked nervously. "Everyone but me?"

"Sure. I mean, Aiko guessed right away that there was something going on between you and me, right? And you and Yoko had a lot more of a history than you and me."

Aiko had been the one to call when the Flower Show arrived back in Tokyo the day after we'd run off. "Well, as long as you're okay," she had said. "What are you two doing?" While I fumbled for an answer, Aiko rephrased the question. "Are you having fun?"

This time, I replied right away, "Oh, sure, loads of fun!"

"It's almost like you eloped or something!" was Aiko's response.

After hanging up the phone, I'd murmured to myself, "How'd she know that?"

Eiko had laughed so hard she fell over.

When I failed to reply to Eiko's statement about Yoko and me having a history, she started firing off one observation after another. "I have to say, it must have been hard for her to ask a girl like you to have sex. I mean, seriously, like I said, you give people the feeling that you have no sex life. If somebody tried to give you some roundabout message, you wouldn't notice. It'd be bad enough for a man unlucky enough to fall for you, but for a woman! That would be a *real* tragedy."

"Don't."

That one word was all I could manage. Because it hurt too much to think that Yoko might have loved me. I certainly didn't want to believe she had, but I couldn't rebut Eiko's take on the situation. I was in pain. Even my toe-penis ached.

"All right, I'll stop," Eiko said. Then, lowering her voice to a whisper, "It's nice that we got together, though, isn't it?"

Eiko didn't regret that she had eloped and had sex with me. The last few days, ever since we came to my apartment, we'd been sleeping in the same bed, preparing and eating dinner together, going out for walks, going shopping, going to the beauty salon, all together. And all that time, she was touching me—taking my hand in hers, pressing her cheek to mine, putting her arm around my shoulder. She felt totally at ease with me; her heart was mine. She liked living with me. And I had the sense it was okay for me to touch her freely, too, without thinking too much about what I was doing.

But I was still trying to resolve the question of whether having sex with Eiko was the same as "being friendly." And I couldn't help wondering, seeing how easy it was for Eiko to show me affection simply because we were lovers—seeing, that is, how smoothly everything seemed to be going for her, as if she were running at a comfortable pace toward the finish line on a fixed course—whether she might just be living out some idealized image she'd had of the lesbian love affair she would like to have. Maybe she was doing things she had anticipated, looked forward to doing, so that the joy she felt came less from being with me personally than from being with another woman.

That said, I couldn't deny that I was quite content with the pleasant, easygoing life we were leading, and the casual physical exchanges that gave it color. Unlike sexual intercourse, our ordinary, everyday touching warmed my heart and left me fully gratified, even when only limited parts of our bodies came in contact. It struck me once again that there was something coarse about sexual stimulation, compared to the happiness that came from ordinary physical contact, which was like soaking in a bath heated to the perfect temperature. Of course, sex with Eiko had been so overwhelming I'd found it impossible to stop once we started, and if we were to do it again, I might change my mind. We wouldn't be able to for a few days, though. The wound on my toe-penis wasn't the only reason; Eiko and I both had our periods.

Eiko, who had just finished blow-drying her hair, came to sit beside me on the bed. I was stretched out, my legs extended in front of me, watching television. I scooted over to make room for her. She settled down just close enough that our arms touched. This wasn't unpleasant. It was far from unpleasant. In fact, the soft warmth of Eiko's arm against me was enough to make me lose all interest in the program I had been watching. I gazed down at our feet, lined up at the foot of the bed. This, I thought, is a much better sight than the scenes of young love on the television screen.

My gaze fell on the nail of Eiko's right pinky toe. I had the impression that this brown, lumpy, deformed bulge had grown larger. The last time I'd seen it, Eiko had just trimmed the fat ridge with a nail clipper; the increased thickness came, presumably, from new growth. The malformed toenail—which had a sorry air, as though it had been chased to the edge by the nine smooth nails—was nevertheless loveable. Several times I had called up an image of that nail while I masturbated, and a desire to touch it came over me.

The first time I'd reached for that nail, Eiko had pulled away, laughing ticklishly. Back then we had just been regular friends, so she might have felt a little tense about it. She was more comfortable with me now that we had made love in the nude. There could be nothing wrong, then, with my touching it. I knew that whatever its texture, whether bumpy or grainy, I'd like it.

I quietly lifted my right foot, crossed it over my left, and stroked Eiko's little toe with the underside of my toe-penis. The nail felt like a small stone, its surface nicely polished. I rubbed my toe-penis across it a few times, shivering at the sensation.

"What are you doing?" Eiko asked, laughing.

Distracted by the tactile pleasures I was feeling, I said nothing. I kept poking around with the tip of my toe-penis. Eiko slapped my knee.

"Excuse me! I don't believe your cut has healed yet, has it?" She seemed to think I was looking to have some fun.

"I'm just admiring your toenail," I said. I *wasn't* looking to have some fun; I was touching her toenail with my toe-penis because I couldn't reach it easily with my hand. And if my nonintentions were not clear, my toe-penis remained limp. Right now my toe-penis wasn't a sexual organ—it was just a toe.

"Admiring *this*?" Eiko said, drawing her toenail across the underside of my toe-penis.

The moment I found myself on the receiving end of the touch, my toe-penis became a sexual organ and stiffened. Eiko thought this was terrific, and started caressing it with her foot. With my toe-penis in this agitated state, I instinctively raised my foot, trying to escape the stimulation. But by then it was obviously erect.

"Now what are you going to do?" Eiko teased.

Under the circumstances it didn't seem appropriate to say, "Do you even have to ask?" so I kept these words to myself. I realized once again how much I loved having Eiko fondle my toe-penis with her hand. The other day I'd felt what it was like to have my toe-penis inside her vagina, but—perhaps because I hadn't climaxed?—her vagina hadn't seemed like the ideal match for it. Her hand was better. When Eiko put her hand around my toe-penis, I experienced a surge of sensation as if my whole body had metamorphosed into a giant toe-penis and was being completely engulfed by a giant Eiko. Nothing like that happened when I did it with her vagina, which had made my toe-penis feel isolated.

It was odd that my whole body should feel satisfied when Eiko touched my toe-penis with her hand, even though she was stimulating only one part of me. Maybe it was because her hand looked so amazingly gentle when she cradled my toe-penis in her palm, and that helped me relax. I felt as peaceful then as when we held hands, wholeheartedly enjoying our love for each other. Of course, the intense sexual rush my toe-penis experienced was quite different from what I felt when we held hands, for instance. But if you discounted the sexual thrill, the spiritual joy I felt when Eiko fondled my toe-penis felt closer to the happiness that accompanied other, more casual forms of physical contact than any erotic stimulation, including of my vagina.

As I lay musing about pleasure, my toe-penis actually began feeling what I was thinking, and I got another erection. All of a sudden I realized that my wound no longer hurt, so I bent my right leg inward to get a better look at the head. It seemed almost entirely healed, with only a small scab remaining. I started to pick at it, but Eiko grabbed my wrist.

"Don't!" she said.

"C'mon, don't you ever feel tempted to pick your scabs?"

"You sound just like Tamotsu. He always picks his scabs. Shin's, I mean."

A cruel scene rose before my eyes, and I let go of the scab.

"Sometimes it'll almost be healed," she went on, "and then he goes and makes it bleed again."

"Do you have to lick off the blood then, too?"

I couldn't believe I had so nonchalantly stuck my nose into their private affairs. Eiko's expression clouded for a moment; then, wrapping an arm around my neck, she replied in a tone as casual as mine had been, "Yeah, I do."

The ache that spread through my chest made my toe-penis wilt.

Eiko, whose gaze had been fixed on it, smiled faintly. "There was this guy, one of the men Tamotsu had me sleep with so he could see what it was like . . . He was a doctor in his early thirties, and he came regularly to our shows. After we did it, he whispered into my ear that he wanted to see me again, just the two of us, and so I went once, and he asked me to break up with Tamotsu and go out with him instead. He seemed like a very nice man on the surface, so I kind of thought about it for a little while, but when I told him what I just told you, about having to lick off the blood, he got an erection."

I burst out laughing.

"Yeah, I know—you have to laugh, right? You can totally imagine the kind of stuff he's into. He got all flustered and tried to defend himself, but I wasn't having any of it, and in the end he just said, 'Yeah, men are hopeless . . .'"

I couldn't stop laughing, but Eiko's expression turned serious again, and she twined both her arms around my neck. "I'm glad you're not a pervert like him."

I planted a kiss on Eiko's arm, which was right below my jaw. "Men like that have something weird going on with their penises," I said.

"You think perversions like that come from weird penises?"

"I think it's easy for these *things*," I said, placing my hand on my toe-penis, "to make men go in bizarre directions. I suppose what happens is that when you go on masturbating all the time, concentrating on an image of a person or a scene, a really strong association develops and pretty soon that person or scene and the pleasure the penis feels can't be separated."

"And it's harder for vaginas to make you get weird like that?"

"I guess it happens, but . . . I don't know, don't you have the impression that men masturbate more often than women? A whole lot more. After all," I went on, adding a note from my own experience, "penises are quite visible, and they're perfect to hold onto, and men consider masturbation a totally normal part of life."

"Hmm, I wonder if it's really that simple."

"I mean, in a sense you could say my toe-penis only responds well to you because you've become a sort of habit for it."

"You're telling me I'm a *habit*?"

"No, no—that's not what I mean! I just mean that all the terrific things you've done for me have created this path of desire that goes from my toe-penis to you. Just think about it. Until I met you, my toe-penis just responded to physical stimulation—it was that simple. Only after I met you, after you became the object of my affections, did it acquire a personality of its own."

"Okay, can I ask you one thing, though? Do you think we would have ended up like this if you didn't have a toe-penis?"

If I hadn't had a toe-penis, Eiko couldn't have touched it, and I wouldn't have had an opportunity to start desiring her, so presumably she and I would just have remained friends. Back then I hadn't understood homosexuality at all. It was hard for me to answer. But I said, "I don't think we would have, no."

The smile vanished from Eiko's face, and was replaced by an achingly lonely, defenseless helplessness. I felt like someone had shot me in the heart. Because the lost expression on her face was exactly the same as the one I used to see on Yoko's face.

♥ ♥ ♥

I realized for the first time after my relationship with Eiko turned physical just how cold the hands and feet of a woman with bad circulation get at the end of October. Her feet, which were even worse than her hands, were so icy from her heels to her toes that I could feel the coldness radiating through her socks. My own circulation was fine, so I put her frigid heels between my thighs, covered her toes with the palms of my hands, and warmed her up. Her feet seemed to suck my body heat from me, making me shiver, but I was soon warm again.

Touching her feet directly, rather than through her socks, seemed like a better thing, and I began peeling them off. Eiko glanced up from the magazine she was reading, and I relaxed, seeing her mild, contented smile. I couldn't help recalling the brittle, forlorn look I had seen on her face the other day—an expression that was like a thin crust of ice—and a faint chill came over me. I hoped I would never make Eiko feel that way again.

But I wasn't confident that I could avoid it. Eiko had wanted me to assure her that we would have had sex even if I didn't have a toe-penis, but I couldn't see why. Maybe she thought I felt nothing for her but a desire centered on my toe-penis. I tried telling her my feelings for her wouldn't change even if my toe-penis were to disappear. But that didn't do anything to cheer her up.

Was Eiko testing to see how much I liked her? Was that it? Suppose I told her I thought we would have had sex whether or not I had a toe-penis—that made it sound like we were bonded by an absolute affection that couldn't be swayed by mere material conditions, and that was very romantic and beautiful. But that was a superficial, verbal thing, not reality. The experience of her doing things to my toe-penis had given me a sexual liking for Eiko, if that was the right thing to call it, and that had transported my feelings for her beyond friendliness. I simply couldn't believe that this friendliness would have escalated, all on its own, into sexual liking.

So was Eiko a romantic? Or was the way she cultivated a sexual liking for someone completely different from my own? Either way, there was no point confusing the issue with hypothetical questions about what might have happened if I didn't have a toe-penis. Why not just be happy that I did, and that we had become sexually close? The truth was, I didn't see why she couldn't be content with the affection I felt for her—why she felt the need to determine precisely how far that affection went.

I didn't understand that, but if she wanted to test the extent of my affection, I wanted to show her how much I cared, and in all sorts of different ways—including, for instance, warming her cold feet with my body. I was afraid, even so, that I would never be able to heal her deep loneliness, when I didn't understand what made her feel that way. Maybe my expressions of affection were no more comforting to her than a dog's devoted licking of its unhappy master's hand.

Eiko's foot seemed to have warmed up, but since my hand and her foot were now the same temperature, I couldn't really tell how warm that was. So I lifted her right foot and pressed her toes to my cheek. Cold. I was about to put her foot back down and warm it some more when my eye landed on the deformed nail on her little toe. I slipped it into my mouth. I hadn't realized how much I had been wanting to do this.

"So you're into this sort of thing, are you? What a weirdo."

I took her toe out of my mouth. "I am not a weirdo," I said. "Look, I'm not even hard."

Eiko pulled off my sock. "You're right," she said.

Running my tongue over the thick, peculiarly shaped toenail, I found myself recalling the small river stones I used to pick up near my parents' home and put into my mouth. There was no sexual excitement involved—just the feeling of fulfillment that comes from being tender to something that deserves to be shown a little tenderness. Eiko was right—what I was doing indeed suggested a sexual act—but the sensations I was experiencing showed no sign of veering in a sexual direction. The tenderness I felt arose not from my sexual liking of Eiko but from my friendly liking of her;

and just as friendly liking could never become sexual liking, no matter how much it escalated, tenderness could never become sexual desire, no matter how much tenderness there was.

Just the same, if I had only felt a friendly liking for Eiko, it's unlikely I would have stuck her toe in my mouth, no matter how adorable I found her oddly shaped toenail. I would have thought it dirty. The reason I didn't think it dirty was that I felt a sexual liking for Eiko. So was my impulse to put her toe in my mouth actually, to some small degree, sexually motivated? No, I doubted it. It was more likely that my sexual liking of Eiko had neutralized the sense of dirtiness I would feel toward another person's foot, allowing me to express my friendly liking of her in this intimate, physical way.

Perhaps you could say that my sexual liking of Eiko had strengthened my liking of her as a friend. And if that was the case, couldn't you conclude that sexual desire plays an important role, even in our nonsexual relationships with other people?

Eiko started playing with my toe-penis, the cut on which was now fully healed. I asked myself: was she was fondling it out of tenderness or out of desire? The slow swell of pleasure soon caused me to forget the question, and Eiko's toe fell from my mouth. Eiko then lifted my right foot and let her tongue slither up and down the length of my erect toe-penis. I stroked the little toe of Eiko's foot with my fingers, thinking, sadly, how unfair it was—if only this toe could have an erection, too.

Just then the phone rang. Eiko stopped moving her tongue and I turned to stare silently at the phone. I reached out to pick up the receiver, but, unnervingly, it stopped ringing.

I had been expecting a call would come sometime. "You think it's Tamotsu?" I asked.

Seven days had passed since we had eloped, and Tamotsu hadn't visited, hadn't called. When Aiko rang, I had asked how Tamotsu was doing, and she'd said he was acting as if everything was just fine—at that moment he was dancing with Masami, seemingly in fine spirits. Eiko hadn't mentioned Tamotsu at all, but how could she not be thinking about him; who knew, she might secretly be seething that he hadn't called. I'd felt a little nervous suggesting the phone call was from him.

"I highly doubt it," she replied brusquely. "More likely it's Shunji."

"Definitely not Shunji."

"How can you be so sure?"

Eiko folded her hand around my toe-penis and squeezed. A burst of pleasure gushed all the way up to my breasts, making me catch my breath. "Shunji doesn't have the delicateness to hesitate," I managed to say. "If he wants to call, he just calls."

Tamotsu and Eiko needed to talk things over during this break. If they didn't, they'd end up facing off at the next performance, which was rapidly approaching, without having cleared up the muddle of their feelings.

Without another word, Eiko went back to fellating my toe-penis. It felt fantastic, but she didn't seem happy about it. She looked pensive. I took my toe-penis out of her mouth and scooted over next to her. She threw her arms around me.

"He's such a child!" she spat out. "He doesn't even have the courage to call!"

"Why don't you call him?"

"But he should be calling me, shouldn't he?"

"That's true, yes, but you don't want to perform with him the way things are now, do you?"

"It's fine with me."

"But you'll have to get naked with him!"

"I'm a professional. I can handle it."

"But . . ."

I fell silent, unable to come up with the right words. I found myself imagining the two of them performing a segment even more gruesome and awful than usual. Eiko turned to face me.

"But what?"

"I'm scared of what Tamotsu might do to you."

"Okay," Eiko said, putting her hand around the back of my neck, "if Tamotsu seems strange on the day of the performance, you can take his place as my partner. How does that sound?"

I felt mud churn in my heart. Stripping off my clothes and performing sexual acts in public was totally embarrassing, but this was even worse. I hated the idea of performing, with Eiko as my partner, an act that looked like lovemaking but was only an exaggerated imitation of sex. I didn't really understand what was going on between us when we had sex as it was, and I had the feeling that I would understand even less if we ended up having imitation sex. The act of making love with her could stop having anything to do with affection or love, but even that would be better than having to watch Tamotsu and Eiko go through with their awful performance.

"Why don't we practice?" Eiko said.

"I don't want to practice."

"What if it weren't practice?"

Eiko drew her hand softly down the front of my body. This didn't bring on any deep pleasure, but I found myself remembering the joy I felt when we embraced in the nude. Both our periods had finished the day before. I puckered my lips, seeking hers.

The second time we had sex I felt hardly any of the discomfort—the sense that something was amiss—that had gnawed at me the first time. Maybe I had gotten used to the idea, and my emotions had evened out. I was fascinated by my body's responses, and threw myself, without hesitation, into teasing and pleasing Eiko. We were putting more emphasis on physical pleasure than on emotional comfort, but that was all right, I was doing it with Eiko, after all, and we could do things that would satisfy both my body and my heart some other time. That's how I saw things then.

Eiko was even more active than the first time, and she tried a move on me that she hadn't used before. It was a first for me. She kept trying, doing her best, but it was like she was scratching a place that didn't itch. Eventually I said, "I don't really feel much there."

Eiko withdrew her finger from my anus. "Yeah, it doesn't do much for me either," she said. "Tamotsu likes it, though."

The sudden image of Tamotsu in the midst of our sex play was perplexing. "I'm not Tamotsu," I blurted out. "Don't get us mixed up."

"I'm not mixing you up!" Eiko said, and shifted position.

When my toe-penis and Eiko's vagina came together, my stomach and breasts, exposed to the air, felt a little chilly, and a loneliness came over me. The wetness and pressure of her vagina felt more intimate than ever, but I had the nagging feeling again that it wasn't the best match. It took some time for the pleasure to intensify, but fortunately Eiko seemed perfectly content to let me take my time.

One thing I discovered was how good it was to climax when my toe-penis was inside someplace warm. When, afterward, Eiko threw herself down on top of me, I rested my hand on her vagina, as if to console it.

After a while, Eiko said, "Is there anything else you want to try?"

"I want to do it in the normal way," I replied. That way our bodies wouldn't have to be apart.

Eiko laughed. "That's the one thing we can't do."

♥ ♥ ♥

Tamotsu never called, even after Aiko got in touch to let us know the date and time of the next performance. Aiko was worried about Tamotsu and Eiko, too; she asked me to put Eiko on the line. Eiko responded to whatever Aiko was saying with phrases like "that's fine" and "I'll be okay." When I asked her about it later, she said Tamotsu had been as evasive as ever, and no one could talk sense into him.

As the day of the performance drew near—the day when she would be brought face to face with Tamotsu again—Eiko became visibly more tense. I told her that she might have to call him, but she only responded with a grimace. Evidently she was prepared to wait him out, and I decided not to say anything more. To tell the truth, I was relieved that we hadn't heard from Tamotsu—especially if that made it possible for Eiko and me to stay together even one day longer.

I hadn't really considered what eloping with Eiko meant, and I hadn't thought at all about the effect the constant presence of a woman who made me feel so unbelievably wonderful would have on me, both mentally and physically. Having her with me meant that I was always delightfully, deliciously intoxicated. I didn't need to be touching her, I didn't even have to see her—just the hint of her presence in the air was enough to make me feel so good my being seemed to melt and everything harsh and hard in me to dissolve. Like a mollusk washed about in the tide, I was limp, a shapeless mass—all from breathing air infused with Eiko's presence. The few times Eiko went out alone to do some shopping, I felt like all the water was being wrung from my body.

It would be fair to say that I was chronically turned on. It was a quiet arousal. I may have felt endlessly woozy, but my toe-penis wasn't always erect. To be sure, it basked in the same overall sense of well-being, but its pleasure was not really different from that of the nonpenile big toe on my left foot. The pleasure of having Eiko near was, in other words, something that my skin felt, and my breasts. And yet it was true that the slightest brush against my toe-penis would get it hard. An erection didn't immediately call up desire, however, or make me eager to dive into sex.

What an erection did call up was the desire to have Eiko give me, crude to say, a hand job, and lead me to an orgasm. My toe-penis was not, in my eyes, a tool intended for the sex act, conventionally speaking. It produced intense pleasure, but it was only one among many elements necessary to satisfy my desire for physical intimacy. Only when Eiko began doing things to other erogenous zones on my body did I begin to feel the urge to have sex.

We had sex again and again once our periods were over. But to be honest, it got a little boring. Being bored didn't make the pleasure less pleasurable, and I still liked Eiko just as much as always, so I didn't feel particularly inclined to stop; but I hadn't developed any deep fondness for the sexual act.

Sex struck me as a highly intellectual game. I had been right to compare the art of lovemaking, identifying what gave a partner pleasure, to figuring out a video game. In sex, as in any other game, it's important to be fair: you have to be sure you aren't the only one having fun, that you're making your partner feel as good as she's making you feel. If you let yourself be carried away by your desire, you can't play the game well, and you blow the important romantic part . . .

Often, while we were engaged in this brainy game, my toe-penis would get soft. My female sex stockpiled the excitement I felt when other parts of my body were stimulated, but my toe-penis didn't appear to be influenced in that way. The toe-penis itself had to be touched. When my toe-penis experienced intense pleasure, my vagina got excited, wet, but the only time when vaginal pleasure had brought on an erection in my toe-penis was that one instance with Shunji. It had never happened like that during sex with Eiko.

All this convinced me that my toe-penis was not fully functional as a sexual tool. Eiko, for her part, seemed to think that whenever my toe-penis got hard it meant I wanted to have sex, and so, when a little caress or some casual stimulation gave me an erection, she immediately leaped into sex. Eiko didn't distinguish between the urge to have sex and the urge to be physically intimate in nonsexual ways. All our desire, she seemed to think, all the pleasure and excitement we had given each other during the course of our intellectual game-playing, should be summed up through the communion of her vagina with my toe-penis. The goal of sexual activity was genital intercourse.

There was no denying, of course, that my toe-penis could be appropriated for use as a sexual tool. If, in the course of the game, it wilted, it could be made hard again by other direct stimulation, and it could maintain an erection inside Eiko's vagina long enough to satisfy her. Personally, I preferred having my toe-penis jerked off, but I recognized that—even if I wasn't all that excited about genital intercourse—it gave pleasure to both of us at the same time, and thus was both rational and convenient. In fact, I tried to get as much pleasure out of it as I could.

I couldn't help looking back fondly at Shunji's approach, though. Sex with him had been a quiet recreation, an extension of other forms of physical intimacy, and the act of uniting his penis with my vagina seemed always to happen almost as if by chance—it wasn't the goal. That was why my vagina felt so good when I was with him, and I found myself wishing sex with Eiko was more like that.

Was it so rare for people, either male or female, to approach sex the way Shunji did? Masao had been like Eiko: coitus was unquestionably the one and only focal point of lovemaking. I, and my toe-penis, was more like Shunji. Like mine, Shunji's penis tended to be passive; it didn't get hard unless you touched it, and while it could function as a sexual tool, it was really only a part of the satisfaction Shunji desired in physical contact, since sex was just one among many ways of being close to his partner.

When Shunji and I were together, we focused on the differences between us, but now I realized how close he and I were in terms of sexual makeup. So close, in fact, that sexual difference—the fact that he was a man and I was a woman—didn't seem very relevant. Eiko and I were both women, but we were sexually very different. I couldn't imagine the pleasure Eiko's vagina might feel having sex in the style she preferred.

I decided to bury this discomfort in my heart, and to adopt the attitude, whenever we had sex, that a moderate pleasure was enough for me. But it was becoming increasingly more difficult to achieve orgasm while my toe-penis was inside her vagina. Finally, after we'd had intercourse several times in a row, it remained standing, exposed, still very stiff, even after Eiko lifted her vagina away.

"Was there something more I could have done?" she asked.

I took her hand in mine without saying anything and kissed it, then guided it down to my toe-penis. With just a few strokes, my organ achieved its peak, contentedly losing its stiffness.

"How eccentric—liking it better with a hand!" She seemed a trifle disappointed. "And we're lucky enough to actually *have* a penis and a vagina."

"It's not like I don't feel *anything* with a vagina."

"I wish we could both come together, though."

"Well, I wish we could share *all* our pleasures."

Eiko pursed her lips, seeming a bit surprised by the sentiment. It had never occurred to her to wonder at—or be frustrated by—the fact that she could never know how I felt when I touched her. "Yeah, I guess that's true," she murmured slowly. "Just sharing genital pleasure isn't enough . . ."

"Besides, the penis and vagina would never climax at just the same time."

Eiko's expression registered bewilderment. "I can't believe how you talk so dryly about these things. Sex could get pretty tiresome that way!" Then she laughed. "Of course, I'm not saying I would give it up."

I smiled, nodding.

"I'm so crazy. When I was with Tamotsu, I felt like I didn't need ordinary sex with a penis, but somewhere deep down I must have been dying for ordinary sex—with a penis that would actually feel what it was supposed to . . . So maybe, even when I was with Tamotsu, I was already betraying him in my heart."

I tried to think of something to say, but came up empty.

"If I hadn't been able to enjoy sex, Tamotsu wouldn't have been so set on using Shin's penis on me. And I wouldn't have betrayed him like this."

I moved closer to Eiko. "Why do you criticize yourself like that? Tamotsu is the one who was always wanting regular sex, right? And because of this, he kept you thinking about it all the time. If he hadn't been so fixated on doing it the way everyone else does, you could have figured out something where you didn't have to rely on Shin, and then you wouldn't have had such a yearning for regular sex."

"I'm not sure it's Tamotsu's fault."

"I am. You wanted to have a lesbian relationship, right?" I couldn't suppress a smile. "Women don't have penises. So that means you'd be perfectly content having sex that doesn't involve a penis, right?"

Eiko finally looked up. "Yes, that's true, but still . . ."

"You and I just happen to have a penis handy, so we use it. That's all there is to it, right? If I had a normal woman's body and no penis, would you not be enjoying sex with me?"

Eiko buried her face in her hands. "Am I just stupid or what?" she said.

When she lowered her hands, her cheeks were flushed and she was smiling. I liked how she looked then, half embarrassed and half amused, and I leaned over and kissed her on the cheek. I didn't want to part with her; I wanted to be with her more. Of course Tamotsu's shadow loomed, and I knew there was no guarantee that Eiko felt as I did. For the moment, I didn't think about it.

That was the night before the performance.

Chapter 14

Before we left the apartment, Eiko took my hand and gave it a squeeze. Thinking she was scared of seeing Tamotsu, I squeezed it back. I felt uneasy myself. I was worried about Eiko, and since Tamotsu had every right to resent me for taking Eiko from him, I couldn't help feeling nervous and guilty at the prospect of meeting him, too. On the other hand, he was probably just as frightened of seeing us. He was so frightened he hadn't called. That thought helped me feel the tiniest bit braver.

Eiko grasped my arm as we stepped through the service gate at that elegant Japanese restaurant in Akasaka where I first met the group. She let go almost immediately, but her face seemed to grow more pale with every step. My heart was pounding so hard it was almost painful. As we approached the room where the troupe would be gathering, one of the paper-paneled doors slid open and Shigeki stepped into the hallway.

"Oh good, you came!" he said, smiling broadly.

"Is Tamotsu here?" Eiko whispered.

"Not yet. Do you think he'll show up?"

Neither of us responded.

"Sorry, dumb question. Only he can answer that question, I guess. He did say he would come, though."

"Either way, we'll make sure everything works out," Eiko said firmly. "If he doesn't show, Kazumi will take his place in the segment."

Shigeki turned to me, surprised.

Aiko, who had stepped into the hallway as Eiko said that, put a hand on my shoulder. "Is that true?" she asked anxiously. "Do you feel ready for it?"

Her concern helped me screw up my courage, because it made me want to make light of her worries. I nodded vigorously. "Sure, I'll do it."

Aiko still seemed anxious for me, but Shigeki's mind appeared to have been set at ease and he ushered Eiko and me inside. Everyone but Tamotsu was there.

When he saw us, Masami hollered, "Thank *goodness*, you two are all *right*! I was scared to death that you'd been kidnapped and sold into slavery in a foreign land!"

"Glad to see you again, too, Masami," Eiko said with a grin.

She seemed to have calmed down at the sight of the troupe's members. Feeling less tense myself, I reached for a cup of tea.

"Here's the latest news, folks," Shigeki began after he sat down. "Lately, the agents who schedule our shows have been acting a little weird, so we've been having trouble ironing out the schedule for our next tour."

"Aren't we supposed to be setting out soon?" Eiko asked.

"It looks like we'll be starting later than usual. The gigs in Kyoto, Osaka, and Kobe are fixed, at least, if nothing else. I have no idea what the problem is."

"Is it because the economy is so bad?" I asked.

"I'm sure that has a lot to do with it, but I have a feeling it's something else. People may just be getting tired of the Flower Show. So we have to be prepared, just in case."

"Just in case . . . we break up, you mean?" Eiko leaned forward.

"Yes. We don't know what's going to happen, but I wanted everyone to know about this. Anyway, I'll be in touch as soon as the tour schedule is settled, so until then you should all just be ready to go."

Eiko turned around to look at me. Hearing that the Flower Show might break up before I had a chance to participate had left me feeling unsure what to think; I couldn't tell what was going on in Eiko's mind. I was still looking blankly back at her when Yukie's shrill voice shook the room.

"Are you kidding me? I'm not old enough for Social Security yet! If the troupe disbands now, I'll have to go back to doing strip shows! At my age!"

"I thought you had savings, Yukie," Yohei said. "C'mon—you've even bought your own apartment."

"I think what the ol' miss is fretting about," Masami said, "is that as soon as the going gets tough, that lover of hers, being seven years younger, is going to run off and leave her. Isn't that right, dear?"

Yukie shot Masami a nasty glance. "I see no need to be so explicit," she said.

"Who cares if you've got a lover or not, as long as you've got enough dough to live a tasteful, elegant life on your own! The whole idea of letting that man *leech* off of you is just *too absurd* anyway. You ought to throw him out."

"Excuse me, but until recently you've been going on about how badly you wanted a lover yourself."

"Well, I've changed my mind."

"Because you don't have to worry. Not with those gay bars you've got in Osaka and Kobe. And you, Yohei! If the Flower Show ended, you'd be able to do very well as an illustrator. You've got nothing to worry about."

"It's not as easy as you think . . ."

Shigeki tapped the table with his finger. "Okay, time to head out," he announced.

As the group rose and filed out into the hallway, Aiko came over to Eiko and me. "Tamotsu still isn't here, huh?"

"I'm sorry," Eiko replied, bowing her head. She had apologized automatically, without thinking—it wasn't as though she actually felt that in some way she was responsible for Tamotsu's absence. She remained pale, biting her lip, even after Aiko told her an apology from her wasn't necessary. Eiko was so occupied she didn't even cast a glance in my direction. I figured her head had to be swirling with thoughts of Tamotsu. I, on the other hand, was occupied with thoughts about my performance.

When we turned the corner, all eyes were fixed on the entryway: Tamotsu was standing in the stone-floored vestibule, taking off his shoes, getting ready to step up into the building. My body tensed. Eiko took a step backward. Tamotsu came striding down the hall toward us, his slippers slapping against the floor, his expression the same as always. Shigeki advanced two or three steps in his direction, as if to welcome him. Tamotsu met him with a cocky smile.

"You're late," Shigeki said.

"Yeah, I thought I'd make more of an impression that way."

My gaze met Tamotsu's as he ran his eyes over the troupe, but he kept smiling. He didn't seem on the verge of going wild. Shigeki must have reached the same conclusion, because he called out "All right, then, let's go!" and started walking. As we made our way down the hall, I was full of unease about Tamotsu, who was right behind us. I kept hearing the slapping of his slippers against the floor, but I didn't have the courage to turn around. Eiko, who was a step ahead of me, was walking with an unsteady gait.

The sound of the slippers drew nearer, and a second later Tamotsu appeared beside me. "You guys are sneaks," he said. "Why did you cut me out like that?"

His voice was loud enough that not only Eiko but even Aiko, who was several steps ahead, could hear him. His tone and expression were both as cheerful as ever, with traces of his usual wheedling dependency. Maybe he'd been telling himself that our disappearance was a whimsical prank, nothing that needed to be taken seriously. Maybe he'd spent the past few days deciding what attitude he'd take when he saw us. The only reply I could muster was an ambiguous "Mmm."

"What do you mean by that? No one likes being ostracized!"

"Are you angry?"

"No. I know you'll just shut me out even more if I get angry, so I'm not going to do that. I'm not a child, you know—much as that may surprise you."

"Keep your voice down, will you?" Shigeki said.

"Hey, do I look angry?" Tamotsu murmured, accepting the scolding.

"If you're not," I said, swallowing my fright, "then you'll go talk to Eiko, too."

As Tamotsu shifted his gaze to Eiko's back, the smile vanished from his face. It was replaced not by a furious grimace but by an achingly forlorn, lackluster look.

"Sure, I can talk to her."

Tamotsu strode past me and took up a position beside Eiko. He looked nervous. He walked for a few moments in silence. Eiko waited for him to speak, making no effort to start the conversation. Finally Tamotsu turned to face her.

"What's up with the outfit?"

"I borrowed it from Kazumi," she replied, leaning cautiously away from him.

"You ought to come get your fall clothes. It must be a pain not having them."

Tamotsu wasn't showing any anger or resentment. He seemed less concerned with his own feelings than with soothing Eiko's—could it be that he had made up his mind not to hurt Eiko anymore and was planning to ask her to come back to him? Watching them from behind, I could see the stiffness gradually leaving their shoulders as they talked. The week that Eiko and I had spent together seemed to blur in my mind, as if it had all been a dream.

Our procession had now arrived at the detached building where we would be performing. Tamotsu and Eiko were still talking. Eiko wasn't exactly smiling, but her expression had regained its customary calm. I should have known all along that Eiko's life with Tamotsu was what she really cared about and that her time with me was simply a detour, but I felt a dull ache in my chest and had to struggle to dam up my emotions. I tried to tell myself that I should be happy for Eiko, since it looked as if Tamotsu was showing he could be a kinder, gentler boyfriend.

One by one, the troupe members stepped up into the building. Last in line, I was about to follow when Eiko came out again. "I'm going to perform with Tamotsu," she whispered. "Please don't worry." She gave me a quick kiss on the lips, then pulled me into the building.

That night, once again, I was in charge of the background music. Eiko's kiss stayed with me, her scent lingering warmly, so that during the first half of the show, I kept picturing her walking out of my apartment, traveling bag in hand. It was a lonely scene—the loneliness of which I would have to start getting used to.

Tamotsu and Eiko must have been in the dressing room, and didn't appear in the room where the show was being put on. Then, shortly after

Yukie started doing her segment, Tamotsu wandered out and plopped down beside me.

"I hear you were ready to take my place in the show. Maybe I should have joined the audience."

What would it be like for Tamotsu to be back with Eiko again after being apart for almost ten days? And what, for that matter, would it be like for Eiko? I tried halfheartedly to call up an image of them as a couple, but my brain wouldn't cooperate.

"Can't do that, though. A bunch of my fans are in the audience tonight, you know, regulars, and they'd be let down if I didn't perform." Tamotsu spoke more slowly than usual. He yawned, scratched his head, then buried his chin in the crook of his arm. "It's only natural, though. Any woman in her right mind would run from an awful guy like me."

"Why didn't you come to see Eiko?" I asked him seriously, ignoring his obsequiousness.

Tamotsu lifted his chin and let his eyes wander. Yukie had just thrown a chewed-up banana into the audience, which was met with shrieks and hoots. "I would have gone to see her if she was with one of her ordinary women friends. But that wasn't the case, was it?"

I couldn't speak.

Tamotsu smiled listlessly. "Don't pretend," he went on. "I know. Your toe-penis got hard the second Eiko touched it. I saw it. And you agreed to take my place performing with her . . . because you've already done it . . ."

On the surface, the facts were just as he said. Eiko had been unfaithful to him, with me, and I was hardly in a position to be asking why he hadn't come to visit. But at the same time, I wanted to say, "No, it isn't like that. I never intended to steal her from you, and in fact I don't think I have." I had never forgotten, even while she and I were together, that Tamotsu was her partner, not me. And it wasn't as if Eiko had thrown Tamotsu over, choosing me instead. Because she and I had never said we loved each other, and we had never discussed the future. I had only started feeling bad at the idea of parting with Eiko a few days ago; prior to that, I too had been waiting for Tamotsu to show up.

Still, there was no denying the facts of the situation. I lowered my head. "I'm sorry," I said.

Tamotsu's expression remained unchanged. "It's not worth an apology. I mean, I've made Eiko screw other men in the past. To tell the truth, I'm kind of glad you and she hooked up."

"And why is that?"

"Because now you can tell me how Eiko feels *down there.*"

"But you already know that."

"My fingers do, not my penis."

I looked down, irritated at Tamotsu's phallic fixation. As long as he believed that the ultimate pleasure came from the union of penis and vagina, he would never stop doing things to make Eiko suffer. Something had to be done to end the cycle. But I knew I could never convince him I preferred Eiko bringing me off with her hand to doing it with her vagina.

"C'mon, tell me. What was her *thing* like? I bet it was really terrific, huh, having your penis squeezed by her vagina?"

"Why do you always—"

"Hey, it's okay! I just wanna know. Is her thing good? Lousy?"

"Would you please stop it!"

Tamotsu moved over until his body was touching mine. It struck me that at the end of each tour, when he used Shin on Yukie, he harassed Eiko with precisely this sort of spiteful persistence, and all of a sudden I grew frightened. As he advanced toward me, I pressed my hand to his chest— not that I actually thought it was going to have an effect. He looked suspiciously at me, relaxing just a little. Just then, a burst of applause erupted from the audience. Yukie's performance was over.

Tamotsu backed away from me, got to his feet, and left the room. Worried, I ran after him as soon as I stopped the tape. There was no sign of Eiko in the dressing room. I realized this even sooner than Tamotsu, who was still scanning the room, so I dashed outside. Eiko was leaning against a wall, gazing out across the garden.

"Am I on?" she asked when she saw me.

As she made ready to go, I grabbed her arm, holding her back. "Tamotsu seems odd."

"Yes, he always does."

"I have a bad feeling about all this."

Eiko laid her left hand over mine. "It's best that I perform with him tonight, trust me. If you and I performed, he'd only get crazier. I'll be fine. I'm used to his violence."

Eiko stepped through the back door and disappeared into the building. I had no choice but to go back to my station. I felt fear. I stared at Tamotsu and Eiko as they took up their positions on the futon before the audience. I prayed that everything would be all right.

Eiko slowly took off her clothing while Tamotsu stood there in his T-shirt and pants. It hurt to see Eiko's body, which I felt such affection for, being exposed to the eyes of others, and I had to turn away. I felt even more anxious not knowing what was happening on stage, though, so I ended up watching anyway. Eiko had just tossed away her last item of clothing. Our eyes met. There was something imploring about them. Tamotsu, who must have noticed Eiko looking my way, turned in my direction. His eyes were empty.

Maintaining an utterly impassive expression, Eiko knelt down before Tamotsu. As she brought her face closer to his crotch, toward the open zipper, my legs went limp and I had to sit down on the floor. It wasn't jealousy I felt, it was sorrow—the sadness of not understanding why Eiko had to be part of such a heart-wrenching scene. I didn't want to watch, but I couldn't tear my eyes away. It was like watching the video of the cat being tortured to death—it was impossible to look away even though I couldn't stand to watch.

At a certain point Masami was beside me. "Tell me, dear—are you in *love* with Eiko?" he asked, his voice unusually soft.

"Yes," I said, and felt like crying.

Masami, keeping his voice down, continued. "Let me give you some advice, honey. Become a masochist. That way you can enjoy the pain."

"No, I'd rather feel pain as pain, and hurt when it hurts."

Masami responded with either a sigh or a laugh, I couldn't tell, as he moved away. There were other whispered conversations among troupe members, but I was too occupied with what I was seeing to pay any attention.

Eiko was down on her knees, doing things to Shin with her mouth. Then, with no warning, Tamotsu knocked her to the ground. My body went rigid. Tamotsu stripped off his T-shirt, his pants, and his boxers, then threw himself on top of her as she tried to right herself on the futon. Startled, she struggled to push him away. He pinned her arms to the futon. When she stopped struggling, he rammed his hips up against her. But Shin had gone limp. Tamotsu heaved himself back up and started frantically jerking Shin.

Ordinarily, Tamotsu went on trying, thinking of nothing else, until he managed to get Shin's penis inside Eiko. Not tonight, however. Twisting his upper body around, he shot a glance in my direction that stabbed me like an arrow. I was frozen, not knowing what would happen next, when he charged at me, grabbed my ankles, and dragged me to the futon. The audience was leaning forward, rows of them, almost as one.

Tamotsu came behind me and hooked me by my armpits. "You do her for me," he growled.

I was tossed up onto the futon. Half of my body landed on Eiko's legs. Raising my head, I saw Eiko staring at me, stunned. My skirt was thrown halfway up my thighs, but I couldn't move. Tamotsu, impatient, pulled my body up with one arm, then stuck his other arm under my skirt and yanked my stockings down.

Then he took my toe-penis in his mouth. This was shocking and unpleasant, but my toe-penis did respond slightly. He stopped sucking and pushed Eiko's head down on it. There was no possibility of saying no. Eiko started doing things to me with her lips and tongue. Emotionally I felt paralyzed, but my toe-penis was faithful to Eiko. It took longer than usual, but my organ got hard.

When Eiko raised her head, a tremor ran through the audience as it confronted my fully erect toe-penis for the first time. I didn't want to see anyone's face. I kept staring at my toe-penis, which Eiko was now straddling. The mouth of her vagina was dry. She grimaced and lowered her hips anyway. Tamotsu got down on all fours to watch as my toe-penis entered Eiko's vagina. I wanted to kick him in the face.

After a few up-and-down movements, Eiko's vagina began to grow moist. When she raised her hips and my toe-penis appeared, it glistened in the light of the lamp beside the futon. It looked like someone else's penis. Tamotsu stretched out a hand and wiped off some of the fluid. I no longer had the energy to be angry. I just kept wishing for the end of this terrible act, in which there was no love being made.

Tamotsu wasn't going to let things end so easily, however. Pushing Eiko out of the way, he grabbed my right ankle, yanked it up, and sandwiched the tip of my foot between his thighs. Viewed from the front, my toe-penis looked like Tamotsu's third penis. He was putting his plan into action. From the knee down, my right leg was being held parallel to the futon, while from the knee up it was practically at a right angle. Unable to support my upper body, I fell back and lay there, face up.

Tamotsu ordered Eiko to turn around and get down on her hands and knees. I emptied my mind, trying not to imagine the scene. I was in a dreadful position; I was on my back, my legs were spread, and I couldn't see a thing. Tamotsu wrapped his hand around the base of my toe-penis and guided it into Eiko's vagina. My right knee pistoned back and forth. Again and again and again.

I don't remember how it all ended. Tamotsu quickly gathered up his clothing and left the room. Shigeki and Yohei hurriedly closed the sliding doors that served as the curtain. Eiko sluggishly put on her clothes. I tried to put on my stockings, but found I couldn't; my toe-penis, which hadn't had an orgasm, was still erect.

Aiko embraced my shoulders from behind. "Thank you for putting up with all that. You too, Eiko."

We were both too dazed to reply.

Back in the dressing room, Tamotsu greeted us with a broad grin. "The audience seemed to like it, huh! You two had fun too, right?"

Without saying a word, Eiko walked over to Tamotsu and slapped his face so hard the air seemed to split in two.

♥ ♥ ♥

That night as we lay in bed, Eiko embraced and kissed me again and again as she cried. She was furious about what Tamotsu had subjected me to, and seemed to think she was comforting me for having to endure such humiliation. But the truth was, I still hadn't emerged from the trancelike state I had put myself into in order to get through that horrible show, and was simply lying there, worn out, feeling neither anger nor sadness. I must have been on edge, though, because even after an emotionally exhausted Eiko sank into sleep, I lay awake, listening to the patter of the falling rain.

The first thing that came to me when I awoke later was the image of Eiko slapping Tamotsu hard on the face. The impact had been strong enough to turn his head; he'd given Eiko a fierce look, then spun around and dashed from the dressing room. The memory of this scene didn't evoke any thoughts worth talking about, but it made my spirits sink. I smelled coffee and pulled myself out of bed. Eiko was sitting at the kitchen table, holding a steaming cup of coffee to her lips. Our eyes met, but she didn't say anything. I walked over to pour myself a cup of coffee, then went back to the bedroom.

I opened the sliding glass doors to the veranda and sat and listened to the rain. I found myself remembering more scenes of last night. I shuddered as I relived the feeling of Tamotsu wiping Eiko's glistening body fluids from my toe-penis. How must Eiko have felt, suppressing her emotions, trying to be professional? I felt like my heart was being ripped out. Strangely, no new anger flared up inside me; I was preoccupied by the question of what Tamotsu had been after.

Had he shown up last night to exact his revenge? Sure, but I found it impossible to believe that a hatred so ferocious it could only be assuaged by violence had lain hidden behind the terrible, sad look he had given Eiko as we walked down the hallway, or behind the feeble smile he had given me later.

Naturally he must have felt resentment. But Tamotsu did want to get back together with Eiko. He might feel anger, he might have wanted a threesome, but what he did, at its root, was really just his childish, twisted way of pleading for love. In other words, it was the same sort of thing he was always doing to Eiko.

Eiko's disappointment in Tamotsu had to have been even deeper than mine. She'd been trying to comfort me, but perhaps it ought to have been the other way around. What actually happened last night wasn't such a big deal. I didn't like the fact that Tamotsu had forcibly appropriated part of my body and used it as a tool, and it had been embarrassing to be exposed in such a ridiculous position, but I hadn't been so deeply hurt that I couldn't recover. Everything had happened so quickly that I had been caught off guard, and hadn't known how to react—that was all. More than anything else, what shocked me was seeing Tamotsu and Eiko doing exactly the opposite of what they needed to if they were going to make up. *That* was traumatic.

When I took my cup back into the kitchen, Eiko had her elbows propped up on the table, her face buried in her hands. I asked if she wanted something to eat; she said no. We hadn't eaten in some eighteen hours, so I thought we ought to have something and went out to buy some fruit.

When I got back, a young man holding a cheap plastic umbrella was standing in front of the building. It was Tamotsu.

He started to back away when he saw me, then stopped. He kept standing there, uncertain, unsmiling.

"Have you come to talk with Eiko?" I asked.

Tamotsu shot me a sharp look. "Drop the Mister Nice Guy act, will you?" he spat.

I wasn't going to argue and tried walking past, but he grabbed my arm. "Sorry, I shouldn't have said that. I know you mean well," he said, as his umbrella bumped into mine and knocked it to the ground. He pressed his umbrella into my hands, then bent down and scooped up mine. Something about the clumsy way he bent over led me, for no clear reason, to feel pity for him. When he handed my umbrella back to me, his expression had softened.

"I understand," he said. "It's only natural to be angry."

"She seems more depressed, actually."

"I was talking about you."

"Oh? I wouldn't have thought that mattered to you."

Tamotsu laughed. "It's funny when you try to get mean all of a sudden."

"You're meaner than anyone."

"I knew you were angry."

I paid no heed to his wheedling tone. His shoulders drooped. "I can't help myself," he muttered, lowering his eyes. "I just do these things."

"You better learn. Unless you're ready to lose Eiko."

"I think it may be too late."

"You won't know unless you talk to her."

"Now?"

"I don't know if Eiko is ready to talk to you yet . . . I'll go ask."

Tamotsu didn't respond, but as I started walking away, he called out, "What are you to Eiko, anyway?" The thin smile on his face might have been ironic.

I wasn't going to answer that, and hurried up to my apartment. Eiko was sitting on the bed.

"Tamotsu's downstairs," I said.

Eiko raised an eyebrow, but didn't immediately reply.

"I think he wants to talk to you," I said.

"About what?" There was anger in Eiko's voice, even if it wasn't particularly fierce.

I was at a loss for words.

"You say he wants to talk to me," Eiko continued, "but that's just your interpretation, right? He didn't actually say that, did he?"

"Not in so many words, no, but . . . he's here, right? He must want to talk."

"Who knows, maybe he just wants to get in a bit of voyeurism?"

I was startled by the bitterness of her tone, but I tried once more. "You don't want to see him?"

"You want me to slap him again?"

I went downstairs to tell Tamotsu to come back another time, but he was nowhere to be found. When I returned to the apartment with this news, Eiko replied with an uninterested "Oh?" Her attitude was so harsh, it scared me. She didn't scare me; what scared me was that she might actually dump him. Which left me feeling like a bystander at the scene of a bloody accident. In a sense, my affection for Eiko put me in the same position as Tamotsu, so that what happened to him almost seemed to be happening to me as well.

I sliced the fruit, and Eiko ate, little by little. She thanked me between bites for going out to get it, which made me feel a little relieved. She was quiet while I cleared the dishes. Then, while we were drinking our second cup of coffee, she asked, "Did you want me to see Tamotsu?"

"No, I didn't exactly want you to see him," I replied.

"Then it's better just to leave him alone. That jerk."

"But . . ."

"I'm amazed you find it so easy to talk to him after last night."

"It's past."

Eiko set her coffee cup down with a bang. "I can't believe you!"

"I guess I'm not very sensitive to these things. Besides, I know what he's like."

"Yeah, so do I. He's a rotten loser."

The hatred in her voice was undisguised. Trying to calm her, I said gently, "What Tamotsu did last night was absolutely the pits, but you know he's just a perverse little kid who doesn't know how to express his love."

The floodgates opened wide. "Tamotsu doesn't have the slightest idea what love is! He thinks to love someone is to have a toy to play with! When people don't do what he wants, he just clams up. That's what happened last night! He didn't care what we were feeling; he just forced us to act out his bizarre fantasies . . . He isn't in love with me. He just misses his girl toy."

Eiko had accepted Tamotsu's selfish, twisted pleas for love for so long that for me to defend him now made no sense. If she was finally fed up with him, well, that made sense. If I hadn't known Tamotsu so well myself, if I had only heard about their relationship from Eiko, I would have thought they should split up. But in my time hanging out with the Flower Show, I had developed a genuine affection for Tamotsu. He was capable of unbelievably terrible things, but he had a genuine gentle side: on our first tour he had brought Shunji a cat to carry; he, and Eiko, had seen me back home the night Oinuma made off with Shunji; he had lent me his video game machine to help me heal my broken heart. I couldn't write him off so easily.

"But don't you love him?" I asked timorously.

Eiko stared at me, her eyes tense. "How can you *say* that?" Her pale cheeks reddened slightly. "Are you that eager to keep us together?"

"I wasn't talking about me, I was asking about you. I thought you loved him. Don't you?"

Eiko stared at the floor quietly; then, as if she had finally decided to say what was on her mind, she said, "If you want me to leave, I can go at any time."

"What are you talking about? I don't want you to leave!"

"Don't pretend. I knew you didn't really like me."

She was the one who was pretending, twisting her lips into a forced smile.

"What are you saying? Of course I like you!"

"A little, maybe. But your feelings for me aren't very deep, are they?"

I was dumbstruck. I knew Eiko was constantly trying to judge the extent of my love, so I had tried hard to communicate my feelings to her as best I could. But I hadn't gotten through to her at all.

"It's obvious," she continued. "It's not like it has to be me, as if you couldn't go out with anyone else. You just think, Oh yeah, she's okay, I guess I can hang around with her. That's the extent of your feelings for me, right? You wouldn't give a damn if Tamotsu and I got back together, would you?"

"Of course I would! I was just hoping the two of you could talk things over and decide what the best solution to all of this is, that's all."

"Your nonchalance does not recommend you."

"All right, then—you prefer that I interfere?"

Eiko looked at me as if she didn't want to hear any more. "Would you please stop pretending! How can you act like you don't know!"

I couldn't answer because I wasn't sure what she was asking.

"How can you act like you don't know I'm *crazy* about you?"

I was hit by a lightning bolt of incomprehension. I stared open-mouthed at Eiko. I could only stammer, "I didn't know. Honest, I really didn't."

Now it was Eiko's turn to be surprised. "You didn't know? You're not lying?"

"I thought Tamotsu was more important to you."

"But if you felt that way . . . didn't it bother you, being with me?"

"It didn't bother me exactly—I just figured that's the way things were."

"And how do you feel now that you understand how I feel?"

"I'm so surprised, I don't know what to think yet." I could think of nothing more to say.

When Eiko spoke next, her voice was full of pain. "It's just as I thought, you don't really like me."

"What?"

"Isn't it obvious? You're perfectly happy thinking I like Tamotsu more than you, you just resign yourself because you think 'that's the way things are,' and when you learn that I actually like you more, you don't even seem to care."

She was picking on every little thing I said. I began to get annoyed. "Haven't I been telling you all along that I like you?"

"People don't usually use the word 'like' to describe feelings as non-committal as yours, at least not in this kind of context."

"Why do you go out of your way to twist everything in a direction that makes you feel miserable?"

"I'm just looking at your attitude, that's all."

There was nothing to say in the face of such obstinacy, so I shut up. How we were having this quarrel when we were saying we loved each other was beyond me. Looking into my heart, at how wonderful the last week had been for me, I *knew* how deep my affection for Eiko was, and I was insulted at having these feelings dismissed as "noncommittal."

Then it struck me: "Are you trying to pick a fight with me because you want to leave? Is that it?"

Eiko opened her eyes wide, then burst out laughing. "What kind of a crazy thing is that to say?"

Relieved to see Eiko laughing, I laughed, too. "As if you haven't been saying crazy things all along yourself!"

Finally the atmosphere relaxed. We stopped arguing and washed the dishes. After lounging around quietly, we went out to a restaurant nearby—Eiko had gotten hungry. At first, as we sat there, she avoided making eye contact, as if she were embarrassed. She didn't appear to be angry anymore.

Maybe fatigue had made her irritable; I tried hard to act cheery and show her that I was having fun. By the time we headed back to the apartment, things were almost back to normal. Until nine o'clock, when the rain let up and the doorbell rang.

I knew instantly it was Tamotsu. Eiko must have thought the same thing, because her expression hardened. I stood. I felt her eyes boring into me, but I couldn't ignore the doorbell.

Tamotsu was standing with the plastic umbrella tucked under his arm. Judging from the puddle of water on the floor, he must have been standing there for a bit. "Can you get Eiko for me?" he asked firmly.

I walked back into the room, propelled by the gravity of his tone. But as I expected, I ended up going back to him to say that Eiko had no desire to see him.

Tamotsu seemed to have been ready for this answer, because he just nodded. "Tell her I'm sorry, please. And that I'll come again."

He was unexpectedly mature. He didn't act like a spoiled child, he didn't goof around. Watching him as he turned without uttering a single unnecessary word and walked away, I found myself thinking I had seen Tamotsu as a new man. And this thought developed almost immediately into an expectation that he and Eiko might be able to make things work. I ran back to Eiko. I couldn't help telling her, not only what Tamotsu himself had asked me to tell her, but about the rainwater on the floor and his new attitude. I may have been a little giddy.

Eiko looked up when I finished my report, expressionless. "Have you fallen for him, Kazumi?"

"Of course not." I shook my head, still feeling happy.

"You sure seem to be thinking a lot about him."

"I can't just pretend he's a stranger, Eiko—he is a friend, after all. Besides, he and I are both in the same position, because we both like you."

"You and Tamotsu are in the same position?" Eiko said, irritated. "Are you sure it's not him you're in love with? Maybe you only started having a relationship with me because it would be too much of a hassle to show him your affection directly?"

"I don't understand."

"I'm suggesting that either you were indirectly enjoying having a relationship with Tamotsu by having a relationship with his partner, or you were mentally identifying with him, thinking that by going out with me you had become him."

"I'm amazed that you can come up with all these things."

Eiko didn't smile. "Sure, that's a great way to brush it off."

"What is it you're so dissatisfied with?" I asked, taking her hand.

Eiko squeezed my hand; hers was cold. "You really want me to tell you?"

We wouldn't get anywhere if she didn't. I peered back into Eiko's eyes. All of a sudden, her hard gaze grew restless. She withdrew her hand. When she spoke, her tone was hollow and her voice so low it was as though I wasn't even there, and she was simply tossing the words out into space. "I just want to know what I am to you," she said.

Eiko and I ended up talking all night, struggling to resist our sleepiness. Our conversation certainly could not have been described as productive—because she insisted from the start that I felt little affection for her, and refused to believe me when I said that simply wasn't true.

At a certain point I began to wonder whether it was possible that, while I couldn't love Eiko any more than I did, maybe by ordinary standards I was missing something. Yoko and Masao had been dissatisfied with the affection I showed them, and I agonized over whether I had just been born that way—cold and unfeeling. But with Eiko it was a different story. When I thought about it, I did not come up wanting.

Eiko and Tamotsu seemed to think there was some rule in love that you had to keep possible competitors as far as possible from your partner, but I couldn't go along with that. Perhaps these rules of thumb applied to someone else, but they sure didn't apply to me. Eiko's rules of love were so deeply ingrained that she ended up assessing reality through them, rather than just assessing reality itself. That, at any rate, was how things seemed to me.

What was Eiko to me? My answer to the question that initiated our long night of conversation was as follows:

"First, you're a friend. Then, if you have no objections, you're my lover."

Eiko immediately took issue with this. "What do you mean if I have no objections? Why hold back?"

I explained that I wasn't holding back, I just didn't want to go around thinking of myself as her lover if I was the only one who saw it that way. Eiko grudgingly conceded that, then took a new tack: "But what do you mean saying I'm a friend *first?* Doesn't that mean I'm not really your lover?"

"I'm just saying I think we could go on being friends even if we stopped being sexually involved."

All night long, Eiko challenged every little thing I said. It was incredibly exhausting, but I responded carefully to each question she lobbed at me. Eiko was the one who fell silent, unable to answer my questions. When she asked me why I bothered with Tamotsu, I responded: "Do you think you can just forget about everyone else as long as you're happy?" She had nothing to say. Time and again I thought I had made her understand what I was thinking. But after a few seconds of silence, she would always either come up with a new question or bring up an issue that I thought had been settled long before, trying to make me admit the poverty of my love.

In retrospect, I could have cut the conversation off, saying there was no point discussing these matters any further, but I was caught in the whirlpool of Eiko's emotions and could not pull away. I was desperate. I related to her in great detail how, in the days since we had first met, I had gradually become conscious of the affection and desire I felt for her, and how I had worked to build up those feelings. I was so determined to make her understand the sort of person I was that I told her about my previous relationships with friends and lovers.

Eiko was very curious about Yoko. Maybe she was comparing our relationship to mine and Yoko's, I don't know—by then the birds were twittering outside and I was exhausted, so I wasn't able to judge accurately. In fact, it was much worse than that: a second's loss of concentration was all it took for me to lose track of our conversation. My brain was functioning at such a low level that I can't remember what prompted Eiko to shoot out the words that remain most vividly etched in my memory:

"It sounds like you started a relationship with me because you felt guilty for being unable to respond to Yoko."

This was so ridiculous that I thought enough was enough. "You're a fascinating person," I spat out as I stood up. "You really are."

Ignoring Eiko, I slid open the closet door and started hauling out the guest futon. I didn't feel like sleeping next to Eiko. "I'm going to bed now," I said. "Maybe you should, too."

I turned the light off and crept under the covers. About five minutes later, I heard Eiko lying down on the bed. It was the first time I was sleeping alone in a while, and the futon seemed very wide.

♥ ♥ ♥

Lifting my head from the pillow in the morning, I instinctively looked around for Eiko. She was up on the bed, asleep, her face to the wall. When my gaze fell on her thin shoulders, which were sticking out from under the covers, I found myself wanting to reach out and touch her. I hadn't completely forgotten the useless conversation we'd had the night before, but there was something vulnerable about the sight of her lying there asleep, like some small, docile animal, and I couldn't help wanting to care for her. Her shoulder was cold to the touch. She knows she has bad circulation, I thought to myself, so why doesn't she get all the way under the covers like she should? I pulled them up over her.

I went into the kitchen and sat down. Eiko kept insisting I didn't care very deeply for her, but suppose I said she was right, would she believe me? She wouldn't accept my professions of love, and she probably wouldn't accept professions of anything else. Of course, she was plagued by anxiety. She had recently given up on Tamotsu, her lover for years, and now she didn't know where to turn for support . . . That's what made my love feel insufficient. I had to find some way to heal her wounds.

I put my anger aside and started preparing breakfast. I boiled two eggs and sliced some fruit and was just about to make toast when Eiko emerged from the bedroom, looking rather unsettled. "Good morning!" I said. Eiko sighed a little and hesitantly took a seat at the table.

We were almost through with breakfast before she spoke. "The desire to be loved is a passion—a passion you're supposed to renounce," she said, almost as if talking to herself. "I realize that."

This unexpected abstraction of the situation took me aback.

She continued, "I know you love me in your way."

I didn't like that qualifier, "in your way," but I didn't say anything.

"Is it all right for me to stay?" she asked.

"Of course!" I said.

Eiko lowered her gaze.

After breakfast, I cleaned the apartment and did the laundry; Eiko helped. Her emotions seemed to have stabilized. When we sat down to a cup of tea, I didn't want to upset her again but felt I had to broach the topic. "You really need to talk with Tamotsu," I said to her. "Even if it's only to break up."

Eiko stiffened slightly, but when she replied, her voice was calm. "I know." Then, laughing, she added, "It wouldn't be like you to say you want me to break up with Tamotsu."

My heart felt like it would tear in two at the sight of her lonely smile.

"No," I said, "I can't say that."

I might have been imagining it, but I thought I detected a hint of sympathy in her expression. I ventured on, "It makes me so happy to hear you say you love me, but I think that, rather than break up with Tamotsu immediately, in the heat of the moment, you ought to take careful stock of your own emotions, then choose which one of us you want to be with, so that—"

"You think I haven't already taken stock of my emotions?"

I slid back in my chair, afraid I had angered her. But she seemed much more at ease than last night, and when she continued her tone was pleasant. "You don't trust me either, but you don't let that bother you. That's the big difference between us."

I hated myself for being unable to love her the way she wanted me to. Eiko ran her hands through her hair, gathering it up into a bundle, as if that would help her clear away her gloom. "I wonder what we should do about the Flower Show. If I break up with Tamotsu, I won't have to be in the show anymore."

This caught me by surprise. It was true. There was the future to think of.

"What are you going to do, Kazumi? Become an official member?"

"I'd rather not."

The words slipped out of my mouth before I had a chance to think. If it ended up that Eiko would be living with me, I wouldn't want to travel with the Flower Show. That was the truth. Besides, if Tamotsu didn't forgive me, life with the troupe could be hell.

"But the thing is, everyone has been so good to me, you know—I feel like I need to repay them somehow."

"Maybe do one tour?"

"I could," I said.

"I could come with you."

I almost dropped my teacup.

Eiko continued, no hesitancy in her voice. "You're not used to it, so you'd feel kind of adrift on your own."

"I'll be fine alone. If you came along, Tamotsu would . . ."

The instant I uttered Tamotsu's name, I was seized by the suspicion that, despite her talk, Eiko might, in some corner of her heart, feel a lingering attachment to him. Maybe she was offering to come along because she didn't want to miss seeing him. A moment later I was ashamed of myself for having thought that. Eiko had spent the whole night seeking some ulterior meaning behind my words, but she had never thought anything as low as that.

"That's true . . . ," she was saying, "Tamotsu is a problem. Shigeki mentioned the other day that the Flower Show might not be around much longer, so we may not even have a chance to do another tour. Let's not worry about it now."

Our discussion of the Flower Show ended there. We started looking further into the future. We talked about finding an apartment where we could live together after we cleared up our current problems, then looking for jobs we could really devote ourselves to. Needless to say, I would have to graduate from college first. Eiko said she wanted to go to college, too. She was once enrolled, but had had to withdraw when Tamotsu dropped out of high school to join the Flower Show. I suggested that she reapply. There should be no problem financially because she had her savings from the show. Eiko beamed.

Our conversation was still in full swing when there was a rough thump on the door. I didn't like the sound of it, but then it was followed by a polite, proper ring of the doorbell.

"Is Tamotsu being a pest again?" Eiko muttered.

I was about to go to the door, but Eiko stopped me, saying, "I'll go." Perhaps she was ready to talk things over seriously with Tamotsu; was that why I was feeling ill at ease? I moved the teacups from the table to the sink and started to wash them, the running water keeping me from hearing the conversation. But before long, Eiko appeared next to me, a very bewildered look on her face.

"What's wrong? Wasn't it Tamotsu?"

"Well, yes, but—" Her eyes signaled toward the door.

I wiped my hands, headed for the door, and opened it. Tamotsu was standing there, and leaning against him, his body smeared with dirt and dust, was Shunji.

"I've brought you a souvenir," Tamotsu said, grinning.

"Kazumi?" Shunji called out, panting. "Is that you?"

I was so shocked I couldn't move. I couldn't speak. Shunji staggered forward a step, one arm still wrapped around Tamotsu's shoulders, one arm stretched in my direction. His fingers brushed my breast. I leaped back.

"That's you, isn't it, Kazumi? What's the matter?" Shunji called out plaintively. "Have you forgotten me?"

"Y—y—yes, I've forgotten you," I said, crushed.

Before Shunji could speak, Tamotsu cried out, "Hey, hey, quit kidding around!"

I wasn't kidding around. I had given up on Shunji ages ago. He had taken so long to get in touch that I now had no idea how to treat him.

Tamotsu began chattering away: "Shunji missed you so badly he skipped out on the Kusakabe Shinobu tour that Oinuma was producing. He came all the way from San'in, alone, with nothing but the clothes on his back. He lost his cane in the crowds at Tokyo Station, so he used an umbrella some kind person gave him instead. When I ran into him he was lost, near the end of his rope! Let the poor guy in to rest."

My head wasn't working at all. I just kept staring at Shunji, who looked like he might burst into tears at any moment, as if he were on pause. Eiko put her arm around my shoulder, and whispered into my ear, "Why don't you let him come in?"

I must have nodded. Shunji and Tamotsu stepped into the apartment. They sat down. I sat down. Eiko brought Shunji a cup of tea. She sat down.

Shunji gulped it down and then turned to me. "I wanted to be with you so badly!" he cried, wringing the words out of his heart. "I was thinking of you the whole time, Kazumi!"

Yeah, that's why you got around to leaving one message on my machine. "Oh really?" I said. "What happened to Oinuma?"

"He lied to me," Shunji replied, trembling. "He said I could play in the concerts, but the tour already had a keyboardist. I didn't get to perform a single time. I just went around with them."

I bet you had your fun with Oinuma, though, didn't you?

"I didn't even get to ghostwrite anything for Kusakabe. I wrote some songs, but they said they didn't fit his image, so they never used them."

"It wouldn't surprise me if they're using them now, kid, without telling you," Tamotsu said. "They really had you duped, huh? I guess that'll teach you to be careful of deals that sound too good to be true."

"But why would Tama want to trick me? We're friends."

"Because, obviously, he doesn't really love you," Tamotsu was quick to answer.

Shunji fell silent.

But Tamotsu wouldn't let him be. "You can't figure out a simple thing like that? Man, what a bozo."

"Tamotsu."

It was nostalgic, hearing Eiko rein him in like that.

"I didn't really love Tama either. I didn't like touching him anymore. I put up with it for a while, but then I started wanting to be with Kazumi so badly. I realized I like Kazumi much more than Tama, so one day I waited until he wasn't around and tried calling, but she wasn't home. Kazumi, you weren't home! Oh yeah, I thought, she's touring, so I made up my mind to sneak away when she would be back at home—to go and see her." He paused for a moment. "I'm so happy we're together again. I really am."

I couldn't take any more of this. "You're too late, Shunji," I said.

Shunji looked puzzled.

"It wasn't right to go off with Tama like that, without telling me!" My voice seemed to rise by itself. "You acted like you didn't like me anymore."

"I thought you knew!" Shunji said, raising his voice, too. "I thought Tama told you we were going out for a drink before we left. He said he told you. I can't believe you didn't know! He was tricking me from the start!"

"You're too careless, man!" Tamotsu said, his tone quiet enough that he almost seemed to be talking to himself, but loud enough that everyone could hear. "Don't leave these things to other people. You gotta tell her yourself."

Tamotsu took the words right out of my mouth. Which filled me with warmth toward him.

"Okay. It was my fault," Shunji said. "I'm sorry. I won't be so careless from now on."

"What do you mean, 'from now on'? I said you're too late, Shunji."

"Why?" he asked innocently.

I glanced at Eiko. Tamotsu tapped Shunji's shoulder. "Kazumi's hooked up with Eiko."

Eiko and I glared at Tamotsu. He shrugged.

Shunji looked astonished. "You can be friends with women now, Kazumi? You always hated that idea."

This was embarrassing—not that Shunji could see.

"So you have no need for me anymore, now that you've become friends with Eiko. Is that it? I thought we were engaged."

I couldn't believe how dense he was being.

Neither could Eiko. "Wow, Shunji," she said, "I guess I don't understand you very well."

I hated having to explain things to him: "Shunji, you left me to go be friendly with someone else. Does a fiancé do something like that?"

"I said I was sorry. I won't do it again."

"But how can I trust you? If someone came along and said something sweet to you, you'd wander off again."

"I absolutely swear I won't do that!"

I couldn't manage a response. A few moments passed in silence. Shunji pressed his forehead against his knees, which were pushed up against his chest, and stayed that way.

Tamotsu peered at him from the side. "Hey, he's asleep."

"He's worn out," Eiko said.

Slowly Shunji raised his head, showing us his tired-looking face.

"Why don't you take a nap in my bed?" I said, trying to set aside my anger.

Murmuring something unintelligible, Shunji found his way to the bed and was soon deep asleep.

"What are you going to do, Kazumi?" Tamotsu asked.

"Do about what?" I was still in a daze.

"This guy is completely, one-hundred-percent pure. He's like an angel. Or an idiot—you could say that, too."

"I hardly think you have the right to talk."

That was Eiko's comment. And hearing it, I found myself succumbing to a feeling of déjà vu. My vision blurred: I wasn't sure whether I had just heard Tamotsu and Eiko talking a second ago, here in my apartment, or whether it had happened ages ago, during the late summer tour of the Flower Show, back when Tamotsu and Eiko were inseparable, and Shunji and I, too. I blinked my eyes and looked around the room, trying to get my bearings.

An odd silence had descended over the room. Weren't Eiko and Tamotsu supposed to be having a conversation? Now that Shunji had shown up, Tamotsu seemed to have forgotten his reason for coming. Feeling perfectly at home, Tamotsu grabbed the television remote and punched it on. A cooking show. Eiko and I reflexively turned our eyes in its direction. All three of us of us were watching a cooking show!

There was definitely something funny going on. The air hung heavy with the expectation that something important would happen, even though nothing was happening. The television helped us mediate the time. The cooking show ended and a rerun of an old drama came on, then the six o'clock news. Still the three of us sat watching.

I found myself succumbing to another wave of déjà vu: Tamotsu and Eiko and I together as "family." A sense of calm. When the wave receded, I remained in a sort of hypnotic trance. I found myself thinking that Tamotsu and Eiko and Shunji and I could just stay this way, spend the next ten years in this one room, and maybe that wouldn't be so bad.

As the news moved on to the second half, Shunji began to stir. "Are you all there?" he called out.

Tamotsu, Eiko, and I exchanged glances. I felt as if I had woken from a dream, and Tamotsu and Eiko looked like they felt the same. Tamotsu turned around and gave the edge of the bed a whack.

"We're here," he said.

"Kazumi, too?"

We were returning to the real world, to the impossible muddle we four were stuck in. Hoarsely I answered, "Yes, Shunji . . . I'm here."

Shunji poked his nose about, this way and that, smelling himself. "I stink," he said. "Can I take a shower?"

I was forced to get up and lead him to the washroom. "These are the only clothes you have?" I asked.

"Yes. I left without anything. It was all just temporary stuff we bought during the tour anyway."

Shunji was small enough that I could lend him something of my own to wear, but I would have to go to the convenience store to buy him some underwear. "There's a basket outside the bathroom door," I told him. "I'll leave a towel and clean clothes for you in it."

As soon as I said that, Shunji threw his arms around me. There wasn't much space in the bathroom, and as my body swerved to the side, my shoulder bumped up against the door, swinging it wide open. If Eiko and Tamotsu were looking our way, they would see us. I struggled to push Shunji away, but his grip was strong. He pulled me closer.

"I'm lonely without you. I like you better than anyone I've ever met."

This called up no emotion in me. I felt nothing but pain—I couldn't bear his body odor, his masculine strength, his heavy breathing. When he relaxed his hold on me, I pulled away from him and closed the door. I went into the bedroom, grabbed my purse, and told Tamotsu and Eiko I was going to the convenience store. Eiko looked pale. Outside, feeling the fresh air, I pictured first Eiko's face and then Shunji's, then Eiko's, then Shunji's. My chest ached terribly; tears welled up in my eyes.

When I came back from the store, Shunji's dirty clothes were lying folded in the basket. I stuck them in a paper bag and, gathering together a set of clean clothes and the underwear I'd bought, placed them into the basket. I took a deep breath.

"Awfully efficient, aren't you?" Tamotsu said.

"I'm not doing this for my pleasure," I replied. "He's here, so I have no choice."

The television was still on, but no one was watching. Eiko's head was down, her hair concealing her expression. Tamotsu didn't say anything more. Maybe, while I was out, Tamotsu had asked Eiko to come back to him? But a glance at them led me to think no such conversation had taken place. I was dying to know what Eiko was thinking, but I couldn't ask her, not with Tamotsu around. If he wasn't going to say anything, I wished he'd leave. I wished Shunji would leave, too.

Finishing his shower, Shunji appeared in the doorway. "I'm hungry," he said. "Can we go get something to eat?"

"Good idea," Tamotsu responded immediately.

Shunji kept standing there grinning, waiting for us to get up. I was hungry myself, I had to admit, and if we went out for dinner, it would be easier to get Tamotsu and Shunji to leave. I took Eiko's arm. She allowed me to steer her toward the front door. I didn't forget to take the paper bag with Shunji's dirty clothes as we left.

After Tamotsu took Shunji's hand and led him outside, Eiko turned to me and whispered, "Why did I have to go and let Shunji in? And Tamotsu, too, as if Shunji weren't bad enough . . ."

I showed her the contents of the paper bag, signaling to her that I planned to send Shunji, and by extension Tamotsu, on their way. She seemed to understand and gave my hand a squeeze.

Tamotsu took active care of Shunji on the street and in the restaurant. I couldn't recall him ever taking pleasure in looking after another person before. I had the impression he was trying hard to keep the mood cheerful, too, counteracting Eiko's and my silence by bantering merrily with Shunji.

Maybe he was trying to show Eiko that he was no longer the perverse, dependent Tamotsu he used to be. But I saw no sign that he was faking it.

When we left the restaurant, I handed Shunji the paper bag.

"What's this?" he asked.

"Your dirty clothes."

Shunji's jaw dropped. "You're sending me home? You're not going to let me stay, even though we haven't seen each other for so long?"

He appeared to be under the impression that I had forgiven him and welcomed him back. It was precisely this astonishing innocence that made him so insufferable. "Yes. You'll have to go home tonight."

"Aw, let him stay—tonight, at least," Tamotsu said. "And why don't you come with me, Eiko? You want to go get your clothes from the apartment anyway, right?"

"No, I don't," Eiko bristled.

"I'm not asking you to stay overnight or anything," Tamotsu said, remaining calm. "You can just pack up the clothes you need right away and then go back."

He was right, at least, that she couldn't just keep wearing my clothes forever.

"But I'm not going alone with you."

"All right, why don't I come along, too?" I intervened. "We can all take Shunji home, then go to your apartment. Once Eiko gets her things together, she and I can go back to my place."

"I guess that's okay," Tamotsu agreed, a bit unwillingly.

"But I don't want to go back," Shunji piped up.

"Better give up. For today, anyway," Tamotsu said, wrapping an arm around Shunji's shoulder and traipsing off toward the station, Eiko and I following behind.

Shunji's house was located on the same train line as mine, and you could get to Tamotsu and Eiko's apartment by changing to a different line at the stop after Shunji's. It would be easy enough to go to one place, then another, and then head home. But when we pulled into Shunji's station, Shunji grabbed onto the rail in the train.

"I'm not getting off," he announced.

The train made only a brief stop at the station and people were watching, so we couldn't pry his hands off. We stood stunned as the train started pulling out of the station.

"You sure are stubborn, aren't you?" Tamotsu said.

Shunji's expression lost none of its intensity, and he did not loosen his grip on the rail. This is not a problem, I told myself. We can just go to Tamotsu's first, then see Shunji off on the way back.

Things didn't go as planned at Tamotsu's either. While Eiko was packing her bag in one bedroom, Tamotsu was bustling around in the other. Before long, he appeared in the living room, where Shunji and I were waiting. A fat duffle bag was slung on his back.

"Where are you going?" I asked.

"Your place, where else?" Tamotsu said. "Shunji's going to insist on going back with you, too. There's no way in hell you're going to be able to get him off the train next time either. Not unless you knock him over."

"That's right," Shunji chirped.

"So you might as well let me stay, too."

"Are you kidding! Absolutely not!" This was Eiko, shouting behind Tamotsu, two bulky bags in her hands. "Are you nuts? You only managed to sneak into Kazumi's apartment in the first place because I got distracted. We'll never let you stay over!"

Tamotsu turned toward me. "Let me come, please? I want to be with you two."

"My apartment's too small, and there aren't enough futons."

"Why don't we all stay here then?"

"But why?" I asked, unable to suppress my annoyance. "What is it that you really want?"

Tamotsu stared fixedly at me for a moment, then took a deep breath and yelled, "I don't want to be apart from Eiko! I don't care if you two are together. It's fine with me if she likes you better than me. I've been such a total loser, all these years, that I'd be happy being her servant! Anything!"

Eiko dropped her two bags and crouched down, hugging her knees. Tamotsu did the same.

"Tamotsu's changed," Shunji said, leaning toward me. "I hear it in his voice. He doesn't have the sniveling, syrupy tone he used to. His voice is big and clear."

Eiko leapt up and ran into the bedroom. Tamotsu fell into the sofa, his face flushed. ". . . So that's that. Please. Stay here."

I couldn't do anything until Eiko came out of the bedroom. Tamotsu's words had found their target. I now found myself willing to spend the night as long as all four of us were there. But how did Eiko feel? She was holed up in the bedroom, her heart in turmoil. Tamotsu seemed distinctly relieved to have gotten his emotions out into the open. He now sat with his arms folded, looking very much at ease.

In the middle of this, the phone started ringing. Tamotsu picked up the receiver. It was a one-sided conversation. He said "yeah" in reply to a question, then just listened, mumbling no more than an "ah" or "mmm" while the person on the other end talked at length. While this was going on, I looked around the apartment. Tamotsu had been living alone for ten days, but there were no dishes heaped in the sink. The place was clean. A stuffed animal, a pig, sat on top of the television in the living room. I didn't know whose it was. The pink fur was faded, and all of a sudden my chest tightened. What was going to happen to us all?

"Eiko? She's here," Tamotsu was saying, a smug smile on his face.

The phone conversation suddenly got interesting.

"Kazumi's here, too," he went on, "and, believe it or not, Shunji has shown up too."

I realized who was on the other end.

"Okay. I'll tell them . . . Yeah, I guess it will, huh?" Tamotsu replaced the receiver, and then he announced, "That was Shigeki! We're heading to Kobe tomorrow!" He turned toward the room where Eiko was hiding and shouted, "We're all going, okay? Shigeki says this is going to be the Flower Show's last performance!"

Chapter 15

"Just out of curiosity, what's up with you all?" Masami asked me as we boarded the minibus at the west gate of Shinjuku Station.

I had to tell him, "I don't really know myself."

It wasn't as if I'd approved of Tamotsu's suggestion that all four of us make the trip to Kobe together. As official members of the troupe, Tamotsu and I were obliged to perform; now that Eiko was no longer involved with Tamotsu, there was no reason for her to accompany us, and of course Shunji had never really needed to come. Presumably no one would mind if Eiko wanted to come along even if she wasn't going to perform, considering how much she had contributed to the Flower Show over the years. Shunji, however, had only been the troupe musician because he was my fiancé, and it was only for a short time; now that we were no longer engaged, it didn't seem appropriate for him to tag along. Not that there was any need for a logical reason: I simply didn't want him around.

As we sat on the sofa in Tamotsu and Eiko's apartment, Shunji had pressed himself against me as though we were still happy lovers. I kept casually sliding over, pulling away from him, only to have him scoot closer the next moment. At first I was so annoyed I could hardly stand it. I was repelled by—and envious of—his natural tendency to get close to people, not worrying about how they reacted. It was the same tendency I had found so appealing at first, and that had later let me down. But when I found myself quickly feeling comfortable with him, even now—with his presence, the touch of his skin—I got scared, thinking I might become trapped in this comfort and be unable to break loose. Shunji was a threat to me. He put so much pressure on me that I couldn't afford to ignore him.

"I don't think there's any need for Shunji to come," I had told Tamotsu, worrying what Eiko would think if she heard me in the bedroom, where she was still holed up.

"No, there's no need," Tamotsu replied casually. "But he might as well come. It could be fun, don't you think?"

"I want to go," Shunji said. "You'll take me, right?"

I paid no attention to Shunji and continued my back-and-forth with Tamotsu. I stuck to my logical approach, since Shunji was sitting at my side and I didn't want to say more, but no logical argument could dispense with Tamotsu's, which was, "It's fine, no one will mind." I decided to call Shigeki and ask him to decide.

"Shunji? Sure he can come. We'll find something for him to do." His tone was glum—his mind was on other things, such as the fact that this performance could mark the end of the Flower Show. "It isn't going to be like our usual shows anyway. Things are flexible. Shunji and Eiko should both come." At this point, he suddenly changed the subject. "I feel really bad about having dragged you around like this. Who knew things would end so quickly?"

This wasn't the response I was looking for. It didn't make the slightest difference to Shigeki whether or not Shunji came along.

When Tamotsu saw my expression after I hung up the phone, he grinned ridiculously, screwing up one eye. Noticing Shunji's anxious frown, he placed a hand on his knee and said, "It's okay, Shunji. I'll take care of you. You'll be with me."

Eiko still hadn't emerged from the bedroom, and by now it was too late to take the train back to my apartment. I went in to check on her, but all she would do was put her arms around my neck as she lay on the bed; she didn't say anything. After I was with Eiko for a while, Shunji started calling for me from the living room. The third time he yelled out, Eiko pushed me away, sending me back out to him. I was furious. But he was like a frightened child—I couldn't just brush him off. It was all I could do not to hug him back when he cuddled up to me.

Once, just once, Eiko muttered something as if she were in a trance: "Man . . . tries to get us."

I didn't understand precisely what she was trying to say, but something in the ring of the words hit me hard. All I could do was sigh deeply, loosing the sense of despondency that churned in my breast.

I ended up sleeping on the sofa that night. The next day, Eiko came out with the two bags she had packed and signaled to me with her eyes. She was indicating that she wanted to go to my apartment; I could see that. But there was something ambiguous in her expression, as if she hadn't really made up her mind what to do, and when Tamotsu came to the door after us with his duffle bag on his shoulder, she just glanced at him, not even attempting to send him back in. We left it up to Tamotsu and Shunji to decide whether or not they would come along.

We were feeling drab and listless; they were bursting with energy. They stuck close to us. That night, Tamotsu and Shunji slept in my apartment, on two futons lined up alongside each other.

Wishy-washy as I was, the next morning I summoned the courage to talk frankly with Shunji. "Shunji," I said, "will you please stay here in Tokyo?"

Tamotsu and Eiko tensed up.

Shunji, on the other hand, did not. "I can't do that!" he replied. "Tamotsu says he wants me to come. He says if the four of us are together, it will be easier for you and me to get friendly again, and then he'll be able to get friendly with Eiko. It's not just for me—it'll be better for Tamotsu, too."

Tamotsu gave Shunji a poke, chagrined to have his plot revealed, although of course this did not come as a surprise.

"I don't want you to come, Shunji. It will be too confusing," I said.

Shunji's face revealed the full extent of his sadness. He was being honest about his emotions, and I couldn't help feeling that I was hurting him. At the same time, for him to hold back so little was pretty calculating. He made me want to reach out and touch him.

He dug his fingers into his thighs, squeezing them, as if this would give him courage. "I'm going with you, because I have a feeling that if I don't, I'll never get to be with you again."

Tamotsu, who had been listening in silence, turned to Eiko. "How about you? You'll come, right?"

Eiko seemed to have recovered her spirits. "Yes, I'll come," she replied. "I've got something up my sleeve, too."

I myself had nothing up my sleeve. I simply made up my mind that, if there was no way to keep all four of us from going, my policy would be to put Eiko first, and consciously try not to look after Shunji when I didn't have to.

But I disregarded this policy almost immediately. When we got to Shinjuku Station, Shunji announced that he had nothing for the trip with him and was going to a department store to buy what he needed. Tamotsu, who was in charge of Shunji, began to head off with him when Eiko pointed out that if Tamotsu was allowed to choose, Shunji would end up with all kinds of outlandish clothes. Shunji yelped, saying he didn't want anything weird. And so, without even realizing it was happening, I said I'd go shopping with Shunji.

To make matters worse, all four of us ended up going, and we had fun. Since his sense of style had been disparaged, Tamotsu intentionally pressed the most ludicrous items on Shunji in every section we visited, from bags to clothing. I laughed a lot. So did Eiko.

We were on our way back to the station when Eiko mentioned to me how Shunji was really blessed with a great personality—you just couldn't help liking him. So where was that supposed to fit with my policy to put Eiko first? I was angry with myself for having broken my own rules, and at the same time was again irritated with Shunji for his exuberant openness. I even started wondering whether it was fair for Shunji to be so "blessed" like that. This made it possible for me to say very curtly, when Shunji was about to sit down next to me on the bus, that his place was beside Tamotsu, and it helped me to steel myself when he stood there shocked. Tamotsu had the good grace to pull Shunji over and sit him down in the seat next to him.

"Are you being so cold to Shunji because of me?" Eiko whispered.

"No," I said. I had a question for her, too: "What about you? The way you're treating Tamotsu . . ."

"Why do you ask?" Eiko smiled sardonically. "You're afraid I've had a change of heart? Please, I can't tell you how many times I've listened to these 'moving' speeches of his . . ."

But if she hadn't had a change of heart, why had she remained holed up in the bedroom all those hours? Eiko looked out the window blankly, her posture rigid. Whatever was up her sleeve, she was keeping it hidden. This trip to Kobe wasn't looking like it would shape up to be much fun, but by now it was too late to get off the bus.

♥ ♥ ♥

On the road, Shigeki announced that we would be appearing as guest artists in another underground theater performance. The details weren't clear—whether it was a new play or a new version of that crazy piece about "stealing back the phallus." All we were told was that members of the Flower Show would appear as guest artists for one night, as part of a special performance, during the normal run of the play. The sponsor, who was also the playwright and director, had promised important parts to every member of the troupe. The venue was in Osaka, but we would be spending the week before the performance learning and rehearsing our roles in the apartment in Kobe where we'd stayed before.

Shigeki said he'd told the playwright about me, and I had been given a part in the script we would be picking up later. I would have to go along and meet the playwright, who would adjust the script as necessary once he had actually met me. Shigeki added that since he hadn't ever mentioned Shunji and Shunji might be able to get a part, too, we would take him with us.

Shigeki said anyone else who wanted to come was welcome, but there were no takers. Tamotsu, who was sitting in front of us, spun around and asked Eiko if she was planning to go; she said she wasn't. She didn't like the playwright. So it was decided that, while Shigeki, Shunji, Yohei—who was the playwright's favorite—and I went to this meeting, everyone else would hang out in a restaurant.

As we were taking our leave, Tamotsu yelled out, "This is your chance, Shunji! Make it count!" Shunji didn't quite understand and replied, "Make what count?" Even Eiko, who had frowned at Tamotsu's little speech, couldn't help laughing.

We hailed a taxi, and Shunji got into the seat next to me. Once we'd arrived at our destination, no sooner was Shunji standing on the sidewalk than he twined his arm tightly around mine. I was going to guide him into the office anyway, so I was willing to let him hold on to me.

At the Utagawa Kin'ya Office, a young woman greeted us. She had long, wavy hair, like a lady in a Renaissance painting, and her face seemed to hover in midair—the effect, perhaps, of her makeup, which was too pale for her complexion. In his office, the playwright sat at his desk, scribbling on a piece of paper. Glancing up, he gave us a chummy wave and called out a warm "Hey!" He gestured us to the sofa—"Go on, take a seat!"—then went back to his writing as the young woman served us Japanese tea.

The woman didn't do anything after that; she wandered over to the counter and leaned on it. She gazed blankly out the window.

After a bit, Utagawa put down his pen, came over, threw himself vigorously into his seat, and said, "Sorry for the wait!" The woman brought him a cup of tea. After taking a sip, he motioned to her and said, "You can go home now. Thanks."

She responded with a simple, "Okay," put on her jacket, bowed, and wafted toward the door like a gentle breeze.

Once the door clicked shut, Utagawa began to speak. "That girl lives nearby. She comes to make tea for me whenever I'm here in the evening. If I want a snack, I just call and she fixes something and brings it over."

"She works for you, then?" Shigeki asked.

Utagawa scowled as if this question were a terrible affront. "I should think not! She does it for free. If I was going to hire her, I'd have her do some meaningful work, not something dull and mindless like serving tea. She does it because she enjoys it. Well, I do give her a little something every now and then, just to let her know I'm grateful. And I introduced her to the people she works for now. And I found her the apartment she lives in. So I guess she feels indebted to me, you know what I mean? Come to think of it, she used to go on and on about how she wished she could pay me back for all I've done. Naturally, I bawled her out for that—I don't do these things because I want to get something in return!"

The last time Utagawa's head had been cleanly shaved, but now his hair had grown out a little so that it resembled a crew cut. Viewed straight on, he looked surprisingly childish, with two plump, rosy cheeks. He was talking up a storm, which made his cheeks bulge even more.

"In truth, she doesn't want to pay me back, she just likes to serve men. Her father was a very domineering man, you see, and now that she has grown up and gotten involved with men, she keeps duplicating her relationship with him. You can imagine how young guys will use a woman like that, I'm sure. She went through hell with all kinds of creeps before she got to know me, let me tell you. The moment I set eyes on her, I realized what kind of a woman she was. And I told myself, Utagawa, you've got to do this girl a favor and give her some psychotherapy so that she won't have to go out with all these young boors. If she can satisfy her desire to serve men by coming to my office and making tea for me, she won't have to throw herself blindly into serving other men, letting them dominate her completely, using her as they wish. That's the story. She's coming here for psychotherapy."

"Does she know about this?" Shigeki asked. "I mean, that making tea is part of a psychotherapeutic process?"

"No." Utagawa made a sour face. "Psychotherapy isn't something you need to be conscious of. I'm a veteran at this kind of treatment, you know. I've helped any number of women over the years. They're all happily married now. In fact, even the members of my troupe perform as a sort of therapy—more or less. I just can't help myself, you know? When I see an unfortunate young woman, I feel I have to give her some glimmer of hope. I've always been like that."

I found myself remembering the young woman's bad makeup job. Maybe what she really needed was a lesson in how to apply cosmetics.

"Let me tell you," Utagawa said, suddenly waxing serious, "life gets interesting once you get your hands on money and connections. It takes more than sincerity to make people happy. You've got to give these wretched creatures support from various different angles all at once, you see. You can only provide that sort of backup when you've got money and connections. You can be as sincere as you want, but that's not going to count for diddly if you can't give them money and introduce them to useful people. Don't take money and connections too lightly is what I'm saying. I used to blow those things off when I was a young buck, but that was just because I didn't know how things work. Looking back now, I can see that in those days, before I acquired money and connections, all I was able to do for wretched women was have sex with them. Well, I have sex with them now, too, of course." Utagawa laughed, crinkling up his face. He kept chuckling for a long time, even though none of us laughed with him. "I'm more popular now, in fact. Unfortunate women seem to like me."

"And that woman who was here earlier? Are you . . . ?" Yohei asked.

"Sure. She says she wants to be my wife. I'm having a hell of a time making her see that it isn't going to happen." Utagawa gave a contented laugh, then added, "I'm not telling you all this because I want to boast, you know."

"Of course, we know that!" Shigeki replied genially. "Now, about the script—"

"I was just responding to your questions, that's all," Utagawa said, cutting Shigeki off. With that, his expression became sullen, rather like a child whose chitchat adults didn't want to listen to.

"It's true, we did ask," Yohei said calmly.

Utagawa's sulk seemed to soften a little. "You certainly did," he said, nodding. Then, as if noticing my presence for the first time, "Who's she?" When Shigeki replied that I was the woman they'd spoken about, Utagawa turned toward me, looking me up and down skeptically.

"She's got a penis on her foot? I expected someone different. Someone who looks more like a guy. A bigger build, bigger bones—someone with male hormones coming out her ears, that kind of thing. You've really got a penis?"

"Yes."

"And who's he?" Utagawa said, referring to Shunji next to me.

"This is Kendo Shunji. He's a blind pianist, and he's Kazumi's—" Shigeki hesitated for a moment, "Kazumi's friend."

"I'm her *fiancé*," Shunji said loudly.

"Her fiancé?"

Utagawa glanced back and forth between Shunji and me. I nudged

Shunji with my elbow, trying to make him shut up, but he misinterpreted this as a sign that I wanted him to be more precise.

"Well, we used to be engaged, but Kazumi fell in love with Eiko while I was away on a trip, so she may not think of me as her fiancé anymore."

"When you say Eiko . . . you mean *that* Eiko?"

Utagawa shook his head in amazement, I grew flustered, and Shunji went on: "I still consider myself her fiancé, though."

Utagawa turned to Shigeki and Yohei, full of curiosity. "What's this about Eiko? She wasn't a lesbian before, was she? What happened to Tamotsu?"

When Shigeki and Yohei failed to answer, Utagawa targeted me. "Were you into this lesbian stuff from the beginning?"

"No."

"What happened then? Eiko went wild over your penis?"

"I don't think so."

"All right then, what was it?"

He hurled this question at me, not bothering to conceal his annoyance. When I hesitated, uncertain how to respond, he threw his back against the sofa and glared up at the ceiling. Then he began preaching: "Forget this lesbian stuff! Nothing ever comes from two women getting together. I guess it can't be helped if a woman is too ugly to attract a man—that's a reason to turn lesbian. But you're cute. Don't you think you ought to just stay with this Shunji kid here?"

I hardly knew what to make of these bizarre statements. True, maybe nothing came from two women getting together, but nothing came from a man and a woman getting together either—nothing but babies. Or did he know something I didn't know? I had no idea whether or not there were women who turned to homosexual love because men wouldn't have anything to do with them, and I couldn't help wondering what led Utagawa to believe there were. And what made him think he could be so arrogant as to decree, even if he wasn't explicit about it, that women who could attract men were better off in heterosexual relationships—that they should mold their sexual proclivities to the needs of men, rather than just stay attuned to their own desires?

I could see why Utagawa was so disliked. He had very fixed ideas, and he was wildly narcissistic. He was selfish and temperamental. He'd gone on and on about how he was giving the woman psychotherapy, making it all sound very clean and nice, when it wasn't so hard to guess just what kind of help he was giving her. I hadn't met such a perfect specimen of a disagreeable person since I was in elementary school. Come to think of it, the wide, beaming smile that kept flashing across Utagawa's face made him look exactly like a kid in the second or third grade.

Utagawa went on lecturing me, his tone now so gentle it was hard to believe he had been angry just a moment before: "Imagine how Tamotsu must feel. Eiko is all he has, you know? How could you be so cruel as to take his sweetheart from him? Not to mention the fact that in order to be with Eiko you've jilted this charming fiancé of yours. It's not right to make men suffer like that. Hey, you . . . Shunji, was that your name? C'mon, be a man! You've gotta win your fiancée back!"

Shunji had been hanging his head, listening in silence as Utagawa spoke; now that he had been addressed directly, he raised his head. "I plan to get her back, but . . . stop bad-mouthing her."

Utagawa blinked a few times. "I didn't bad-mouth her!"

"Yes, you did. You said she's cruel, and that what she's doing isn't right, and that she ought to stop . . ."

"That's not bad-mouthing! I was just giving her a bit of advice."

Shunji thought for a few moments. "If you give someone too much advice, you make it sound like she's bad."

Shunji reached out and took my hand in his. It felt reassuringly warm. Moved, I gave it an unintentional squeeze.

Utagawa scratched his head, then slapped his knee. "Shunji," he cried passionately, "you're a good man!"

Had he given in so quickly because of Shunji's loveable character or because he was easier on men than he was on women? Turning toward me, a scornful look in his eyes, he declared, "He's a fine young man! Heaven forbid you should dump him!" Then shifting his gaze back to Shunji, his face relaxing into a smile, he said, "You'll definitely have a role in the play, Shunji!"

Utagawa stood up and handed a large envelope to Shigeki. In it was the script, a thin booklet with pale yellow covers. He went on about how his image of my character had changed as a result of our meeting, and so he would have to rewrite certain parts; he needed to add a part for Shunji, too—but we needn't worry, the final script would be delivered to the Kobe apartment within a day or two. He worked fast, so it would only take him two or three hours to revise the script—in fact he could write a whole play in two nights, no sweat, and all it took was a phone call from him and he'd have a piano for Shunji to play, and . . . There was no end to his pomposity.

Finally, Utagawa turned his attention to me again. "I was forgetting. I'd better have a look at your toe-penis."

At the sight of his beady eyes and his fat, childish face, I had the urge to refuse—not out of embarrassment, but out of disgust. For its part, my toe-penis had shriveled in my sock. I knew I had no choice but to show it to him, and yet my body refused to move.

"Are you shy?" Utagawa said. "You're still a woman, I guess. That's a relief. But I'm afraid you're going to have to let me see."

I rested the heel of my right foot on the sofa arm and peeled off my sock. Utagawa bent over and peered at it in its withered state, then gave a surprised grunt—something along the lines of *Phrnugt!* I could feel his warm, repellent breath and forced myself not to pull my foot away. It wasn't only his breath—it was his leer, which oozed over my toe-penis. The poor organ was slowly being drowned in the gutter. Utagawa, whose lips were twisted in a frown shaped like an N, demanded that I show him the underside, and so, barely able to breathe, I lifted my foot.

When he had ogled my toe-penis to his heart's content, he stared at my face. "Doesn't really match your features—not that that's a surprise. How long have you had this *thing*?"

"Almost eight months."

"And how many times have you used it for sex?"

". . . I'm afraid I can't say."

"Not an awful lot, I'd bet. Am I wrong?" Utagawa started declaiming again, obviously proud of his keen intellect. "You don't have the unique shadow that the penis creates, you see. So I can tell that you haven't made much use of it."

"I don't have . . . a shadow?"

"When a man goes through hell for having done some stupid thing, something he didn't really mean to do, that he got dragged into by the insatiable appetite of a penis that can't be controlled by rationality—when a man has experienced that, he acquires a certain aura of pathos. You don't have that."

Utagawa's expression took on a rapturous look, as if he were imagining the aura of pathos he believed he, too, possessed. "You say that you and Eiko have gotten into this lesbian stuff, but let's face it, you're not getting much sex, are you? If you'd been really deeply involved with a woman, exhausted all your love and hatred, even managed to get tired of having sex for pleasure alone, and yet kept on going until you couldn't help reviling your own penis for its greed—let me tell you, you wouldn't be sitting there with that happy-go-lucky look on your mug. I can see it all. Forgive me for saying this, but even as a woman, you haven't had too much experience with men, have you? You've got the face of a girl who's still playing house."

I looked again at Utagawa's face. His skin wasn't really sagging, but it wasn't firm either, so that when his expression turned serious the abundant flesh of his cheeks lost its rotundity and drooped down around his lips. There was a certain seductive charm in the worn-out appearance of his skin, but the seduction wasn't exactly sexual—it was the sort of allure you feel when you see the deepest core of a person's being, a part that normally doesn't get put on display, laid bare. Perhaps "seductive" isn't the right word—"lewd" might be better. I certainly didn't detect any pathos. The gleam in his eyes was irritable and aggressive, and seemed to harbor a kind of strength—not the sort that would be useful for anything, however, unless it was to help Utagawa satisfy his narcissism and act on his misogyny.

I had no desire to look like that, or to be close to a person who did— I'd rather look like "a girl who's still playing house." He repulsed me. I despised this man who wanted to force me to accept a view of sex and human existence that was tailored to fit his own desires.

Utagawa must have seen something he didn't like in my expression, because he sat up and barked, "All right, let me see you get it up!" When I didn't immediately jump to it, he went on, "It's necessary for the play. I want to see how big it gets when it's hard. Go on, let's see you jerk off— you can do it right here. You've got to be able to do that much if you want to make a woman happy."

It made sense that, for the sake of the play, I would have to show him my toe-penis erect. But I hated him for that vulgar comment about making a woman happy. Still, unable to refuse, I squeezed my fingers tightly around my toe-penis. I started rubbing it, hoping the movements of my right hand would get the job done.

"Well, well," Utagawa said, "I can see you're used to *that*."

I kept massaging the penis, not saying a word. But since I wasn't feeling at all sexy and I was filled with loathing for Utagawa, the results were poor. I gave up when, after a heroic struggle, I managed to get it half erect. Utagawa, who still had no idea what it looked like fully erect, offered his amused evaluation. "Well, it's not bad. It'll serve the purpose."

At this point Shigeki spoke up. "Fully erect, it's about seven inches long."

"Seven inches!" Utagawa was stunned.

Shigeki nodded, then turned to me and said, as if he, too, were sickened with the proceedings, "Don't give up. Get it hard."

I was annoyed with Shigeki for having told Utagawa more than he needed to know, but I set about stimulating my toe-penis once again. But after a while, realizing that it wasn't going to work, I gave up. "I can't do any better than this right now," I said.

"Don't think you can weasel out of it like that!" Utagawa shouted. "A pro has to be able to get it up anytime, anywhere. Don't stop! I want to see your seven inches!"

My toe-penis had started to hurt, and I stopped, looking up uneasily at Utagawa.

Slowly, Utagawa's face broke into a smile. "Ah, I see. Masturbation doesn't work, huh? All right. Let's have that boy next to you help out."

I shielded my toe-penis with the palms of my hand. My mouth was dry, and I couldn't speak. The thought of being touched by my former fiancé on someone else's orders was about the most noxious thing I could imagine.

"You've fondled her toe-penis before. She can't get it up. This is where you save the day."

"Please, Mr. Utagawa," Shigeki intervened, "don't tease them like that—they're young."

Utagawa didn't so much as glance at him. "She might change her mind about you if you make her feel good right now. This is your big chance to win her back!"

I was totally unnerved. Shunji had no sense of shame; he was always wonderfully innocent and carefree, and when he felt desire, he acted on it immediately. Goaded like this by Utagawa, he was almost certain to put my toe-penis in his mouth. He hadn't said a word, but I could see that he was preparing to act. Was I going to have to sit here and endure this?

Shunji stretched out his right hand in my direction. I held my breath. But his hand didn't grab my toe-penis; he grabbed my wrist. "I'm not going to do that," he said loudly, his voice shaking the heavy air. "I only get friendly with Kazumi when it means something. I don't enjoy it when there are people around. And I don't like when someone tells me to do it either."

Shunji pressed his shoulder into mine. Since his return, the thought of physical contact with him was oppressive and scary, but as we sat here next to each other, I felt his passion flowing into me, from his body into mine, encouraging me, making me braver. Startled by this new sensation, I pressed back. The firm bulge of his shoulder and the heftiness of his arm were as I remembered, and I felt a twinge of nostalgia at their touch, but there was, somehow, a new resilience in his muscles. I wasn't about to forget everything that had happened between us, but he had definitely changed during the time he was with Oinuma.

"Don't be so serious, kid!" Utagawa smiled with half his face, looking ill at ease, then continued rather hastily. "Didn't you hear what Shigeki said? I was poking fun at you two youngsters, that's all. What you did just now was really something, I've got to say. Your former fiancée is looking all starry-eyed, too. The truth is, it was a trick—I was only trying to help you two get back together."

"In that case, it's okay," Shunji said, a trace of his former earnestness still evident. Shigeki and Yohei smiled.

But the tenor of the meeting had changed, and Utagawa, hoping to salvage what he could, now launched into a speech. "Well, you're really helping me a lot, Shigeki, finding such a fascinating individual. I bet I can shock the living daylights out of the petite bourgeoisie with this performance—even more than usual, I mean. Of course, it all depends on how far I decide to go with the material. This chick with the toe-penis isn't quite what I thought she'd be, but I have a feeling the play could be even better for it. I'll get to work on the script tonight! A lot will be riding on my shoulders, but don't worry, I won't let you down! I'll make the final performance of the Flower Show a night to remember! That's that, then. I've got to work now, so you can buzz off."

♥ ♥ ♥

The apartment in Kobe was completely different from the last time we were there. The terrific audio-visual system, the suspicious drugs, and the chest holding the collection of videotapes had all been carted away, leaving depressions in the carpet and dust everywhere. The expensive dishes had vanished from the cabinets, the phone was gone, and while the sofa beds were still there, they did nothing to relieve the cold, cavernous look of the space. Everyone worked together to clean the place up the night we arrived, but we couldn't do anything about the forlorn air.

Clearly some catastrophe had befallen the apartment's owner, but Shigeki said he didn't know the details. "The police or someone must have gotten wind of the funny stuff that was going on here. I'm sure he didn't want to have anything to do with us anymore, but Butakin asked him to let us stay here as a personal favor to him. Butakin repeated this three times, trying to make it seem like he was doing *us* a favor."

Butakin was the nickname the troupe had given Utagawa Kin'ya, mashing the "uta" from his family name together with the "kin" from his given name and changing the "uta" to "buta," which meant "pig."

Utagawa's script was basically the same sort of thing as last time—

an "underground play," if that's the word, with shocking content and no story, made up largely of lines that were a sort of incantation and suggestive actions that didn't seem to be suggesting anything. The scenes for the Flower Show in the special, one-night-only performance were in italics. My character was a woman who, flying into a rage when her boyfriend is stolen by another woman, murders the man and chops off his penis, only to have it show up on the big toe of her right foot; there, like a parasite, it starts living a life of its own. Her deceased boyfriend's parasitic penis has an erection every night, hot for the new girlfriend's vagina, and so night after night she has to masturbate to calm it, lamenting her fate all the while.

"What the hell is this?" I muttered. I was sitting on the sofa bed in the living room.

"A defense of the man's wantonness?" Aiko replied.

"You're too generous," Yohei said. "He's trying to punish the woman."

"For killing the man and chopping off his penis?" I asked.

"No. For becoming obsessed with sex. Or if you want to be even more specific, you could say she's being punished for having gone beyond simply accepting the man's desires, making the man suffer by cultivating desires of her own."

"But that's not fair! I mean, how the—"

Yohei smiled at my indignation. "Exactly," he said. "He's a selfish, unfair, phallicist judge."

Yohei had been given the same role as last time: "a man who, because of his unusual appearance and physical characteristics, is unloved by any woman, and is thus filled with bitterness toward all women." His partner, Masami, had been given a new scene in which crowds of ordinary people jeer at him, calling him a pervert, and then stone him. Shigeki would try to force himself upon a woman (Aiko) who refuses to accept his love, then, seeing her break out in painful rashes because she turns out to be allergic to sex, repent, and drown himself in a pond. Immediately after her suitor's suicide, Aiko was to go to the pond in which his body lies submerged and do her laundry, humming all the while. Yukie, in addition to her usual routine, would come alongside me, while I diligently tried to pleasure the parasitic penis, and growl, "Shall I eat that *thing* of yours?" The only members of the troupe who did their usual thing without any extra additions were Tamotsu and Eiko, who were going to perform together after all.

I tossed the script onto the floor, disgusted. "I can't play a role like this."

"I doubt you'll have to," Shigeki said. "The gentleman said he'd rewrite the play, right? And you don't look obsessed with sex at all."

With that, Shigeki turned to Eiko, who was sitting with me, and to Tamotsu, who was sitting next to her. "Your roles may change, too, now that Utagawa knows you're no longer . . . well, I don't know the situation. At any rate, Utagawa knows things aren't what they were between the two of you."

"Speaking of which—what *is* the situation?" Masami cried giddily. "I'm *dying* to hear, you know! I'm just *wild* about love stories."

The four of us, including Shunji, who was sitting on the other side of me, simply sat there fidgeting, saying nothing.

Masami didn't give up, though. "The way I see it," he said, aiming a finger in our direction, "this is *exactly* the sort of problem that bisexuals have to deal with."

Tamotsu, who had never been sexually involved with another man, took on a slightly sullen look.

"Bisexuals don't settle down. First they go for a man, then a woman, then a man, then a woman, *etcetera*. When they're with someone of *one* sex, they start telling themselves they actually prefer someone of the *other*—and they have *no compunctions whatsoever* about having affairs, because they can justify it! If they get tired of lover number one, they just go flitting off to someone else, as if they're not doing anything wrong, saying, *Yes, it's true. I like men better*, or *I guess I'm more of a woman person, after all*. Oh, it's just *awful*. I've had some *terrible* experiences with bisexuals."

"Aren't you bisexual yourself, Masami?" Eiko asked gloomily.

"You just leave me out of this!" Masami snapped, baring his teeth.

This was our second night in Kobe, but there had been no real change in the situation with the four of us. Tamotsu appeared to have relaxed a bit now that we had settled down in the apartment, because he was taking it easy, not trying to force himself on Eiko, and earlier in the afternoon he had even talked Shunji, who kept wanting to get close to me, into going out somewhere. They seemed to have had a nice time: Shunji looked content when they came back, and he no longer clung to me all the time. That said, I could tell without looking that Tamotsu was constantly keeping an eye on Eiko and me, and that Shunji was always listening.

It was perfectly clear how Tamotsu and Shunji felt. Eiko and I were the ones who had to make up our minds. Although Eiko denied being moved when Tamotsu said he still wanted to be with her, her attitude toward him had obviously relaxed a little. She didn't strike up conversations with him, but she laughed at his jokes and she didn't seem unwilling to sit next to him. I was probably right—she hadn't completely given up on him. It isn't easy to hate someone that you've loved for so long. Eiko had stated explicitly that she loved me more, but considering Tamotsu's sincerity, I wouldn't have been surprised if her affections were tilting back in his direction.

And yet, while I could imagine her wavering like this, I had no idea whether or not that really was the case. Maybe I wanted to believe that Eiko was wavering because my own heart was undecided. I couldn't get Shunji out of my mind after he had risen to my defense at Utagawa's office. He was a different person now, and I wanted to get to know him more. The wall I had built around my heart to keep Shunji out was crumbling. Needless to say, I felt guilty about this, and I was tortured by my pathetic wishy-washiness. Guilt was also what kept me from asking Eiko straight out how she felt.

The previous night, when we were all cleaning the apartment, I had taken charge of the area around the front door. I had swept the dust out into the hallway and was scooping it up when Eiko, who had been working in the dining area, slipped out and gave me a hug. Our first embrace in two days left me in a state of bliss.

"I thought Shunji had stolen you from me," she whispered.

Had my expression, after she said that, betrayed me? Because Eiko, who was looking into my eyes, went pale.

"You're so honest," she said. Then she vanished into the apartment.

I felt terrible. My heart was so changeable, so fickle. While Shunji and I were together, I hadn't given a moment's thought to Eiko. And when Eiko and I embraced, I totally forgot my feelings for Shunji. My tendency to lose myself completely in whatever was happening in me at the moment was an embarrassment. I was the lowest of the low, an animal, a creature with no steady core. On the other hand, if I thought of Eiko and Shunji at the same time, I was able to feel, bubbling up inside me, the deep love I had for both of them. I wanted to believe that this wasn't a sign of frivolousness—that it just proved my body was being honest when it reacted to both of them.

Despite my fears, Eiko didn't harbor a grudge. When bedtime rolled around, she quickly took my hand and led me to the sofa bed. The sound of us walking away prompted Shunji to call after us, "Kazumi? Where are you going?"

Eiko replied, in a tone that was mild but left no room for argument, "Kazumi is sleeping with me. You'll be sleeping with Tamotsu."

She had stayed with me the whole day—our second in the apartment— and never once pressed me about what had happened between Shunji and me. She was nice to Shunji, too. She seemed to have figured out what was going on in my heart. I, on the other hand, didn't have the slightest idea what was going on in hers.

The situation, in short, kept growing more and more tense, but there were no upheavals. A few times each day the four of us would have a good laugh together, as if nothing were amiss, but the gaiety didn't last for long; sometimes I would lose myself in my thoughts and realize, when I came to, that all four of us had been sitting there silently, hanging our heads. It was bound to seem like an extremely odd state of affairs to an outside observer.

Naturally, Masami was eager to hear every little detail. "All right, then— let me get this straight. Tamotsu loves Eiko, and Shunji loves Kazumi. Eiko is torn between Tamotsu and Kazumi, and Kazumi is torn between Shunji and Eiko, right? That means—"

"I am not torn," Eiko said, cutting Masami off. Pointing at me, she said, "This woman here is the only one who can't make up her mind."

I was taken aback by the objective, almost indifferent tone in which she delivered this judgment.

Masami's curiosity was piqued. Looking me in the eyes, he declared, "My my, so *you're* the one burning the candle at both ends!"

"I am not! I'm hardly adept enough to—"

Without waiting for me to finish, Masami began shrieking. "That's *enough* out of you! You can dress it up in whatever language you like, that doesn't change the fact that you are one *very* lucky girl. Oh, it's *unforgivable*! To think that not one but *two* people have fallen in love with you!"

I kept silent, overwhelmed by his fervor.

But Eiko burst out laughing. "Go on, Masami," she said, "let her have it!"

"Philanderer! Coward!" he cried, as his tongue moved into high gear. "Yes, I see now that *evil* lurks behind that mild-mannered exterior of yours. Go on and keep *pretending* you're suffering—you'll get what's coming to you! Oh, how I *envy* you! What I wouldn't give to have the experience, just *once* in my life, of having a flower in each hand! Oh, you idiot, you idiot, you *idiot*!"

The whole troupe was listening and laughing. Eiko, too. Maybe this was just a casual way to blow off some steam, but I had gotten a glimpse of the anger behind her smile. I winced. She was using Masami to do the dirty work rather than confronting me directly, which suggested she was keeping me at a distance. It made me feel lonely.

On the surface, she didn't seem distant, but she'd been withdrawing from me, keeping to herself, refusing to share her feelings with me, ever since we got on the bus to come to Kobe. Now, she was claiming the problem was mine and nobody else's. Masami kept piling it on, even in his false hysteria.

Then, softening his tone, he added, "You don't fight back, do you? You just sit there letting yourself be bullied . . . I must say, you sure do take my mind off my troubles. You'd be a very handy tool to have around. Tell me, darling, how would you like to stay with *me* for the rest of my life?"

"No thanks," I replied.

"Well, you sure don't seem torn where I'm concerned!" Masami said, pursing his lips dramatically. He didn't seem to have been offended, and went on. "Seeing how things are, I think you three might as well just move in together: you, Eiko, and Shunji."

"What about me?" Tamotsu cried.

"You can live with Shin, darling."

"What! He's not good for anything!"

"Then why don't you scoop him out and get rid of him?"

The repartee, however serious the matter, had been at a joking level, but this last statement of Masami's was radical and it brought on a sudden silence. His shrill voice reverberated through the cavernous living room. Masami was utterly unfazed. He glared at Tamotsu out of the corners of his eyes, waiting for a response.

When Tamotsu didn't reply, Masami spoke again, even more harshly. "The whole reason Eiko ran away from you in the first place is that you're so hung up on ordinary sex, you can't get over it, and you take out your frustration at your inability to do it on her! Isn't that so? And *why* are you so goddamn hung up on ordinary sex? It's because you've got Shin's penis there, so it looks from the outside as if you ought to be able to have ordinary sex. If you could just steel yourself and say goodbye to him, you could give that fantasy up. Find a surgeon and have it done."

Tamotsu gave an ill-tempered laugh. "Leave it to a man who goes and cuts off his own penis to come up with a plan like that."

Masami wasn't the slightest bit disturbed by Tamotsu's irony. "It seems to *me*, my dear, that right now you and I are just about evenly matched in our perversions."

Tamotsu swallowed his anger, and for a few moments he remained silent. Then he spoke again. "If I got rid of Shin's penis now, what chance would I stand against Kazumi? Just think, I wouldn't be able to do anything for Eiko."

"That's not true," I blurted out. "This is not a penis issue."

"Oh, isn't it? You sure have a lot of confidence in your humanity."

"I never said anything about my humanity!" I shouted.

"All right, then, tell me why Eiko loves you."

"I have no idea!" This was frustrating. I was unable to make myself clear, unable to make Tamotsu understand.

Masami, intent on giving Tamotsu advice, didn't wait to take over the conversation again. "If you change your body, your state of mind changes, too. Think how *awful* it is for Shin, being abused forever. Surgery is the best option for *both* of you."

"But . . . ," Tamotsu protested without looking up, "he'll die if I cut it off."

"Let him rest in peace. What's wrong with that? You won't have to put up with him stealing nutrition from you anymore."

Tamotsu's head had now dropped so low it was almost touching his knees. He muttered something, but his voice was too quiet for him to be understood.

"What was that?" Masami asked.

Tamotsu didn't respond. Masami asked again.

This time, Shunji answered for him. "He said he can't."

One moment all eyes were on Shunji, the next we were all looking at Tamotsu.

"I may be a terrible person," he said quietly, "but I don't want to commit murder."

"But I thought you hated Shin?"

"That's because I can't talk with him. We can't fight, we can't make up, we can't play together. He doesn't do anything with me, even though he's my brother."

"So let him die! What's the problem?"

Tamotsu looked up and shouted, "He's my brother! Our two hearts beat as one, literally!" Tamotsu wasn't crying. He was shrieking—with the unintelligible cry of a baby, straining its lungs, its whole abdominal cavity vibrating. "He's always been with me! From the first day of my life. Of course, I've wanted to kill him, many times, but I can't do it. We'll live together and we'll die together." He leaped from his seat, stormed across the room, and went out onto the dark balcony.

The group sat stunned, overwhelmed by this cry from the heart. All of us, that is, except for Masami, who had a weirdly gleeful grin on his face. "Even a brat like him has emotions, it seems!" He patted Eiko's knee. "I'm sure he cares very deeply for you, too, sweetie. What are you going to do?"

"What do you mean, what am I going to do?" Eiko said firmly, as if trying to crush her uncertainty. "I'm not in love with Tamotsu anymore."

"Yes, that's *true*!" Masami looked even more delighted. "No matter how much another person may care for you, if you don't care for them . . . well, their love just isn't worth a *fart*, is it?"

Masami was clearly making fun of Eiko, whose expression soured.

But in the last few moments, telling things had happened. When Tamotsu had rushed out onto the balcony, Eiko started to stand up, to go to him, but she sat back down almost immediately, averting her gaze. I knew it all along—she still has feelings for Tamotsu! I laughed grimly to myself. She makes it seem like it's my fault, but she's just the same! An instant later, the echo of my laughter turned cold. It was selfish of me, and I was in pain.

Eiko sat stiffly. She had to be hurting too.

♥ ♥ ♥

I was on the balcony feeling the wind when Eiko came out and put her hand on my arm. "Lunch is ready," she said. She was giving my arm a little tug when she changed course and pinched the flesh above my elbow. I yelped, but she had already let go, and looking like she hadn't done a thing, she went back into the apartment. I was entirely puzzled. She had pinched my arm and then feigned innocence earlier that morning, too.

Eiko seemed to be in a good mood, so she might have just been playing with me. Plates of pasta that gave off a delicious aroma of olive oil had been set out on the dining room table. Yohei, who was a very good cook, had prepared the meal for Shigeki, Aiko, Eiko, and me. Masami had gone out to eat with the rest of the group—Tamotsu, Shunji, and Yukie. Tamotsu, who had been so shaken by Masami's goading the previous night—I could still hear that terrible, bloody shriek—had been quiet all morning. He had been so quick to accept Masami's invitation that the word "docile" came to mind.

As we ate, Shigeki read the rewritten script of Utagawa's play.

"How is it?" Yohei asked Shigeki.

"I'm not sure yet how it's different from the old version."

Shigeki was about to hand the script to Yohei when he reconsidered and looked at Eiko and me. "I think you two should have a look at it first."

The "you two" did not bode well. I took the script and read where Utagawa had added parts, scrawled into the margins. When I was done, I silently thrust the script to Eiko.

"The lesson here," Shigeki said, "is that rewriting a play doesn't deprive it of any of its Utagawa Kin'ya—esque qualities."

I didn't feel like saying anything. My role was no longer that of the woman who chops off the penis of the man who betrays her, only to have it show up living on her like a parasite. The new premise was that I took the penis from the pervert, played by Masami, when he cut it off. After that, I threw myself between Tamotsu and Eiko, two lovers who had trouble having sex, stole Eiko from Tamotsu, and flung myself wholeheartedly into having sex with her. In his agony, Tamotsu makes an enormous dildo, intending to kill Eiko and me with it by crushing us under its weight, but in the process of transporting it, he stumbles and is himself flattened beneath it. Eiko and I go on having sex, completely oblivious of what has happened, and the stage goes black. Shunji makes an appearance as a blind pianist in the scene, too: he stops his piano-playing as Eiko and I start having sex, then comes over and runs his hands over our intertwined bodies.

Just the thought of Utagawa made me sick. His flashing eyes, his flabby face, his know-it-all position on high, judge of the theater and the world. From meager tidbits of our lives, he had thrown together this simpleminded homophobic crap. It was beyond malevolent, his dyed-in-the-wool homophobia, and his attempt to denigrate us and deny us private lives by making us perform on stage. It was sadistic. It was unbearable.

"I see," Eiko muttered coldly, and tossed the script onto the floor.

Yohei got up, went over, and scooped it up.

"What right does he have to use our lives as his material?" Eiko said.

"He doesn't have the imagination to do anything else," Shigeki responded. "He can't coach his actors, so he brings their real lives into the foreground and has that take the place of acting. And of course he's excited at the thought of seeing you two get it on."

"Disgusting," Eiko spat, her hatred of Utagawa undisguised. "Your part was bad in the old version, Kazumi, but it wasn't *this* bad, was it?"

I didn't disagree. "Do we really have to do this?" I asked.

"We have no choice," Shigeki said seriously. "Utagawa's the boss."

"But what if we *did* tell him we don't like the parts?" Aiko said. "We've never once refused him. I'm sure he'd be thrown for a loop if we did."

"And then he'd go into hysterics." Shigeki turned to face Eiko and me. "This is one of those times to pretend you're obeying, even if in your heart you're not."

I guess I must not have looked very pleased, because Shigeki addressed me next. "Do you not want to do it? There's no need to put private things on display, you know. Just act like you are. He could never understand us anyway."

"It's not that . . . I just don't want to do anything that will satisfy Utagawa's sick desires. And I don't want to play a part in his homophobia."

Shigeki seemed dubious, but Aiko nodded, saying, "I agree. This script goes too far—he's making a mockery of you. My part—the woman washing clothes in the pond with the drowned lover the bottom of it—at least it's neutral."

Shigeki picked up the script and began skimming it again. "You're talking about the fact that you've been put into the roles of disgraceful, whacked-out women? I can see you might not like it, but regardless of Utagawa's intentions, there's only one thing we can do. We just have to grin and bear it."

"Why?" Aiko said.

Shigeki glanced up at her.

"Why is grinning and bearing it the only option?" she repeated, smiling, but with an edge.

Shigeki didn't let this trouble him; he responded with an air of mature resignation. "Because Utagawa has the money, and that keeps us in line."

"That doesn't mean we can't try, does it? We can just tell him we don't want to do it this way. I'd love to give him a piece of my mind this once, at least, for our final performance. I think it'd be fun," Aiko said, an odd giddiness entering her tone.

Shigeki stared at her, looking uncertain how to respond, then heaved a sigh. "This may not be our last performance," he said.

"What do you mean?"

"Utagawa says he's interested in buying the Flower Show. He's especially keen on having Yohei, you, and me."

Aiko's face flushed. "You never told me that."

This was the first I'd heard of it, too. Eiko seemed startled also.

"I was waiting for the right time to bring it up, because I knew you'd object."

"You were planning to try and convince me—to get me to go on playing that stupid role of the woman who washes her laundry in the pond?" Aiko was furious. "Since when are you on Utagawa's side!" she shouted.

"I'm not on his side," Shigeki answered feebly. "But you have to get by somehow, right?"

"Getting by isn't a problem, Shigeki! All you have to do is work! We've been talking about opening a coffee shop! What happened to that? We should be able to raise the money to open it."

"You seriously think we can make that work? We've gotten used to a rather flashy lifestyle, in case you haven't noticed! I want to earn a little more working with Utagawa's troupe, then start a business with Yohei."

"And what about me! I have to go on playing this idiotic role Utagawa cooked up out of his hatred for me, all for the sake of some male dream?"

"If you don't want to do it, you can go back to Tokyo."

Aiko's face flushed with anger, but all at once, her passion cooled. Her eyes kept burning wildly, but a smile appeared on her lips. "You're very careful to respect the feelings of the people around you, and yet beneath that careful, diplomatic outer layer, you're nothing but a cowardly pragmatist." Shigeki's face went pale. "I hate that side of you," she said. "I really do."

With that, Aiko kicked her chair out of the way and stormed off into the back bedroom. Shigeki sat for a few seconds looking down, his hands clasped, then got up and followed her. A few moments later, Aiko flew past in her coat, heading for the door, Shigeki rushing after her.

Shocked, Yohei, Eiko, and I sat in silence.

"I've never seen Aiko so angry before," Eiko finally said.

"Me neither," I said. "But Aiko told me once that her relationship with Shigeki was less warm than you might think . . ."

"She said that?" Eiko asked.

Yohei, however, nodded knowingly.

"She also said Shigeki would eventually fall in love with a normal woman."

"No, there's no way that could ever happen," Yohei said. "Aiko is the first woman Shigeki ever really fell in love with."

"But the love isn't getting through to Aiko?" Eiko asked. "Is that it?"

"I don't know if it isn't getting through, or if she's denying it . . ." Yohei shook his head sadly.

"Doesn't Aiko love Shigeki?" I asked him.

"I don't know." Yohei chose his words carefully. "Even if there are parts of him that she hates, I wouldn't say she doesn't love him at all."

"Poor Shigeki," Eiko murmured.

"No, he's okay with that. He's decided he wants to be with her even if she doesn't love him as much as he loves her."

Eiko fell silent when she heard this. Yohei's words gave me food for thought, too. Aiko had said some pretty harsh things to Shigeki, writing him off as a "cowardly pragmatist." When did she discover this side of Shigeki that she hated? Had she gradually developed a pessimism about their relationship because she couldn't get past that aspect of his personality? It would be much easier if you started hating everything about your partner, because then you could simply split up—but it had to be exhausting to remain with the person, keeping that discomfort locked up inside of you, since you didn't hate him through and through. That sort of thing was bound to warp the love you had in the first place.

I was less sensitive than Aiko, and I wasn't at all observant; generally speaking, I could sum up my feelings for a person with a single word: "like" or "dislike." My reaction when Shunji came back had felt complex to me at the time, but in retrospect I was only sulking. My view of Eiko had changed a good deal as I got to know her more intimately, and I had discovered aspects of her personality that were far from admirable—the way she kept coming after you so persistently, her inability to be forthright, her streak of slyness—but there had been no change in my affection for her. And that was something to be grateful for.

The three of us were still sitting there, depressed, when Masami and the rest of the troupe came parading gaily back into the apartment. Tamotsu had completely recovered his spirits. He came over and stood in front of me, his arm wrapped around Shunji's neck.

"Hey, you guys had spaghetti, too?" he said, looking down at the unfinished food on our plates. "Mine was squid-ink!" With that, he pushed Shunji down onto my lap.

"What are you doing?" I said.

"Mmm?" Tamotsu feigned ignorance. "Just putting him where he belongs."

He sat down across from me. Shunji moved over next to me.

"What's up?" Masami asked, taking off his muffler. "You all look like you're at a funeral."

Yohei said nothing about Shigeki and Aiko. "Utagawa's new script arrived."

"Hear that, Shunji? You better read it, I guess, huh?" Tamotsu said.

"Why don't you read it out loud to him. Your part's changed, too."

Yohei opened the script to the page where the changes began and handed it to Tamotsu. Tamotsu began reciting the lines mechanically, at the top of his lungs. He commenced with the stage directions: "We see the bodies of two sinful women writhing with eerie sensuousness, illuminated by the flames of hell (scene reminiscent of Baudelaire)."

It was hilarious to hear this read aloud in Tamotsu's wooden tone. I couldn't help laughing even as the nauseating scene rose up vividly before my eyes. I could picture Utagawa relishing the games he was playing with us as he wrote, taking spiteful glee in imagining our humiliation.

Tamotsu finished reading. "I die?" he mumbled. "Man, I don't want to die crushed by a penis."

Without losing a beat, Masami shot back, "Aren't you *already* being crushed by a penis, Tamotsu darling?"

Tamotsu didn't protest. "Yeah—that's exactly why I don't like it. Can't I hop on the dildo and zoom off into the sky or something?"

"Still obsessed with *the penis*, I see. Try telling us that you'd like to hold Eiko's shoulders and fly through the sky with her—something like *that*."

Tamotsu's cheeks flushed. Eiko's cheeks had reddened too, though her expression remained as prickly as before. I had to grit my teeth to keep from laughing, amused by her stubbornness.

"I like Shunji's role better. He gets to tangle with two women . . . It's bound to be a crowd-pleaser."

This line was a disappointment. Tamotsu had just shown us the endearing side of his personality—why did he have to act so obnoxious the next moment?

Masami looked disgruntled, too, and was just opening his mouth to speak when Shunji cut him off, leaving him gaping.

"I don't want to play a role like that."

"Huh?" Tamotsu said. "Why not?"

"I don't like to get involved when people are getting friendly. That happened when I was traveling with Tama. He and some young guy were being friends, and he told me to touch them, and then—"

"That's enough," Eiko said. "We get the picture."

Shunji gave a sad little shiver. I couldn't know what bizarre sexual games he'd been put through with Oinuma, but I wanted to show Shunji support in the way he'd supported me in Utagawa's office. Shunji leaned back, pinning my arm to the chair. This seemed like an odd way to be intimate—squashing my arm rather than squeezing my hand. Suddenly it hit me: Shunji didn't want to upset Eiko.

This then led me to worry what Eiko was thinking. She was staring at the table, her face blank. Lately, I'd learned that she was most volatile when her expression said least. I needed to keep her more in the picture, but on the other hand, why couldn't I be solicitous of Shunji when he seemed in need? I didn't know how long I'd be able to bear this tangled web of relationships.

"So you don't like it either, huh?" Tamotsu said. "I should just rewrite the script. I'd make everyone in the Flower Show happy, at least on stage."

"Do that. I'd like to be happy."

This was Eiko, her tone so rigid and serious it was like a body slam directed at Tamotsu's vague, optimistic daydreaming.

Tamotsu unlocked his hands, which had been clasped behind his head, and sat up straight. "You want *me* to make *you* happy?"

"Me and everyone else. I'd like to be happy," Eiko repeated quietly.

"Why? You aren't happy with your role, either?"

"Absolutely not."

"Why? You don't have to do anything bad, do you?"

Evidently Tamotsu understood as little of Utagawa's intentions as Shigeki did.

"I have no desire to appear on stage as a sinful woman illuminated by the flames of hell, and I don't want Shunji to come and run his hands over us, and I don't want to be the sort of idiot who wouldn't even notice you had died."

Naturally, Eiko was referring to the script, but since so much of our personal lives was reflected in what Utagawa had written, our lives and the play were blended into one. Even if she hadn't meant it that way, her words must have sounded very sweet to Tamotsu.

"Yeah, if only I could write the script. I'd make everyone happy."

Suddenly Yukie spoke up. "You're naïve, Tamotsu. As if you could make me happy! It's hopeless."

"Sheesh, how *gloomy* you are," Masami said, as if he couldn't believe his ears. "It's beyond me how you can say *you're* unhappy. You've got money and a man. Even your *name* means happy, for goodness' sake."

Yukie's name was, I realized, written with the character for "happiness."

"Strange. If that's the case, you ought to be beautiful."

Masami's name contained the character for "beauty."

"Excuse me?"

Masami and Yukie barreled on with their argument, getting further and further away from where they'd started. They were bitter and funny at the same time. We were all laughing uproariously. Yohei had been dragged into the argument now, and the hilarity was escalating. Tamotsu, though, had gotten up, gone to the bathroom, and was now quietly making his way out the door.

I got up and went out onto the balcony. I stood there, looking down, and after a few moments, I saw Tamotsu walk out of the building. I called to him, unsure that he'd hear me from the fifth floor. He didn't. But after he'd gone seven or eight yards, he turned to look up at the apartment and saw me standing there. I waved to him, and in response, he propped one knee on the ground and crossed his arms in front of his chest, like an alien in a children's TV program. Then he got to his feet and kept going.

I found myself thinking about all the pieces of our lives that would fall neatly into place if only Eiko could bring herself to go back to Tamotsu and I could bring myself to return to Shunji. There had been a time when I dreamed, all too simplemindedly, that it might just be possible for the four of us to make things work out, but these past few days had made it clear how difficult that would be. Basically, the following things, in no particular order, had to happen: Eiko and I could keep seeing each other as friends even if we stopped being lovers. I would abandon what Masami had described as the "extremely lucky" state of having not one but two persons in love with me. The two couples would split up, no one person therefore having to be too deeply hurt.

That said, I hated the thought of losing Eiko as a lover. Nothing much would change if we went back to being friends and stopped spending every hour of the day together, and stopped having sex. But I would never again feel her naked skin on mine, her hand resting on my toe-penis . . . an image of her deformed toenail rose in my mind. And it wasn't only sex . . . I would no longer have the opportunity to be alone with her in a room, utterly comfortable and relaxed and vulnerable and free to accept, ever so naturally, parts of her body I wouldn't have dreamed of touching when we were only friends.

During the time we spent living together, the act of taking her deformed toenail in my mouth had become associated with my sexual liking of Eiko, and that feeling had stripped me of the sense of uncleanness I would ordinarily have regarding feet. And so, over time, I had come to express the liking I felt for her as a friend by putting her toe in my mouth as well. As I saw it, my sexual liking of her had reinforced my friendly liking of her. If I had to suppress my sexual liking of her, then, I would also have to suppress that extra liking I had developed for her as a friend. The thought weighed upon me; a knot formed in my chest. *I don't only want to be friends with her—that isn't any fun.* These words echoed clearly through my mind.

I tried once again to reason with myself: So being friends isn't any fun . . . That isn't a very nice thing to say, is it? How would Tamotsu feel if he heard you say that, or the other members of the Flower Show, or any of your other friends for that matter? Above all, how would that make Yoko feel, after all the kindness she showed you? . . .

The moment Yoko's face flashed up in my mind, I was overcome by remorse. This was the feeling that had troubled me for some time after her death—the sense that all along I had simply been basking in the warmth of her gentleness, and had never given her anything in return. Now that I had gotten to know Shunji and Eiko, and learned what it meant to care deeply for another person, I had to admit that the affection I had shown Yoko was colorless, a little lacking. Why couldn't I have developed a sexual liking of her? The question of whether or not Yoko had felt a homosexual love for me, as Eiko and others had suggested, wasn't irrelevant. The point was that if I had loved her in a homosexual way, I would have been able to give her something in return.

The glass door rattled open behind me and Eiko stepped out onto the balcony. "What are you doing?" she asked. My heart was still filled with remorse, and I found it hard to turn my thoughts in another direction, so I blurted out a response that didn't have anything to do with the question: "Tamotsu just walked down the street." Eiko peered down the road, then restated the question: "Who were you thinking of?"

This time I answered. "Yoko."

Looking out across the city, Eiko began talking: "You saw Tamotsu walking on the street there. You started realizing how exhausting this three-way relationship is—or maybe it's a four-way relationship. And you started feeling nostalgic for the simple clarity and openness of your friendship with Yoko. How's that? Pretty good, don't you think?"

I was impressed by her guesswork, I had to admit, but she was wrong about my nostalgia for Yoko.

"Yes, but it's no fun, just being friends."

"It's no fun, but it's easy. You don't have any of this trouble. You wish things could be easier, don't you?"

She was right I wanted things to be easier, but that didn't mean I was going to take the easy path. I was thinking of explaining this to her when her hand slipped into the crook of my arm. Ouch! It was the third time she had pinched me today. She was expressionless as she did it; so if she wasn't kidding around, maybe she was trying to communicate. I wasn't sure what she was communicating, but I thought I'd try some body language myself. Seizing her hand, I brought it to my lips and kissed it.

From this position, I couldn't see Eiko's face, but I could see her breasts, and they trembled. Wrapping her arms around me, she pushed me against the wall where we couldn't be seen from inside the apartment or from down on the ground and pressed her lips to mine. My body responded to this communication. Joy gushed through me, and my arms squeezed her tightly to me. I didn't say it, but I knew what I was feeling at this moment—that I didn't want to be apart from her, even if we lived in a state of endless tension and had to put up with all kinds of trouble, as long as I could feel a few moments of joy like this . . . Yes, yes, I wanted to be by her side forever.

Taking her lips from mine, Eiko whispered, "You're so sociable. You just can't refuse—not Shunji, not me."

I was stunned. Her words were so cold I could hardly believe my ears.

"You're a very nice girl," she went on, "but . . . or maybe it's because you're such a nice girl, I don't know . . . you can only feel moderately fond of other people—you aren't capable of real love. You feel the same fondness for Shunji and me both, don't you?"

"What about you? You love Tamotsu, too, don't you?" I asked, a bit offended.

"Me? Not at all. I stopped loving him ages ago." Eiko drew her face slowly away from mine. She seemed utterly sad. "I love you, Kazumi, but I feel so alone when I realize that you will never care for me as deeply as I do for you. This has nothing to do with Shunji, but I'm going to have to let go. I hope you can work things out with Shunji. I don't plan to stay with Tamotsu."

She turned and started to walk back into the apartment. I tried to grab her arm, but she shook me off. I whammed the hand that had been left floating in midair against my thigh.

Even after I stopped crying, I couldn't summon the energy to go back into the apartment. I looked down at the ground, gazed up at the sky; my eyes roamed over the city, and down to the cars driving down the street. It looked like scenery on a stage. The fierce November wind whipped against me. I grasped the handrail of the balcony. She'd said this before, that night in my apartment—that I didn't love her. You couldn't argue against something like that. I inhaled, but ended up choking.

I walked the length of the balcony, trying to recover. Something hit the sliding glass door behind me, and I turned around, startled. I found myself outside Yohei and Masami's room, in which Masami stood, wearing nothing but panties and a bra, mouthing something to me. I couldn't hear what he was saying. Masami slid the door open, and shouted, "I'll thank you not to spy on me, you dirty Peeping *Tom!*"

The absurdity of this scene brought a smile to my lips. But Masami noticed the state I was in. "Dear me," he said, "do I detect a certain *melancholic* air about you?"

He pulled me into his room. The outfit he had worn to lunch lay on the floor, so the sound I'd heard must have been him hurling his clothes against the glass. He had me sit on the bed while he changed clothes, then took a seat next to me on the bed.

"Living your youth, I can see—happy girl."

"Actually, I've just been dumped."

"How *divine*—being swept up in such *drama*! That is what youth is all about, my darling. There's no such excitement in my life."

I had the feeling he wanted me to laugh, so I did. He seemed pleased.

"I take it Eiko is going back to Tamotsu?"

"No, she says she has no plans to do that."

"Surely you *jest!*" Masami cried mockingly. "She's got spunk, hasn't she?"

Lately Masami had been provocative in the things he said to Tamotsu and Eiko. It was his way, I knew, but he was doing it for a reason.

"Do you think Eiko loves Tamotsu, too, Masami?" I thought I'd ask.

"Indeed I do."

So it wasn't just me—no one thought Eiko was telling the truth about her feelings. Why couldn't she admit it? Was she simply being stubborn, sulking over Tamotsu the way I'd been sulking over Shunji? What was behind her convoluted behavior? I didn't dare speculate—me, a dullard incapable of experiencing "true" love—but perhaps Eiko enjoyed the tension, confusing her own feelings and her relationships with other people, lying.

"On the other hand . . ." Masami shook his head. "Even if she decides to give up on a lover or two, there are still plenty of men out there besides Tamotsu, and plenty of women besides you."

"No, not really—I think there are very few people someone would want to have as a lover, or as a friend."

As I said this, the faces of Shunji, Eiko, and Yoko came to mind. Yoko most clearly. I wished I could see her now. Maybe a certain part of me did want to escape into an easy, clear friendship, but it was more than that. I recollected with pleasure the innocent affection I had felt for Yoko. Because I really had enjoyed being with her *even if*—and I felt, as this thought came to me, as if I had woken up to a new truth—that enjoyment hadn't been sexual.

"I never would have expected a line like that from you," Masami was saying. "You don't seem all that choosey about people—you seem like you could get along with anyone."

"That's what people always think. But I don't fall in love with everyone."

"No, I suppose not. A lover is a different story." Masami sat still for a few moments, lost in thought, then looked at me very solemnly. "You know, darling, I like women better than I like men."

He'd said that before, that he didn't really like men. "Then why did you change sex?" I asked.

"I wanted to love women as a woman, not as a man. I wanted to be a lesbian."

"So badly you were willing to change sex? Wouldn't it have been easier finding a girlfriend as a man than as a woman who'd changed sex?

Wouldn't it have been less trouble to let that dream of becoming a lesbian stay a dream?"

"Yes, that would have been less trouble," Masami replied, his expression dark but strong. "And as it turned out, I never did find a woman who was willing to love me for long. Or a man either, for that matter. But I was willing to sacrifice myself to the dream. And the thing is, I knew right from the get-go that in the real world no lover is perfect. I knew that at the end of the day I couldn't make my dream come true by telling myself that deep down I was actually a woman who just happened to have a penis between my legs, and then going off and having a sex change to make things right. You must think I'm an idiot."

I found myself deeply moved by the choice Masami had made—to sacrifice so much, following his dream to the end.

"I was an idiot, but I was still rational. I had them make me a vagina, but I didn't have them make me a clitoris. You knew that, right? Do you know why? Because I never wanted to let myself forget that I'm actually a man. You're finished if you lose sight of reality, letting yourself drown in a dream."

"You're hardly an idiot, Masami."

"You think? But I constantly regret having chosen this way of life. Do you realize I've never once had sex with any love in it? Most people just want to sleep with me out of curiosity. I'm sure you're hurting right now because you've broken up with Eiko, but you two had sex because you loved each other, didn't you? And you were happy, right? Don't mourn those happy things as if you've lost them. Enjoy the memories as something you gained."

Tears welled up in my eyes as he said this. Masami gave my hand a squeeze.

Then, in a singsong voice, he started to chant, "I want to have sex with love." He twirled the hand he was holding mine with. "I want to have sex with love. I want to have sex with love."

As it got dark outside, Masami and I returned to the living room. Shigeki and Aiko were there, too, looking exhausted, sprawled on the sofa. Eiko poked Shunji to tell him I had returned.

"Kazumi! Where were you?" he said, stretching out his hand.

I gave his hand a light squeeze and sat down next to him. Eiko didn't look at me. I didn't have the courage to say anything. Masami took a seat beside me, put his arm around my shoulder, then cried out in a voice loud enough to banish the gloom, "Oh, baby, we sure have *stunning* sex, don't we!"

Eiko turned to look at me, dumbfounded. I shouted at Masami that he shouldn't joke, but my voice was shaking with laughter, and we ended up guffawing together. Eiko averted her gaze. I was gratified for the glimpse of her sadness, but that happiness immediately faded into a pain that shot through my heart.

"I'll be bunking with you and Tamotsu from tonight on," I whispered to Shunji. "I won't be sleeping with Eiko."

"Really?" he whispered back, his face glowing.

Suddenly the door to the apartment flew open and Tamotsu burst in. He looked bright and energized. Masami, happy for the cheer, called out, "Where were you?"

"Osaka." Tamotsu ran his eyes over the entire troupe as he took off his jacket, then, pleased with himself, loudly told us what he had done. "I got Utagawa to change the script! I don't have to be crushed to death by a dildo anymore! I'm going to have Shin make love to Yukie instead. And then, right there on stage, I'm going to castrate him!"

Tamotsu smiled proudly.

Chapter 16

The day before the actual show was to take place, the group drove together to Osaka for a dress rehearsal.

Shigeki seemed to have lost weight, and his tone was listless. Ever since the day Aiko blasted him and ran out of the apartment, a chill had fallen on their relationship. They never had overt disagreements, but Aiko was brusque and Shigeki was always trying to placate her. I worried about their rift, but it was their private life and they were both adults. It would have been presumptuous of me to show too much concern.

I was occupied with my own issues, three of them, all related to Utagawa's play: First, I would be having sex with Eiko on stage, even though she and I were no longer lovers. Second, Shunji would be groping Eiko and me while we had sex. And third, Tamotsu would be hacking off Shin's penis.

I wasn't hardened enough, spiritually or mentally, to sail through sex with an ex-lover, taking a strictly professional attitude, like Eiko— although she probably hadn't been thinking about this performance when she dumped me. If she was so determined to end things between us, she might as well have waited until after this performance. I was fed up with this side of her—her inability to put up with anything she didn't like, even for a short time. She had been keeping her distance since our breakup, so one day I approached her and asked her how we were going to do this. Her response: "We have no choice, do we? Think of it as a ceremonial way of saying goodbye." Her flexibility amazed me.

I hated the idea of Shunji running his hands over us as we did it, too, but that was a minor concern compared to my horror at Tamotsu's plan to castrate Shin. We all tried to convince him to change his mind. But he was not to be dissuaded.

"It's too late to back out—I've already promised that shit Utagawa that I'll do it. Besides, what I'm going to do is perfectly reasonable. I thought and thought about all the options and finally decided this is best, both for me and for Shin."

"Oh *please*. What *good* is there in this plan of yours!" Masami screeched.

"But you were completely right, Masami—having Shin's penis around has made it a struggle for me to move on. It's just made my complex even worse. I don't think I could live with myself if I had Shin taken out of my body, if I just let him die. The best solution really is to cut off his penis, but keep the rest of him in me."

Tamotsu would feel no pain when he cut the penis off because it was part of Shin's body, not his. Utagawa would have a doctor standing by in the dressing room to stop the bleeding, sterilize the wound, and suture it after Tamotsu emasculated Shin with a jackknife on stage. That Utagawa was blithely helping this along made me furious.

Masami felt dreadful. It was his outrageous suggestion that Shin be surgically removed from Tamotsu's body. The only reason he had even mentioned it was, he said, to show Tamotsu what was wrong with the way he was living—who would have thought Tamotsu would take him seriously? "Oh, oh, oh, I really *am* an idiot," he moaned.

Eventually I came up with an argument to change Tamotsu's mind. When Tamotsu, Shunji, and I—just the three of us—went out for a meal, I brought it up: "All you have to do is just not use Shin's penis anymore and the problem will be solved. You don't need to castrate him."

"I've got no willpower. If it's there, I'll use it."

"How can you be so sure the problem will be solved once you cut it off? Isn't the real difficulty within you? It's a matter of perspective. Will you really be able to forget Shin's penis, pretend it was never there, just because you've cut it off? I'm afraid you're going to continue to be haunted by visions of that penis, which won't stop until you yourself stop obsessing over ordinary sex. And if that ever happens, then you're going to realize that Shin's penis is gone forever, and it's going to be very hard to recover from the loss."

"I'll get over the visions eventually. When you change your body, your state of mind changes, right? Isn't that what Masami said?"

"That's just a generalization! I'm sorry to say this, but I think you've made a rash decision—you're just tampering with your body to distract yourself from your real issues about sex."

"I gotta say, Kazumi, that's a pretty wild misreading of the situation. I'm not as hung up on sex as I used to be. After all, you've got a penis, and that still didn't save you from getting jilted by Eiko."

"The fact that you're even thinking of castrating Shin proves that you're still hung up on sex. You're just frustrated and confused and can't find a way out!"

"That's the whole point. Castrating Shin is a way out."

The conversation had started going in circles, and I wasn't clever enough to do anything about it. "There's no guarantee Eiko will come back to you after you castrate Shin, you know," I said, trying one last approach.

"If that's the case, I'll deal with it."

There went my grand argument. I thought that maybe Eiko might have some success, even though she had voiced no objection when Tamotsu announced his decision to the group—which irritated me. "Have you talked to Tamotsu?" I asked her.

"No."

"You've got to! Make him stop this craziness!"

"I have no influence over him."

"So it's fine with you if he castrates Shin?"

"Personally, I don't think it's a good idea, but . . ."

Eiko's apathy only made me more incensed. "You just can't make up your mind where Tamotsu is concerned, can you? Funny, considering how quickly you decided to break up with me."

"You're hardly one to talk. How long did it take you to make up with Shunji after we split up?"

"Yes, yes, I know, you think I'm incapable of love, but that's not what we're talking about. I want you to say something to Tamotsu that will make him abandon this scheme of his. You have to try at least!" I blurted this out, then turned my back on her and walked away.

I don't know whether or not she actually spoke to Tamotsu. But in the bus to Osaka, when I saw how on edge he was about the rehearsal, I knew he hadn't given up the idea. I decided I had to appeal straight to Utagawa.

The venue for this performance was even more spacious than the theater in the basement of the office building where the troupe had performed the last time; it even had its own parking lot. We arrived thirty minutes before the rehearsal was scheduled to begin, but already Utagawa's voice could be heard thundering through the theater as he shouted out directions.

"Look, I told you that's no good! You know what you're doing? It's like you're coming out here with two pairs of underpants on, and then you strip off one and try and act like, Hey folks, look, it's me, in the buff! Take off that second pair, kid! You think you can move an audience without feeling humiliated?"

Utagawa was standing on stage waving a rolled-up script; a young man in a black Japanese-style outfit with a short-sleeved top and matching shorts was standing in front of him, hanging his head. Was an actor supposed to understand such abstract direction? Other actors and actresses were scattered across the stage. They must have been exhausted after several days of rehearsal; they were so quiet you hardly noticed them.

At the left of the stage, two platforms had been constructed from wood planks. There was a grand piano on the lower platform—presumably that was where Shunji would be playing. A flight of stairs extended to the higher platform, where a few trees stood at the back, suggesting a spot on a mountain. This had to be the mountain path where Tamotsu had originally been slated to die, crushed by the giant dildo. Over toward stage right, there was a Shinto torii. Two mattresses had been set out in different places at the foot of the mountain. Eiko and I would be doing our sex act on one of them.

At a certain point, Utagawa glanced over his shoulder toward the rows of seats, and Shigeki raised his hand in greeting. Utagawa called out a

"Hey!" and jumped down off the stage. I tagged along after Shigeki and Yohei as they went over to greet him, dragging Shunji behind me.

The moment Utagawa noticed me, he said, "Hey, Miss Big Toe P! Did you like the script?"

The man was beneath contempt, but I wasn't going to let him see that. I was going to flatter him into doing what I wanted him to do. "I enjoyed it very much," I said, then added gratuitously, "except that some scenes were so frightening . . ."

As expected, the insolent smirk on Utagawa's face morphed into a self-satisfied grin. "Ah," he said, "but the work wouldn't have force if it didn't scare people! I bet *you* found it especially frightening, Miss P? My plays aren't exactly intended for women and children, you know. You must be happy you get to tangle with Eiko, though, huh?"

"Actually, I wanted to talk to you about that," I said. "Eiko and I have broken up."

"What?"

"So I'd be grateful if you could put the script back the way it was."

Utagawa's expression soured. "No can do. How the hell am I supposed to rewrite it now? The original script had a man who betrays you and a woman who makes that man betray you. We've been rehearsing the new script, which doesn't have any of those roles."

"In that case, how about cutting that bit out and just having me play a woman who's been cursed and had a penis grow on her foot? Would that be okay?"

"Use your brain. If I take out the scene with you and Eiko, Shunji won't have a role to play anymore! I ordered the piano for him specially!"

"Can't you just have him play the piano at some other point? Shunji's great, he can improvise any kind of tune, as long as he knows the atmosphere of the scene."

"She's right, I can," Shunji assured him.

Utagawa's annoyance was starting to show. "I don't think you're getting the message. There are all kinds of reasons I can't change the play now. Take Tamotsu's castration scene . . . that won't make any sense without the romantic interlude between you and Eiko."

"So why don't you call that off, too? Tamotsu can come over to where I am and jerk off Shin. We can have a masturbation competition! How does that sound?"

"What the hell is up with you?" Utagawa spat, then turned to Shigeki and Yohei. "This woman is trying to write the script for me! I'm the playwright! Who the hell does she think she is?"

"Oh dear! I'm so sorry!" I said. "That's not what I meant to do at all!"

Utagawa went on grumbling at Shigeki and Yohei, choosing not even to glance in my direction.

"Actually," Yohei interrupted, "we're not really sure we like the idea of having Tamotsu hurt Shin for real, rather than just making it seem that he is."

Utagawa stared at Yohei, his face registering surprise. "Tamotsu is the one who asked me to let him do it! I agree that it's dangerous, but if Tamotsu is actually willing to go through with it, he'll make this play into something magnificent, absolutely unrepeatable. You guys may not understand this, but when it comes to the theater, I have no emotions. Even a little bloodshed doesn't bother me."

Then why don't you be the one to shed the blood, I thought bitterly.

"At any rate, Miss P, do me a favor and forget the crazy suggestions, okay?" Utagawa said, seeming a bit deflated, perhaps because the apple of his eye, Yohei, had offered a contrary opinion. "I worked in this one idea of Tamotsu's as a favor to him, but I was willing. It had pizzazz. He had another idea, but it was worthless."

"What was that?"

"He wanted to cut your scene with Eiko, too. Maybe you two were still together then? I thought he was being a wuss because he didn't want to see you two going at it right in front of him, so I told him so. Didn't make him very happy . . . Well, the good news is, you two have given up playing your silly lesbian games. Women are better off with men; they just need to find that out. The bad news is, the script can't be changed. Not possible, no way. You'll just have to gird up your loins, honey, and do it like a pro."

That went over real big, I mumbled to myself as I walked away with

Shunji. "I wasn't able to get him to change your role either," I said to him.

"That's okay," he said. "I'll just stay at the piano anyway."

"I don't think that will work."

"Sure it will. You two don't want me touching you, and I don't want to touch you either, so I'll just play the piano."

Shunji had no understanding of the theater, the roles actresses and actors play, or what it was like to be in the position of an employee. Sometime before tomorrow, I was going to have to explain that he couldn't just do things the way he wanted.

Immediately before the dress rehearsal began, the members of the Flower Show changed into light white cotton kimonos of the sort provided for guests at hot springs. Shunji was given a walking stick. Utagawa had gone through his steps with him—from the edge of the stage up to the piano, then back down to the mattress where Eiko and I would be having sex.

Tamotsu had somehow gotten hold of a glass goldfish bowl, which he was fooling around with in the dressing room. When Masami asked him about it, he said it was for catching Shin's penis when he severed it. Utagawa's aesthetic sensibility was beyond belief. And those aesthetics informed the whole play. From the monitor in our dressing room, I watched as several men and women, also in light cotton kimonos, ran around the stage with an enormous dildo on their shoulders, led by the man in black whom Utagawa had been scolding earlier. They set the dildo down on the stage, made a circle around it, and began kowtowing, worshiping it. Yukie appeared on the higher of the two platforms and began doing her stunts, putting teeth marks into cucumbers and bananas.

Unable to see what was happening on the monitor, Shunji wiggled his fingers in the air, practicing his number. I stopped watching the screen; but when Shigeki and Aiko made their appearance, I could no longer keep from looking. Theirs was a scene in which Aiko refused, time after time, to respond to Shigeki's advances, and he then forced himself onto her, pinning her down. Shigeki wasn't the sort of person who would take pleasure in raping someone, and obviously Aiko wouldn't enjoy being raped;

it seemed unlikely that they would have wanted to perform a scene like this even when things were going well between them.

As I watched, I realized that Shigeki had found a way out: he made no effort whatsoever to be realistic, simply taking Aiko's arm in his hand or lifting his fist in the air, doing the absolute minimum in a style that seemed almost dancelike, leaving it up to Aiko to show that she was being raped. Thanks to his approach, I could bear to watch the scene. I couldn't bear to watch them have sex, though, because it reminded me that my own sex scene with Eiko, in full view of everyone, would be next.

"We're supposed to have a hard time having sex, right?" I heard Tamotsu say behind me. "It's not supposed to be going well, so I don't have to penetrate or anything, do I?"

"I have no idea." Eiko's voice came from another direction. "Why don't you just do whatever you feel like? You'll be on stage, why hold back?"

These words were clearly intended as not-so-subtle jabs at Tamotsu, who had never been one to restrain himself. Tamotsu had no response to this.

The atmosphere in the dressing room was dismal. I felt like I was going crazy.

The play went on. Masami, Tamotsu, Eiko, Shunji, and I would all be making our entrance at about the same time, so we gathered ourselves and left the dressing room together.

"My, my, I can hardly *breathe*," muttered Masami, as he, Shunji, and I split off to the wings on the left side of the stage. Masami's role had him getting a male-to-female sex change, so he wasn't wearing blush or lipstick and he had gathered his long hair up into a bun. Without makeup, except for an even layer of white grease paint, his large nose and mouth seemed unmistakably masculine. It was this man who had sung to me the other day, "I want to have sex with love."

Tamotsu and Eiko walked out from stage right holding hands like ordinary lovers and sat on the mattress at the center of the stage. Masami and I went up onto the higher platform and peered down at the two lovers. It was surprisingly high and a little scary looking down. Tamotsu put his arm around Eiko's shoulders, then slipped his hand into her kimono.

"All of you, your faces are stiff!" Utagawa screamed. "You two up on the mountain are having fun spying on them. Let's see some smiles!"

I had no choice but to show my teeth. I can't say whether or not it looked like a happy face. Down on stage, Eiko was lying down with her breasts bared, and Tamotsu was exhibiting his naked body. Masami ran down the stairs, sailed by Tamotsu and Eiko, and disappeared behind the mountain, where he applied blush and lipstick and let down his hair. When he returned to stage as a woman and began prancing around, it was my turn to go behind the mountain. I was supposed to be taking the penis he had thrown away and grafting it to my foot, so I had to get my toe-penis hard before coming out again.

Tamotsu was jerking off Shin. The action today was different from usual: Eiko hadn't put Shin's penis in her mouth, and Tamotsu gave no indication that he was frustrated with Shin for being unable to get it up. I was glad not to have to watch that drama again. Behind the mountain, among Masami's scattered cosmetics, I was sitting down with my toe-penis in my hand, trying to get it hard.

The script called for me to go on stage and begin my sex segment with Eiko when I heard Tamotsu, having given up all hope of having sex, run off stage right. I wasn't feeling very in-the-mood, but my toe-penis did respond—it started expanding, pressing against my palm. I hadn't touched it in almost ten days, not since my demonstration for Utagawa, so it must have been extra sensitive. The sensations could hardly be described as pleasurable, however, and the organ grew little more than an inch.

Soon I heard the sounds of Tamotsu whacking Shin, and an image of the castration that would take place tomorrow rose before my eyes. Immediately, my toe-penis withered. It was hopeless. I heard Tamotsu dashing off stage, but I wasn't ready to go out. I hadn't been told what to do in the event of an incomplete erection. I put my toe-penis in my mouth, but that didn't get it big enough to be of any use. How much time had passed? Completely at a loss, I peeked out from behind the platform at Eiko, who was sitting up, perhaps in an effort to buy time. She looked around, as if acting, trying to buy even more; our eyes met. Guessing what the situation was, she gestured quickly for me to come to her.

I walked on stage, my eyes trained on Eiko. I stepped onto the mattress. Eiko welcomed me and began stroking my toe-penis. The realization that it was Eiko's hand on me brought on waves of deep emotion, more so than pleasure. She pulled me down onto the mattress, and as she wrapped her hand around my toe-penis, blood began flowing into it, titillating nerves that had been beset by anger and sadness and loneliness. I felt as if my whole body and even my heart were being massaged, and pleasure washed over me. I loved Eiko, I really did. Needless to say, my toe-penis was now fully erect.

Eiko covered my body with hers as she kissed me, pushing me down against the mattress. I wanted to forget all about the play, to surrender fully to my emotions and my desire as I touched her and she touched me. There was a passion in Eiko's hands, as they darted over me, that went beyond mere playacting. I had to get it into my head, though, that what we were doing was no more than a "ceremonial way of saying goodbye."

"Utagawa said Tamotsu asked him to cut this scene yesterday," I whispered.

Eiko's hands froze.

♥ ♥ ♥

"This is the second-to-last time we'll be having sex, so I was hoping to make it nice and emotional," Eiko said with a laugh, "and then you go and say something like that and ruin the mood." I supposed she was half joking. Utagawa kept hollering out instructions, telling us to "Be more dynamic!" and "C'mon, get on with it!" so there was no way either of us could have lost herself in the act.

Even so, she was probably half serious. My chest tightened with joy the moment she touched me, and as we embraced on the mattress I was overwhelmed again with emotion. Physical intimacy with Eiko apparently thrilled me under any circumstances, whether it was part of a play or not. Even if we kept being interrupted, even if our joy kept being cut into pieces, I could still pour my heart into each caress and kiss, relishing each momentary pleasure. I suppose when you're starving for physical contact with a person and know you'll never again be able to have sex with them under ideal conditions, you can't help throwing yourself body and soul into any sort of sexual exchange.

Eiko said I had ruined the mood, but she had only stopped moving her hands for a second when she heard what Tamotsu had done; then, in a truly professional manner, she started up again. Her mind must have been occupied by thoughts of Tamotsu, because her expression remained empty. It wasn't just him: I'm sure she was also disturbed by Shunji, who had come timidly over to where we were, in accordance with the script, but was just waving his hands around midair, unable to get up the nerve to grope us; and by Utagawa, who kept berating Shunji, screaming at him, "Go on, kid, touch them! Run your hands over them!" As we continued caressing, however, Eiko's mind seemed to focus on the matter at hand— which is to say, on me. The moment before I slipped my toe-penis into her vagina, she looked down at me with pity in her eyes, as if I were some small animal on the verge of death.

My own thoughts weren't entirely focused on Eiko. All sorts of things flashed through my mind. But since she was right there with me and we were caressing each other, my feelings for her remained foremost in my heart. By the time I sensed the soft pressure of her vagina on my toe-penis, my longing and desire for her had risen to such a peak that I was eager to use the pleasure I was feeling—even if vaginal stimulation wasn't what my toe-penis liked best—to release the sexual tension inside me. When she began raising and lowering her hips, I experienced a surge as intense as any I felt when she used her hand. This time her vagina would be able to bring me to a climax.

Precisely as I was about to come, Utagawa yelled, "Cut!" The reason he gave for interrupting us was that the whole point of this scene was to express the pathos of Tamotsu's impairment by parading my toe-penis before the audience in its fully erect state. One could also have interpreted it as spite. Either way, Eiko and I both felt as if we'd been left hanging in midair, both physically and mentally—not a nice sensation. Of course, we ended up forgetting all about our frustrated desires a moment later, when Tamotsu came out with his jackknife and goldfish bowl and practiced castrating Shin.

Despite these difficulties, I felt refreshed after having gotten naked with Eiko. I had been struggling to suppress my affection for her ever since she told me our relationship was over; and the whole reason I had been afraid of performing with her on stage was that I loathed the idea of simply going through the motions of sexual intercourse, coldly and lovelessly, and worried that maybe, right in the middle of the act, my regrets would burst out in a flood of tears, as if a dam had broken. My fears turned out to have been completely unfounded. In part, no doubt, this was because Eiko had been so gentle, beckoning to me to come out on stage, but it was also because physical contact with her had totally eclipsed my resolve not to care for her anymore, allowing my heart to fill with a pure longing. I started feeling better when I stopped struggling and accepted the fact that when you love a person, you just love them. And Eiko seemed to be feeling the same way.

"Our bodies certainly were truthful, weren't they?" Eiko said, her expression more relaxed than I had seen it for some time. We were sitting on the balcony at the apartment, wrapped up in blankets against the night chill. "I realized that if I kept sulking," she said, "I would lose you even as a friend."

Without her defenses up, Eiko might be more willing to talk, and so I asked her, "Do you love Tamotsu?"

"I realized I missed him when he touched me. And he was so considerate this time. He was gentle with me . . ."

"And all along you kept pretending that you hated him!" I teased, feeling warmer under the blanket.

Eiko gave me a shove with her shoulder. "I cared for you more," she said.

It hurt to hear that—because I myself couldn't decide who I loved more, Shunji or Eiko.

"It's really too bad," she murmured, laughing as she saw me fidget, "but there seems to be a certain logic to monogamy."

I asked her if she thought it would be possible to stop Tamotsu from castrating Shin.

She shivered, pulling the edges of the blanket together in front of her.

"You can't do anything with him once he's made up his mind . . . nothing but physical force can stop him."

"What if we call the police and have them put a stop to the play?"

"We'd all be arrested," Eiko said, then broke off, leaning against me. "Please don't think I'm cruel. I think that to some extent Tamotsu is probably right—cutting off Shin's penis may be the best thing, both for him and for Shin."

"You really think castrating Shin will help Tamotsu get over his obsession with ordinary sex?"

"If it doesn't help, it doesn't help. Who knows, maybe he'll make some other discovery. It takes Tamotsu a long time to change the way he thinks about things, so I kind of think going along with him one step at time, trying to find ways to make him feel comfortable with new ideas, is the best approach."

Eiko's long association with Tamotsu had, not surprisingly, given her a deeper perspective. I felt ashamed of my shallowness, acting as if I were the only one who knew what was right. "I'm sorry I tried to tell you what to do yesterday."

"It's okay, I don't mind things like that."

Eiko peered into my face, a gentle light in her eyes. We weren't touching each other, and yet I felt like her arms were around me. It's not bad being friends, I thought, not bad at all.

Having spent a pleasant evening with Eiko, I made up my mind just to stand by and watch as Tamotsu castrated Shin, accepting it as something inevitable. But on the day of the performance, I couldn't help wishing there was a way to stop him. He had been in a nasty mood all morning, and by the time evening rolled around and he stormed into the dressing room, his face wore an expression darker and fiercer than any I had ever seen on him before.

At first, everyone put up with the harrowing noise of him drawing the tip of his jackknife over the surface of the goldfish bowl, which he held on his knees. But after this went on for longer than was bearable, Masami shouted, "Would you stop making that *awful* noise!"

Tamotsu stopped moving his hand and fixed Masami with a lifeless gaze. He twisted his lips into a frown, then hurled the knife to the floor. The knife landed upright, its blade embedded into the floor.

"Tamotsu!" Aiko shouted.

He answered with a smirk, then bent over to pull out the knife. But before he could reach it, Shigeki's hand closed around the handle. "I'll hold on to this until the performance."

"What!" Tamotsu howled. "Why do you want to do that!"

Shigeki retreated to the rear of the dressing room, ignoring him. Tamotsu dropped his head and wrapped his arms around the goldfish bowl again.

"If it hurts you so much to castrate Shin," I blurted out, "don't do it!"

Tamotsu cocked his head for a moment, then looked up wearily. "You—are—really—getting—on—my—nerves," he growled.

"Yes, and you're getting on ours, too!" Aiko said.

Tamotsu's eyelids twitched. Troupe members had always handled him delicately whenever he acted up over something having to do with his body, and he seemed completely taken aback. "It's not my fault!" he cried. "Kazumi's the one sticking her nose into things that don't concern her!"

Aiko looked down coldly at him. "And I'm going to stick mine in, too. This is your last chance to call it off."

"You're telling me I should ruin the play?" Tamotsu said with another smirk.

"You can just act out the castration—you don't actually have to do it."

"I highly doubt Utagawa will be satisfied with that." Tamotsu's grin widened. "And we can't afford to anger Utagawa, can we? Shigeki and Yohei say they want to join his company! If I don't go through with the castration, Shigeki will be held responsible as our manager, right? And who knows, with a little bad luck Utagawa might decide not to let him join!"

Aiko, displeased, said nothing. But Shigeki replied, "You don't have to worry about us. Utagawa really wants Yohei and me, so he'll let us in regardless of what you do."

"So it's okay for me to violate my agreement with him?" Tamotsu exclaimed, growing more agitated. "I'm going to tell Utagawa you said that! Sure I violated our agreement, because Shigeki told me to!"

With Aiko's eyes on him, Shigeki responded, without bravado, "Fine with me, tell him."

Tamotsu looked surprised for a moment, but quickly started leering again. "It looks to me, Shigeki, like you're trying to look cool so you can get in good with Aiko again."

"You're free to think whatever you like."

Tamotsu rested his chin on the goldfish bowl, annoyed that he hadn't been able to get a rise out of Shigeki.

A knock on the door, and Utagawa stuck his head in. "Hey, I'm counting on you all today! You've made mental notes of everything we talked about yesterday, right? And you, Miss P! You remember the new bit I added to the script? Don't forget to poke your head out from behind the mountain and look at Eiko before you go out to the mattress."

Utagawa had loved the way I peeked out at Eiko during the dress rehearsal, looking helpless, and had told me to perform the part exactly that way. "You looked perfect—miserable and cowering. You've got a great sense of comedy, Miss P!"

He glanced around the room. "As for you Shunji, today you do everything just like it says in the script—you got that? I won't let you get away with a halfhearted performance like the one you gave me yesterday."

Shunji squirmed on his chair. He had only given Eiko and me a few perfunctory pats in the scene during rehearsal. Utagawa must have assumed all was under control now that he had pressed the point home, even though Shunji hadn't said anything in response, because he moved on to the climactic scene. "Tamotsu, give 'em your all, okay! The doctor will be here at seven, so you've got nothing to worry about." And then he left.

I had been on pins and needles, afraid Tamotsu might blab that Shigeki had encouraged him not to go through with the castration, but he didn't even seem to be considering it. On the contrary, the manic state that had prompted him to challenge Shigeki had passed, plunging him once more into a sullen silence. What was he thinking?

"You know, Tamotsu," ventured Shunji, "I'm not planning to go touch Kazumi and Eiko when they're doing it, so why don't you forget about cutting Shin?"

Tamotsu heaved a miserable sigh. "Yeah, you have it easy."

"Yes, *darling*," Masami said, "and you ought to take it easy yourself."

His tone had been unusually mild, but it still got on Tamotsu's nerves. "You're trying to stop me, too?" he growled. "As if you weren't the one who told me to go have Shin scooped out in the first place!"

Masami's lips trembled, and I intervened: "Having Shin surgically removed and castrating him are not the same thing."

"I'm not in the mood for your logic right now, thanks." Tamotsu glowered at me. "If you're so opposed to my castrating Shin, why don't you cut off *your* toe-penis instead?"

When I fumbled for a response, Tamotsu laughed triumphantly. "Make you a deal: If you get rid of your thing, I'll leave Shin's alone. How's that sound?"

Eiko, finally, said something: "Why should another person have to sacrifice so much for you?"

Tamotsu bit his lip; evidently Eiko's words had hit home. But he went on anyway: "If you're going to meddle in other people's lives, you ought to be willing to sacrifice your own."

"That's just narcissism, pure and simple," Eiko said.

Tamotsu's face twisted into a grimace. "It pisses me off when people like Kazumi and Shigeki, who have splendid, working penises, try and tell me what to do!" he shouted.

This was more than enough to shut my mouth.

Tamotsu glanced at me, then continued his rant, as if emboldened. "You don't just have a penis, Kazumi, you have a vagina too! A person who can enjoy sex twice as much as ordinary people has no right to give me advice!"

Eiko walked over and stood directly in front of Tamotsu. "So you can't enjoy sex, huh? That sure wasn't the impression I got."

Tamotsu went scarlet. Eiko's cheeks were flushed, too, but she seemed unable to hold back. "No, I remember you falling asleep with a contented smile on your face while I licked your penis—yours, not Shin's. You don't have a vagina, but you enjoy anal sex well enough. Didn't I do things to any part of your body you wanted me to—your nipples, the side of your stomach, your ears? And didn't you always love it when I hugged you from behind? You had all these preferences, all these demands, and you're telling me you're incapable of enjoying sex? What the hell was I doing all these years, huh? You tell me that!"

The goldfish bowl rolled off Tamotsu's lap. "But I wanted us to be united," he croaked, "penis and vagina."

"Kazumi doesn't think it's so hot."

I was staggered by her frankness, but I didn't deny it. Tamotsu shifted his dull gaze from Eiko to me, then from me down to his feet. After a moment, he kicked the goldfish bowl on the floor.

"Yeah, I think you ought to forget about this castration thing," Yohei said. "If the only thing that's motivating you is your envy of ordinary—"

Before Yohei had even finished, Tamotsu was on his feet, shouting. "Shut up, all of you! I'm not going to let anyone tell me what to do! You all say you're against castrating Shin, and yet you sit and watch quietly every month while his penis gets shredded by Yukie's vagina!" He grabbed the folding chair he'd been sitting on and hurled it at the door. The room echoed with a metallic clatter.

And then, almost on cue, the bell announcing the start of the performance rang. Tamotsu picked up the goldfish bowl from the floor and held his open hand out to Shigeki. Shigeki placed the jackknife in it, and Tamotsu dropped it into the bowl. Then, kicking the chair out of his path, he stomped out of the dressing room.

I went and stood by Eiko, who remained frozen in place. Her hand was damp with sweat.

"I guess I shouldn't have said that," Yohei muttered.

"You were right, Kazumi," Shigeki whispered, sounding as tortured as Yohei. "We shouldn't have allowed that segment between Tamotsu and Yukie."

The room was drowning in forboding and regret. But then Yukie, who'd been quiet all this time, spoke up: "Personally, I was a little grateful for the opportunity to have Shin's penis inside me. After all, I can't have proper sex with my body either."

No one had anything to say in response to this. Yukie had to be on stage next, so she stood up, but as she walked by me, she stopped and asked, "Is it really true that genital sex isn't what it's cracked up to be?"

I wasn't sure how to take this, but Yukie was serious. She wanted to know. "I like hugging and kissing and having my penis fondled better," I said.

"Isn't that just because you're a woman?"

"I wasn't raised as a boy, so my penis probably feels things differently from most men's. But I think that some men might agree with me."

"I'm like that, aren't I?" Shunji said. "Don't you think our penises are kind of similar, Kazumi?"

This made me smile. And in order to let Shunji know I was smiling, I took his hand and pressed it against my cheek.

"Even supposing there are such men," Yukie said, watching this, "it doesn't mean anything to me unless they're willing to be my men." With that, she headed out toward the stage. A short while later, she appeared on the monitor, sliding the cucumbers and bananas into her vagina.

Time kept flowing relentlessly on.

The moment arrived for Masami, Eiko, Shunji, and me to go on stage. It took a lot of energy for the four of us to stand up. I felt as if my muscles had atrophied, and I had difficulty making my body do what I wanted it to. Eiko's hand seemed to have gone limp, too: she was having trouble turning the doorknob.

"Just so you know, I'm not leaving the piano," Shunji announced once we were in the hall.

"Utagawa's not going to be happy," Eiko said.

"Yeah, but he wouldn't hit a blind man. And I don't need the money. He can't control me. I'm not going to do anything I don't want to do."

As we were walking, a man who had "doctor" written all over him passed us in the hall. He was dressed in white and was carrying a black medical bag. The sight of him was enough to silence us.

Yukie, who had finished her solo act, came over to us. She was waiting for her part with Tamotsu in the pre-castration scene and reported that he seemed to have calmed down. "At least," she said, "I don't think he'll be waving the knife around and going wild or anything."

"Is he in the wings?" Eiko asked.

"I don't know. When I saw him, he was wandering around."

Eiko bit her lips, then walked off with Yukie toward the wings at stage right. Masami and I exchanged glances, then locked arms with Shunji and headed for the wings at stage left. The house was packed, unlike last night; even from our position at the side of the stage we could feel the heat radiating from the audience. I was minutes away from putting my naked body on display before the public for the first time in my life, but the distress I felt at the thought of this couldn't have seemed more trivial. My thoughts were with Tamotsu, who was waiting on the other side of the stage, and the glittering blade of the jackknife in his hand.

Tamotsu walked out onto the stage. He was leading Eiko by the hand, a broad grin on his face, but it had a manic quality. Eiko wasn't smiling, but she didn't look particularly sad either. Her expression could only be described as cool. She had conquered the horror she felt at the thought of Tamotsu castrating his brother, decided despite herself not to intervene, made up her mind to remain by his side through thick and thin, no matter whether the castration led him to an emotional breakthrough or left him even more messed up than he already was . . . She was an unbelievably strong, good person. I realized again how much I had loved her, and how much I still loved her.

As soon as Tamotsu and Eiko had sat down on the mattress, Masami and I walked out on stage. The gaze of the audience was palpable. But by the time we had climbed to the platform and I looked down at Tamotsu and Eiko, I had blocked out all thought of the audience.

Eiko took the initiative, leaning forward, taking Tamotsu's head between her hands and kissing him. Normally, she confined herself to fake, dramatic kisses. This was a real kiss, one that belonged to private life, the sort she used to give me. Tamotsu's body seemed to go limp. The kissing continued. Eiko removed her hands from Tamotsu's cheeks and began stroking his arms and chest, incredibly gently. This wasn't playacting either. Eiko was showing Tamotsu, right out there on stage, how she felt about him.

Tamotsu seemed to come to his senses somewhat when Eiko removed her thin cotton kimono, and he began undoing his obi. His confusion was apparent in the awkwardness of his movements. Naked, he stood at a loss, his face blank. Under usual circumstances, Eiko would have begun stimulating Shin's penis with her hands and mouth, but today she just knelt there, gazing up at Tamotsu. His hands, which had been hanging at his sides, began to shake. He raised them, not to Shin's penis, but to his heart. He knelt on both knees. Then he put his arms around Eiko, covering her body with his.

According to the script, Tamotsu was supposed to be jerking off Shin's penis when Masami and I took turns dashing behind the mountain, but tonight he didn't touch Shin's penis at all. He lay on top of Eiko, moving his hips at an unusual angle, not in a way I'd seen before. It looked as if they were having sex with an imaginary normal penis of Tamotsu's own—not Shin's. They seemed to have dispensed with the plot of the play . . . A bit at a loss, I went behind the mountain, trying to follow the script in some way. I sat on the floor, getting ready to go on stage as soon as I heard Tamotsu rush off. But I couldn't stop myself from checking to see what was happening.

Tamotsu was no longer going through the motions of an imaginary sexual act; he had sat up. He lifted Shin's still-drooping penis and stared at it; then he leaped to his feet and ran off the stage. He had made no attempt to get Shin's penis hard. The point of this scene was to show that Tamotsu was incapable of ordinary sex, so the play was still on track, even though they weren't following the script.

I walked out from behind the mountain. Eiko welcomed me with open arms. She hadn't done this in the previous day's dress rehearsal either. Without realizing what I was doing, I found myself folding her in my arms.

"I told Tamotsu I would stay with him forever," she whispered, "whether or not he castrated Shin."

So you finally did it, I thought. I asked how Tamotsu had responded.

"He didn't say anything."

"Will he go through with it?"

"I don't know."

Eiko wrapped her hand softly around my toe-penis. I felt a delicious surge of excitement, and my toe-penis expanded, eager to fill the palm of her hand. She kissed me as she stroked it. She was as gentle and sincere as she had been with Tamotsu a moment earlier. This awareness only intensified my pleasure, and love for Eiko bubbled up inside me.

In the midst of this onstage sex performance, I found myself thinking that you couldn't be too cavalier about the erotic pleasure of a penis. I realized that I loved my toe-penis and the pleasure it was feeling. And I realized, out of nowhere, that if it should ever happen to disappear I would miss it dearly.

"Shunji doesn't seem to be coming down, does he?" Eiko whispered, as she took her lips from mine.

Now that she mentioned it, the moment for him to come down and start groping our tangled bodies had passed. His piece on the piano continued unabated. The sequence of actions Shunji had willfully ignored was meant to make homosexual lovemaking seem like something outlandish—Utagawa was sure to be very angry about this.

In character, Eiko smiled, then drew her body away from me where I lay on my back, moving down toward my feet. My toe-penis was about to be united with Eiko's vagina for the last time.

I had the impression that, unlike the audiences that came to see the Flower Show, the audience for tonight's play was in some way more refined, or more serious, or at least that they were keeping any lewd excitement they felt under wraps; but when my toe-penis appeared under the spotlight, fully erect, there were unmistakable signs of agitation in the crowd—the sounds of people shifting in their seats, of irregular breathing. As Eiko prepared to insert my toe-penis in her vagina, the atmosphere of surprise changed to one of tension; then, once my toe-penis was inside her, the tension dissipated, and everyone relaxed.

All at once, I was overcome by the hilarity of the entire situation. The oh-so-proper audience was relieved that our genitals had finally gotten together. Utagawa, who was so proud of his bombast, had staged an oh-so-proper play that pandered to the properness of the audience. And Eiko and I had gone along properly with Utagawa's script without a word! The whole evening had come together seamlessly—including the fact that my toe-penis and Eiko's vagina came together so neatly, as if it were the most natural thing in the world. The whole thing, from start to finish, was pathetically, ridiculously silly.

Admittedly, my toe-penis felt good being squeezed by Eiko's vagina, and yet I was seized by dissatisfaction. The single most important lesson I had learned from my toe-penis was that, more than anything else, I loved the overall feeling of my nakedness against Eiko's nakedness. I preferred this closeness—the way it made my whole body and heart thrill with excitement—to the cookie-cutter version of sex that took small pleasures and desires that each partner elicited from the other, greedily and intellectually, and stuck them together, subjugating them to a single large burst of pleasure. I badly regretted that I had been unable to communicate this to Tamotsu.

The spotlight that had been shining down so brightly on Eiko and me dimmed. This was the sign for us to separate our genitals, and for Tamotsu and Yukie to begin their segment. Eiko lifted her hips up from my foot, but as Utagawa's script had us fooling around with each other until Tamotsu had carried out the castration and the stage went black, she lay back down on top of me. Shunji had stopped playing by then, but he was still at the piano.

Yukie walked onto the stage from the left, a chewed banana in her hand, and sat down on the other mattress. Tamotsu walked out from stage right. He set the goldfish bowl with the jackknife in it on the stage, in front of Eiko and me, and ambled slowly over to Yukie. According to the script, the bloody castration scene was now to begin. Eiko buried her face in my breasts. I closed my eyes. But the moments kept passing, and nothing seemed to be happening.

I looked over at Tamotsu and Yukie. Tamotsu was standing stiff as a rod, his hand prepared to untie his obi. Yukie was looking up at him, puzzled. Her lips moved . . . She was saying something to him. Tamotsu's face took on a ghastly, twisted expression.

Eiko had raised her head, too, and was watching Tamotsu and Yukie. She grabbed my arm; she was trembling.

"He doesn't want to do it," I muttered.

This was the first time I had ever seen Tamotsu hesitate when it was time to perform with Yukie. He was standing slumped over, the tension totally gone from his body, and his expression showed none of the mania that had been there earlier. Instead, there was simple undisguised sorrow. Having been caressed with such tenderness by Eiko, having been told that she would remain with him forever whatever he chose to do, he had finally let down his guard. His heart was bared.

Then, all of a sudden, he seemed to make up his mind. He stripped off his kimono, reached out for Yukie, and tumbled down onto the mattress. He caressed her mechanically. He seemed to have given up, decided it was impossible to call off either his segment with Yukie or Shin's castration. Eiko's fingers dug into my upper arm. She had said she wouldn't prevent Tamotsu from castrating Shin, but what if he himself had changed his mind, if the whole time he was doing it he were wishing that he didn't have to? In my heart, I screamed out to Tamotsu to stop. He began rubbing Shin's penis, agony written on his face.

I could feel Eiko's pulse quickening. I couldn't understand why Tamotsu wouldn't stop. Surely he wasn't just being stubborn—not at a time like this. Did he feel he owed it to Utagawa? But Tamotsu hated Utagawa! Then, all of a sudden, it hit me. He was simply sticking with the program because he couldn't figure out how to break free from it! Maybe all we needed to do was give him the chance.

I had to act. There was no time to sit around thinking through the options. Tamotsu was on the verge of shoving Shin's penis into Yukie's vagina when I leaped up, dashed over to them, and knocked Tamotsu out of the way. I turned to Yukie and gave her a small bow. "Let me take his place," I said.

Yukie stared at me in amazement, but she didn't refuse. Maybe she was just too surprised to speak, I don't know. I clenched my fingers around my toe-penis, which was still somewhat enlarged after my encounter with Eiko.

I didn't let myself imagine the pain. Supporting my body with both hands, I poked my erect toe-penis toward Yukie's vagina. Tamotsu, who had gotten up, grabbed hold of my right knee and pushed it back. I kicked him out of the way and shoved my toe-penis into the folds of Yukie's flesh. At first I couldn't tell whether it hurt or not. I had the impression that my toe-penis was hitting up against little hard toothlike objects, deep inside her vagina, but the sensation of moistness and warmth took precedence. I jerked my right foot rapidly back and forth to keep from losing my erection.

I didn't know exactly when the teeth in her vagina broke the skin of my toe-penis. The pain that knifed into me came from body fluids seeping into the wounds. If this is as bad as it gets, I thought, it's not much worse than the pain I'd felt having sex with Eiko when I had that cut from the broken bottle. I kept moving my foot. Each new burst of pain made my vision flicker. I didn't let that stop me. But when the pain of the body fluids seeping into the wounds was joined by that of deeper cuts, more and more, I began at last to moan. It was unbearable.

My toe-penis shriveled, making it impossible for me to keep it inside any longer. It slipped out of Yukie's vagina, bloody, still bleeding, and glistening with fluids.

Tamotsu had knelt down; he was staring at it.

"Phew, that hurt" I said.

"What are you saying!" Tamotsu cried. "What the hell were you doing?" Then, with a bewildered smile, he lowered his head and tried to lick my toe-penis.

I pushed his head up away. "I said it hurts."

He nodded, looking as if he had been thrown off-balance. Eiko wrapped her arms around my shoulders from behind. Tamotsu shifted his gaze from me to her, on the verge of tears.

The play had ground to a halt, but the audience didn't know this. Everyone's eyes were glued to the stage. We needed to bring the scene to an end. Tamotsu, Eiko, and Yukie seemed to be in a daze, so I would have to take matters into my own hands. Shunji, in the unexpected silence, had begun making his way over to us with the aid of his stick.

"Let's get out of here," I said.

I threw on my kimono, slipped my hand into Shunji's, and we all walked off the stage—just as the quick-thinking floor manager killed the lights.

♥ ♥ ♥

The deepest teeth marks on the head of my toe-penis went in about an eighth of an inch. The wounds were concentrated in three distinct areas. The pain itself had been terrible, but the sight of the wounds up close after they had been cleaned up was almost as excruciating. I had to turn away. When the doctor was done bandaging my toe-penis, he cracked precisely the sort of stupid joke one would expect from an acquaintance of Utagawa's: "Your mushroom has turned into a cauliflower."

Tamotsu kept circling around the whole time I was being attended to, but he didn't say a word until the doctor had left. Then: "Gee, I never realized you wanted Yukie so badly, Kazumi." It was pure Tamotsu, complete with undisguised affection on his face. There was something tender in the elbow-jab Eiko gave him, too.

The tension of the evening gone, it occurred to me that I had treated Yukie rather presumptuously, and I apologized to her. She told me in an indifferent tone not to worry about it, then added wryly, "You're even worse than Tamotsu." I laughed, and Tamotsu struck a pose, putting up his fists. The members of the troupe who had been watching us on the monitor made various comments—about how pathetic Tamotsu had looked rolling across the floor when I rammed into him, and about how, during my encounter with Yukie, my expression had looked less heroic than droll. No one said anything outright about Tamotsu's not going through with the castration of Shin, but it was clear that everyone was relieved.

The one big concern was whether Shigeki and Yohei would have to pay for the havoc I had wreaked on stage, forfeiting their place in Utagawa's company. As the manager of the Flower Show, Shigeki in particular might be held responsible. And yet he showed no sign of displeasure when I returned to the dressing room. All he said was, "You did it."

Although one scene had been eliminated and the transition to the next scene somewhat shaky, the play had continued uninterrupted. The suggestion was made that we skip out and flee to Kobe right away, but Shigeki said we should see things through to the end.

Minutes before the play ended, after Yohei and Masami had finished their segment, Utagawa burst into the dressing room. His rage was palpable. He turned to Shigeki first: "Have you thought up a good explanation?"

"I'm extremely sorry," Shigeki said, making a very low bow.

Utagawa's lips twisted into a smile. "That's all you've got for me? How pathetic. You ruined my play and you can't even make up an excuse?"

Utagawa looked over the members of the troupe, then noticed me in the corner. "Ah well, there's no point blaming Shigeki and the rest of you. *She's* responsible."

"*I'm* responsible!" Tamotsu piped up. "I didn't do what I was supposed to."

"Damn right you didn't!" Utagawa screamed. "I feel like slapping you! . . . But the one I really want to throttle is that self-righteous brat hiding in the corner, this pussy with a dick who gets all infatuated with her humanism and starts whining her head off about what a terrible thing castration is—it's her, that girl! She's the one I blame!"

"But she doesn't seem to have done any lasting damage to your play, has she?" said Aiko, unintimidated, pointing to the monitor. The final scene of the play was being performed, a crowd of men and women writhing around the giant dildo, when the stage lights went dramatically dark. After a stunned silence, a thunderous roar of applause rose from the audience.

"Of course not!" Utagawa shouted, raising his voice to be heard over the noise of the applause. "A little meddling from the likes of you isn't going to ruin a play of mine!"

"I don't see the problem, then," Aiko said. "You lost one bloody scene, big deal."

"You know, I never did like you," Utagawa said, glaring at Aiko. "I wish I had the time to have a nice, leisurely chat, just you and me, but unfortunately I have other fish to fry right now. I think you know who I'm talking about, don't you, Miss P?" Utagawa heaved himself to his full height and stared me straight in the eyes.

Shigeki blocked his path, but I actually felt fear. Shunji, next to me, noticed me squirming and protectively put his arm around my shoulder.

"Ah, what a lovely picture," Utagawa snorted. "Two children playing house. Hmm. Maybe you had something going with Tamotsu, too? Is that it? Or did you just interfere because you felt guilty? No, no, forget it—I don't give a shit what your motive was. Do you have some excuse for yourself? Some explanation for why you decided to make an *ass* of me?"

This jerk didn't have a shred of decency. I hated him—and this made me bold. "I'm sorry I inconvenienced you, but I couldn't just stand by and watch."

"Such arrogance!" Utagawa sneered. "Such self-righteousness! What a baby you are. Tamotsu wanted something so bad he was willing to shed his own blood for it, and you butted in and screwed it up for him."

"If Tamotsu seriously wants to castrate Shin, I'm sure he'll do it on his own, someplace where he won't have to worry about being interrupted by me or anyone else."

"Wait a minute, wait a minute! You're forgetting who you're dealing with! *Me!* Tamotsu was willing to shed real, bona fide blood for *my* play— a work I poured *my* lifeblood into! That's something you'll never understand . . . I feel like I've been castrated myself! Do you have any idea what you've done?"

"Now that you mention it," I said, "I shed a bit of blood myself."

"The blood from your so-called penis? You call that blood? I'm sure it must have been painful for you, but think about it: Blood from a fake penis just looks like red paint! Your *thing* isn't the same as a man's penis."

"Why, because it isn't bloated up with 'an air of pathos'?"

"Yow, so that brain of yours works!" Utagawa sneered some more. "In a word, yes, that's about it. You may have something that looks like a penis, but ultimately you are clueless—you have no understanding of the male penis."

"I know that this *thing* of mine isn't a man's penis. It's *mine*, for god's sake! But men like you invest the penis with all kinds of ideas of 'male dignity' and your own personal narcissism, even though when you get right down to it the penis is just another bodily organ. You said you were castrated, having your play messed up, but the only thing that's been damaged is your pathetic self-image and the illusion that you were in control. Or am I missing something? Maybe it's just *beyond* me."

Utagawa trembled with rage. "You think you can make a fool of me like that? Come over here and try saying that again."

Utagawa's wild face was terrifying, but I stepped forward. He took a step toward me, as Shigeki and Yohei held him back. Eiko put a hand on my shoulder.

"C'mon, don't worry!" Utagawa said, feigning mildness. "I'm not saying we should settle this like *men*—with a duel or anything! You tell them, Miss P. Tell them you're not scared of me."

"I certainly am," I said.

"Well you shouldn't be. I see your point of view," Utagawa said, taking a half-step backward, continuing his act. Shigeki and Yohei let him go. He cocked his head to one side, as though he couldn't see what all the fuss was about, and scratched his ear. "I learned as a boy that a man should never hit a woman, you know. That's nice for women, of course, because they don't ever have to get hit."

I would have loved to tell him he could shove his old-fart chivalry and hit me if he wanted to, but I didn't have the guts.

Utagawa turned his back to me and spoke to Shigeki. "Considering how things have turned out, I won't be able to pay you the full amount we had agreed upon."

"Yes, that makes sense," Shigeki replied.

"Tamotsu and Shunji will get half pay. Miss P gets nothing. She ought to be compensating me! I was so angry when I saw what was happening on stage that I considered withholding all your pay. I won't do that. But forget about the Flower Show. I'm not buying it."

"Actually, that's fine with us. The feeling is that people want to go back to living ordinary lives," Shigeki said.

"Oh. They do?" Utagawa's brow clouded. "So you and Yohei will be the only ones joining my company?"

"No, we've decided to pass on that, too."

Utagawa blinked. Aiko's lips parted slightly—evidently this was news to her, too.

"But why?" Utagawa asked Shigeki, his tone completely different. "We had an agreement!"

"We were against the castration, too," Yohei said.

"The same girly-man sensibilities! Did you catch it from Miss P?"

"Oh please! You've got the most infantile sensibilities of all!" I shouted, unable to stop myself.

No one was quick enough to stop him this time. Utagawa sprang forward two steps and he was upon me, his arm raised over his head. I was still on my feet at that point. Then, all of a sudden, the world spun and my body crashed into Shunji. The two of us tumbled to the floor together, sending a metal chair flying. I thought I heard the dull thud of Shunji's head hitting the floor. I jumped off Shunji, who lay there not moving.

"I hit a woman if she needs to be hit! Because women like this one here think they can show a man any kind of disrespect, knowing they're protected by the belief, endemic among the vulgar herd, that only the vilest of the vile would ever hit a woman! No, I won't let her get away with it!"

Utagawa's words passed right over me. I didn't even hear them. I pressed my hand to Shunji's cheek and called his name. He didn't respond. Eiko crouched down beside him, too. A groan escaped from Shunji's lips. I looked up at Utagawa, furious, completely forgetting the sting on my cheek where his punch had landed, just in time to see Tamotsu bringing a chair down on his head. Utagawa staggered, then fell to his knees. Tamotsu brought the chair down on him once more. Then, as Utagawa clutched his head, Tamotsu kicked his back.

"C'mon," Tamotsu shouted, "let's get out of here!"

Eiko and I helped Shunji to his feet. He shook his head, and his sunglasses fell to the floor. With the two of us supporting him, we hurried for the door. The rest of the troupe followed. Tamotsu, taking a last look at Utagawa lying on the floor groaning, closed the door.

"You think he's okay?" I asked. "He won't die, will he?"

"He'll be fine," Tamotsu replied, as he glanced down at Shunji's feet. "Look, he's able to walk on his own."

"Huh? I'm not talking about Shunji. I'm talking about Utagawa."

"Aw, there's nothing to worry about—a little bump like that? He won't even need stitches."

He scampered off then, waving his arms around and doing a peculiar little jig. He looked like a somewhat awkward elf.

Shunji's feet had started dragging by the time we reached the parking lot. He tried to keep up, but he took his arm from Eiko's shoulder and covered his eyes—a peculiar thing to do, which made me worry he was feeling sick after getting hit in the head. We stopped in our path, and after a second Shunji took his hand off my shoulder and covered his eyes with it, too. Then, ever so slowly, he removed his hands from his face.

"What's wrong?" I asked, getting very concerned.

He turned to face me. Somehow his expression seemed different. "Kazumi?" he asked anxiously.

"Don't worry, I'm here."

When I touched his arm, he brought his face so close to mine that our noses were practically touching. His lips trembled. "I can see," he mumbled.

"Huh?" It took me a moment to understand what he was saying.

"I don't know, but I think what I'm doing right now is *seeing*."

"You mean you can see?!" Eiko shouted.

Aiko, who was just climbing up into the minibus, came running over. Shunji stretched out his hands, touched my face, and closed his eyes. He felt the structure of my bones with his fingers.

"It is you," he said.

He opened his eyes and smiled. I couldn't believe it! Shunji could actually see! He was now inspecting the bruise on my left cheek.

"That red blotch is where Utagawa punched her," Eiko said.

"So this is red?"

Shunji stared at me for a moment, as if trying to fix the color in his mind, then turned his head. "You're Eiko?"

Eiko nodded, a big grin on her face.

"That's a smile, isn't it?"

I threw my arms around Shunji, as the members of the troupe crowded around. Tamotsu tugged Shunji's sleeve. "Hey, do you know who I am?"

"Tamotsu, of course. I can tell."

"Yup. Quite a handsome young man, aren't I?"

"Is that the kind of face people call handsome?"

"Nope," Eiko said, laughing.

Shunji inspected everyone, matching each face with a name.

"How did hitting his head fix his eyesight?"

"I've heard that happens sometimes. Something in the eyeball that was keeping the person from seeing gets broken up by a blow, and the person's vision clears."

"I guess we ought to be grateful to Utagawa, then."

"I hardly think we need to feel grateful to *him*. It's all thanks to Kazumi, because she made him angry enough to punch her!"

We ambled toward the bus, chattering back and forth. Shigeki and Aiko were walking together, exchanging smiles for the first time in ages. Eiko, who had started walking off with Tamotsu, turned around and beckoned to us. Shunji had to be nudged along; he was standing in place looking around at everything, eyes full of wonder. He took his first step forward without holding onto me for support.

"The scenery moves. It feels funny."

I was overjoyed. I held out my arm to him. "You can close your eyes while we walk, if that helps."

Shunji didn't shut his eyes, but he did take my hand. He strode confidently toward the bus, walking in front of me, pulling me along.

♥ ♥ ♥

On our last night in Kobe, we had a feast to commemorate the breakup of the Flower Show. It opened with a clichéd speech about what a long journey it had been for all of us, and there were lots of fond memories, including many that preceded my joining the troupe. Shunji was less interested in the talk and alcohol than in the fascinating new experience of seeing, and he kept slipping out onto the balcony to count the stars. He found it fresh and wonderful that after he had reached a certain number, he lost track of which stars he had already counted and which ones he hadn't. I stood with him on the balcony until it got too chilly and then came back in, leaving him to his stars.

"It's just *marvelous* that Shunji can see now," Masami said to me. "But life is going to be harder for you. Sooner or later he'll start developing tastes where appearance is concerned. What will you do if it turns out you're not his type?"

"That would be a problem."

"Shunji is *bound* to change, sweetie. Be happy, but be prepared."

Masami was wiser than he tried to seem. But I didn't see any need to start worrying. When he was blind, Shunji had been perceptive enough to pick out the things that were essential to him, and he had picked me. I wasn't going to be overconfident in myself, but I wanted to trust Shunji to know what was right for him. Call me wishful; I didn't care.

When Shunji came back in from the balcony, Masami spoke to him, too. "You're simply *bound* to change, young man, now that you can see. But don't get too wacky—because Kazumi might stop liking you! Be careful, okay?"

"If I think she's starting to dislike me," Shunji replied, "I'll just shut my eyes."

"You two must be the most blissfully *idiotic* couple in the *world*," Masami said, beaming.

Tired as everyone was, the party continued until late. Even Yukie, who tended to go to bed early, seemed reluctant to head off to her bedroom. It was hard to let the party end, even though the excitement was wearing down. No one wanted to say goodbye. I began to feel an undefined sadness. But apart from the wounds on my toe-penis, what was there to be unhappy about?

Toward midnight, Shigeki, his eyes bloodshot, started talking to Tamotsu. "There's no excuse for my failing to intervene, to stop you from abusing Shin's penis that way, month after month. I couldn't make up my mind to stop you even after I started thinking it was bad myself, you know, because it went over so well with the audience."

"It's okay," Tamotsu said, perfectly cool. "I was just taking my anger out on you earlier, that's all. I'm the one who came up with the idea for that segment with Yukie in the first place."

"Mmm," Shigeki murmured, musing. "Thanks, but I'm afraid that, after all, when push came to shove, I really was a cowardly pragmatist."

Aiko, who had used that phrase first, put a hand on Shigeki's shoulder. "Don't hold that against me, please?"

"No, no—it's true," Shigeki replied. "I didn't *mean* to look at the Flower

Show as a simple commercial enterprise, but somewhere in my mind I was . . . I saw my friends as products to be sold."

"It doesn't matter. You helped us all out a lot. Nobody is *always* perfect."

"It made me feel so ashamed of myself," Shigeki went on, turning toward me, "seeing what you did for Tamotsu."

"Oh, it was just something I did on an impulse," I said, feeling a bit embarrassed with all this attention. "The idea of trying to help Tamotsu didn't even really occur to me."

"I don't believe that," Yohei said. "But in a way, maybe Kazumi's like a character in a science-fiction novel I read a long time ago. An alien lands in a village and takes it over because he can read minds. The villagers are helpless because every time they try to do anything to get rid of him, the alien knows what they're going to do. Then one day, the village fool, who really is a little low on intelligence, takes out the alien with one shot. The villagers are saved! And when they ask him how he did it, he says he just acted without thinking. Kazumi is that kind of fool. Not that I think she's lacking in intelligence, of course."

"I think you've got me pegged," I told him, "except I'm not so sure about the intelligence part!"

"Well that sucks," Tamotsu said. "I'd rather believe she stepped in because she's secretly in love with me." Then, after the laughter had died down, he cocked his head, looking perfectly serious. "The weird thing is, even after what she did for me, I don't seem to be falling in love with Kazumi. I mean, I love her, but not like that."

"That's because you have Eiko!" I said perkily.

No sooner had I said this than a feeling of loneliness swept over me. I couldn't believe myself—hadn't I gotten over losing her yet? I could ease the pain a little by telling myself I'd still have her as a friend, but that did nothing to ease the sense of loss.

Then, for just a second, the pain in my toe-penis seemed to lessen. My toe-penis is going to go away, I thought. I quickly grabbed hold of it, feeling it through the bandage. A burst of pain shot to the top of my head.

The wounds were certainly there, but was my organ there too, underneath all the bandages? Before I inserted it into Yukie's vagina, it had struck me that since I was going to lose Eiko as a lover anyway, my toe-penis might as well vanish along with her. It had occurred to me, however briefly, that if I were to castrate my toe-penis, I might be able to save Shin's penis. And then I had purposely stuck it into Yukie's vagina. Perhaps, after all that had happened, my toe-penis had had enough. If I were to undo the bandages right now, maybe all I would find would be a wounded ordinary big toe.

I had no idea why I had acquired this toe-penis whose loss I now dreaded. It had played such a significant role in my life, led me to places I could never have imagined before, and I didn't want my honeymoon to end. But maybe it had done all it had come to do. Even if my toe-penis *was* still there when I undid the bandages, this feeling of loss would remain.

While I sat there wallowing in my sadness, the party continued. Masami was addressing the entire group: "If you had to choose between having enough money to live on happily for the rest of your life, or a single, perfect sexual experience, which would you choose?"

"Sex," Tamotsu answered immediately. "I would definitely take the sex."

"Sex," Yukie agreed. "I won't be around much longer anyway, and I've got enough money."

"How about you, Yohei?" Masami asked.

"If it's sex or money, I'd go with sex. You can earn money."

"I'd be happy with the money," Shigeki said, after a quick glance at Aiko.

"Hard to give up that sex, though, isn't it?" Aiko said.

"I wouldn't need either one," Shunji murmured. "I can earn money, and I have sex all the time."

"Come here, you *awful* man! I'm going to give you a spanking! . . . Who hasn't answered yet? Eiko—how about you?"

"No comment," Eiko said crisply, laughing. "I can't answer."

"Coward. How about you, Kazumi?"

I ended up giving a dumb answer. "Hmm, I wonder."

Masami didn't press me any further—perhaps he took my response as another "no comment." This came as a relief. To tell the truth, when Masami first asked the question, I almost blurted out, "Perfect sex!" I had no particular image in mind what perfect sex was, but the idea was very enticing. So I was stunned when Shunji said he had sex all the time, making it clear by his indifference just how little the notion of perfection concerned him. The fact that I had chosen "perfect sex" made me realize two things: that I was greedy, and that I had never had perfect sex.

What was perfect sex? "I want to have sex with love" was Masami's mantra, so naturally his idea of perfection was sex between partners who loved each other. I'd had sex with people who loved me as much as I loved them, but it hadn't been perfect. Stylistically, sex with Shunji suited me, but it didn't get me wildly aroused or provide intense pleasure. Sex with Eiko had all the excitement and pleasure I needed, but it wasn't exactly my style. Combining the best points of each experience would, I supposed, be my way of coming up with an image of perfect sex. Love wasn't enough.

So Masami wasn't the only one. I myself might never experience perfect sex. That would be true whether my toe-penis stayed with me or vanished. But I had been fortunate to have love. The sense of loss faded. I hoped everyone in the Flower Show would find happiness.

The party finally broke up, and we all slipped off to our respective beds. Eiko started for the sofa bed she would share with Tamotsu. "We'll see each other again, right?" she asked, turning around.

I smiled. "Of course."

She smiled back, then ran after Tamotsu.

Shunji was already in our sofa bed, sound asleep, breathing deeply. When we get back to Tokyo, I thought, I'll take off these bandages. And then maybe I'll have sex with Shunji, with love. For the time being, I was happy.

Epilogue

"And was your toe-penis gone?" I asked.

Mano Kazumi smiled and lowered her gaze. "No, it's still there. These things don't just vanish when you get to a convenient stopping place, I'm afraid."

A year had passed since Kazumi's last visit to my apartment. She had followed the same procedure as the previous year: she phoned early in the morning, when I was still asleep, then came and knocked on my door an hour later, awakening me from the slumber I had fallen into after hanging up the phone. This time, her purpose in visiting had been to fill me in on the developments that had taken place since she met the members of the Flower Show.

"Nothing much has happened with my toe-penis since the troupe disbanded and I came back to Tokyo. Shunji and I are living together, just passing the days, taking it nice and easy, not doing much of anything." She would be going back to school in a month. Shunji was struggling to learn to write music on the computer.

In June, Shigeki and Aiko would be opening a coffee shop. Masami had moved to Kobe, where he was devoting himself to the management of his chain of gay bars. Yukie was officially married to her boyfriend, who was seven years younger. Yohei had been showing his illustrations to publishers and was finally starting to get some work. Tamotsu was helping with the family business, learning to be an electrician, and Eiko had enrolled in a language school. As for Chisato, she and Haruhiko had decided, after arguing back and forth, to break up.

"Do you ever see Eiko?" I asked.

"From time to time. She's a great friend. We don't get naked together anymore, but I'm still happy to be with her—we were lovers, after all." Despite her resolve, she spoke with a hint of loneliness.

"I have to say, I really am glad I got this toe-penis of mine. I wondered, as you know, if this *thing* was a curse from Yoko, but if she did have something to do with it, I think it's just as you said last year: this isn't a curse, it's a gift, her way of teaching me, making me see new things. I feel very grateful."

Already, when we met last summer at the hotel with the pool, there had been something different about Kazumi. And now I could see it more fully: she'd been growing up. Her cheeks had fallen a little, losing their childlike plumpness—in part, no doubt, because she had aged another year, turning twenty-three in December. She was as adorable as ever, but every so often I caught glimpses of a new complexity in her personality. She was becoming an adult. If Yoko could see her now, looking down from heaven, would she be thrilled? Or would she miss the old Kazumi— her perfect naïveté, her complete obliviousness to worldly matters?

Thinking of Yoko, I had another question.

"This is the last time I'll ask, I promise. What would you do if Yoko came back to life and she asked you to use your toe-penis on her? Would you do it?"

Kazumi looked as if she might burst into tears. "No, I couldn't. Just because I've experienced lesbian love doesn't mean I can go out with anyone just because we're the same sex. Things didn't work out between us, as you know—I never had a chance to develop a sexual liking for her. I regret that terribly, but it's a fact, and I can't change it. Do you think I'm horrible?"

I admired her honesty, her sincerity. But I felt sorry for Yoko, who had, I suspected, loved her.

"Did you find my story interesting?" Kazumi asked as she gathered her things to leave.

"Extremely."

"Well, then, I'll let you know if anything more happens. Feel free to use this in a novel if you want . . . if you don't have anything better to write about."

"How would we split the royalties?"

"I don't need any. I think I've got more money than you."

"Thank you!"

The young woman with the toe-penis went home.

And I wrote this novel.

（英文版）親指Ｐの修業時代
The Apprenticeship of Big Toe P

2009 年 8 月 24 日　第 1 刷発行

著　者	松浦理英子
訳　者	マイケル・エメリック
発行者	廣田浩二
発行所	講談社インターナショナル株式会社
	〒112−8652　東京都文京区音羽 1−17−14
	電話　03−3944−6493（編集部）
	03−3944−6492（営業部・業務部）
	ホームページ　www.kodansha-intl.com
印刷・製本所	大日本印刷株式会社

落丁本、乱丁本は購入書店名を明記のうえ、講談社インターナショナル業務部宛
にお送りください。送料小社負担にてお取替えいたします。なお、この本につい
てのお問い合わせは、編集部宛にお願いいたします。本書の無断複写（コピー）
は著作権法上での例外を除き、禁じられています。

定価はカバーに表示してあります。